Books should be returned on or before the
last date stamped

02

27 DEC 2002

10 JAN 2003

-1 MAR 2003

30 APR 2003

06 JUN 2003

11 JUL 2003

26 SEP 2003

-1 MAY 2004

16 OCT 2004

15 DEC 2004

- 2 MAR 2005

30 Mar 05
HEADQUARTERS

3 1 AUG 2005

- 7 OCT 2005

17 JAN 2006

1 0 JUN 2006

17 AUG 2010

28 MAR 2011

- 9 JUL 2011

- 6 SEP 2011

3 1 JUL 2012

1 0 JUL 2013

- 3 MAR 2014

2 6 MAR 2014

2 3 FEB 2015

1 4 DEC 2015

1 JAN 2016

Nicholas Coleridge is also the author of *With Friends Like These*.

'In this acidly smart thriller, Nicholas Coleridge takes the lid off the glossy magazine business ... Coleridge writes superbly with both pace and depth – never an easy combination. He leaves you feeling you know everything there is to know about periodical publishing and more than a little about the stink of corruption that is power's closest companion' *Sunday Times*

'I was glued to the thriller ... the plot grips to the end' *Literary Review*

'*With Friends Like These* is a book with everything going for it: style, surprise and a considerable amount of substance. Kit Preston is a hero who might well lay James Bond to rest. Readers will cheer him, quite deservedly, all the way' *Washington Post*

'Pacy, polished and exciting, it gives a riveting insider's view of a fascinating and frenetic world. Nicholas Coleridge, whose beady eye misses nothing, is expert at putting across unpatronisingly a great deal of inside information. Much of it is extremely funny' *Evening Standard*

'A riveting and well-informed read' *Spectator*

'Mercilessly accurate, great descriptions. All the drama and glamour is here. It's as funny, in its way, as *England Their England*' *Mail on Sunday*

'Coleridge is an elegant writer, light without being flip, never self-regarding ... He handles the plot perfectly' *The Times*

'Thrillers come and thrillers go, but this one is something else. What raises Coleridge's novel to a far higher level of sophistication and charm is the author's special combination of the knowing and ironic' *Daily Telegraph*

StreetSmart

Also by Nicholas Coleridge

StreetSmart

Nicholas Coleridge

ORION

Copyright © Nicholas Coleridge 1999
All rights reserved

The right of Nicholas Coleridge to be
identified as the author of this work
has been asserted by him in accordance
with the Copyright, Designs and Patents Act 1988.

First published in Great Britain in 1999 by
Orion
An imprint of Orion Books Ltd
Orion House, 5 Upper St Martin's Lane,
London WC2H 9EA

A CIP catalogue record for this book
is available from the British Library

Typeset by Deltatype Ltd, Birkenhead, Merseyside

Printed in Great Britain by Clays Ltd, St Ives plc

This one for Tom Coleridge

PART ONE

[1]

New York

Saskia Thompson, the most famous magazine editor in the world, glared at somebody way across the ballroom.

'I don't believe it, *he's* here.'

'Who's here?' asked Kitty. There must have been eighteen hundred people in the room, half of them famous. That night, it would have been simpler to draw up a list of who wasn't there.

'Just someone I hoped wouldn't have the bad taste to show up.'

Saskia pressed her lips together grimly. Kitty knew better than to question her editor further. With Saskia, it was generally prudent to keep a little distance.

Newspaper profiles of Saskia Thompson invariably referred to her highly calibrated social radar, which registered all sources of human power within a distance of a hundred feet. Tonight, in the ballroom of the Waldorf Astoria, it was functioning like air traffic control over a busy metropolitan airport. Turning on her heel, Saskia paused to kiss Ted Turner of CNN, before moving with the precision of a chess piece – a knight, Kitty felt, two paces forward, one to the side – across the geometric carpet of the ballroom. Calvin Klein, Isabella Rossellini, Steven Spielberg, Isaac Mizrahi, Mrs Leonard Lauder, Demi Moore: ninety seconds' conversation for the double A list, sixty for straight As.

'Stay close, but not too close. I may need you,' she hissed, motioning Kitty to follow her as she weaved between the tables.

'Saskia!' Someone wearing a white tuxedo was bearing down on her.

'Oh, Tom, it's you.' They embraced, and then, after a tiny pause, Saskia turned to acknowledge Tom Cruise's wife, Nicole Kidman.

'*Great* new issue,' said Tom.

'Thanks,' said Saskia. 'It was you guys who made the difference. That cover should do a million.' Then she added, 'That's over here. We shift a further four hundred thousand a month in London now.'

'*Bazaar* were spitting,' said Nicole. 'We'd kind of promised that next time we did a double cover it'd be for them.'

'They're down the tubes anyway,' said Saskia. 'Creatively, it's over. I'm sure your agent told you that. Sad. It's a great name. *Was.*'

Subsequently, when Kitty was asked to describe Saskia's mood on that fateful evening, all she could think to say was that she'd been on sparkling form, the toast of the gala, the toast of New York. How else could she describe her almost royal progress, the relentless exchange of compliments, as Saskia surfed on breakers of success across the dark Manhattan sea?

With her truculent, intelligent face, feral green eyes and air of perpetual alertness, Saskia reminded Kitty of a wild fox – sleek, meretricious and predatory, alive with sexual energy.

Kitty had been surprised when Saskia included her, at the last possible moment, on the *StreetSmart* table. In the office, Saskia restricted her circle to a tight cabal of the most senior editors and contributors, from which Kitty was excluded. Now she realised her role tonight was to provide a discreet safety net for Saskia to bounce against in case she briefly missed her footing on the celebrity trapeze.

'*StreetSmart* goes from strength to strength, I hear.'

Saskia was eyeball-to-eyeball with a grizzle-haired Australian. 'What do you mean, "I hear"?' she snapped. 'Don't you *read* it?'

'I guess not as often as I should. I've been travelling.'

'Well, I'll have my office courier it in future. Kitty,' she said, 'remind me to have Mr Murdoch added to the comp list.'

Saskia was gliding ever closer to the stage, where a twenty-piece steel band was setting up for dancing. A *New York Times* profile had once described Saskia as 'the eagle ray', for the way in which she seemed to float, weightlessly, on deep currents, soaring above those she wanted to avoid, and sweeping down on elegant, determined wings on those she wished to encounter. The Eagle Ray. The nickname stuck. Eagle Ray or Sting Ray. But never to her face.

'Kitty, there's a man over there I need to meet. The tall, bald-headed one.'

Aloof and well groomed, he looked European more than American, Kitty reckoned.

'Étienne Bercuse,' said Saskia. 'Head of Bercuse SA, the luxury-goods group. That's Tranquilité, Gaia, Serène: all those French scents. And all those French vineyards. And the Lockerjock sportswear brands over here in the States. Mega important. Stick close now.'

'Good evening, Monsieur Bercuse. Saskia Thompson. Editor-in-Chief of *StreetSmart*. I want to thank you for advertising in my magazine.'

M. Bercuse bowed his head stiffly.

'Actually, I *don't* want to thank you,' said Saskia. 'I've come over to complain. Your companies are screwing up.'

'In what way?' he asked.

'Budgets. Your media planners must be deaf and dumb. They don't seem to have clocked how big *StreetSmart*'s become. We're not getting our fair share of your ad-budgets.'

'I do not place advertising personally,' replied M. Bercuse, 'but it is my understanding that we do support your magazine.'

'Yeah, but not enough,' said Saskia. 'We're as big as *Vogue* and *Vanity Fair* now, but we get half the space. I tell you, it's outrageous.'

For a moment, Kitty thought the French businessman was going to walk off. His eyes had gone very cold. He had devoted the past fifteen years of his life to building up a global luxury-goods conglomerate, and a muscle in his cheek twitched irritably.

Then an extraordinary thing happened. Saskia looked him straight in the eye and smiled. It was a smile with the precision and intensity of a blowtorch. Kitty had seen it before in the office, though never directed at herself. It was the look that Saskia deployed on people who mattered, who could do things for her.

Kitty watched as Saskia took the Frenchman by the arm, and moved closer to him. 'I do think, Monsieur Bercuse, that you should at least review the situation. We can do a lot for your company. May I take it that I can ring you tomorrow, at your hotel?'

'Er, at my office. After seven o'clock. But I make no promises.'

'We'll speak tomorrow at seven,' she said, letting his arm fall gently back to his side.

'Right,' said Saskia, when he was out of earshot, 'let's not waste any more time. Help me find my driver, I'm going back to the apartment.'

They recrossed the ballroom, faster this time, Saskia acknowledging only the most prominent of the film stars, fashion designers and moguls who rose like phantoms in her path.

For an instant, as they neared the coat-check, Kitty felt Saskia hesitate, as though she was avoiding somebody ahead of her, among the large crowd jostling for their wraps.

They emerged into Park Avenue to find it was snowing. The first snow since Christmas. The street was double-parked with limousines, their drivers on the sidewalk muffled up against the February chill. A small crowd of photographers and rubberneckers was waiting behind a rope barrier, to catch a glimpse of departing celebrities.

'Miss Thompson?' A driver holding a name board was waiting by the open door of a Lincoln town car.

Saskia was about to climb inside when her social radar alerted her to activity behind her. Mr and Mrs John Kennedy Jr were emerging through the revolving doors.

'Wait,' Saskia told the driver.

Kitty watched as Saskia edged backwards, while somehow contriving to give the impression she was quite stationary, until she was positioned directly between the Kennedys. One shoulder pressed against the sleeve of John Kennedy's camel coat, the other partially blocked out Carolyn Bessette Kennedy's diaphanous dress.

Seconds later, the flashbulbs started.

For Kitty, it was a tableau that remained forever frozen in the strobe-like sheen of a hundred shutters.

Saskia Thompson with her short red bob and red Versace swing-coat, pressed against the arm of John Kennedy. The world's most famous magazine editor leaving a star-studded party at the Waldorf. That was the intended impression, and who could reasonably say that she hadn't pulled it off? In photographs, Saskia always looked absurdly young anyway, infinitely younger than her thirty-four years. Kennedy, in this much-syndicated last picture, looked far from unhappy at the sudden imposition of the girl in the couture coat.

The picture over, Saskia bolted, head down, across the sidewalk for the open door of her limo.

Kitty tried to peer inside to say good night, but the windows were darkly tinted and the car already edging out into the traffic of Park Avenue.

It was the last time that Kitty would see her editor alive.

[2]

London

Max Thompson had lived in the same flat off Ladbroke Grove for nine years, but each time he returned from an assignment, he recognised the area less. There used to be a late-night Cypriot delicatessen at the top of Oxford Gardens, but that had turned into a designer handbag shop. And the whole neighbourhood round the Harrow Road was suddenly full of independent record companies and steel-and-concrete tapas bars.

He was inclined to blame his sister's magazine, *StreetSmart*, for most of this. They had been the first people to run a big article on the area. Saskia had had her secretary send him round an early copy by motorbike. Inside was a brusque typed message, attached with a paperclip: 'You owe me one. I'm putting you on the map.' There was a list in the article of notable people who were moving in, and for some reason they'd included him: 'Max Thompson, war correspondent'. Max would have preferred photojournalist. In fact, he'd have preferred not to have been mentioned at all. He didn't regard himself as famous, and there was something embarrassing and trivialising about appearing on a list like that.

He had bought the flat because it was the first basement he'd seen with sufficient ceiling height to enable him to walk about without stooping. It was also cheap. You could make quite decent money in his job, but it wasn't regular and was slow arriving. First his agency, Bullet in New York, had to collect from the publication, and then they forwarded it less their forty per cent. Some of the Asian news magazines took six months to pay. Not helpful for the mortgage.

Max heaved the cameras down the area steps and let himself in with the key that had been to Kabul and back; then braced himself for what he might find. He'd been broken into so often while out of

8

the country, he was almost more surprised when he hadn't been. There wasn't much left to take anyway, apart from the Herat rugs. Those he'd miss.

The flat looked just as he'd left it. There was a pile of post on the kitchen table, mostly junk mail it looked like. And the place felt warm, which meant the boiler hadn't broken down this time. He found a note from the Caribbean lady who stopped by once a week to check the joint and maybe clean. 'Max, your boiler busted down again. I got my brother to fix it OK for £120.'

The display on the answerphone showed there were twenty messages waiting, which seemed a lot, but first he needed a hot shower and a fistful of painkillers.

He removed the sling and peeled away the dressing. It was surprisingly painful to do. His arm, once he could see it properly in the mirror on the bathroom cabinet, was white and withered. Flecks of lint and patches of yellow antiseptic were stuck to the wounds, which looked deeper and nastier than he'd envisaged.

He remembered he hadn't had a proper hot bath since the morning he'd set off with the Mujahedin almost a month earlier. He kicked off the rest of his clothes and ran the shower. The pressure of the water jet against his arm made him flinch, as rivulets of dirt and old sweat trickled down his legs on to the floor.

The telephone was ringing in the sitting room, but he ignored it. The machine could pick it up, and he heard it whirr into action.

Less than a minute later, it began ringing again. This time he struggled to get it, dripping water across the carpet as he went.

'Hello.'

'Is that Max Thompson? Greg White, *Daily Mail* news desk here. Sorry to intrude at a distressing time, but I'm ringing for a reaction about your sister.'

A reaction about Saskia. This was all he needed, fifteen minutes after arriving home. Hadn't the world read enough already about brilliant Saskia Thompson? And why the hell did they always ring him? He'd spent much of the last decade avoiding her long shadow.

'What kind of thing do you want? I'm never much good at this, you know.'

'Oh, just a first reaction. How you're coping. What your parents make of it all.'

'My parents? Why not ask them yourself? I'm sure they'll tell you they're very proud.'

Down the line, the journalist tapped away at a keyboard. 'Your parents aren't taking calls right now,' he said. 'In fact their house – that's down near Farnborough – seems deserted. Unless they're ignoring the doorbell. We've got a couple of freelancers outside, in case they do show up.'

'I'm sorry, I'm not with you. I only arrived back from Afghanistan a few minutes ago.'

'Are you telling me,' said Greg, 'that you haven't heard what's happened? You haven't seen today's papers?'

Max wanted to tell him to piss off, but some instinct told him this was significant. For the first time in two weeks, he forgot the throbbing in his arm.

'I just can't believe you haven't heard,' said Greg. 'It's a huge story. Front pages everywhere.'

'I've been up a mountain with the Mujahedin. I can tell you it didn't make any impact there, whatever it is.'

From the sudden silence of his keyboard, it was clear Greg had no idea who or what the Mujahedin might be. 'Well, I'm sorry to be the bearer of bad tidings, but your sister's dead. They found her the day before yesterday in her apartment in New York. She'd been out to a function the previous night, wall-to-wall celebs and all that.'

Afterwards, when he had a chance to analyse it properly, Max saw that his reaction – on first hearing the news – was distinctly mixed. Shocked, of course. Amazed. Staggered was probably the word. Even horrified. But dismayed? Not completely. You don't have control over your reactions in situations like these. The fact was, he experienced something close to relief, just for an instant. One shameful instant. It felt like a large black cloud had lifted from the face of the sun.

'What do you mean, she's dead? What the hell's happened?'

'That's just it,' said Greg. 'No one's saying much at the moment. Sounds like she topped herself. She was in the bathroom when they found her.'

Max felt numb. His brain was shutting down. Saskia was dead.

Greg asked, 'Any explanation you can think of, as to why she might have done it?'

Max paused. 'None at all. I just can't believe this, I'm totally shocked. My sister was one of the most fulfilled people. I can't think of any reason.'

'Look,' the journalist was saying, 'the editor's asked me to put together a major analysis job for tomorrow's paper. Probably centre pages. We see this as the definitive piece. Intelligent, sympathetic. Any objections if I ask you a few questions?'

'Go ahead.' Max was hardly listening to what Greg was saying, his mind was reeling. Their parents would be distraught. And Cody. The whole thing was unbelievable. He must call them, soon as he could shake this guy off the line.

'One theory that's going round,' said Greg, 'is that Saskia was suffering from COS – Celebrity Overload Syndrome. Do you have any reaction to that?'

'I've never even heard of it. What the hell's that?'

'Oh,' said Greg, 'it's all very kosher medically. We've got a professor at Bedford College of London University who can stand it up. It's a stress-related condition that afflicts high-profile achievers. Women especially. I mean, looking through the cuts and the photo library, your sister was photographed with an awful lot of celebrities, wasn't she? Eric Clapton, Ralph Lauren, Tony Blair, Larry King. Princess Diana. And according to this doctor, excess exposure to celebs can erode a sense of self-worth.' Even Greg began to sound unconvinced by his daft theory. 'Over a period of years, of course.'

'I'm sorry,' said Max. 'I just haven't got anything to say about that.' He sat down on a leather footstool he'd brought back from Somalia, adapted from a tribal drum, the stitches digging into his bare ass.

'Well, let me ask you about the kid, then. Cody. Saskia never revealed the identity of his father, did she?'

'No, she didn't.'

'Any ideas?'

'None.'

'No objection if I run a few names past you?'

'Look, I've already said I don't know. She never told anyone. Not my parents, not me, maybe not even Cody's father.'

'The kid didn't live with his mother, did he?'

'No. With my parents.'

'Why was that, then?'

'Work, really. She edited a magazine in London and New York. She visited Cody at weekends.'

'Though not frequently, I hear.'

'I'm sorry, what are you getting at?'

'Saskia's relationship with Cody. She hardly ever saw him. The editor's got this theory that Saskia was kind of this idealised modern mother, put on a pedestal if you like. Successful, famous. But she couldn't relate to her own child. It's kind of a post-feminist problem for all high-achieving female bosses . . .'

Max put the telephone down on Greg and dialled his parents. He let it ring thirty times – where the hell were they? Come on, come on – then gave up. They had evidently been hounded out of the house. He doubted they'd go far, because of Cody's school. Not unless they really had to.

It was his parents he felt saddest for. They were going to be devastated. His parents adored Saskia, their father especially. Even as a child, Max had recognised that Colonel Thompson would never feel the same intensity of love for him as he felt for Saskia. It was a realisation that had crept up on him, at first unconsciously; but later, by the time he was seven or eight, he knew it as an objective truth. There was a bond between father and daughter that was stronger than anything between his father and himself.

In time, Max had come to understand that his father, in many respects an emotionally constrained man, found it easier to open up to his gregarious daughter than to his diffident son. Post Grozny, post Angola, post Bosnia, everything about Max's relationship with his father was better. Even now, however, Max knew that Colonel Thompson took special pleasure in being Saskia's father. He had heard him more than once, on running into an old friend at the club or out shopping, saying with his particular combination of irony and pride, 'Expect you saw the photograph of Saskia in this morning's *Express*. Out on the town with Liam Neeson, that Irish actor chap who doesn't shave properly.'

His parents sometimes liked to describe themselves as 'chips off the young block'. They pasted all the articles about Saskia into a big cloth-bound scrapbook which was kept on a round table in their drawing room, even the American articles, which she arranged to have sent to them by a clippings service.

Max couldn't imagine how his parents would cope with the news of her death.

He played back the answerphone and, apart from the odd message from friends who didn't know he'd been away, it was all calls about Saskia. *The Sunday Times*, *The New York Times*, *New York Post*. Please call. Then a confusing message from his father sounding close to tears, first telling him to ring the minute he got back, then saying they wouldn't be answering the phone. A tragic accident, he said, as I expect you've heard by now.

Max dialled his parents' number three more times, but no one ever answered.

He threw on some clothes and walked to the shops at the end of the street. Max was a tall, solidly built man with the kind of impassive face that doesn't show emotions easily. Built for stamina rather than speed, broad chested, with large long arms and legs. His dark brown hair was thick and curled over his collar, his neck and hands were leathery and tanned from the sun. He shivered. After Afghanistan, London felt bitterly cold. There was a Portuguese chemist in Ladbroke Grove where he knew the woman in the dispensary would sell him a sling and tie it, and a newsagent where he could pick up all the papers.

Even before he'd paid, he saw Saskia's face across half the front pages. 'MYSTERY OF SUICIDE SASKIA.' Most of them had used a photograph of her posing with the Kennedys outside a New York hotel. 'The last picture', it was invariably captioned.

He carried the papers home, to find the phone was ringing. A fact-checker from the *New York Observer* wanted to confirm the exact date that Saskia had launched the American edition of *StreetSmart*. And would it be accurate to describe her father as a retired soldier?

Not sure about the first one, Max told the fact-checker, but yes, Colonel Thompson had retired from the army nine years ago. He had been Commanding Officer of the 1st Battalion The Cheshire Regiment, sometimes known as the 22nd of Foot.

The news reports of Saskia's death in the broadsheets had a remorseless sameness about them and Max guessed that most had relied on agency reports.

Saskia Thompson, 34, the British-born President and Editor-in-Chief of *StreetSmart*, the trans-Atlantic lifestyle magazine, has been found dead in her New York apartment.

The circumstances surrounding the death of the editor credited with founding the independent publishing phenomenon of the last decade, are not thought to be suspicious. It is understood that Miss Thompson took her own life. Her body was discovered by a maid at the Upper East Side apartment building.

StreetSmart, which is published in separate monthly editions in London and New York, with a combined circulation of 1.4 million, has been one of the fastest-growing magazine titles in both markets, measured by readership and advertising revenues.

Her last appearance was at a charity benefit at the Waldorf Astoria hotel on 26 February, to raise money for research into ovarian cancer. Other guests at the event included Mr and Mrs John Kennedy Jr, Rupert Murdoch, Ted Turner, the fashion designers Calvin Klein and Donna Karan, the actress Sharon Stone, and Mayor of New York Rudolph W. Giuliani.

A statement on the circumstances of her death has been promised by the office of the Chief Medical Examiner of the City of New York.

All of the broadsheets ran obituaries too, universally glowing. Max spread the papers out on the carpet and just let it wash over him. From the way they wrote, you'd have thought Saskia had invented an antidote for AIDS or repaired the ozone layer, rather than started a fanzine for Hollywood stars. To be fair, it had more in it than that. Popular ecology and profiles of Aung San Suu Kyi. Or some twenty-page thesis about the death of modern art. Everything and nothing.

The obituaries claimed she'd changed the way magazines were read and designed. The *Independent* said she'd managed to harness the ten-second attention span of the MTV generation with the post-digital literacy of new global urban culture. *The Times* suggested Saskia had tapped into a particular mindset, freeform more than geopolitical, that had compelled all other publishing houses to re-examine their own print offerings.

All were in complete agreement that Saskia had invented the hottest, hippest magazine there had ever been, and that no other word but genius would do. Creative genius, business genius.

Estimates of the value of *StreetSmart* were put at anywhere between seventy and one hundred million dollars. Max did a double-take when he read that. He'd never thought of *StreetSmart* being worth anything. He realised that Saskia must have paid herself well, otherwise she couldn't have bought her enormous flat, but beyond that, it was a revelation.

The tabloids' take on Saskia was a further revelation. The more he read, the less he felt he'd known his sister. Inevitably there was a lot of speculation about Cody and who his father might have been. One of the papers had even got hold of a school photograph; Cody must be six, nearly seven now. Saskia certainly seemed to have had her fair share of lovers. They'd linked her with several rock stars, some quite famous, others whose names meant nothing to Max.

There was a lot of fantasy stuff, which he knew for a fact was inaccurate, about how she'd started *StreetSmart* on the kitchen table with a budget of £1,000. In fact, he remembered her getting a loan of £40,000 from their father, and renting an office up near the Westway, before the area became corny. It had always slightly annoyed him, that loan, because at around the same time, when he needed to buy his first proper cameras – a pair of Canons – he was told he had to earn the money himself.

Another myth was that *StreetSmart* was an instant success. 'The first issue, edited and designed on her kitchen table, sold more than 250,000 copies. And the rest is history.' Max didn't remember it quite like that; rather, he had an idea that the first issue had performed disappointingly, and that their father – the reluctant backer – had discouraged her from publishing a second. But somehow she had talked him round, and that issue did do better. It got a lot of media attention too. Saskia was always smart at self-publicity. One of the papers printed an old picture of Saskia from around that time, and studying it, Max felt intensely moved. He found it easier to relate to the earlier pictures, before she'd changed her hair and learned to dress like a Hollywood film star. She was standing on the pavement outside the first office, wearing some kind of denim smock, with her hair long and brown and loose across her shoulders. She was beautiful. Not glamorous and polished, as she later became, but beautiful none the less.

There were a lot more pictures in the tabloids of Saskia with celebrities, mostly taken four years earlier at her thirtieth birthday party. She had actually invited Max to that one, and he remembered having felt relieved to be safely in Mogadishu, covering the aftermath of the American invasion of Somalia. He always felt irritable at Saskia's parties, guessing that he'd only been invited along to be impressed. Anyway, he was hardly going to fly to New York for dinner, even to see Madonna close up. The other guests sounded gruesome: Martin Scorsese, Quentin Tarantino, Damien Hirst, to name but three. Apparently you could hardly eat for all the camera lenses being poked in your face.

However, the thing that upset him the most that morning was all the speculation. 'The last desperate hours of a gloss princess.' No one knew anything, it was all guesswork. You'd never get away with it on a news magazine, he thought angrily. According to one report, Saskia had been found naked on her bed 'with her £10,000 designer ballgown in a heap on the floor'. Another revealed she'd been discovered, partially clothed, in the bathroom, others said the kitchen. None were shy of knee-jerk explanations. Saskia had gone to pieces without a lover. She was concerned that *StreetSmart* might be off the boil. She was addicted to slimming pills and had fallen victim to a 'lethal cocktail' having combined them with alcohol.

Reading this stuff, it was enough to make Max question whether popular journalism had any integrity at all.

[3]

Whenever Max went away on assignment, he left his car in a garage in Kensal Road. Not strictly speaking a garage, more a razor-wired parking lot, but at least it was off the street, and they kept a mad dog on a chain as a deterrent.

He redeemed his old white Citroën and drove down into Ladbroke Grove. The car was second hand when he'd bought it five years ago, and had 119,000 miles on the clock, but after the dented wrecks of Peshawar it looked brand new. Thank God it's automatic, he thought, which meant he could drive one-handed. He headed south, gingerly at first, past Olympia and down the North End Road. When he hit the A30, he really let rip. Something he missed about the Third World – and this went for just about everywhere – was driving at speed.

He made Farnborough in fifty minutes flat. The old family homestead was a mile and a half outside town. School of Lutyens, his father always said, if he were trying to impress. Which meant gables, leaded windowpanes, an in-and-out driveway. Some desirable later additions: conservatory, up-and-over garage with two extra bedrooms on top, ornamental birdbath on classical pedestal. Max never returned to High Hatch without a certain foreboding. Quite irrational, since he had been perfectly happy growing up there, on the family's periodic postings back to England. It was just that he always felt eleven years old again, whenever he reached the top of the lane.

The grass verge across from the house was thick with cars. There must have been a dozen. Standing by the gate was a crowd of men with cameras, drinking tea out of Thermoses. Inside the garden, at the front of the house, he could see two men in parkas peering through the sitting-room windows. The curtains appeared to be drawn tight.

He drove on without slowing up and hung a right at the signpost into Holly Lane. From there he could circle the whole hamlet and park up in a lay-by near the top of the garden, behind the house. As he passed the Drovers, the local pub, he noticed another journalist and a photographer questioning the landlord in the car park. If they were hoping for material about Saskia they'd be lucky: she'd hated pubs and never went near the place.

He left the Citroën behind a clump of rhododendrons and let himself in by the picket gate. There was a path down a bank of azaleas, which led round a lumpen croquet lawn to a small greenhouse and oil tank. Now he could call up to his parents' bedroom window, which overlooked the back garden. If they were at home, he guessed they'd be holed up there.

The bedroom curtains were drawn, an encouraging sign. He collected a handful of gravel from the path and lobbed it up at the window. The stones ricocheted against the pane. The curtains didn't even twitch.

He took a second handful and tried it again.

The third time, he thought he heard something. There was no question. A child's voice, followed by a sharp reprimand not to go near those curtains. Cody and his grandfather.

'Dad, it's me. Max. I'm down here.' He was shouting, but softly. 'Dad, Cody. It's Max.'

At last the curtains moved and he saw his father's face peering narrowly through a chink. Then, just as abruptly, he disappeared. Max guessed he would come down the back stairs to the utility-room door.

Now his father was fumbling about with the keys and drawing back the bolts, top and bottom, breathing heavily. How old was the Colonel now anyway? Max was thirty-six, and his father had been in his mid-thirties when he was born. He must be seventy.

Colonel Thompson was opening the door when he heard the camera.

The two men Max had seen looking in at the windows were round the back of the house, standing in the flowerbed. The photographer must have taken a dozen shots already. His father stood paralysed in the doorway, not knowing what to do. For a moment Max thought he must have believed the men were something to do with his son.

'Dad,' Max yelled, 'get back inside. And *you* –' he turned on the journalists – 'get the fuck out of this garden. *Now*. You're trespassing.'

The photographer didn't miss a beat. He kept his finger down hard on the motor drive, strafing Max and his father, who was dithering on the back step.

'You Saskia's brother, then?' shouted the journalist. 'Heard anything yet on why she gone and done it?'

'Look, I told you already, fuck off out of here.'

'Keep your hair on, mate. We're only doing our jobs. Listen, is the kid in there too?'

Max didn't answer, just tried to manoeuvre his father back indoors.

'Cody, I'm talking about. Come on, who's his dad really, then?'

That did it. Something inside Max snapped. Before he knew it, he'd swung a punch. His right fist connected with the journalist's pepper-and-salt beard, and he stumbled backwards, knocking his head against the protruding overflow of a drainpipe.

All the time, the photographer continued taking pictures.

'All right, Jim, you saw that,' spluttered the journalist. 'You're my witness.' He turned on Max. 'You've had it, mate. I've got you. You thumped me, unprovoked attack. I'm taking it all the way.'

'If you don't want another one, I advise you to leave my parents' garden now. Get out.'

For a moment, Max thought they were both going to take him on. If they had, he didn't know what he'd have done. The exertion of one punch, even with his good arm, had taken its toll. His bad one was throbbing in its sling. His father had backed into the house, shaking. Max followed him inside, and bolted the door behind them both.

'Sorry about that, Dad. I was intending to slip in without being seen.'

'They've been outside for two whole days. We can't go anywhere. All they want is to ask upsetting questions about Saskia. Your mother hates it.'

'Can't the police do anything?'

'Apparently not. First thing I did was ring the station, but there's nothing they can do. The lane's a public right-of-way.'

They went upstairs and Max saw how his parents had turned their bedroom into a refuge. The curtains were drawn tight on both sides, reducing the room to a wintry half-light. His mother was washing up cutlery in the basin and the carpet was strewn with Cody's toys and computer stuff. There was a toaster on the dressing table and cardboard boxes of provisions: jars of Robertson's marmalade and Marmite, a variety pack of cereal.

He was shocked by his mother's appearance. She looked drawn, her skin grey, and the light had gone out of her eyes. It was obvious that nobody had got a proper night's sleep since the news about Saskia. Looking at her exhausted, bewildered face, Max wondered if it was all in reaction to Saskia's death, or whether, bit by bit, and unnoticed by himself, his mother had simply grown old. She had always been frail, a pale shadow to her husband. As the Colonel's wife, she had made no strong impression on the regiment. Max's main memory of her was of an attractive, self-effacing woman with a small waist and a quiet, rather faded prettiness. Max found it difficult to reconcile it with this parchment-skinned old lady at the basin, in her brown stretch ski-pants with elastic stirrups beneath her feet.

'I'm so sorry, Mum, about Saskia. I don't even know where to begin. It's terrible.'

Margaret Thompson made a face. *Not in front of Cody*. They couldn't have told him yet. Max didn't blame them, with the pariahs parked up outside. They'd have loved a picture of Cody crying.

Max stooped to kiss his nephew on the head. 'Hi, Cody.'

Cody hardly looked up. 'Max, have you seen my Buzz Lightyear anywhere? I *know* Granny's hidden it somewhere, but she says she hasn't.'

'I really *haven't* touched it, Cody. Truly,' said Margaret Thompson. 'Have you looked in the toy chest?'

'I've looked there *already*. You *always* say look there. Come and look yourself if you don't believe me.'

'Cody, don't be cheeky to your grandmother,' said Colonel Thompson, quite sharply.

'Don't *you* be cheeky, more like,' said Cody. 'You're the cheeky one, butthead.'

Max's mother shot him a look which said, 'What can we do?' If they'd been cooped up in this room for two whole days, no wonder Cody was fractious. Saskia had said he was hyperactive. His grandparents did their best for him, but it wasn't easy.

'I can offer you a cup of tea,' said Margaret. 'And what on earth have you done to your arm?'

'It got grazed by shrapnel. A landmine.'

She looked at Max, but he could tell she wasn't listening.

'In Afghanistan. I flew back this morning.'

'That's nice,' she said vaguely. 'I expect you had good weather. It's been bitter here, this winter. Ice on the windscreen most mornings. You have to take such care in the lanes.'

'I suppose they'll go away sooner or later,' said the Colonel, nodding meaningfully outside. 'They wouldn't stay put for ever. We kept Cody out of school on Friday, but he's got to go tomorrow. And the rations won't last out much longer.'

Cody went to the bathroom, and Max said, 'Dad, quick, while he's out of the room. What on earth happened? I only know what I've read in the papers.'

'We hardly know more ourselves,' replied the Colonel. He sounded weary. 'It's bewildering. It's difficult to get any information. I've spoken to a Detective someone – a Polish name – in New York and he promised to let us know when they have anything to tell us. Max, this is a tragedy. It's heartbreaking. Your sister meant so much to me, you know that.'

Max felt desperate for his father. 'The newspapers said they found her in her flat.'

'Maid found her, apparently. She'd been out late the night before, got back around midnight, porter remembers seeing her. From then on, no one seems to know a damn thing.'

'But how did she kill herself? I don't even know that.'

'Sleeping pills. They found a bottle of them next to the bed. Half full apparently.'

'And what about identifying the body and all that?'

'That's already taken place,' said Colonel Thompson. 'I'm afraid it's definitely her. One of her magazine colleagues in New York made the formal identification.'

Margaret Thompson came over with the tea, and Max perched on a hoop-backed chair at her dressing table. The chair had belonged to his mother for thirty years but this was the first time he'd ever sat down on it.

'We heard about it first from Saskia's office,' his mother said. 'They were the ones who told us. A very nice-sounding man – Bob – he's Saskia's second-in-command. He telephoned us here on Friday evening, about eleven o'clock at night. We couldn't think who could be ringing so late. It turned out he was calling from the magazine office, and he told us he was very sorry but Saskia had killed herself. Nobody seems to know the whys or wherefores. She wasn't unhappy. So why would she do it? Your father and I have been asking ourselves over and over.'

'You know, Max,' said the Colonel, 'this is an odd business all round. Saskia didn't seem to you the kind of person who'd take her own life, did she?'

'Hardly. Though one can never know what's going on inside someone else's head.'

'Well, it makes no sense to me. Not someone like Saskia, at the top of her tree.'

'She certainly never struck me as depressed,' Max said. 'I thought she adored her success.'

'And quite right too,' said Colonel Thompson. 'She had an exceptional talent. I've been remembering how, even as a child, one knew she would one day go on to do great things. There aren't many Saskia Thompsons around. She was well aware of that, we talked about it. That's why it astounds me she'd ever have killed herself.'

The cistern roared next door, and Cody came back into the bedroom. He sighed. 'I want to play outside now. It's *boring* being inside all the time. *Please* can I go out? I want to see if the trough is frozen over.'

'Sorry,' said the Colonel. 'No playing outside, it's too cold. You've got school tomorrow. You don't want to be ill for school, do you?'

'But I'm not cold. I've said that a million times.'

'Why not play with your computer? Or Meccano?' Max suggested. 'We could build something together.'

'Meccano's boring. Anyway, we lost most of the bits.' Then he said, 'Why are all those people *still* taking photographs of our house?'

His grandparents exchanged glances. 'Which people are those?' asked the Colonel.

'Those men on our lawn, the ones you don't like. You can see them if you stand up on the loo seat, through the little window. They were all waving at me with their cameras. And I waved back.'

Max remembered the atmosphere at High Hatch around the time Cody was born. He'd been abroad for the birth itself but had returned to England a week or two later. Cody was already installed in Max's old bedroom. The Colonel had been struggling to assemble a flat-packed wooden cot that he'd purchased that morning from the Army and Navy in Guildford.

In those early weeks of Cody's life, it was still assumed that Saskia would take him to live with her in Holland Park, once she'd engaged a suitable nanny, but three months passed, then four, and Saskia showed no inclination to collect him. On her weekend visits to High Hatch, which soon became day trips, she displayed little interest in Cody.

Margaret Thompson was exasperated by her daughter's indifference. She would stand in the kitchen, waiting for a bottle of powdered milk to cool down, and proclaim herself 'too old to be doing all this. I am a *grandmother*. I had my fair share of sleepless nights with my own children.'

However, as the weeks and months slipped by, and Saskia's visits to High Hatch were overriden by the fashion collections and her New York commitments, it became generally accepted that Cody would be brought up by his grandparents. Max stopped asking about it and Margaret became almost resigned.

Colonel Thompson, for his part, seemed energised by the turn of events and strenuously resisted the accusation that Saskia had dumped her unwanted son on them. 'Makes perfect sense to me,' he would declare. 'In many cultures round the world, that's how *all* children are raised, by the grandparents. Parents are too busy working. With someone like Saskia it would be a heinous waste of her abilities. Much more sensible to have Cody down here with us.'

Max remained at High Hatch until dusk, when they heard the journalists start their engines and drive off. Three of them, however, seemed to be hunkering down for an all-night stake-out. Across the dark garden, he could see them on their mobile phones checking in with their news desks. The Saskia story must still be regarded as hot, if they were being kept at their posts.

Margaret Thompson coaxed Cody away for a bath, and the Colonel tipped a finger of whisky for Max and himself into toothmugs. 'The curse of this thing,' he said, 'is that we're almost out of Scotch. I'd been meaning to get some anyway, and then this happens.'

Max said he'd slip out later and buy some. 'Now that it's dark, there'll be no problem. And I'll pick up some milk and bread.'

Colonel Thompson placed his toothmug on the night table and sat down on the side of the bed. For an instant, Max thought how incongruous his father looked, his tan corduroys against the bedcover with its pattern of coral-coloured ribbons and grapes.

'Until this whole ghastly business is cleared up,' the Colonel said, 'I wonder if I could ask something of you, Max? Try and find out what had been going through Saskia's mind. Ask around a bit, will you? Easier for you to do than me, stuck down here.'

'I'll give it a go, certainly,' said Max, uncertainly. 'Though, as you know, I don't really move in her world.'

'It's important, Max. We need to know, however painful. Promise me you'll try.'

Max passed undetected through the garden back to his car. The Esso garage on the bypass sold the basics, and then he pulled up outside the Drovers. There was an off-licence, with its own separate entrance between the public and saloon bars, where the landlord sold spirits across the counter. There was nobody in the narrow room, and he could hear the landlord serving a boisterous group in the saloon next door.

'Ten to one on it was drugs related,' a man was saying. 'It all adds up: celebrity lifestyle, rock stars, illegitimate kid. Old story.'

'Don't you believe it, mate. This one's sex related. That's what we're hearing, and we're going big with it. Providing the lawyers don't go ape-shit.'

'Sex related in what way?' asked a third man, who Max could see nursing a whisky. He remembered him from earlier, lurking on the verge opposite High Hatch.

'Oh, too murky for your readers, mate. This is specialist stuff. Let's just say, it's significant they found her in the bathroom. There's a lot more that's going to come out yet.'

The landlord saw Max at the counter and called out that he wouldn't be long. 'Terrible business about your sister,' he added, though evidently it had been rather good business for him personally.

Max made a face, to shut him up. He must have got the message because he came through looking conciliatory. He packed a couple of bottles of Bell's and some mixers into a bag. 'Give my best to your parents,' he said. 'We're all thinking of them in the village. They're a nice couple, and were always cock-a-hoop about your sister. Your father passed on a copy of her magazine once or twice,' he went on. 'Can't say I found a lot in it, but they do say it was very popular.'

Max arrived back at his flat to find three new messages on the machine. Stefan, his picture editor at Bullet, had rung from New York with a message to ring him urgently. Max shrugged. He liked Stefan, but everything at Bullet was always urgent, except when you needed them to pay you in a hurry.

The second message was from someone called Bob Troup. 'Hi, we haven't met,' he said, 'but I'm Saskia's deputy at *StreetSmart*.' He was almost whispering into the receiver, as though he didn't want to be overheard. 'I'm just ringing to reassure you that everything's under control here during this difficult time. I've rung all the staff and told them no one's to talk to the press except me. As you can imagine, the phones have gone berserk. We're besieged by journalists. But the important thing's to get the next issue out. I talked to New York earlier this evening, and told them the same thing. Anyway,' he said, 'maybe you can give me a call? A lot of people are quite jumpy, not knowing what's happening, but I wanted you to know I'm in charge.'

Instinctively, Max disliked the sound of Bob Troup. Presumably he was the same guy who'd rung his parents. He had a voice like that snake, Ka, in Walt Disney's *Jungle Book*, it slithered down the line. Yuk! Saskia's parties were always jam-packed with men like that. And he wondered why Bob was bothering to tell him all this. Because he was family, presumably. Maybe I'm being unfair, Max thought. Bob was probably pretty shaken up himself, if he'd been close to Saskia.

The third call was a lot brisker. 'Philip Landau speaking. I hope I've got the correct number for Max Thompson. I'm Saskia Thompson's lawyer. Could you ring me at your earliest convenience at my office? Or leave a message with my paging service.'

He left a number ending in three noughts that sounded like a West End switchboard. Max remembered Saskia mentioning that she'd signed up with some super-charged solicitor. She'd said he practised in both London and New York, 'which is ridiculously hard to find considering it's so crucial.' He assumed that this essential resource was Philip Landau.

[4]

Étienne Bercuse was suffering a bad attack of the advanced corporate petulance that had long ago become his most identifiable human characteristic. Today, he felt especially put-upon: his Gulfstream IV was laid over for routine maintenance in Savannah, which meant that he had to use a scheduled flight from Houston to LaGuardia.

Then, no sooner had the United Airlines 727 attained cruising altitude above the Revlon-red Texan prairie than he noticed a Chinese businessman in the adjacent first-class seat across the aisle had snapped open a Louis Vuitton briefcase. Étienne Bercuse experienced an emotion that hovered somewhere between envy, fury and disdain. It began in the shallow membrane behind his domed, bald head, then conducted itself like an electric current to the bile-lined pit of his stomach.

'I'm not believing this,' he muttered. 'That fat Chinese fuck has a Louis Vuitton.'

The main reason Bercuse disliked flying on commercial flights was that he ran the risk of seeing his competitors' products in action.

The seat next to his own was empty, since he had a rule, well understood by the seven personal assistants in his various offices around the world, that two seats must always be reserved and paid for, ensuring him a cordon of privacy. However, in the seat immediately behind his own sat Jim Marciano, Chief Operating Officer of his North American subsidiary, Bercuse Inc.

'Jim,' said Bercuse, turning and peering through the narrow gap between the seats. 'You have seen it, *non*?'

'The briefcase, Étienne? Sure I've seen the briefcase.' Jim had noticed the Louis Vuitton 'Président' – the biggest in the range – with its distinctive chocolate and café au lait monogram design, and had spent the past four minutes hoping against hope that his boss hadn't spotted it too.

'Any idea why he might have made that purchase, Jim? Why he bought that case in preference to one of ours?'

Marciano thought, How in Christ's name does he expect me to know that? But he replied, 'Couldn't tell you for sure on that one, I'm afraid, Étienne. From the look of him, I guess he's Chinese. Could have bought it anywhere – Taipei, Hong Kong, Shenzen. Vuitton has wide distribution in the Pacific Rim.'

What he meant was, 'He didn't buy it here in North America, so kindly get out of my face.'

Jim Marciano had eleven thousand employees and six executive vice presidents reporting to him in North America, was paid in excess of two million dollars, and had grown the business by seven hundred per cent in four years. But when his French chairman was about, sometimes he just felt like some kind of big Girl Friday.

Étienne was still regarding him accusingly through the gap between the seats. 'You *guess* he's Chinese? He *could* have bought it in China? Jesus Christ, Jim, don't you *know*?' He jabbed at a button above his seat and then, as a stewardess began swaying her way up the aisle from the galley, rapped, 'Fetch me a telephone that works international.'

Marciano closed his eyes and counted slowly to ten. Two more days and Étienne Bercuse would have left New York for Geneva. If he could only keep his cool until then. Jim had made a promise to himself and to his wife that, if he could stick it out for another two years, they'd be in blue skies financially. Then he'd do himself a favour and walk.

If he could only keep his cool. Right now, he wasn't sure he'd even last out until tonight. This trip had been the worst. Five metropolitan centres in ninety-six hours, with Étienne criticising every detail along the way. There was an expression in business for men like Étienne Bercuse: corporate seagulls. Every year they fly in, shit all over you and fly out again. Except with Étienne it was worse. He came quarterly.

The architect of the nearly completed Bercuse concession in South Coast Plaza, Costa Mesa, the world's largest shopping mall, had almost walked out too. All those drawings had been signed off months ago, though Étienne chose not to remember that now. The revisions he'd insisted on weren't in the spec and he'd made it clear the project couldn't go over budget or open late.

Jim Marciano sighed as he reviewed the trip. The gala dinner at the Waldorf had been the low point. Étienne had complained about the positioning of the Bercuse table in the ballroom, claiming that it had been geographically less prestigious than the Chanel table. Jim hadn't seen it himself, but had nevertheless contrived to get them switched.

The only time all evening that Étienne had looked interested was when the British magazine editor, Saskia Thompson, had come up and talked to him. She'd made quite an impression in her red dress, that had been obvious. Jim had known for a long time that the only route to Étienne's heart, always assuming that he had one, was via his underpants.

'So, you're telling me he bought the Vuitton briefcase in China?'

'That's my best guess, Étienne.' Jim shrugged. He hoped his irritation didn't show. 'It's an assumption, nothing more.'

They were both staring across the aisle at the Chinese man, trying to establish where he was from: Hong Kong Chinese, Mainland Chinese, Taiwanese or even American-Chinese, it was impossible to say. All Chinese loved Vuitton; in fact all the Pacific Rim countries had a regard for Vuitton merchandise that Étienne Bercuse took as a personal affront. His own Étienne Bis briefcase in a rich tan redolent of old bridle hide, with its polished aluminium fittings and interior built on a frame of burr-walnut, was an equally good product, and yet his market share in Hong Kong, Seoul, Shanghai, Taipei and Singapore – the briefcase capitals of the Tiger economies – had never come close.

At that moment, the Chinese businessman did something that made Jim Marciano shudder. He shot the brass catches of the briefcase, reached inside one of the document pockets, the colour of old armagnac, and produced a calculator and pair of spectacles. Both were encased in matching Vuitton monogrammed slipcases.

Étienne cursed and his eyes narrowed. It was the look that meant he was about to have someone's ass. He picked up the mobile the stewardess had delivered and began punching out numbers.

Jim blanched. He didn't need to ask. He guessed it would be two, three o'clock in the morning in Hong Kong.

'Li, is that you? This is Étienne. I'm sorry, Flora, I didn't wake you, did I? I did? That's too bad. Let me speak with Li, please.'

There was a pause while Li Fah Hsiang, President of Bercuse Asia-

Pacific, was awakened by his wife. Étienne drummed his fingers impatiently on the fold-down table.

'Li, that you there? I'm glad.' He listened for a moment while Li Fah Hsiang said something, and then broke in, 'I understand that, Li. You flew in overnight from Manila, that's fine, Li, we are all entitled to some rest in this organisation. But the reason I am calling you now, Li, is I want to describe something – a vignette – I'm seeing from right where I'm seated on this aeroplane. I am thinking you might find it illuminating.'

Jim listened with his eyes closed while Étienne described the unidentified Chinese businessman across the aisle and his Louis Vuitton luggage.

'So you understand why I'm calling you, Li? It is important, I think. Whatever marketing initiatives your people are taking over there, they don't seem to be working. This is first-hand research I'm giving you. So, maybe you could take a look into this for me, Li, and let me know what you come up with. *Ça va?* You will ring me in Geneva?'

After he'd terminated the call, Étienne shook his head and shrugged. Étienne Bercuse had a vision. And he knew exactly how long it was going to take to turn the vision into reality: one more year.

In one year he would be running the biggest luxury-goods conglomerate in the world.

The statistics in his Apple PowerBook, which he reviewed and extrapolated several times a day, were unambiguous. If Bercuse SA continued to grow as he anticipated, he was on course to move from number five to number one. Bigger than the Wertheimer family's Chanel, with its global fashion, fragrance and cosmetics business; bigger than the South African Johann Rupert's Vendôme group, with its cigarette brands, Dunhill and Rothmans, plus Cartier, Chloé, Piaget watches and Montblanc pens; bigger than Francois Pinault's Artémis Group, owner of Château Latour, the Au Printemps department stores, Christie's, Saint Laurent, Samsonite luggage and the Colorado ski resort of Vail; bigger even than Bernard Arnault's Louis Vuitton–Moët Hennessy (LVMH), generally regarded as the most aggressive and acquisitive luxury-brands empire of modern time, owners not only of Étienne's bête noir, Louis Vuitton, and half the great champagne houses of France, but Dior, Givenchy,

Guerlain, Christian Lacroix, Kenzo, Loewe, Celine, Berluti shoes and the giant Pacific duty-free shoppers' network, DFS.

Étienne Bercuse loved flying. At 37,000 feet the cabin pressure made him feel cleverer, bolder, omnipotent. He had all his best ideas in the sky. It was as though, suspended above the earth's crust, like Christ up the exceeding high mountain, he could see all the kingdoms of the world in perspective, market by market, and decide which were ready for the next brand invasion.

He knew that the tide of progress was with him. More frequent travel, the communications revolution, satellites beaming identical channels of entertainment into every territory, the degradation of communism and the triumph of western consumerism: everything was driving the world, remorselessly, to brand culture. Already, one third of the earth's population had access to Bercuse brands. His twelve-storey Manhattan department store on 57th and Park was the most impressive shopping emporium in North America. Built by I. M. Pei and fitted out by Peter Marino at a cost of $290 million, Bercuse Plaza showcased every one of his much-advertised products. Tranquilité, Gaia and Serène occupied a whole floor each, with spas and restaurants in the image of the brand. There were departments for the Lockerjock sportswear lines – Homeboy and D Troit Denim – and for Sensi, the Milanese fashion label he had recently acquired. There was a *cave de luxe* devoted to brandy, wine and champagne, and emporia selling Étienne briefcases, evening purses with linked EB gold chains, cigarette lighters, watches, eternity rings, marine chronometers and silver-plated Bercuse powerbooks. Every piece of merchandise was manufactured by one of his own companies.

He pressed a key on the powerbook and a computer-assisted graphic of the world's surface came up, indicating Bercuse super-stores, malls and offices in each continent. Beverly Hills, San Francisco, Bal Harbor, Manhattan, Tokyo, Shanghai, Guangzhou, Rio de Janeiro, Toronto, London, Paris, Berlin, Moscow. Each city had retail space of 140,000 square feet or more.

He hit a second key and sites under construction were illuminated: Osaka, Sydney, Manila, Bangalore, Dubai, Prague, Costa Mesa, Johannesburg, Sao Paolo, Mexico City, Taipei, Guam. All would be open for business within eight months from today. They had better be, Étienne reflected coldly, or their respective general managers would be seeking alternative employment.

Two million square feet of new selling space, all within one year. The following year, two million more. He had hardly scratched the surface of China or the old Soviet Union. Or Malaysia. He needed to be in Kuala Lumpur. That was a priority. Cartier was there already and so were Vuitton and Hermès.

He snapped shut his powerbook and picked up a newspaper on the seat next to him. He grimaced: it was *USA Today*, a paper that, with its gaudy weather maps and colour printing like a too-bright television, Étienne instinctively recoiled from. He preferred the chilly asceticism of *Le Monde* and the *Wall Street Journal*.

He turned the pages, hardly troubling to focus on the parochial nuggets of world news. Then he noticed her picture. Saskia Thompson photographed on the sidewalk with John and Carolyn Bessette Kennedy. The headline said, 'MYSTERY OF MAGAZINE EDITOR'S LAST HOURS.'

Étienne Bercuse tensed and then read the item very carefully.

By the time he'd finished reading, he felt that his scheme was not so impossible. In fact it was shaping up as one of his better strategies. He permitted himself the most fleeting of smiles. Nobody but he would ever know when he first conceived it, and now he was certain that it could play an important part in his plan to be Number One.

[5]

There was a Greek greasy spoon at the top of the Harrow Road which served sausages, houmous and stewed tea, and this was where Max had breakfast when he was on his own.

The woman who ran the place, Ariana, always put on this great phoney welcome when he showed up, though Max guessed she hadn't got a clue who he was. She probably thought he was a sound engineer from Rabbit Records, round the block.

On the way, he picked up the newspapers to see if there was anything more about Saskia. The *Daily Mail* had four whole pages: 'Gloss girls: when the heat gets too hot to handle. Greg White explodes the myth of the modern media superwomen who think they can have it all.' The theory behind the article, if you could call it that, was pretty much as Greg had outlined on the telephone: how women in high-powered jobs fail at everything else. It incorporated several manufactured or out-of-context quotes from Max, even though he'd said practically nothing. 'Her brother, Max, 36, commented last night that, despite the tragic circumstances surrounding her death, Saskia's parents "were very proud". He could throw no light on a motive for her suicide. "My sister was one of the most fulfilled people. She loved the high life and celebrities. Madonna was one of her closest friends." ' Later in the article he was credited with saying, 'None of us knows who Cody's father is. Not even my parents. It's a secret she's taken with her to the grave.' The *Mail* published a picture of Cody waving happily through the lavatory window.

'What in mercy's name have you done to your arm?' exclaimed Ariana, delivering pitta bread. 'Here, let me put the butter on for you. You need two hands for that job.'

Max allowed himself to be bossed around by Ariana for a while, and got his sling sorted out, then dialled Philip Landau from the payphone in the corner.

He was put straight through, and after ten seconds of statutory condolences about Saskia, Landau came to the point.

'Any prospect of you meeting me here at lunchtime today? We can have something to eat at my desk. Easier to talk freely than in a restaurant. Shall we say one o'clock?' It was one of those invitations that don't allow for the possibility of refusal. He gave Max an address off the Strand, on the Covent Garden side.

The offices, when Max arrived, in no way corresponded with his preconception of a lawyer's set-up. The walls in reception were lined with silver- and gold-framed discs, like a record company, and a series of glass portholes allowed you a glimpse into conference pods beyond. A moment later he was collected by Philip Landau himself and escorted down a modern-art-lined corridor to his office.

Landau was a well-preserved man of fifty, fit and sleek in a dark suit with a black rollneck jersey. Max had never been any good at noticing what other people were wearing, but even he could tell that Philip Landau dressed with enormous care to achieve this degree of informality.

For the first time, Max was conscious of how scruffy he looked himself. He still had on the lace-up boots that he'd worn to Kabul and back, and a combat jacket he'd picked up years ago from a soldier in Bosnia. His hair needed a trim, and he wasn't sure he'd shaved all that carefully either, what with the arm and everything.

The two men went into Landau's office, which was dominated by a serpentine desk made of inky-blue glass. The only picture, which was vast and took up one whole wall, was a charcoal drawing of a chilli pepper, framed in inch-thick steel.

Landau crossed the room to a narrow black-lacquered sideboard with a tray of drinks. 'We have various interesting beers, Badoit, or I can build you a Bloody Caesar – vodka and clamato juice.' Max chose a beer. 'Mexican,' said Landau as he poured it into an octagonal tumbler. 'From the Baja.'

Landau was a pretentious sod, but Max couldn't help liking him. He said a lot of his work was for the record industry, hammering out contracts and copyright issues to do with electronic publishing. 'That's how I first came across your sister. When she set up the *StreetSmart* website, she needed advice on rights and drafting new contracts for contributors.'

Two lacquer boxes of Thai food arrived from a place across the street, and a bottle of Sancerre, opened by his secretary with the aid of some aerodynamic corkscrew.

'Now,' said Landau, when they'd both eaten a little, 'how much, if anything, did Saskia tell you about her businesses?'

'Her *businesses*? I thought she owned a magazine.'

'She did, in one sense. There's only one registered trademark, but you probably know there were independent editions of *StreetSmart* in London and in the States. Also, as I've mentioned, a website on the Internet. Each division was set up as a separate entity. Each was structured and financed in a slightly different way. I can give you chapter and verse later to take away with you. Suffice it to say that, four or five years back, Saskia approached me to represent her in a reasonably complex financial restructuring of the company. Particularly with the American operation, she needed help. Which, I'm happy to say, we were able to provide. After the restructuring was completed, she continued to retain this firm for all legal and tax matters.'

'I see,' said Max. He knew nothing of any of this. He associated Saskia with parties, and newspaper articles about her success.

'If I'm telling you things you already know, for goodness' sake stop me,' said Landau. 'As a breed, I'm afraid lawyers have a tendency to do that. Probably because we charge by the hour.' He chuckled throatily.

'To be honest, I don't know that much about Saskia's world,' Max admitted. 'It's something I'm pretty ignorant about. I've spent most of the past ten years out of the country, taking photographs.'

'I know. I've seen some of them. You took a remarkable one of about twenty young boys posing on a multicoloured jeep. In Liberia, I think it was. All wearing those reflective sunglasses and waving machine-guns. Big smiles across their faces. What made it so chilling was that corpse in the foreground, lying in the dust. No one giving a damn.'

'You've got a good memory. It was in *Time*. How did you know it was by me?'

'Saskia pointed it out. We were lunching the day it was published.'

'That surprises me too. That she'd have noticed it.'

Landau snorted. 'Saskia noticed *everything*. She showed me your stuff several times. She rated it. You were in Grozny too, weren't you?'

'Yep.'

'How was that?'

'The lunches weren't as good as this.' Max laughed. He felt uncomfortable talking about his trips, because he felt that he'd never found a way of describing them without coming over as some kind of *Boys' Own* hero, or else as a complete prick. Or both.

Landau must have sensed this, because he said, 'Max, you're most probably wondering why I asked you to drop by.'

'I am rather.'

'You need to read this. It's Saskia's will.'

He handed over a slim typewritten document with acetate covers. Max flicked through it, noticing Saskia's signature, witnessed by two names he didn't recognise.

'It's quite straightforward,' said Landau, 'but if you'd like me to paraphrase, your sister has left everything to her son, Cody. Not until his twenty-fifth birthday, however. Until then, it's just his running costs. You're one of his two trustees, by the way. I'm the other. The important part from your point of view is paragraph 3.2, on the fourth page. To put it simply, in the event of your sister's death before Cody reaches the age of twenty-five, Saskia has asked you to run the whole shooting match, her entire business.'

'*Me?* You're not serious.' Max gasped. 'That's about the craziest idea I ever heard.'

'Well, I can only say that your sister evidently didn't think so. She gave this will a lot of consideration.'

'*When* did you say it was she wrote it?'

Landau turned to the frontispiece. 'February twelfth, this year. I believe she gave us her instructions about five weeks before that.'

Max cast his mind back to a particularly dismal Christmas at High Hatch. For once, all the family had been there. Normally Saskia took Cody to the Caribbean with a nanny for Christmas, where she had friends on St Barts, and Max tried his hardest to find an assignment – any assignment – over the holiday. 'Christmas returns to Latvia' was one, he remembered. This year, however, they had all descended on the Colonel and Margaret for a dose of old-fashioned family bonding.

Saskia had looked morose from the moment she arrived. She'd announced she'd come straight from the Hotel Bel-Air in Beverly Hills, and the contrast was getting to her. Max had argued with her about magazines for five solid days; for some reason, which in the aftermath of her death he now found inexplicable, he'd just felt like goading her. He'd told her he thought *StreetSmart* was glib when it attempted to be serious, and was embarrassing in the way it pandered to movie stars. Saskia, enraged, had said that he didn't understand the politics of Hollywood, and that if a million people bought the magazine, including Henry Kissinger, it couldn't be that bad. Max had replied that the very fact Henry Kissinger bought it confirmed it was rubbish. They had carried on in similar vein until the *StreetSmart* offices reopened on 29 December.

It must have been a fortnight later that Saskia had drawn up her will.

'You do realise this is one of Saskia's jokes,' Max told Landau.

'I hardly think so,' he replied. 'In fact it's rather a serious obligation. You will need to think very carefully indeed before deciding whether to take it up.'

'It's out of the question, I can tell you that straight away. I have a contract with Bullet, the photo-agency. I'm away half the year.'

'Obviously, were you to run *StreetSmart*, you'd have to give all that up.'

Max stared around the office, floundering for additional ammunition to say no. 'Tell me something,' he said. 'Can you think of one good reason why I'm even remotely suitable for the job? I don't read this kind of magazine. I don't know anything about business. I haven't even *heard* of most of the people *StreetSmart* writes about. Nor am I particularly interested in them.'

'Put like that, you certainly don't sound like a headhunter's dream. All I can tell you is that Saskia had the highest regard for you. And, as you'll appreciate, she didn't suffer fools. She talked to me more than once about you. She said you were single minded and courageous, and a good judge of character. If she didn't believe you could do it, she wouldn't have offered you the job.'

'The job I've turned down.'

'The job you're seriously considering for the next few days. And I mean *seriously*. I've put all the relevant paperwork into this bag: consolidated results for the past four years, trading statements for the different divisions. I've marked which are in dollars, which are sterling. Also payroll, accruals and deferred debt. We have some junk financing on the American operation, which I can talk you through some time. So, here it is: homework. If there's anything you feel you're missing, give me a call. Oh, and I've taken the liberty of including both the latest issues of *StreetSmart* in here too, just in case you somehow missed them . . .'

Landau stood up, and smiled. 'I don't want to hear from you until Friday at the earliest,' he said sternly. 'In fact, I recommend you use the weekend to think it over. You'll probably want to pay a visit to the *StreetSmart* office too, to see what you're getting yourself into. Call Jean, Saskia's secretary, and take a look around.

'Two final things,' said Landau as he walked Max to the lifts. 'Saskia's instructions are very thorough. As you know, she always thought everything through to the last detail. Nothing's been left to chance. She's even left details about your own remuneration, in the unlikely contingency of her death. They're actually very simple. She wants you to be paid the same as she paid herself.'

'How much was that, by the way?' Max asked.

'Last year, the package worked out at one point seven million dollars. And there's a company apartment in Manhattan.'

Max started. It was a mind-blowing amount of money. For some odd reason, his first thought was, Did Dad realise she made that much? The Colonel probably hadn't earned that in thirty years in the army. As a family, money had always been in short supply. Max remembered how much Saskia had always resented that. When she was seven or eight years old, they'd lived in Kiplingweg, outside Berlin, when their father was 2ic of B Company. There'd been an officer's furnished house, complete with china, linen, bedding, penny-dreadful sticks of furniture. Saskia had cried when they moved in.

'Why is everything always horrible and sad and brown wherever we live?' she had wailed, shoulders heaving with emotion. The outburst had become a family joke.

As she grew up, it seemed to Max that his sister had quite consciously recoiled from everything that reminded her of that period. Apart from last Christmas, it was years since she'd stayed overnight at High Hatch. She had once told him, matter of factly, that there wasn't a single piece of furniture, picture or ornament in their parents' home that she had any interest in eventually inheriting. 'When the day comes,' she had said, as they walked in Indian file across the flattened bracken of the common behind the house, 'you can have the lot.'

If she was paying herself more than a million pounds a year from *StreetSmart*, Max thought, he could understand why she didn't need anyone's castoffs.

'You said there were two things,' said Max. 'One was the salary. What was the other?'

'A letter,' said Landau. 'Saskia left it here for you, to be handed over if anything ever happened to her.'

'What's it say?'

'Couldn't tell you. It's addressed to you. My instructions were to lodge it in the strong room until required.'

Max slipped the letter into the pocket of his jacket and Landau helped him into his overcoat.

As they waited for the lift, Max asked, 'Philip, how well did you know my sister? Away from the office, that is.'

Landau considered the question. 'A lot of people knew her for much longer – I've only represented her for about five years. We beat the same paths socially, and had working lunches together.'

'So, what's your reaction to the suicide? Does it surprise you?'

'It does, yes. Very much. I don't know what to make of it. I guess it only goes to show how little one really knows about one's clients, even clients one imagines one knows well.'

'So you didn't have any premonition that something like this could happen?'

'Not the slightest, not for one moment. I saw Saskia ten days ago at a film premiere, and she looked a million dollars. She said business was good, *StreetSmart* was booming.'

Max shrugged. 'A mystery, then.'

'A mystery,' said Landau, then went on, 'So we'll touch base later this week or on Monday morning. Feel free to ring me at home at the Barbican over the weekend, if you'd like to.'

[6]

It was five minutes before three o'clock and Marcus Brooke was awaiting the daily image review with his boss, Freddie Saidi, the Lebanese business tycoon. He was not looking forward to today's meeting because most of the news was negative, and nobody responded less well to negative press than Freddie Saidi.

Marcus gathered up the sheaf of newspapers and magazines and crossed the hallway of the Rutland Gate headquarters. The mahogany double doors to Saidi's office stood less than twenty feet away. He could see three attractive young secretaries sitting at their workstations outside the door. One of Marcus's many responsibilities was to ensure that the supply of strawberry-blonde personal assistants never ran low, despite their exceptionally high turnover.

As he approached along the corridor, Marcus watched the CCTV surveillance cameras buried in the cornice lock on to him, one by one; the pictures, he knew, were being tracked by three different monitors, including the one directly beneath Freddie Saidi's desk, and by the four-man security team in the adjacent office.

Ten yards from the door, he reached the armoured Plexiglas cordon. Invisible from a distance of more than five feet, Marcus knew that it was 200 millimetres thick, built to take anything from a sniper rifle with a muzzle velocity of 838m per second to a full-blown combat shotgun like the Remington or Franchi special-purpose automatic. When he'd commissioned the security upgrade at Rutland Gate two years earlier, Saidi had told the security consultants, 'I don't want one fucking thing past here, you understand. Not a mortar, not a surface-to-bullshit-air missile, not nothing, OK?' So they had installed what they described as a Bespoke Personal Security Cocoon (BPESC), similar to, though Freddie Saidi liked to claim superior to, the BPESC the same company had built for Saddam

Hussein in his six-storey bunker beneath the al-Sajda palace in Baghdad.

Marcus stood for a moment before the entrance to Saidi's inner sanctum, and heard the whoosh of displaced air as the suction mechanism slid a second Plexiglas door shut behind him. Now he was sealed in a transparent compression chamber until one of the girls punched the code that would allow him to proceed. He knew that he was being screened for clearance by Security.

'Get on with it, *come on*, come on,' he muttered under his breath. Sometimes he thought Security intentionally kept him waiting, which was impertinent, considering how close he was to Mr Saidi in the organisation.

He smiled ingratiatingly through the glass at the secretaries. One of his many insecurities was that he always felt somehow inferior to his boss's personal assistants. First he hired them, then he sucked up to them: one day, they'd know before he did when his number was up.

There was a second whoosh of air – slower this time, more like the gentle exhale of a Gravitron machine reaching equilibrium in a gym – and Marcus was in the outer office.

'Morning, Ann-Marie,' he said cheerily to Freddie's senior secretary. She had long blonde hair and a childlike face, just as Freddie liked them, and she was discreet. 'How are we all this morning, then, girls? Full of the joys of spring?' Marcus noticed a new Cartier tank watch on the wrist of the latest recruit, Gemma. She had only been there a week, as junior secretary. He smiled. He had evidently chosen well.

'All right to go on in?' he asked Ann-Marie. He disliked having to ask her permission since, as Mr Saidi's London Head of Corporate Relations, he outranked her in the hierarchy.

Ann-Marie glanced at the telephone panel, where a narrow slit of red light could just be seen above an extension. 'I'm sorry, Mr Brooke, but Mr Saidi is still occupied on a call. I'll tell you when he's free, if you'd like to take a seat.'

Marcus preferred to stand in front of a Louis XIV looking-glass, its frame carved and gilded with a procession of dancing fauns and satyrs. He was a short, corpulent man, with sleek black hair brushed back vertically from his scalp and coated with some florid eucalyptus-based unguent. He removed from his inside jacket pocket an ivory comb, which he slid gloopily through his hair a couple of times, before patting the wings with his palms.

Fifteen minutes later, just as Marcus was starting to fret that his personal status, in the eyes of the PAs, was being permanently eroded by this undignified delay, there was a splutter of expletives from the intercom. Freddie Saidi was on the squawk box from next door.

'Eh, Ann-Marie. Is that fucking useless PR man of mine with you out there?'

'Yes, Mr Saidi.'

'Then send him in right away. He's meant to be here for a meeting, not sniffing around your pussies outside.'

'Of course, Mr Saidi.'

Marcus Brooke went into the office and laid his pile of papers on a polished walnut table. The centrepiece, cast of solid silver, was a perfect scale model of a Soviet-built MiG 1100 jet fighter. Made by Asprey, it was the sole reference in the room to Freddie Saidi's principal occupation as an arms dealer. Each time Marcus saw it, he winced. Marcus's own job, explicitly explained when he had been hired six years earlier, was to ensure that nobody ever referred to the fact that Freddie Saidi's fortune had been made through arms dealing in Beirut.

'I don't give one fuck how you do this thing,' Saidi had said, in what passed as a job specification. 'That's your problem. You fix that. You tell me, "Freddie, go here, don't go there, buy this thing, give money to these peoples, this charity, another charity." If I like the idea, I go along with it, why not, no problem. I want people to think, when they see Freddie Saidi come along, they think, "What a great guy. He build this hospital. He own this thing, that thing." But nobody mentions nothing about the special deals, OK? Nothing. That's your job. Don't let me down, Marcus, I am warning you.'

Freddie Saidi rose this morning from behind his desk and regarded Marcus non-committally from beneath hooded eyelids. He was a slight, rather scrawny man, in a grey suit made of a slinky shimmering cloth that he had ordered from Brioni in Manhattan. His hair was cut short and lay close to the scalp in a succession of tight grey curls, like rolls of wire wool.

'So, what have you got for me today?' he asked, as he crossed the carpet with its pattern of yellow crescents against a royal blue background.

'Bit of a mixed bag today, Freddie,' said Marcus. 'Plenty of positive mentions, but a couple of pieces where the journalist rather lost the plot, I'm afraid.' Saidi's face darkened, so Marcus added hurriedly, 'On balance, you definitely come out ahead.'

'Show me,' said Saidi. He leaned against the table where Marcus was arranging the day's media exhibits. Post-It notes marked the pages where there were articles mentioning the boss. Green Post-Its had been attached to opportunities that might interest him for high-profile charitable donations.

'There's a nice one here in the *Express* this morning, Freddie,' Marcus began. 'A picture of you presenting the cheque to the South London hospice for incurable diseases. Two paragraphs praising your benevolence. They used that quote from Nelson Mandela that you'll remember I asked him for.'

'OK, no problem,' grunted Saidi. 'What's this one here?'

'Ah,' said Marcus uncertainly. 'The interview in the *Independent*. You remember the girl they sent over? You talked to her here in your office.'

'The ugly one with a face like a fucking monkey's anus?'

'Yes, the girl who moved over from the business section. Now writes general features.'

'OK, what she go and say about me? That I'm giving all this money to charity and hung like a fucking donkey?

'She does touch on your charity, very much so,' said Marcus. 'You'll remember I gave her the complete list of your gifts, strictly off the record and unattributable of course. But I'm afraid she's tried to be a bit too clever, silly girl, and has included some unhelpful stuff about the Fournels et Fils polo tournament, and some of the other activities.'

Saidi put his face very close to Marcus's and said, 'I thought you told me this girl was OK. You checked her out. You said she'd write good things.'

'Indeed, Freddie, and that's what I was assured would happen. I briefed her myself. But, as I always tell you, you can't control journalists, not one hundred per cent. They're unpredictable and capricious by nature.'

Saidi's eyes narrowed and he hammered the table with his fist. 'That is what I fucking pay you for, Marcus. Eh? Don't I? To take care of all this. So, what can you do about it now? Now is too late.'

'Freddie, let me assure you that I've already spoken to the editor of the newspaper, and to the girl's immediate superior, her section editor, and I've told them both that the whole piece is shot through with factual errors, misquotations and deliberate falsehoods, and that you are urgently consulting your lawyers on possible legal redress. I told them that I have personally identified forty-three errors of fact, and that I believe the article to have been provoked by malice. You can take it as read, Freddie, that neither the journalist nor the newspaper will be publishing anything similar about you for a long time to come.

'Furthermore,' he went on, 'I have secured an undertaking from the editor that next time you make some newsworthy private charitable donation, they will be given an exclusive in return for prominent coverage. There's a possible contender in today's *Daily Mirror* I was about to draw to your attention.' Marcus scrabbled about in the pile. 'Here you go, look. Six-year-old kid with a respiratory problem, only the local health authority won't pay up for the operation. Best clinic is in Lausanne. Looking for Father Christmas.'

Saidi shrugged. He was sifting through the marked-up pages on the table, folding broadsheets inside out and jabbing with his finger at the tabloids.

'What's this say here anyway?'

Marcus blanched. It was a photocopy of a faxed paragraph from the Intelligencer gossip column of *New York* magazine, and he had purposely buried it at the bottom of the pile, hoping Saidi would overlook it.

'Ah, yes, Freddie. Another rather unhelpful item, I regret to say. I'd fed them the story about your generous gifts of food to the homeless, and how you personally instructed the management of the East River Hotel to distribute seasonal delicacies over the holiday. But I'm not happy with their angle, nor the way they've chosen to describe you.'

Freddie Saidi picked up the inky photocopy. Whenever he read anything – a contract, a menu, the press – his expression became watchful and contemptuous, as though he expected each line to include some buried conceit or trap, which he alone had the perspicacity to detect. He read slowly, interrogating each word for any derogatory nuance, and as he read, his eyes narrowed.

'Marcus, you fucking read this thing, this piece of bullshit?'

'Regrettably, Freddie, it's a mendacious attempt to defame you. And I can only say that as soon as America opens up, I'll be demanding a retraction.'

'You'd better get one,' said Saidi. 'Sometimes I don't know what you do all day, except sit on your arse.'

Marcus knew not to protest. He had long ago given up trying to justify himself or explain. Sometimes, in those increasingly rare moments when he dared reflect on what had happened to his life, when he tried to recover the sequence of events and shameful compromises that had borne him to this point, he had a fleeting memory of life BS: Before Saidi. Lately, he tried not to think too deeply about anything, he lived day to day. Sufficient unto the day. It was an old saying that had implanted itself in his brain, like a scrap of food trapped between the back teeth and impossible to dislodge.

Saidi was still turning pages of the tabloids, and had stopped at a news item headed, 'Mag queen Saskia. Police probe cocaine connection.' There was a photograph of Saskia, that couldn't have been less than ten years old, accompanied by a few nebulous paragraphs about a possible drugs angle.

'Tomorrow we start,' said Saidi. 'It's enough time now. You ring the magazine, what's the name again – *Streetwalk, Streetwise* ...'

'*StreetSmart*, Freddie.'

'*Streetfuck*, who gives a fuck, whatever. Ring them and tell them Freddie Saidi, he is buying them, and how much they want?'

'Of course, Freddie,' said Marcus. 'I'll be on to it right away. I'll take some soundings later today.'

'Just get on with it, OK?' said Saidi. 'Don't fuck this one up. Now the girl's out of the way, it's no problem. And you know something? After I've bought my own magazine, I might even get some good press. Is that possible? In my own magazine? Even you could arrange that, Marcus. At least I hope so.'

[7]

Max didn't feel like going straight home, so he walked up from Philip's office towards Covent Garden to stretch his legs a bit.

The narrow lanes in that part of London were lined with clothes shops, their windows crammed with sharp-looking suits and knitwear, and mannequins wearing dark glasses. For the first time, Max found himself noticing the cardboard showcards propped up in the windows: 'As seen in *StreetSmart*.' The Paul Smith shop had several 'As seen in *Vogue*'s and 'As seen in *Arena*'s, but no *StreetSmart*s at all.

He had already resolved to say no to Landau.

God knows what mischief had possessed Saskia when she made that will. No one seriously expects to die, and he supposed it just seemed a neat jape at the time, since he'd been so dismissive about her magazine over Christmas. Serve him right, he could hear her thinking, if I land him with it. Like bequeathing a rottweiler to someone who hates dogs.

There was a pub Max had always liked at the top of Sackville Street, the Sedan Chair, and he wandered inside to get out of the cold. It was one of those pubs that lays claim to half of English history, with a display of quill pens and pewter tankards and cockfighting spurs behind glass. There were some Italian tourists consulting guidebooks, otherwise the place was deserted in the middle of the afternoon. He bought a pint and sat down in a booth. The last time he'd been at this pub, it had been for a reunion drink with some French photographers from Gamma, whom he'd met the previous year in Mogadishu. They'd seemed more earnest and less entertaining out of context.

He delved into the bag Philip had given him, and extricated the British and American *StreetSmart*s. At first glance they both looked exactly the same, with Tom Cruise and Nicole Kidman on the cover, Cruise in the top half of a pair of white pyjamas, Kidman wearing only the bottoms. Then he noticed that one of the issues was chunkier, and more compact, than the other, and was different in other ways too. The words down the front of the cover flagged different articles. The slightly smaller format one was American and had some big exposé about the mistress of a Democrat presidential aide. The British issue didn't include that one. Instead there was an article about an Ayurvedic doctor from Kerala, who was secretly treating the Duchess of York and Kevin Costner.

The more Max studied the magazines, the less qualified he felt to make any judgements at all.

There was a great deal of fashion, most of it photographed on a blonde stick-insect he recognised from scent advertisements. Elsewhere there was a photo essay about a Mexican architect who designed eco-sustainable houses in the desert, and an article about American women who had chucked well-paid jobs on the corporate ladder to become high-class hookers. There was a colourful interview with a former attorney from Baltimore who reputedly turned ten thousand bucks a night, whenever trade-show delegates hit town.

There was a long profile of a Caribbean novelist, interviews with Tibetan women persecuted by the Chinese, movie gossip, a survey of ergonomic lip brushes, and twenty ways to make yourself instantly happy. On the back page of both editions was some new method for telling your fortune, based on the length and shape of your big toe.

The more Max read, the more he found the whole package disorientating. Half the articles struck him as trashy and aimed at the lowest possible denominator, and the rest rather pretentious and obscure. He couldn't visualise the sort of person who was meant to read it.

Towards the front of the magazine, about twenty pages in, he discovered a list of all the people who worked on it. At the very top, in giant type, it said SASKIA THOMPSON, President, Publishing Director and Editor-in-Chief. That was the American edition. In the British one, she was slightly more modestly titled: Editor, Chairman and Chief Executive.

He read down the long list of staff, with their complex-sounding job titles. Many were four or five words long: Executive Managing Editor/News, or Associate Special Projects Director/Cosmetics. Apart from Saskia, it was impossible to work out who was senior to anyone else. The hierarchy was obfuscated by a plethora of different type sizes. If someone's name was printed in bold black ink, did that make them a bigger fish than someone with their name in a lighter type, but further up the roll of credits?

Bob Troup was there on the line directly below Saskia's but not, Max noticed, titled as her deputy. He was called Senior Editor. On the same line were two other people: a Managing Editor named Gina David and an Associate Editor/Features, Marie-Louise Clay.

He ordered a second pint and returned to the magazines. The American issue had more pages than the British, but somehow didn't feel as substantial. Of course, the paper was thinner. If you pressed down hard, the type showed through from the page before. And the American one had more advertisements for mail-order CDs, printed on thick card. It was quite interesting to spot the differences. About half the articles, he reckoned, were exactly the same in both editions.

He left the Sedan Chair feeling nauseous. At first he attributed it to his painkillers reacting badly with the real ale, but came to the conclusion that it had more to do with the clouds of scent that wafted out of *StreetSmart*. He had always hated the way the pages were impregnated with the stuff. He remembered feeling so hacked off about it once that he had rung Saskia in her office, and told her, 'I wish you wouldn't send me your magazine if it's going to stink out my whole flat.' He had been away on a trip, and the copy had sat on the doormat, leaking noxious fumes.

Saskia had been unsympathetic. 'They pay us a fortune to insert scent strips, and most people like them anyway.'

He kept walking in the direction of Piccadilly and then headed up Regent Street. His arm was throbbing badly and he was looking for a chemist. He knew the whole area was thick with them, but all he seemed to pass were games arcades and dingy tailors' shop fronts selling bolts of men's suiting. Before long he found himself in Conduit Street, heading down towards the old Time-Life building on the corner of Bond Street. Until they shipped the staff out to somewhere near the airport, Max used to drop in regularly on *Time*'s London bureau, because they let him use the phone and fax with no questions asked. He even remembered fixing up some trips for *Newsweek* from there.

After *Time* left, the building had stood empty for ages, and then *StreetSmart* moved in. He knew that Saskia had originally hoped to rename it the StreetSmart Building, but the planning authority wouldn't allow it, because Time-Life was chiselled into the façade. She was furious. '*Time*'s history now,' she had raged. 'It's a brand in terminal decline. Can't they see that?'

On impulse, Max wandered into the lobby.

'Can I help you?' asked a receptionist, looking him up and down. He got the feeling that her offer of help was insincere.

'I'd like to speak to Jean, Saskia Thompson's secretary. Is it possible to ring her from here?'

'Have you an appointment?' asked the receptionist, doubtfully. She reminded him of an obstructive functionary in the Taliban information office, only much more attractive. She had thick black hair cut to her jaw, a shiny black suit and black nail varnish.

'No. But I'd still like to talk to her.'

She sighed and dialled an extension. 'Who shall I say it is?'

'Max Thompson.'

There was a muttered conversation which he could only half hear, and then she said, 'God, I'm really sorry, I didn't realise you were Saskia Thompson's brother. You should have said. Anyway, go straight up to the third floor. Jean will meet you by the lifts.'

When the lift doors opened, he didn't recognise the place. Saskia must have had it gutted. It was instantly intimidating, which was probably the intention. Ahead lay an enormous open-plan room with a steel floor, divided into sections by shiny silver mesh suspended at angles on tensile wires. It couldn't have been less than twenty windows across. All the desks were black and lacquered.

'Mr Thompson? I'm Jean Lovell, Saskia's PA.'

He didn't know what he'd been expecting, but not this small, mature, bustling senior secretary in a tweed suit with a brooch.

'I'm so sorry about your sister. She was a remarkable person. We're all desperately sad and shocked.'

'Thank you,' said Max. 'It's been a big shock for us too.'

'If you'd like to follow me, I'll take you along to her office. It's down at the end of this corridor.'

She showed him into another echoing suite with a view across Bond Street into the Donna Karan boutique. A table and most of the floor was covered with baskets of flowers.

'Tributes to Saskia,' said Jean. 'Lots of well-known people and companies have been sending them. It's very thoughtful, though what we'll do with them all, I'm not sure. Another whole lot arrived at the New York office. We've been noting the names of course, so we can thank them.' She offered him tea, then left him alone in the room while she went to make it.

Idly, Max examined the tags on some of the flowers.

'Deepest condolences, from all your friends at Cartier.'

'Editor of genius. Always, Fran Leibowitz.'

'Giant steps are what you took – walking on the moon, love Sting and Trudie.'

'To a great lady. With respect, from everyone in the print room at Gërstler-Begg plc (Doncaster).'

'So very sorry – Donatella and Santo Versace.'

Seeing all the flowers moved Max to a degree that took him by surprise, and he felt tears pricking his eyes.

Jean returned with the tea and a glass containing some effervescent drink. 'I don't know whether this would help, but it contains paracetamol. I noticed your arm, it looks painful.'

He thanked her gratefully.

'Your sister used to swear by it too,' said Jean. 'Not that I altogether approve. You can get hooked on pain relief, even the mild variety. I told Saskia as much, many times.'

'How long did you work for Saskia?'

'How long? It must be getting on for eight years. When I joined her, we were still in the Soho Square offices. A long while.'

'I'm sorry we haven't met before.'

'Well, we've spoken on the telephone on several occasions. And I always ensure your copy of *StreetSmart* gets sent off to you each month. And your party invitations.'

Max reddened slightly. He had never been much good at replying to Saskia's invitations; they'd always struck him as too much like royal commands. 'I'm afraid I missed most of them,' he mumbled. 'I'm abroad a good deal.'

'Oh, we knew that,' said Jean. 'We know you're a difficult man to pin down, but Saskia was always so delighted when you could come.'

There was a tap at the door and a man appeared in the office. He looked about forty, somewhat overweight, with pale ginger hair and eyebrows. He was wearing a green wool suit with a white T-shirt.

'Mind if I join you? I heard you were in here. Max, I'm Bob Troup. We spoke on the phone.'

'Ah yes. My sister's deputy editor.'

Max saw Bob's eyes dart guiltily to Jean and then back again. He really was like a snake.

'Senior Editor is my official job title,' he said quickly, 'but I was certainly her effective number two.'

'Good to meet you,' said Max, then, feeling that he should say something about Saskia, added, 'It must be quite difficult for everyone here at the moment.'

'It is, but people are getting on with their jobs. They have to. We're on deadline with the next issue. Ironically,' he went on, 'the April issue we're all working on looks like being particularly strong. I've commissioned some last-minute, very topical stories.'

'Great,' said Max. 'I was reading your latest issue in the pub just now. Some of that seemed surprisingly good and topical too.'

Bob raised his eyes at the mention of a pub, and didn't seem to appreciate the compliment either. '*StreetSmart* could be even more topical and newsy. Sometimes we're too slow to react. That's the way forward.'

For some reason, Max suddenly got the feeling he was being exposed to a job pitch.

'Max, could I have a word with you in private?'

'Sure.' He looked round for Jean who was watering a pot of white lilies. 'Jean, would you mind . . . for one minute . . . ?'

Jean left the office, giving Bob a hard stare. Max got the impression she didn't much care for him.

When they were alone, Bob said, 'Look, I hope you don't mind me speaking out, but a lot of us are feeling quite unsettled, not knowing what's going on.'

'In what way?'

'Well, now Saskia's dead. She owned *StreetSmart*, or most of it. Who'll own us now? And when will they appoint a new editor?'

'I'm afraid I don't know the answer to those questions, but I'm sure the thing to do is carry on as usual. Nothing's going to happen overnight.'

'Is that really fair on the staff though?' asked Bob. 'The magazine can't function indefinitely without an editor. We need to make changes. We can't just churn it out to Saskia's old formula.'

'Presumably you can for a while. Everyone tells me *StreetSmart*'s a big success.'

'*Now* it is, yes. But whether it's as hot as it was a year ago, I'm not sure. People are starting to question that. Are we going stale?'

Bob had lost him there. Everything Max had ever read about the magazine suggested it was booming. And it won awards all the time. From where he was sitting, he could see a shelf-ful of trophies and citations along Saskia's bookcase.

'Look, there's two things I have to know,' said Bob. 'Is the magazine for sale?'

'For sale? Not that I'm aware.'

'And am I a candidate to be the next editor?'

'I really couldn't tell you. I'm only her brother.'

'I have the support of the staff,' said Bob. 'Well, most of them. The talented ones. And I understand the magazine. I'd bring continuity and change.' He stared at Max, bug eyed. 'I need an answer quickly,' he said, 'because there are other offers. Ever since Saskia killed herself, my phone's been ringing. People saying, "You're bound to get it, Bob, but if they're stupid enough not to give it to you . . ."'

He was half threatening, half pleading. Max found the whole experience embarrassing.

'Listen, Bob,' he said. 'Nobody knows what'll happen yet. Genuinely. I hope you won't walk out at this critical time. My sister's only been dead a few days. But if you feel you have to, I can't stop you. You must do what you think's best.'

Bob looked at him, crestfallen. This wasn't the reaction he'd been looking for. He stood up. 'What about this rumour about Freddie Saidi, then?'

'What rumour?'

'Everyone says he's going to buy *StreetSmart*.'

'They do?'

'And what Saidi wants, he generally gets.'

'Well, maybe he'll be disappointed this time.'

'He wouldn't be a bad owner,' said Bob. 'He'd invest in the titles, he's got deep pockets. And he wouldn't interfere editorially.'

'You know all this, do you?'

Bob coloured. It was obvious he felt he'd said too much already. 'Anyway, I hope you didn't mind me telling you where I stand. It's just that I'm passionately committed to *StreetSmart*. It's a special magazine, and I know it intimately. It wouldn't be easy,' he added meaningfully, 'for anyone to come in from the outside.'

Then, to Max's immense relief, he backed out of Saskia's office, smiling thinly.

Jean was through the door a second later. 'Well,' she sniffed, 'I suppose he was putting his hat in the ring to be editor, was he? The presumption of the man.'

'So you don't think he'd be suitable, then?'

'I most certainly do not. Editor, indeed. I wouldn't trust him to walk my Airedale round the block.'

'Then why did Saskia put up with him? He seems to have had quite a lot of responsibility.'

'Oh, Saskia knew exactly how to handle Bob Troup. He had his uses. He was always in the office, all hours. That's because he doesn't have a private life,' she added, damningly.

'And Saskia did.'

'Gracious yes, out every night,' said Jean proudly. 'Launches, first nights. And all those dinners. A good part of my day was spent organising Saskia's evening engagements. And sending flowers the next morning.

'By the way,' she went on, 'I've got Saskia's spare key to her flat. She always kept one with me here at the office. It occurred to me that someone should go round there, to make sure everything's all right. I'd go myself, but I thought her brother . . .'

'I'm happy to. Is the flat alarmed?'

'I've typed the code on to a card for you. The keypad is just inside the front door, as I recall.'

This woman was so efficient, no wonder Saskia's life was so easy.

'I'll go round this evening. If there's anything important, I'll let you know.'

'But you'll be dropping into the office tomorrow, I expect,' Jean said.

'I hadn't planned to.'

'It would make such a difference if you could. It's been a great morale boost for the staff, your visit here today.'

'But I haven't even seen anybody. Except Bob Troup.'

'Next time I'll introduce you around the office,' said Jean, walking him to the lifts. 'The staff adored your sister, and they're finding it painful to come to terms with it all. Everything that's happened is so . . . out of character.'

As they passed the newsroom, about thirty heads turned to stare at Max. And, for the second time that day, he regretted not looking more the part.

[8]

Whenever Étienne Bercuse was in New York for longer than a few hours, he liked to treat himself to a hooker.

He maintained that the choice of women in the city was more comprehensive than in any other place he visited. Texan girls, blacks from Brownsville, browns from Blackwell Park, Latinos, Koreans, Slavs and Polaks, blondes from Miami, French girls – though Étienne instinctively avoided these, on the grounds that his face was well enough known in his own country to pose a remote security risk.

Each time the helicopter ferried him into the city along the East River from the airport, Bercuse first had the pilot tip the chopper so he could admire Bercuse Plaza from the air, then he liked to stare down across the Art Deco spires and dark canyons of the Manhattan skyscape. It turned him on to think that somewhere way down below, amidst the twinkling lights of the office buildings and gridlocked traffic, were thousands of hookers of every nationality and race, all biddable through a single telephone call to hang off the end of his dick.

Bercuse's brand of free-market capitalism demanded an ample supply of everything, at all times, everywhere. French scent, Italian leather handbags, Mexican or Thai pussy. It should make no difference where in the world you happened to be, geographically, it was all a matter of distribution. If a businessman needed a 50ml bottle of Tranquilité to bring home to his wife, or an atomiser of Gaia for his mistress, or felt like screwing the fat ass off some Haitian tart, it should all be possible in a developed service economy.

Had he bothered to glance outside from the windows of his wraparound suite on the fifty-third floor of the Four Seasons Hotel, Bercuse could have seen half the landmark buildings of midtown Manhattan: the verdigris copper and slate roof of Henry Hardenbergh's Plaza hotel; the mirrored vulgarity of Trump Tower; the

54

coarse white granite spurs of the old General Motors Building, like the grille of a giant radiator, soaring above the canopy of diesel-laden trees of Central Park, and the Edwardian turrets of the Dakota apartment house beyond. But Bercuse never once raised his eyes. Instead his narrow face was buried in the NYNEX yellow pages for Area Code 212, in the fifty-three-page section headed Escorts.

Two things made Étienne Bercuse hard, and neither of them was women. The two things were air travel and success. After any flight, however short its duration, he always needed sex; success – or more accurately the anticipation of success – had the same effect. When he had a great idea, the adrenalin that pumped around his system went straight to his testicles.

'There is no question,' he reflected to himself as he dictated over the phone the credit card numbers that would secure the arrival of two Hispanic girls within one hour maximum, 'this will be one of the great deals of my life.' He was inclined to place it on a par with his landmark acquisition of the St-Cyr-le-Châtel vineyard, five years earlier, from the daughter of France's oldest aristocrat, the Marquis de St Cyr, in a secret deal conducted entirely behind the beady old man's back.

By his feet on the floor lay a schedule of advertising for all his brands in *StreetSmart*, on both sides of the Atlantic. A second schedule detailed the page investments of Chanel, Vendôme and LVMH. Bercuse could see that his own companies invested on average $6 million a year on advertising in *StreetSmart* – seventy pages in the US edition at $60,000 a page, plus 107 more in Britain at £15,000 each – a total of $30 million over the past five years. Some of his competitors had invested even more, because they were paying higher rates for special positions in the magazine: inside front covers, back covers, first cosmetic advertisement and first fragrance. For Bercuse, one of the frustrations of building up the newest luxury-goods conglomerate was that the premium advertising sites had already been reserved in perpetuity by his rivals.

All this will change, he thought. When I acquire *StreetSmart*, all the positions will be exclusively reserved for the Bercuse brands.

He could hardly wait for the day when LVMH, Chanel, Vendôme and the others received notice to quit. A fax, not even a letter, would be the most satisfying way of communicating his victory. An unsigned fax. Dictated by Étienne Bercuse and sent unread in his absence. 'Owing to a change of ownership, *StreetSmart* magazine is henceforth unable to accept advertising or promotional material from the following brands: Louis Vuitton, Dior, Givenchy, Christian Lacroix, Chloé, Chanel, Cartier, Dunhill, Montblanc, Piaget, Baume & Mercier, Vacheron . . .'

Wasn't that what every luxury-goods company secretly desired, a powerful glossy magazine from which all its competitors were excluded? Competitive advantage at its most explicit. How many times had he picked up the new issues of *Vogue, Elle* and *StreetSmart*, and turned eagerly to the campaigns for his latest launches, only to find their impact neutralised by the proximity of competitors' advertisements?

When he'd launched the Bercuse Reverso sports watch, with its reversible face for deep-sea diving and high-altitude snowboarding, the impact had been undermined by the presence of rival products like the Rolex Oyster and Cartier's Pasha Chronograph. And the American launch of Tranquilité Pour Homme, which Jim Marciano had insisted run everywhere with scent strips and tip-ons, had been swamped – there was no other word for it – by Calvin Klein's CKbe and Chanel's Allure.

Étienne Bercuse had worked it all out. He had constructed a model, and the logic was irrefutable. The loss of advertising revenue when he booted his competitors out of *StreetSmart* would be painful, but it was nothing, nothing at all, when you quantified the impact of solus advertising for his own brands. The margin on increased turnover would more than compensate for the lost revenue.

So far he had told nobody about his plan. Not Jim Marciano, not Li Fah Hsiang, nobody. They'd be angry with him for not consulting them, but it was only their pride that would be hurt. It made no difference. All the big ideas in this company were his. And only he would ever know how it came about, and how he had made it happen.

Anyway, he thought, if he shared this with Jim and Li, they'd never keep their mouths shut. One of them would blab. They could read about it in the business pages, as a done deal, along with everyone else.

Already, he knew exactly how he was going to explain it to the world. 'Think of it this way, *hein*? From today, when Vuitton or Cartier or any of our competitors launches something new, the seven million readers of our magazine *StreetSmart* will not even know about it. It is perfect, *non*? They will remain *entirely ignorant*. All they will be seeing in the advertisements, when they open the magazine, is our products. It is enough.'

Every step, it was all planned, as it had been from the day he thought of it. Right now, *StreetSmart* wasn't even on the market. But it would be. And he knew exactly how he was going to accelerate the process even further.

The doorbell of the suite rang softly, and Étienne Bercuse rose to his feet and padded stiffly across the carpet. He consulted his wrist watch: there were precisely two hours until he needed to leave for the airport.

Waiting outside in the beige corridor were two sullen-faced girls in plastic imitation-leather jackets.

'So you two really are sisters, *non*?' asked Bercuse, as he shepherded them into the suite.

[9]

Max had only visited Saskia's flat in Holland Park once before, for a party she'd given in honour of a Jamaican poet. *StreetSmart* had extracted some verse from a new collection, and had him photographed by David LaChapelle looking like Jimi Hendrix in a patched sheepskin coat. By the time Max had arrived, there were already a couple of hundred people there, drinking rum hooch and eating goat curry out of coconut husks, all prepared by some expensive catering company. He remembered hacking his way through a thicket of celebrities, none of whom had any interest in talking to him, and getting the hell out again as quickly as he decently could.

He hadn't appreciated, on that earlier visit, quite how large the flat was. It occupied two floors of an immense lateral conversion, spanning the width of three stuccoed mansions at the top of Holland Park Avenue. He let himself into a flagstoned hall, deactivated the alarm and groped about for the lightswitches. He pressed a black pad and at once the whole room was bathed in pinhead beams of halogen light. There must have been fifty bulbs in the ceiling.

He scooped up a pile of post and newspapers from the mat and placed them on a black marble hall table. Then, feeling uncomfortably like a burglar, he entered the drawing room. His boots clattered loudly across the wide wooden floorboards. There was very little furniture, other than six long white sofas. On the walls were some large canvases, mostly white, and a big circular spin painting by Damien Hirst in bright purple and lime green.

Jean Lovell had suggested he made sure everything was all right. He supposed he could have collected the letters and made a note to cancel the newspapers and left it at that, but now that he was there, he was curious to see the place. He felt it might give him some steer, if not to his sister's death then at least to her life.

There were no other rooms on the first floor beyond a small

soulless kitchen full of steel appliances, and this huge white drawing room. It was like a New York loft space transported from SoHo and installed behind a Holland Park façade. It was a room that made a statement: I am seriously cool. But if it said anything more intimate about Saskia, then Max missed it.

A stone staircase from the hall led upstairs to a corridor, off which led several doors. The first one he opened must have been Saskia's bedroom. A pile of clothes was thrown across the back of a chair, presumably the ones she had changed out of before leaving for America. There was a wide, low double bed with a white bedspread, and at the foot of the bed, a big-screen television.

One wall of the room was given over to cupboards and, feeling guilty, he opened a door and peered inside. The rails were overflowing. Max had never seen so many clothes in one place in his life, not even in a shop. They were squeezed flat against each other, hangers tangled together on the rails, sleeves of dresses sticking out from lack of space. The cupboard was a complete mess. With difficulty, he jammed the door shut again, and the room reverted to minimalist order.

A surprise awaited him in the bathroom; he saw it the moment he opened the door. One of his photographs was framed above the bath: the only picture in the white room. It was one of those lucky shots you don't really expect to work at the time, just take on the off-chance. It was in Sarajevo and Max had been returning from the press information bunker at the end of Sniper Alley. A Croat woman was sitting in the passenger seat of a beaten-up old banger. He was just walking past when a single shot rang out, shattered the windscreen and bore straight through the woman's skull. He'd taken the picture on reflex, focusing on the windscreen rather than the person inside, and when developed, it had turned out to be rather great. Just a single bullethole in the middle of this expanse of shattered glass, which had fanned out like an op-art painting, almost an optical illusion, because you couldn't quite work out the perspective. In the background you just saw the horribly distorted face.

God knows where Saskia had got it from. Actually, it wouldn't have been that difficult, she had probably just ordered it through Bullet. But she'd had it beautifully printed up and framed; exhibition quality. Max was quite flattered that she'd gone to the trouble. Maybe Saskia really had rated his work, as Philip Landau had said.

Next door was a smaller spare bedroom and another bathroom, and finally a study. This was a complete contrast to the drawing room. He imagined no one ever got near it except Saskia herself. There were old magazines and newspapers stacked on every surface, especially the floor, and towers of books, some in half-open Jiffy bags. Underneath the window he could just make out the shape of a desk, covered by drifts of paper.

He sat down at the desk and stared outside into the darkness of Holland Park. How many times had Saskia sat here like this, all alone in her big, empty show flat? Or was she never alone? He realised how little he really knew his sister, despite the many articles he'd read about her in the papers. There were whole areas of her emotional life that he just didn't know about. It struck him that the study was the only room in the flat that had anything of the real Saskia about it. Downstairs was public space. State rooms, practically.

There was a display of photographs along the windowsill, some in frames, others propped up against the pane. Several of Saskia herself. Suddenly he thought: Where's Cody? Surely she has a picture of her son. He hadn't spotted one in the bedroom either. The absence of Cody worried him. There *must* be one, he had to be there somewhere. He rifled through the display, found rock stars, a film director, but still no Cody. There were more photographs in a desk drawer. And there – at last – a little snap of him on the beach, it looked like the West Indies. He was sitting on the shoulders of a Rastafarian, clinging on to his dreadlocks while they waded in from a banana boat.

It made Max wonder where she kept his toys. Although Cody lived in Farnborough with his grandparents, he came up for visits. Saskia must have a cupboard full of toys somewhere.

The thought nagged at him. He opened all the cupboards in the study, then in the spare room and Saskia's bedroom, searching for anything gross and plastic that Cody played with in London. And he couldn't find one damn thing.

His sister's attitude to Cody had always bugged him. Sometimes she was all over him, assuring profile writers that her son was the most important thing in her life, and how she made quality time for him. Max remembered one interview in which she'd claimed that she'd turned down dinner with Kiefer Sutherland at Mezzaluna, because Cody was staying with her at the Château Marmont in LA and she'd promised to stay in and watch Cartoon Network with him that evening. If it had happened at all, it was definitely a one-off. Most of the time she seemed to forget about Cody, and he would be left at High Hatch, while Saskia devoted herself to becoming ever more famous.

Until she was nine or ten, Max had known everything about his sister. Her toys, her tantrums, the places she'd visited and not visited, the food she liked and didn't like, the way she couldn't get off to sleep without the light left on in the passage and her bedroom door precisely six inches ajar. After that, she had simply drifted further and further away from him, like a lilo on a strong ocean current, until one day she was so far beyond reach that they were subject to the pull of different tides. He could only guess at the demons and ambitions that had driven Saskia.

However, when other people criticised her, or described her as a starfucker, Max always found himself hastening to her defence. He knew the distance she had travelled to attain her success. Virtually everything she stood for, the people she mixed with, the magazine: all struck him as worthless and shallow. But when he remembered her as a teenager – the moon-faced adolescent at Episkopi Garrison in Cyprus, turning the pages of a movie fanzine on the steps of their house on the base – and then thought of the woman she'd become, he admired her determination, the way she had done it all on her own.

A couple of years back, he had been staying at a hotel in Amman, lying on his bed with his boots on and half watching CNN, when they'd shown a segment from the Oscar ceremony with actresses and film moguls stepping out from their limousines, half a world away on Sunset Boulevard. And suddenly, arriving on the arm of Richard Gere, there was Saskia, wearing some incredible beaded dress that she later told him she'd borrowed for the night from Giorgio Armani. Max remembered thinking then, Hey, that's incredible, that's my sister up there at the Oscars with Richard Gere.

Max was putting Saskia's photographs back in the drawer when he remembered the letter. He had thrust it into his jacket pocket in Philip Landau's office, and it was still there. On the envelope was typed, 'Max Thompson, c/o Philip Landau & Associates. To be opened by addressee only.'

Inside was a single sheet of paper, typed double space, with Saskia's signature at the bottom.

Dear Max,

Chances are you'll never read this. I hope you don't, because that means something's happened.

You may already have spoken to my lawyer Philip Landau, or you may not. I've asked him to explain to you that I want you to run *StreetSmart* until Cody's old enough to take over himself.

I know the idea won't appeal to you. You told me often enough how little you think of my magazine. In fact you were bloody dismissive and patronising. The only reason I'm writing this letter now is because you're the right person.

You've always been wrong about the magazine world, and I hope one day you'll recognise this. One reason I want you to take over *StreetSmart* is because of everything you learned in Afghanistan, Bosnia etc. It should help. The magazine business is like guerilla warfare. You'll understand what I mean if you take the job.

I need someone strong to follow me. I've never said anything like this to you before – for some reason I never could – but I admire you, Max. I admire the way you went off and did your own thing.

You're also brave, and I've got a feeling that's going to be a big advantage over the next few months. I may be wrong about this, but for the first time since I started *StreetSmart* I'm nervous. There are a lot of predators out there.

Max, I really need you to give it your best. If not for me, then for Cody. I'd like to believe that one day he'll follow me on the magazine. It'd be kind of neat.

Best,

Saskia

The letter was dated 14 February, just over a fortnight old. She must have written it just before leaving for New York on this last trip.

Max read it a second time, folded it in half and slipped it inside his wallet, then he turned out the lights, reset the alarm and ventured out into the inky black February night.

As he walked home up Ladbroke Grove, he couldn't get a thought out of his head: he was being well and truly manipulated. And he didn't like it one bit.

[10]

Max passed the corner of Arundel Gardens, which made him think of Ken Craig. Ken was another photojournalist, who, when he was in England, lived on the top floor of a tall, peeling house permanently clad in scaffolding.

They had met in Peshawar shortly before Max's first trip across the border into Afghanistan, and they had subsequently worked together in Liberia, Chechnya and Rwanda. Max thought of Ken as his closest friend in the business.

Ken had also once pretty much saved his life. They had gone into Rwanda together for Bullet, and got involved in a situation with trigger-happy Hutus manning a roadblock outside Butare. Max had always believed that they were within five minutes of death that afternoon, and it was Ken Craig who had somehow talked their way out of it.

Max pressed the entryphone in Arundel Gardens and it crackled into life. 'Max? Greetings, stranger, I'll buzz you in.'

Five flights of stairs and he was up at the flat. Ken had once challenged him to find a smaller flat in the whole of West London, and so far Max hadn't even got a contender. Ken's place was one of those cowboy conversions in which an already modest space is subdivided, with sheets of hardboard and mdf, into several monkish cells. Highly desirable studio apartments is the euphemism they trade under.

Max stepped inside into a bedsit, with a sofabed along one wall, and a sink and microwave in a louvred cupboard. There was a water tank on top of the wardrobe, and a Formica table at which Ken worked and ate. Squeezed into another, windowless closet was a shower and lavatory with an extractor fan that roared like a jet turbine.

'Fortunate I'm just a Scots midget, isn't it?' Ken used to joke, when he welcomed guests home for the first time.

Max had always partly attributed Ken's considerable success with women to the fact that, once they'd crossed the threshold, there was no place to go except bed.

It was true Ken was small, barely five foot three, and stocky like an army sergeant. He didn't actually wear a moustache, but he might well have done. There was something military, too, about Ken's place in its precision and orderliness. His books, CDs and box-files were ranged in descending order of size along a shelf, and a dozen perfectly folded khaki shirts and jerseys stood in a pile. Max was sure if he'd called out, 'Kit inspection, Ken,' he could have displayed the entire contents on the bed in ten seconds flat. Even the stainless-steel taps on his sink gleamed from polishing.

'So, Max,' Ken said, when he noticed the sling, 'they weren't having me on then, when they said you'd taken on the Taliban single handed. You're only there to report the war, remember, not grab a starring role.'

They both laughed. It was good to see Ken again. Max had missed his utterly predictable Scots humour. One of the best things about Ken was the way you always knew what he was going to say next.

'But seriously,' he said, 'you should get that arm looked at. A gentleman like you needs both his elbows in working order.'

How many times had he heard Ken tell that one? Ken always maintained that the only true definition of a gentleman was someone who took his own weight while screwing.

Max described the trip to Afghanistan and Ken handed over a pile of newspapers and magazines that had used his pictures while he was away. The two men always acted as a clippings service when the other was out of the country. The *Observer* Review had run six or seven of his shots of Taliban moral police in Kabul, including a spread of a mullah beating a woman who'd ventured outside without her chador. For once, they'd chosen the best picture. There were some others in *Newsweek* and the *Corriere della Sera* magazine, used much too small.

'And then the minute I arrive back,' Max said, 'I discover my sister has gone and killed herself. God knows why, she's the last person I'd have expected it of.'

'I read about that in the papers,' said Ken. 'In fact I thought of trying to contact you on your trip, but then I reckoned, well, maybe not.'

'Why was that, out of interest?'

'Well, you know, I'd never thought of you two as all that close.'

'That obvious, was it?'

'You didn't exactly make a secret of it.' Ken rinsed a couple of glasses in the sink, shook them dry and poured two generous measures of whisky. 'That evening in Grozny, when we couldn't leave the hotel and sat up late in the bar. The things you told me about Saskia, your opinion of her.' Suddenly Ken looked embarrassed. 'Probably that was insensitive of me, to remind you of that. She was your sister. I'm sure you're very cut up about her, I'm sorry.'

Max shrugged. 'I guess we're all a bit ambivalent about our families, aren't we? With Saskia, more than anyone. I don't know what I thought really. I've just been round to her flat and, you know something, it was like the home of a stranger. A weird experience. I suppose we were just very different.'

'You certainly were that,' said Ken. 'Your sister was a seriously fanciable bird. No way I'd have said no to her, I can tell you.'

Max laughed. 'Dream on, Ken. She'd have been more likely to make it with Boris Yeltsin than you. Far more likely, in fact.'

Ken looked momentarily crestfallen. 'And what's wrong with *me*, then? Too small?'

'No, it's your flat that's too small. About three dozen rooms too small. And I don't think you've won an Oscar yet, or edited a national newspaper, or won a Pulitzer prize, or played Madison Square Garden, or ruled a country. I could go on.'

'I see. Bad as that, was she?'

'Worse. But, as you said, she was my sister so she can't have been all bad. Actually,' Max said, 'I had this weird meeting today with Saskia's lawyer.'

He told Ken about his visit to Philip Landau's office, and Saskia's will, and the letter she'd left for him.

'It's all very odd. From the letter, she sounds genuinely keen I should run her magazine. I thought it was a wind-up at first. In fact, I still half think it's a joke. I don't know what to do about it.'

'I'd have thought it was a complete no-brainer,' said Ken. 'The easiest decision of your life.'

'OK. *What*, then?'

'Don't touch it with a barge-pole, mate. You'd hate it. You told me in Chechnya about your contempt for that magazine. You said it represents everything you despise.'

'It does, but, there again, I was reading it in the pub this afternoon, and there are a few articles that aren't bad. I was quite surprised.'

'Oh yeah,' said Ken sceptically. 'Five new hairdos for spring. How to make a cherry cheesecake. I don't really see you choosing the knitting patterns, Max.'

'Seriously, there are some worthwhile articles in there too. They had one on human rights violations of Tibetan women by the Chinese. It was good stuff.'

Ken was unconvinced. 'I can't believe anyone reads those articles. Not under the hairdryer. And they'd never get proper journalists writing for them.'

'That's not true either, as a matter of fact. John Updike had contributed something. And so had Gabriel Garcia Marquez.'

'Sure. Gabriel Garcia Marquez on "How to reactivate your sex life. Ten fail-safe tips." '

'I'm perfectly serious: *StreetSmart* isn't all crap. You should take a look some time.'

Ken refilled his glass, then said, 'Max, you asked my advice and I've told you what I think. We've always been straight with each other. My considered opinion is that you'd be bored rigid. I'd give you a month, two at the outside, before you chucked it in. It would be a total waste of your talents. I'm not just flattering you – you know me, a misanthropic old Scot, I don't go round telling my friends they're wonderful all the time – but you're a bloody good photojournalist. The dog's bollocks. Everyone recognises that. I hate to admit this, but you're a lot better than me. We go to the same places, point our cameras at the same things, but your pictures are that bit sharper and stronger, every time. It's bloody irritating.

'Another thing,' he went on, 'wouldn't you find it a bit humiliating, telling the world you were working for something like that? Don't delude yourself: all those magazines are rubbish, read by uptight housewives during their coffee breaks.' Ken put on a silly, female voice. 'Ooh, I've finished my vacuuming, I'll just put my feet up for five minutes and have a nice read of my magazine. Ooh, cherry cheesecake and Tibetan women. What a treat!'

Max laughed, but he was annoyed too. 'Now you're being pathetic,

Ken. *StreetSmart* sells a million and a half copies a month: it's a big deal.'

'So your sister always used to insist. And in those days *you* weren't impressed either. I'm just saying that, next to reporting wars, magazines are nothing. Not in the same league. The work you're doing now – Grozny, Kabul – it means something. You're telling the world what's really happening. They may not care half the time, but it's still important. It makes a difference. Don't you remember how elated we all felt when we got pictures out of Afghanistan of the Mujahedin fighting back against the Russians? That first photograph of a rebel shooting down a Soviet helicopter with a Stinger? It encouraged the Americans to continue funding the whole resistance movement, which eventually led the Russians to pull out. That was partly you, Max. You should be proud. Don't sell out now.'

'It's confusing,' he replied. 'I'm torn myself. I just don't know where my responsibilities lie. Half of me wants to get on the next plane out of town. There's the civil war in Eritrea, up near the Sudanese border . . .'

'Great,' said Ken. 'Let's go together. Bullet owes us a trip. We haven't been on an adventure together for a year.'

'I've got to think. There are a lot of different aspects to this. Cody, for one. Saskia wants me to caretake the magazine until he's old enough to inherit it.'

'But he's only a kid,' said Ken. 'There was a picture of him in the newspaper. It'll be twenty years till he's ready, and he might not even want it. He might prefer to do a man's job.'

'Thanks, Ken. Why I ever thought of asking a Scottish misogynist for impartial advice, I can't imagine. I'd have done better asking Fred Flintstone.'

'Well,' said Ken, 'I'm sure you'll make up your own mind. You always do, you're that stubborn. And if you're looking for a partner for a trip to Eritrea, I'm up for it. Any time you like.'

Max walked the rest of the way home, cursing silently. Ken Craig had always known how to wind him up.

The telephone was ringing as he let himself into his flat.

'Hello. Can I speak to Max Thompson?' A female voice. Quite young, not yet thirty, he reckoned. It could have been another tabloid journalist and he was tempted to put the receiver straight down.

'Who wants him?'

'Kitty Marr. My name won't mean anything, but I work at *StreetSmart*.'

'It's Max speaking.'

'I guessed it probably was,' said Kitty. 'Your voice sounds like I expected. It matches what you looked like when you came into the office this afternoon.'

'You were there, were you?'

'I work in the fashion room. You went past with Jean Lovell when she took you to Saskia's office. I hope you weren't too embarrassed, with everyone gawping.'

'I was slightly, as a matter of fact.'

'You should have been there when Keanu Reeves came in to visit Saskia,' said Kitty. 'Everyone was hanging out of the windows when he arrived, and then kept walking past her office. Jean was furious, she kept shooing everyone away.' Kitty laughed. 'Bob Troup was *just fuming* not to be introduced to Keanu. He probably fancied him.'

'I met Bob at the office. He came and said hello.'

'Predictably,' said Kitty. 'Everyone was just so annoyed about that. The minute he heard you were there, he practically ran across the office.'

Now it was Max's turn to laugh. He found it easy talking to Kitty Marr, and he wondered whether she'd be as fun in real life.

'It's Bob I'm calling you about actually,' she said. 'About ten of us in the office wanted to say something, and I sort of drew the short straw. So it's my job to ring you.'

'What about him?'

'Well, you're not about to appoint him editor, are you?'

'Not another one,' Max said. 'Why does everyone imagine I'm some sort of kingmaker all of a sudden?'

'Bob's going round saying you virtually promised him. He's drawing up lists of who is going to be kept on and who'll be fired.'

'Which list are you on?'

'No question. The second. I'm on the fast track to the exit.'

'Well, don't clear your desk yet. Nothing's decided. And you can tell your nine friends that too.' Then, on an impulse, he said, 'I'm planning on dropping into the office again tomorrow afternoon. Do you want lunch first? Then you can explain the magazine to me and everything else.'

'You sure?' said Kitty. 'That'd be great. I'm out on appointments all morning but they'll be over by lunchtime.'

'Is there somewhere close to the office to meet? I don't spend a lot of time in England, so restaurants aren't something I know about.'

'There's a place just down the street,' said Kitty. 'In the basement of the new Givenchy boutique. Chow Bene – it's Chinese Italian. I can book a table if you like.'

'See you there at one o'clock, then. I don't have to dress up, do I?'

There was a pause down the line. 'Not really. But, you know, in that part of London . . .' She sounded embarrassed.

'I get it,' Max said, laughing. 'You're reminding me I'm not still on the front line, am I right?'

'Something like that, I expect,' said Kitty. 'But don't worry about it.'

Max was gingerly removing his sling before turning in when the telephone rang again.

'Max? It's Stefan.'

'Stefan! Sorry I haven't rung you back, but things have been rather hairy here, one way and another.'

'I can imagine,' said Stefan. 'I saw the news about your sister on *Good Morning America*. I'm sorry, it must be a terrible time.'

'It's not great. For my parents especially.'

'Well,' said Stefan, 'what I've got to tell you isn't great either. We've run into problems over here at Bullet. Not long term, it's just a temporary cashflow problem.'

Max tensed. 'How long have I got to wait to be reimbursed? You guys owe me a fortune already, plus all my expenses from Afghanistan.'

'Like I said, I'm sure there won't be a problem, once the new equity comes through, but we've been told to put a stop on everything. No payments, no new assignments. We're pulling everyone out of the field.'

'Thanks, Stefan,' said Max. 'That's just tremendous. And your timing's impeccable too, with my arm shot up and everything.'

'Don't mention it,' said Stefan. 'I'll get back to you when the situation changes, if they don't sling me out too.'

Afterwards, Max thought, Terrific. I'm wounded and flat broke, and I can't go to Eritrea. It's a straight choice between that damn magazine and busking on the Embankment.

[11]

To enter Chow Bene, Max passed first through the white boutique, past rails of clothes and cabinets full of handbags and earrings, before arriving at a spiral of tubular-steel-and-glass stairs. Each step, as he descended to the basement, was individually lit by pinhead bulbs encased in glass bricks, like eggs in aspic; at the foot of the stairs, a concrete lectern was manned by a Calabrian maître d', who looked Max up and down with obvious disdain, as though searching for a pretext on which to turn him away. Max's efforts at looking presentable – even taking his combat jacket for a high-speed clean in the Harrow Road – were evidently insufficient.

'I'm joining Kitty Marr.'

'She has just arrived,' said the head waiter, before striding ahead across a vast expanse of wooden floor, to a table at the rear of the restaurant.

'Hi, I'm Kitty,' she said, standing up.

She had long fair hair that looked bleached by sunshine, and big round blue eyes. Her figure, he could see, was terrific: slender greyhound legs, small satsuma breasts, neat ankles. She was wearing a short cream-coloured coat over a plain cream-coloured dress.

'Max.'

They shook hands across the table, and the waiter ushered him next to her inside the booth, before pushing the table back in on them, like a fairground attendant securing the safety bar on a wild ride.

'So you worked with my sister?'

'Worked *for* her is more accurate. And, listen, there's something I want to say to you. It's something I feel quite bad about. When I rang you at your home last night, I should have said how sorry I am about Saskia, instead of just launching in about my job.'

'And *are* you?'

'Am I what?'

'Sorry about my sister? Genuinely? People keep telling me they're sorry. Were you close to her?'

'Well,' said Kitty, 'put it this way, she gave me my job. Or, at least, she was the editor when I was hired by Racinda, the fashion director. I never got to know Saskia that well, but she was a great editor. A superstar really. She had the best life.'

'Then why go and kill herself?'

Kitty looked at him. 'That's what everyone's wondering, isn't it? At the office, people talk about nothing else. In fact, everywhere you go.'

A waiter arrived to take their order and Max chose a veal chop with garlic mash. Kitty went for something involving lamb's lettuce, sesame seeds and beansprouts in soy. Chinese rabbit food, exactly the kind of thing Saskia used to order, Max noticed.

'So how long have you been on *StreetSmart*?' Max asked.

'Nearly seven years. I'm in the fashion room.'

'You're going to think me very ignorant, but what exactly does that mean? Being in the fashion room. Is that choosing the clothes to be photographed?'

'Sure. You call in the clothes, set up shoots. Get the right girl – the model – photographer, location, hair and make-up. All of that really.'

'And which of you gets to keep the clothes afterwards? You or the model?'

Kitty laughed. 'You know, that's the first question people always ask: "Do you get to keep the clothes?" Well, dream on. They all have to go back to the designer's PR. Anyway, they're samples. Size tens. I couldn't get them over my shoulders.'

'Sorry my question was so obvious.'

'Well, at least you didn't ask what Stella Tennant looks like in her knickers. That's what men usually want to know.'

He must have looked blank because Kitty said, 'You know Stella, don't you? Was the Chanel model. Took over from Claudia Schiffer. English, punk, aristo. The one who had the nose ring and pierced navel. Did those pictures with Steven Meisel. She's everywhere.'

None of this meant anything to Max. 'I've been out of the country. And, anyway, most of these models just look emaciated to me. They're so thin, they're not even that attractive half the time. Can't you persuade some decent, pretty girls to model for you?'

'My God,' said Kitty. 'You certainly have been out of the country. I don't mean to be rude, but where were you, *Mars*?'

'Afghanistan. Before that, Rwanda and Chechnya.'

'Wow,' said Kitty. 'I've always wanted to do a shoot in Afghanistan. In fact we were talking about it the other day, at a fashion planning meeting. Do you have any contacts in the government who might help us get sponsorship?'

'Probably best to write to the Chief Mullah of the Taliban in Kabul,' said Max drily. 'It could be good timing. They're particularly keen on bikini shoots at the moment. You should take that model you were talking about, the one with the navel ring – Stella.'

Kitty looked at him sharply, gauging whether or not he was teasing her, then rabbit-punched him on the arm.

He let out a yell. 'For Christ's sake, don't touch my arm. Jesus, that was fucking agony.'

He told Kitty about Afghanistan and the landmine on the pass and how the whole country was reverting to some kind of repressive medieval state. He told her that it sickened him and, what was worse, no one seemed to care that much.

Kitty nodded sympathetically. When she was serious, she looked surprisingly grave. She said, 'There was one other thing I thought I should mention, to do with Saskia. It probably isn't important. I could have imagined it.'

'Go on.'

'Well, the night she died, I was at the same party at the Waldorf. I wasn't going to be there, but I was doing a sitting in New York, and they needed another person, so I got roped in. Anyway, Saskia asked me to stay close to her all evening, and I kind of got the impression she was avoiding someone. Nothing definite, it was just an impression, and something she said.'

'What was that?'

'Oh, right after dinner, she spotted someone across the ballroom and seemed annoyed he was there. Then later, by the cloakroom when we were leaving, it happened again. Maybe I'm attaching too much importance to it.'

'Maybe. Maybe not. Any idea who it could have been?'

'None. When she first spotted him across the room, Saskia said, "I don't believe it, *he's* here." She seemed pretty annoyed.'

'And you didn't ask who she was referring to?'

'I didn't get a chance, because just then Tom Cruise came up. Anyway, she was more talking to herself. She didn't encourage questions.'

'Did my sister have any enemies?'

'Enemies?'

'People who didn't like her.'

'Well, I suppose she wasn't always very tactful. She did alienate a few people.'

'What sort of people?'

'Writers, celebrities. She changed her mind a lot about what went into the magazine, though I'm sure she was right from an editorial standpoint. She'd get us to photograph ten pages of clothes on some actress, then cool on the project and drop it. And she usually forgot to tell the person. So they'd be looking out for the story and it'd never appear. We had a thing like that recently with Jackie and Joan Collins. There was this big shoot in LA with the sisters wearing Valentino couture. It cost a fortune to set up, and when it came in, Saskia hated it and killed it. When they eventually found out, everyone went mad: Joan's agent, Jackie's agent, Valentino, the photographer. So she did make enemies.'

'What about inside the office? The staff all liked her, didn't they?'

For the second time, Kitty was evasive. 'Saskia was very impressive. You learned so much, just by working there.'

'That's not what I asked. I asked, "Did they *like* her?"'

Kitty looked troubled. 'Well, you probably know there was quite a lot of coming and going.'

'I don't know anything. Tell me.'

'It's just that the staff kept changing. People didn't always stay long.'

'Because Saskia fired them?'

'Or they left. She didn't usually need to fire them. Most jumped before they were pushed. If Saskia went off you, you just sort of got frozen out. None of your stories got published, you weren't included in meetings, so you might as well leave. People said it was Saskia's way of saving on severance payments. Sorry, I don't mean to be negative about your sister.'

'Listen, Kitty,' Max said. 'There's one thing you'd better know about me and Saskia. I admired her a lot, and she was my sister and everything, but we didn't always get on. We're very different people.

So nothing you've told me comes as a surprise. There, I've said it. That's for you, incidentally, not the whole world.'

'I promise, I won't tell anyone.'

At that moment, he felt a bond had been established between them. In some strange way, he felt unburdened having told her. He was either going to have to spend the rest of his life pretending to everyone that Saskia and he had been soulmates, or tell the truth. And, having come clean, he felt better about it.

'Now,' he said, 'this afternoon. I think I promised Jean Lovell I'd drop by the office, so I suppose I'd better. I'm not that keen to.'

'She'd be very put out if you didn't. There's a full editorial meeting in your honour. The whole office has been tidied up.'

'You're joking.'

'I'm not. It's a big ideas conference, to come up with stories for May and June. All the section editors: news, features, fashion, health and beauty. Jean's rung all the freelancers who work from home and summoned them in too, the reviewers and stylists and so on.'

'But that's absurd.'

'Not really. They want to see you, and find out what's happening. You're Saskia's brother. People are curious.'

'They must have very little to think about.'

'You should see Bob Troup,' said Kitty. 'He's come in today wearing a shirt and tie. A *tie*! He hasn't worn one ever before, at least not while I've been at *StreetSmart*.'

'Why's he done that?'

'Because he thinks you're going to confirm him as editor. He's even shaved. Goodbye designer stubble.'

'If I'd known, I'd have shaved more carefully myself.'

'I shouldn't bother,' said Kitty. 'On Bob it just looks pretentious, but on you it's actually quite macho.'

[12]

They arrived at *StreetSmart* to find an arc of metal chairs arranged in the centre of the editorial floor. Some were already occupied by contributors, while groups of section editors milled about in the lobby and around a coffee machine.

As soon as Max arrived, Jean Lovell, who had been watching out for him, came over. 'There you are, good,' she said briskly. 'There are a lot of people wanting to meet you. It's probably best if I start by introducing you to the senior members of Saskia's team. Gina!' She summoned a raven-haired woman with scarlet lipstick and a determined jaw. 'Max, this is Gina David. Gina's the Managing Editor.'

'Hello,' said Gina. 'Terrible about your sister.'

'Thanks. Had you worked together long?'

'From the beginning virtually, I joined her on issue four. That was in the original Westway offices. A long journey from here, in every sense.' She rolled her eyes at the steel floor and silver mesh.

'So you don't find these surroundings sympathetic either?' he said.

'Like working in an industrial kitchen. That's what I told Saskia. But she loved it.'

While they were talking, Jean had been lining up the next encounter. 'Marie-Louise Clay, Associate Editor/Features.'

Marie-Louise, like Gina, was an impressive woman in her late thirties, with ash-blonde hair and an algae-coloured trouser suit.

'Forgive my ignorance, but what's the difference between a managing editor and a – what was it – associate editor/features?' he asked.

'Easy,' said Gina. 'Marie-Louise does her best to bust the budget, and my job's to restrain her.'

Marie-Louise laughed. Max got the impression they were good friends as well as colleagues.

'And how do you manage that?'

'Restrain her? Oh, we managing editors have our methods. Threats, trade-offs. Usually it comes right in the end. It's easier working with Marie-Louise than some people I could mention. Especially since they're coming this way now.'

Bob Troup, dressed as Kitty had described in jacket and narrow black tie, managed to look both ingratiating and vaguely confrontational as he sidled over towards them. 'Hi, Max. Jean says you want to sit in on this meeting, which is fine by me. Just to warn you, these things can be a bit overwhelming if you haven't experienced them before, so don't feel you have to contribute.'

Bob clapped his hands together for quiet and said, 'Gather round, everyone, *please*. We are going to make a start. *Lisa*, this isn't a mothers' meeting. Are you joining us or aren't you? If you're not, perhaps you'd care to leave the office. For good.'

A girl in a padded Mao jacket scuttled nervously to her place.

There were forty of them sitting in a half circle, Bob in the middle with a file containing some kind of agenda, Gina taking minutes, Marie-Louise marshalling lists of ideas. Max found a chair at the edge of the arc, intending to keep shtum and spectate.

Opposite him sat Kitty next to an unhinged-looking older woman with mocha-brown lipstick and leggings – Kitty's boss, probably. Kitty looked cool and was chewing gum.

Looking further round the circle, he tried to work out what everyone's job might be. There was a guy in grey cords who could be the news editor, or maybe travel, and a woman with cropped grey hair and a metal attaché case who must be design. He thought he'd identified the arts and health editors too, when Bob kicked off the meeting.

'This is the first editorial conference since Saskia's death,' he began, 'and I know a lot of you are feeling quite unsettled by it all. However, in a business as competitive as ours, it's important to keep moving forward, and we need to come up with a lot of fresh ideas this afternoon. I trust you've all come along prepared with two great ideas each. I'm going to start by going round the room. Lisa – since you were so full of hot air before the meeting – perhaps you'd like to start us off.'

All eyes turned on Lisa, who shifted uncomfortably. She was a whey-faced anaemic, who either hadn't seen daylight for several months or was suffering from some advanced wasting disease. 'For the May health and beauty notebook,' she said, 'we were planning on doing something about macrobiotic diuretics. There's been some quite interesting research done at UCLA in California.'

'That counts as interesting, does it?' said Bob. 'Macrobiotic diuretics.' He rolled the concept disdainfully around his tongue. 'Well, as an idea it doesn't make *my* dick hard.' There was a titter from a section of the group. 'Any other great scoops, Lisa, or is macrobiotic diuretics your sole submission this time for a Pulitzer prize?'

She gulped and looked down at her notes.

'Come on, Lisa,' said Bob. 'Wake up and smell the coffee, will you? You've had twenty-four hours to get with the programme. Don't keep us in suspense. Surely some other American quack – excuse me, Californian professor – has produced some crap research you can plagiarise for your page. Well, haven't they?'

'There is another possibility,' stuttered Lisa. 'Shark-liver oil. It's being developed in capsule form as a cure for certain forms of cancer. Apparently the Japanese have been using it for years, but now it's being taken seriously. There's a professor at Osaka University ...'

'You're making this up,' said Bob. 'Got to be. That or you're gullible. Shark-liver oil. You want to rub some into your brain, Lisa. Morning and evening for about thirty years and you might come up with a publishable idea.'

He eyeballed the meeting for approval and Max noticed several sycophants smirk back at him. 'The talented ones', as he'd no doubt classify them.

'All right, who's next? We've had macrobiotic diuretics and shark-liver oil. Who has any other bright ideas to make *StreetSmart* jump off the newsstands?' Nobody seemed anxious to volunteer. 'Marie-Louise?'

Marie-Louise Clay was a confident presenter. 'Three ideas,' she said. 'All very different. Suttee in India – that's the tradition of the widow throwing herself on to her dead husband's funeral pyre. Apparently it's making a comeback in certain areas, in particular the State of Bihar. Except that there's evidence it isn't generally voluntary – the widow's parents-in-law are usually implicated. They force the girls to cremate themselves. It's a dowry thing. Any interest, anyone?'

There was a murmur of assent, but Bob moved quickly to quell it. 'Sorry, old idea. I've read that story before.'

'You *have*?' said Marie-Louise. 'I must have missed it. Where was it?'

'Oh, some Italian publication. Maybe American. Anyway, I've read it. What else?'

'Jacqueline Onassis. There's a big new biography coming out in the summer which implies—'

'Marie-Louise, I cannot believe you are seriously suggesting Jackie O for an article in *StreetSmart* this close to the third millennium. Get real, darling. What's the third idea? Greta Garbo? Joan of Arc?'

'Madonna actually,' said Marie-Louise. 'I mentioned this one to Saskia, and she was very excited by it. We may have come up with an interesting scoop. This man everyone says she's seeing – the Russian industrialist, Igor Sergov – well, he's definitely got a shady past. He was apparently involved with all kinds of dubious people in Chechnya, gun-running, currency-smuggling. He was known as the hard-currency king of Moscow.'

A ripple of excitement ran through the meeting, and mutterings of 'great story'. Max was intrigued himself, and it rang distant bells. He'd definitely heard the name, Igor Sergov, when he was in Grozny, but hadn't made the connection when he'd read about him in this new superstar context.

Bob curled his lip. For some reason he was reluctant to endorse Marie-Louise's scoop. Even without knowing the internal politics at *StreetSmart*, you could tell they detested each other.

'The thing about Chechnya,' said Bob, his voice becoming silkier by the syllable, 'in fact the thing about all those Russian satellites, is this: who gives a toss? No one even knows where Chechnya is, do they?'

'Oh, come on, Bob, yes they do,' said Gina David. 'Our readers know.'

'Well, they sure as hell haven't been there. It's not Barcelona or Nevis.' He looked round the circle. 'Anyone been to Chechnya on their summer hols? Nice two-week vacation in a Soviet-Muslim condo? Anyone?'

'I've been to Chechnya,' said Max. 'I've travelled across it. Several times.'

'I see,' said Bob, feigning delight at his interjection. 'Saskia's brother Max has been there. Typical of a Thompson to be blazing the trail, if I may say so.' Then, with obvious reluctance, he asked Max's opinion on the Sergov idea.

'If true, it'll get picked up by all the national newspapers,' Max said. 'A genuine scoop. And, I must say, I agree with Gina that people are interested in Chechnya – in the gang warfare at least. It's the only place I've been with no concept of law at all. Pure Wild West. You can gun a man down in the street and no one will stop you, or try and arrest you. I saw that happen. I took some horrific pictures while I was there.'

'Maybe we could see them,' said a man in jeans and a vest. 'I'm Spiro, by the way, the picture editor. Do you have agency representation?'

'Bullet.'

'Great,' said Spiro. 'I'll call them in.'

Bob, looking furious, said, 'OK then, Marie-Louise will progress the Sergov story to the next stage and see if it stacks up. Personally I have my doubts, but we'll defer to Saskia's brother. Why not? We always deferred to his sister.'

Max caught Kitty's eye across the room and she smiled and mouthed, 'Well done, Max.' He held her gaze for a moment. Somehow he felt that, by challenging Bob, he'd achieved something useful and significant. It was just that he couldn't work out what it was.

'Now,' Bob was saying, 'who's next above the parapet with the stale buns?'

'I've got an idea,' volunteered a young guy in black chinos. 'This might sound boring but it's not, so don't yawn, anyone. Data protection violation ...'

'God, I'm yawning already,' said Bob. He emitted a porcine snore.

'Go on, Tim,' said Marie-Louise. 'I'm listening. Data protection is very current.'

'The thing is,' said Tim, 'there are some important ramifications of the new data protection legislation that have been overlooked. I mean, areas that weren't intended to be covered when the legislation was drafted, but have nevertheless been caught up in it. Take the international hotel chains and auction houses. They all compile detailed databases on their top clients – preferences and quirks, names of wives and husbands, personal details and notes about their

banking and screwing arrangements. Whether they prefer a peppermint on their pillow at night or a call-girl. Sometimes these files are
really comprehensive. Well, the fact is, under the new data
protection act, people can demand to see what's been written about
them. Just like you can request your medical history, credit rating
and life insurance profile. It's against the law now for any business or
institution to compile a personal profile on anyone and not allow
them to inspect it on demand.'

Bob, glassy eyed, was making a big show of yawning behind his
hand, but Tim pressed on.

'The point is,' he said, 'we could encourage well-known people to
request their files, and then ask them how accurate they are, maybe
even print them with their comments. Wouldn't you like to read the
secret Marriott hotels file on Bruce Springsteen? Or the Ritz-
Carlton database on President Clinton? Or the auction houses,
Christie's and Sotheby's; apparently their files are incredible. A
hundred pages each on Heini Thyssen, Prince Al-Waleed of Saudi
Arabia, the Rothschilds, Mick Jagger, anyone who's ever bought a
serious picture. All stored in retrieval systems, so available for
scrutiny. Couldn't it be great?'

'Riveting,' said Gina David.

'Totally impractical,' said Bob. 'Not even worth discussing. If you
think you can get Al-Waleed to collaborate on something like that,
you don't know what day of the week it is. You could spend six
months on that story and get nowhere.'

'Oh, give us a break, Bob,' said Marie-Louise. 'You're being
negative. Even without any input from celebrities, it's still a good
story. The secret VIP files. I'd read it.'

'But not in *StreetSmart*. Now, moving on, who haven't we heard
from? The fashion department haven't contributed anything so far.
Kitty Marr. Give us your ideas.'

Max felt himself tense as Kitty consulted her list. It surprised him
that, on such a short acquaintance, he was so anxious for her to shine,
or anyway to get through her turn with minimum humiliation.

Kitty looked remarkably composed. If she were apprehensive, it
didn't show. The cream dress suited her, showed off her figure.

'My idea is basically visual,' said Kitty. 'A group photograph by
Yando of the fashion world's financial analysts. Now that half the big
fashion companies have got stockmarket quotations – Donna Karan,

Ralph Lauren, Gucci, Tommy Hilfiger, Givenchy and Dior via LVMH – all those analysts from Merrill Lynch and SBC Warburg are suddenly very influential. You must have spotted them at the shows. They get front row seats. If they hate a collection, they dump the stock and the price drops. No one seems to have caught on to them or done anything about them. Anyway, my idea is to dress them up in the clothes of the companies they've taken big positions in. All those smooth young analysts wearing Givenchy, DKNY, Hilfiger, et cetera. It could be fun.'

As an idea, it sounded original to Max, and he could see Gina nodding as she minuted it. Kitty looked at Max enquiringly, as if to ask, 'Was that OK?' and he smiled back. He felt relieved for her. The ordeal was over.

But he had reckoned without Bob.

'Don't you feel these group pictures are rather Been There, Done That?' he began in a slow, petulant voice. 'We've all been publishing them for several years and, as a concept, they're looking tired. I wish,' he said, 'that for *once* – just once – you could push the envelope, Kitty. It's actually getting rather boring having to listen to your derivative suggestions, meeting after meeting.' He was working himself into a fury now; the veins were bulging in his neck. It was sickening to watch, and rather frightening. 'And that goes for everyone else, too. A lot of you are just as bad as Kitty: recycling ideas, coming up with total crap at meetings. Well, I won't stand for it. No, it's got to change. Saskia might have thought it was acceptable, but I don't, OK? If I have to change the whole team, every single one of you, then I'm perfectly prepared to do that. Starting with you, Kitty. You can just get out of here. Go on, fuck off out of it.'

The whole meeting had moved into shutdown mode, people were avoiding each other's eyes.

Bob glared at Kitty, his neck blotchy with anger. 'I said get out. Don't you people in fashion comprehend English, or must I express myself visually?'

'Actually, Bob, that won't be necessary.' Before he knew it, Max was on his feet, his voice sounding unnaturally loud.

Bob turned to him in surprise. He might even have forgotten Max was there.

'Kitty won't be leaving the magazine,' said Max. 'As a matter of fact, however, I will be accepting one resignation this afternoon: yours.'

Bob stared at Max, then laughed nervously. 'I'm sure there's no need for any more change on *StreetSmart*,' he said. 'We've had enough disruption already, with your sister . . .'

But Bob had misread him. When Max lost his rag, he really lost it. 'We'll just have to put up with a bit more disruption, then,' he said. 'I'm sure we'll manage somehow, even without your morale-building leadership. Right now, I'd like you to collect your things and leave.'

Afterwards, Kitty told him that he looked completely in control throughout the whole spiel; inside, he was shaking. In a way, he was more frightened taking on Bob than he'd ever been on a foreign assignment. At least he'd always had a camera to hide behind. And the enemy was generally way out of sight, even when they were in range.

Very slowly, Bob rose to his feet and walked towards the door. When he reached the stairs, he turned to address the room. 'You do realise *StreetSmart* is finished,' he said. 'Everyone knows I've held it together. Without me, it's over. I *am StreetSmart*.' He paused dramatically. 'I give the magazine six months. If you're sensible, you'll all get out first, before it goes under.'

After he'd gone, Max stood up, looked at the shocked faces and let out a long sigh. 'Anyone keep a stiff drink in this place? I feel I deserve one. And anyway,' he added, 'we need to celebrate, don't we? He's gone.'

There was relieved laughter, followed by a small cheer.

Many of the staff looked stunned or disbelieving, and kept eyeing the door as though Bob would at any moment reappear. The younger ones hardly knew who Max was, and were probably wondering if he even had the authority to dismiss him. It was a valid question. Legally, Max was sure he was on dodgy ground.

Gradually, however, as they began to see it was for real, an extraordinary euphoria swept the room.

Gina and Marie-Louise came over, beaming with delight.

'That was *so great*,' said Gina. 'Now I know how the Romanians felt when they booted out Ceauşescu. Or the Filipinos after Marcos. Pure joy.'

Marie-Louise said, 'Without Saskia to slap him down, the power turned his head. Poisonous little jerk.'

84

Jean Lovell appeared down the corridor with a tray of glasses, while her assistant struggled behind with a case of wine. 'Nothing stiffer than Chablis, I'm afraid,' said Jean. 'Saskia was never one for strong liquor. But, if you agree, we could all have a glass of this.'

'Great,' said Max. 'Though I'm feeling quite spacy already after that showdown. It wasn't premeditated, it just happened. It was the way he was so negative and was obviously getting off on ritual humiliation.'

Jean handed him a glass and he felt a soft hand on his back. 'Thanks for saving my job,' said Kitty.

'Any time. Actually, I'm already having serious misgivings. Not about firing Bob Troup, but about interfering at all. It's all very well playing the hero, but what the hell happens next?'

'That's easy,' said Kitty. '*You* edit it.'

Gina grasped his elbow and he flinched. If one more person touched his damn sling . . .

'As I keep saying, I don't know the first thing about magazines.'

'The staff will unite behind you,' said Jean. 'I mean, you *are* Saskia's brother.'

'Seriously, I've got strong reservations.'

'Jean's right,' said Gina. 'It will be like old times working with a Thompson. And you were brilliant getting rid of Bob.'

'Go on,' said Kitty. 'You know you've got to say yes. Otherwise who's going to save my job for me next time?'

'OK,' Max heard himself saying. 'I'm going to wake up tomorrow regretting this – and so will you probably – but I'll give it a shot. Not longterm, just a few weeks, until we find someone permanent.'

Max felt as though the whole staff took two steps forward, until his legs were pressed flat against a desk. Jean Lovell shook him by the hand, while Gina David pumped his sling and Kitty kissed him full on the lips. He hadn't been jostled this much since covering a lynch-mob in Kabul. Everywhere were smiling faces. At least almost everywhere. Over by the window, he noticed Bob's acolytes in a mutinous huddle. He hoped they wouldn't resign too quickly. After all, as Bob kept insisting, they were the talent.

Gina David stood on a desk and proposed a toast. 'This last week has been a really rough time for all of us on the magazine, with the awful news about Saskia,' she said. 'I know how cut up about it everyone is, and how, right now, it's impossible to imagine the magazine without her, because Saskia is irreplaceable. I know we all feel that, but I also know that she would have wanted us to keep going, to continue her work, as a kind of memorial to her. So I'm asking everyone to raise their glasses to a fresh chapter in the history of *StreetSmart*. Max, we're proud to have you on board. And, as Saskia's brother, we have no doubts you can do it. It's in the blood.'

There was another ragged cheer and then Jean paraded him round the room, introducing him to the rest of the team. It wasn't hard to tell, from the build-up she gave them, who Jean did or didn't rate. The man in cords, who Max had earlier marked down as news or travel, turned out to be the production director, who launched into a not-very-condensed briefing about developments in web-offset printing.

'Do shut up, Tod,' said Jean sharply, as she extricated Max from his orbit. 'Mr Thompson has only been editor for ten minutes. He'll be on the first plane back to the Killing Fields if you bang on like that.'

The boy in black chinos – Tim – came up and introduced himself as the features assistant, and Spiro the picture editor said he knew various people at Bullet. Max was reassured by how friendly everyone was. Just then Kitty appeared, looking put upon, closely pursued by the older woman in brown lipstick.

'This is my boss, Racinda Blick. She's fashion director. She's very keen to meet you.'

A bony hand covered in rings brushed Max's own. 'We need a new lightbox,' she stated. 'I've been saying this for months now. One lightbox is not enough. This morning, we had the Ann Demeulemeester catwalk pictures spread out, and then Yando's showgirls sitting came in. The situation's untenable. I told Saskia that. I memo'd her.'

'I'm not a hundred per cent sure what you're talking about yet,' Max said, 'but I'll look into it right away. Give me a couple of days. If your request's reasonable, I'll sort it.'

'Of course it's reasonable,' snapped Racinda. She sighed. 'I don't know why I put up with this. I'll show you the correspondence, all the memos. Oh yes, you'll be surprised.'

'Thanks,' he said uneasily. 'I'll look forward to them.' Then he dived into the throng, wondering what Saskia would have done in that situation.

He surfaced at the far side and found himself next to the talented ones: Bob's sycophants who'd so relished his public demolition of Lisa and Kitty. They were loitering stroppily by the windows, two youths and a girl with a cigarette.

Max introduced himself, and came out with some platitude about looking forward to learning what everyone's job was.

'Hardly matters, does it?' replied the girl, sourly.

'Why's that? Aren't you planning on staying long?'

'No, it's *you* who won't be staying long.' The youths glared at him. One of them had a shaven head and a short black goatee. He was stocky and aggressive.

'Why's that, out of interest?' Max asked coolly.

'Freddie Saidi's buying us. That's what everyone says.'

'As a matter of fact, he's not.'

'Yeah?' said the shaven-headed one. 'I wouldn't bet on it.'

This reference to the ownership of *StreetSmart* reminded Max that he ought to inform Philip Landau what had happened. Things had moved on more rapidly than he could ever have imagined. Yesterday, at lunchtime, he'd agreed to think over Philip's offer until after the weekend. Now, barely twenty-four hours later, he'd mounted a coup and seized the throne.

He asked Jean if he could borrow an office to make a call.

'Why borrow one?' she said. 'You have a perfectly good corner office of your own.'

It took him a moment to understand what the cryptic old dragon was driving at. 'Oh, you mean Saskia's office.'

'The editor's office.'

He shut the door of his large new suite and tried to figure out how to use the phone. There was a mini-switchboard on Saskia's desk with two handsets, speakers for conference calls and a digital display screen like the dashboard of a Lexus. Several glowing green bars kept rising and falling, to no obvious purpose, and there was a pre-dial memory facility for a hundred names. He picked up the receiver and a green icon flashed, 'Enter password.'

He cursed. It was somehow typical of Saskia to have installed a state-of-technology telecommunications centre that he couldn't even access.

Jean put her head round the door. 'Dial nine for an outside line. Ignore everything else. Saskia didn't understand it either.'

Philip Landau took his call and asked him to hold while he turned the music down. In the background he could hear some catchy pop song about girls just wanting to disco.

'Sorry about that,' said Philip. 'They're the new Spice Girls. In theory, anyway. I'm preparing a contract for Rabbit Records.'

'I'm ringing you from *StreetSmart*,' Max said. 'Things have moved rather fast here. I appear to have appointed myself Acting Editor.'

'That's fantastic,' said Philip. He sounded genuinely delighted. 'I wasn't sure you were going to.'

'Me neither. When I left your office yesterday, I was determined to turn it down. In fact I nearly caught the first plane to Eritrea. But I've decided to give it a go. For a few weeks, anyway.'

'All I can say,' said Philip, 'is that Saskia would be proud of you.'

'You know, it still amazes me. That she wanted me to do it. I think she was nuts.' He told Philip about the contents of Saskia's letter, and how she seemed to be worried that someone was trying to prise the magazine away from her. 'People here keep mentioning Freddie Saidi. Who is he? His name's come up a couple of times.'

'The thing about Saidi,' said Philip, 'is that he's invoked as a potential predator for everything, whether he's interested or not. He's Lebanese, but mostly lives here in London now. Owns various prestige businesses, including a hotel in New York. We certainly haven't received an overture from him. Not yet. If I do hear anything, I'll tell you right away.'

'Thanks. Starting tomorrow, I'll be fulltime at *StreetSmart*.'

'Later in the week I'll drop round and ask you to sign various papers. Bank mandates, et cetera. Meanwhile, good luck and don't panic. You've got some experienced people there to help you. Saskia always said she had a strong deputy in Bob Troup.'

'Ah. That's something else I was going to mention. I've just fired him.'

'You *have*? You're becoming more like your sister every minute. What severance have you agreed?'

'None, so far.'

Philip laughed. 'If it weren't a male voice at the end of this line, I'd believe I really was talking to Saskia. This is the sort of conversation we had all the time. She was always canning staff and leaving me to clean up the mess.'

'I don't think this is the same at all,' Max replied, quite sharply.

These constant comparisons with Saskia were beginning to annoy him. After all, Saskia was a prima donna and a bitch in the office; that was the script. And he didn't find it flattering to be cast as some kind of reincarnation.

'Max, I wonder if I could have a word?' said Gina David, as he was leaving the office.

'Sure,' replied Max.

'Up at the end of the hall. It's quieter there.'

They found a deserted stretch of corridor, and Gina said, 'I hope you don't mind me asking this, but having worked with Saskia for such a long time, there's something I need to get off my chest.'

'Anything. Feel free.'

'To be blunt, do you really believe she committed suicide?'

Max looked at her sharply. 'Why do you ask that?'

'Because it doesn't ring true. Not Saskia's style.'

'The newspapers seem pretty convinced.'

'I'm telling you my own reaction. Marie-Louise feels the same. The minute we heard, we said, "This doesn't add up. Saskia would never walk off the set like that."'

'I don't know what to think,' said Max. 'My whole family is baffled. We can't imagine why Saskia would have done it. Maybe when the post mortem comes through we'll learn more. One of the papers suggested she was depressed about her job or love life or something.'

'I read that, and it's crap. She wasn't depressed. If anything, I'd say she was hyper. She was planning a lot of new things for *StreetSmart*, and was excited about them. She liked the new issue. We biked about a thousand copies.'

'How do you mean, biked them?'

'Got them couriered by motorcycle messenger. When Saskia was pleased with an issue, she liked to have it hand-delivered to opinion-formers, to create a buzz. Actors, politicians, socialites, I can show you the list if you like.'

'And they were all delivered by *messenger*? It must cost a fortune. What's wrong with the mail?'

'It is extravagant, sure, you need about eighty bikes. But Saskia thought it made more impact, having the issue arrive by courier. She was a great believer in word of mouth.'

[13]

That evening at home, Max tipped all the reports Philip Landau had given him on to the sitting-room floor, poured a large whisky, and made a start on trying to read them. He found it difficult to concentrate, because his mind kept returning to his conversation with Gina. She didn't believe Saskia would commit suicide, any more than his father seemed to believe it. But if it wasn't suicide, what had happened that night at her apartment?

It took Max a while even to work out what each document was. There were spreadsheets of numbers, cashflow, advertising reports, bad debt provisions, statistics about payroll and headcount. Also a lot of stuff he didn't understand about accruals, deferred profit and midterm debt. He made a mental note to set up a meeting with Philip, and get him to take him through it line by line.

The most complicated documents were to do with the ownership structure. As far as he could tell, the British company was pretty straightforward. Saskia owned it outright. StreetSmart Ltd was a private company, with 99.9 per cent of the share capital registered in the name of S. H. Thompson. The H stood for Henrietta, after their father, Henry. It had always slightly annoyed Max that the Colonel had saved his own Christian name for Saskia, his second child. Aside from Saskia, the only other shareholder was Philip Landau who had 0.1 per cent and was listed as company secretary. Max imagined that his token shareholding was a statutory requirement, rather than an investment. He'd check that out when they next met.

The American edition was far more complex. Saskia Henrietta Thompson had forty per cent of StreetSmart Inc. with the remaining sixty per cent held by a handful of funds or institutions that meant nothing to Max: the Firemen's Fund, the State of Wisconsin, Veronis, Suhler & Associates Communications Partners Fund. A list was attached to a fat document, described as a private placement memorandum. It seemed that Saskia had raised money by placing equity four years earlier. This must have been the major restructuring Philip had referred to yesterday at his office. He found it slightly embarrassing that all this had passed him by. Four years ago he'd been with Ken Craig in Grozny, then in Angola. He'd not seen much of Saskia that whole year.

He read through the list of stockholders. Most were American, though some seemed to operate via offshore vehicles in Bermuda and the Cayman Islands. Somebody called Burt Sugarman of the Giant Corporation had a position. Great name! The second largest investor, after Saskia, was an outfit called Vision Capital Partners with thirty per cent, followed by the California State Pension fund with seven per cent. Nobody else held more than five per cent of the stock.

What exactly was a private placement anyway? And who were all these different investors? Their names meant nothing to him. Business was one of those alien areas of newspapers he'd never studied, even when stuck for reading matter on a foreign assignment. If I'm supposed to understand all this in my new job, he thought, then Saskia really has picked the wrong guy.

The third element of Saskia's empire was the Internet operation: StreetSmart Interactive Inc. This was also an American company, registered in Hartford, Connecticut. But SII, as they abbreviated it, was a semi-private company, a fifty per cent subsidiary of StreetSmart Inc. with the remaining fifty per cent held by a separate group of investors. There were a few of the same names, but also some cooler-sounding outfits with ten or twelve per cent each: Grand Junction Webmaster Inc., Cyberbahn GmbH, with an address in Berlin, and RedWeb in Moscow. Saskia was named as CEO of SII, with someone called Chip Miller as Chief Operating Officer.

Max wondered what kind of person Chip would turn out to be, and what he would make of his new boss. It struck him that there must be a lot of people who worked for *StreetSmart* in the States who didn't even know he'd agreed to take over. Or if they'd heard by now, certainly hadn't heard it from him. He delved about in the folder for the American payroll and counted the names. Seventy-nine people worked for the American edition of the magazine, and forty-three for StreetSmart Interactive. It seemed an enormous number. The surnames were Italian, Chinese, Hispanic, Jewish, African and

Japanese. It was reading this great roll-call of strangers that brought home to him the absurdity of what he'd taken on. Who on earth were Silas Cheung, Anka Kaplan, Ilsa Jane Pezzimenti and Jonny Tannenbaum?

The moment he'd got a fix on the London office, he'd head over to the States and introduce himself. Maybe he could go for a few days next week, and try and discover more about Saskia's death at the same time.

Gina's scepticism about the suicide was starting to get to him. What was the expression she'd used? 'Saskia would never walk off the set like that.' She was right, it was out of character. Saskia was a fighter.

He was contemplating a second malt, to counteract the throbbing of his arm, when he heard the sound of heavy boots on the basement steps outside. The doorbell rang. He looked at his watch and saw it had just gone midnight.

'Who is it?'

'Package for you. Mercury Despatch.'

A biker in leathers with a radio-controlled helmet was standing in the area, bearing a large brown envelope. The label showed that it came from *StreetSmart*.

Max signed for it, and took it inside. The first thing he saw when he tore it open was a card from Marie-Louise Clay.

'Max. Sorry to burden you with this on your first night as editor, but these pages need to go first thing tomorrow, so it would be great if you could take a look. They are all for the StreetLife notebook section at the front-of-book. If you haven't any changes to make, please sign them off at the bottom of the proof.'

Attached were six single-page proofs, each comprising several separate items. Max read:

Suddenly Arne Jacobsen's iconic 1958 moulded-wood stacking chair has become the must-have design classic of babyboomer-meets-millennium post-modern chic. First manufactured by the Danish firm Fritz Hansen, and available in lemon, black, stained vernal green, natural beech veneer and stained azure, the Jacobsen classic has become a trademark accent of East-meets-West stylemaker Kelly Hoppen, as well as evergreen taste guru Sir Terence Conran.

What's hot and what's not? *StreetSmart*'s cutting-edge barometer to the far side of cool.

HOT	NOT
Mixing new and vintage china	Matched sets of china
Croatia	Zanzibar
Perrier Jouet	Perrier water
John Cusack	David Duchovny
Pushkar	Push technology
Hilfiger	Hillwalking
Salt cellars	Salt shakers
SoHo	Soho

Hot Lips. *StreetSmart*'s top ten tips for top toned lips: for every day, Estée Lauder Deep Blackberry, Revlon Raisin Rage, MAC Sheer Plum and Clinique Double Fudge add drama and depth, and are as flattering and subdued as a cashmere turtleneck. Elizabeth Arden's Breathless, L'Oréal Spiced Up and Christian Dior Mauve Inspiration stay loyal for hours. For sheer shimmer, Chanel Silver Mauve, Benefit Hold It! and Revlon Toast of New York.

Max sat on the sofa, dumbly contemplating the sheaf of pages on his knee. If anything proved his total unfitness for the job, this was it. He had never heard of Arne Jacobsen's iconic 1958 chair, nor did he have any idea what millennium post-modern chic might be. Nor could he think of one good reason why Croatia should be categorised as hot, and Zanzibar not. He had been to both, and Zanzibar was a lot hotter in every respect, not least climatically.

He wondered how Saskia would have reacted, faced with the same homework. Maybe it was a test, and the staff of *StreetSmart* had included a couple of bouncers, to see if he knew what he was doing. Maybe John Cusack wasn't hot at all, and there was no such thing as MAC Sheer Plum, and the only person on the magazine not to realise this was the editor.

Had Saskia really known all this stuff about fudge lipsticks and iconic chairs and style etiquette, as well as Tibetan women and Caribbean novelists and running three separate businesses? If so, then he wished she were here now, to explain how she did it. In all those years, he'd never once sat down with her and really asked her about the magazine, and how she put it together, month after month. There was evidently more to it than he'd realised. He was angry with himself for having been so dismissive and narrow minded.

Later that night, before turning in, he altered the message on his answerphone. 'There's nobody here right now, but you could try ringing me at my office.' He recorded the number for the *StreetSmart* switchboard.

The whole idea of having an office telephone number rather depressed him. For the first time in his adult life, he had a regular job.

[14]

The next morning at eight o'clock he emerged up the area steps and set off in the direction of the Tube.

'Mr Thompson?' A black man in a chauffeur's cap called out to him from the kerb. He was standing next to a silver S-series Mercedes. 'Car service for you, man.'

'What?' Max was amazed.

'Belgravia Limousines. Booking on the *StreetSmart* account.'

He held open the back passenger-side door and Max clambered into the leather interior. For some reason he suddenly felt like a member of the Soviet politburo. He'd once seen a whole line of cars like these ferrying Russian generals from Severny airport to the outskirts of Grozny, when they'd flown in for the final push.

'Is it to Bruton Street?'

'Exactly. To *StreetSmart*.'

'Well, let's move it, then, man. Nice 'n' easy, OK.'

Max looked around uneasily, hoping none of his neighbours had seen him get into the car, but the curtains along the street were still tightly drawn. In this neighbourhood, nothing happened much before ten.

'Do you drive a lot of people from the magazine?' he asked as they headed up Ladbroke Grove.

'Sure. All the time, man.' Max could see the driver watching him under the brim of his cap in the mirror. 'I drove the older woman – the one with the rings – to dinner last night. You know, the fashion lady?'

'Racinda Blick?'

'She's something else, that one.'

'Is that another way of saying rude?'

The driver laughed. 'She didn't seem to have enjoyed her evening much.'

'How do you know that?'

'Well, she was with that other man from *StreetSmart*, Bob – the one who's been running it all since Saskia wasted herself – and they neither of them seemed happy. Apparently some motherfucker has been brought in over them.'

'That's what they said, is it?'

'In this job, you can't help overhearing things. I'm telling you, Bob was *not* a happy man last night. Apparently he's been canned by the new guy. It must have been one o'clock before they came back out of the restaurant.'

'What about Saskia?' asked Max. 'Did you ever drive her?'

'Did I drive her? I was her main man. She used to request me by name from the company, like "Get me Bartholomew." I drove her everywhere she needed to go. She had so much energy, it freaked me out. When I heard what happened, it was like "What? You're kidding, man? Saskia's done that?" '

Jean Lovell was already at her station in the outer office when Max arrived. She was wearing a different tweed suit today, with a different brooch: a silver poodle.

'I've put a tray of coffee on your desk and a couple of paracetamol,' she said. 'In five minutes I'll come in for a diary conference. A lot of people are agitating for your time, we need to prioritise.'

Max sat down behind Saskia's desk and surveyed the office properly for the first time. The baskets of flowers had been cleared from the carpet, which made the room appear even larger. One whole wall was devoted to a display of magazines, propped up on special shallow shelves. British, American, European and Asian covers jostled for attention. There were twelve different foreign editions of *Vogue*, all overlapping, and twenty *Elle*s. There were American supermarket tabloids, a shelf devoted to decorating titles, with country cottages and Sutton Place apartments on their covers, and Eastern European fashion monthlies. The largest section of the display was given over to *StreetSmart*. There must have been two years' worth of back issues, each with their American and British circulation results stapled on to the front on squares of yellow card.

Across the room was a beechwood conference table with ten suede chairs, the bookcase lined with trophies and awards and several framed photographs of Saskia with celebrities. There was one of her with Hillary Clinton and two other women Max couldn't recognise, and another with Jack Nicholson and Alicia Silverstone.

Jean appeared with a diary and a tower of post in a wire basket. 'At nine o'clock this morning,' she said, 'you've got an advertising sales review. Saskia had them monthly – but the commercial director has requested a special meeting this morning. Apparently there are some problems you need to be aware of.'

'And the commercial director is?'

'Kevin Sky. Saskia rated him. He joined us eighteen months ago from Weiss Magazines, around the time they were taken over. After lunch,' Jean went on, 'I've arranged for a video conference for you with your two principal executives in America. Chip Miller is down in New York City today from Hartford, so we can link you up with him along with the American publisher of the magazine, Anka Kaplan. I've scheduled that for two thirty our time which is nine thirty over there.'

'Great. Anything I ought to know about Chip and Anka?'

'Only that they're American,' said Jean.

'Which means?'

'That they'll constantly surprise you with the depth of their general knowledge – lack of depth, that is. Never assume an American knows anything, unless they've specifically confirmed it.'

Max laughed. 'When I began working for Bullet, their New York bureau fixed me a flight to Azerbaijan in the old USSR, and they booked it to Abidjan – in the Ivory Coast, Africa – instead. When the ticket arrived and I rang to point out the mistake, the operations officer asked, "Is that close by? Do we need to adjust that reservation or could you take a cab on over?"'

'Chip Miller is actually a very smart young man, that's what Saskia always said,' said Jean. 'I wish he could learn to construct a proper letter though, instead of these rambling e-mails he sends us. All their lines of different lengths, like poetry.'

They were about to tackle the post when a man appeared through the door carrying two buff files, followed by a determined-looking blonde. She was a well-above-average looker, Max thought.

'Kevin Sky. Commercial Director.' The man gripped Max's hand. He was about ten years older than Max and well preserved. His tie was covered with little blue cornflowers on a purple background. 'Your sister and I were mates as well as having a good professional business relationship,' he said. 'I had a lot of respect for her. It blew me out when I heard what happened.'

'Thank you,' Max said. 'Do we normally have meetings like this one sitting around the table?'

'Correct,' said Kevin. He introduced the woman as his advertisement director. 'Between us, we're charged with leading the sales effort,' he said. 'Basically, we flog space.'

'And how's it going?'

'Not good, I'm afraid,' said Kevin. 'We received some disturbing news yesterday evening, about six o'clock.'

The blonde slipped some sheets of paper from a slim plastic folder, and passed them around the table.

'To come straight to the point,' said Kevin. 'Bercuse, the French luxury-goods company, has cancelled its entire advertising schedule. The whole damn lot. Every single brand.' He paused dramatically for the news to sink in.

'And how important is Bercuse?' Max asked. 'The name doesn't mean anything to me. I mean, it's not exactly Pepsi Cola.'

Kevin and the blonde exchanged glances. It was a look that said, 'Is this guy a complete gonzo or what?' However, when Kevin replied, he just said, 'Bercuse is a hugely significant account. Big, big revenues. In fact, when you add together all their different divisions, they rank fourth for *StreetSmart* after Estée Lauder, Vendôme and LVMH. Slightly ahead of L'Oréal and Ralph Lauren.'

'Then how come I've never heard of them? Even I know Estée Lauder and Ralph Lauren.'

'Bercuse is a holding company,' said Kevin. 'French and very aggressive. It acquires and operates luxury brands. Over the past ten years they've bought out one company after another. Tara, why don't you talk Mr Thompson through the schedule?'

The blonde smiled thinly. She radiated a chilly competence. There was nevertheless something distinctly sexy about her. She was one of those women Max could imagine grabbing exactly what she needed in bed, and booting out her partner the minute she got it.

'I'm Tara Keane,' she said. 'As ad director, Bercuse is one of the accounts I handle personally. If you take a look at the top sheet, you can see how the Bercuse business has increased over the past four years, from thirty-three pages in 1995 to 107 last year, plus twenty-six scent strips. This has been achieved partly by market share gains –

see Venn diagram – but, objectively, Bercuse has grown by acquisition, absorbing existing brands, and by an aggressive programme of launches.'

She turned to the second sheet, and Max followed suit. 'You can see the list of individual brands in the left column,' said Tara, 'and how their spend has grown incrementally year by year: Serène was the biggest print launch of a new fragrance since Chanel's Allure – you remember those twenty-four-page black and white inserts, the photographs of eco-warriors? And now there's the Sensi fashion label too in Milan, which they're about to start marketing heavily. They had optioned forty pages. Then they bought Tranquilité last year from Mouchette. Plus, of course, we pick up all the champagne business from St-Cyr-le-Châtel, the Reverso sports watch and some of the Lockerjock sports brands – D Troit Denim and Homeboy.'

'And you're telling me they've cancelled all that advertising at once?' Max said. 'Why've they done that?'

'That's just it,' said Kevin. 'No one knows. The agency informed us last night, but they're as mystified as we are. We've been ringing round the different Bercuse marketing departments in London, and they don't know either.'

'Then who made the decision? Someone must have.'

'Paris. That's all we've established so far. And it was taken pretty high up. Maybe even by Étienne Bercuse himself.'

'Can't we just ring him and ask?'

Kevin sighed. 'Wish it was that simple. The fact is, we can't get near him. He's not like other clients. He doesn't do lunch, seldom even attends his own company's fragrance launches. He sets the strategy, but that's it.'

'If you telephoned his office, what would happen?'

'I just did,' said Tara. 'Some stroppy cow harangued me in French, saying Monsieur Bercuse was unavailable and I shouldn't have rung that number anyway.'

'Did my sister know Étienne Bercuse?'

'That's what we were about to suggest,' said Kevin. 'That you might give it a go. Everyone's talking about Saskia at the moment for obvious reasons. If you said Saskia Thompson's brother wanted a word, you might get through.'

'OK,' said Max. 'But before I make the call, we'd better just think this through. Why *might* they have done this – pulled all their advertising?'

Kevin looked thoughtful. 'I've been chewing over it all night. Normally there are only three reasons a company pulls out on this scale. The first is they're about to go belly-up, or have serious cashflow problems. That clearly isn't the case with Bercuse. They're heavily geared, sure, but their business is booming. The second is if we've offended them in some way. Slagged off one of their products, or said Étienne Bercuse is an anally retentive asset stripper. Or suggested one of their rivals is better than them. A couple of seasons ago we burned our fingers when Racinda Blick wrote that Ralph Lauren is better made than Tommy Hilfiger, or maybe it was the other way round, I forget now. Anyway, Saskia had to smooth that one out over there. But I can't see anything this time. I've been through the three most recent issues, and they seem fine. Plenty of editorial credits for Bercuse, all positive.'

'Well, that's two reasons. If it's neither of those, what's the third?'

'The other possibility is that some competitor – some rival magazine – has made a pre-emptive strike.'

'How do you mean?'

'Well, for argument's sake, let's imagine Incorporated Periodicals – who own *Town Talk* – has gone to Étienne Bercuse, and somehow got in to see him, and said, "Listen, Étienne, you're booking 107 pages in *StreetSmart* at an estimated net of 1.4 million pounds. We'll offer you – as a one-time volume deal – the same 107 pages for £600,000. But there's a condition: you mustn't book a single page into *StreetSmart*.'

'Why would Incorporated propose that?' Max asked. 'I mean, I can see they'd want the £600,000, but why make it conditional upon cutting us out altogether?'

'Status,' replied Kevin. 'Bercuse business is market-making business. Advertisers have a tendency to behave like sheep. If there's a big presence in *StreetSmart* from Serène, Sensi, D Troit Denim, et cetera, it draws in others. Safety in numbers. Critical mass. Sometimes agencies complain there are too many other advertisements – too much clutter – but they don't really mean it. A few years back, the fragrance companies all went overboard for outdoor – that's billboards and posters in bus shelter – but then they all went off them again. The market shadows itself.'

'So you're saying Incorporated might have done a cut-price deal, to exclude us, specifically to attract other advertisers into *Town Talk*?'

'Exactly.'

Max felt oddly elated at having grasped this first time. It was like penetrating the mangled thought-processes of some voodoo culture. He had felt a similar satisfaction the first time he'd been able to explain, to someone else, exactly what the Christian Phalangistes really wanted in Beirut. Magazines evidently worked by similarly circuitous means. In order to strengthen *Town Talk*, its owners could be prepared to inflict short-term damage on themselves, providing that the damage to *StreetSmart* was greater.

'So, who runs Incorporated Periodicals?'

'Caryl Fargo,' chorused Kevin and Tara.

'And what's she like?'

'Impressive,' said Tara.

'A bullshitter,' said Kevin. 'Talks the talk, but can't walk the walk.'

'What sort of age?'

'Forty-eight. Maybe a bit older. Extraordinary blonde hair: like she's wearing a plastic motorcycle helmet. If you touch it, it's solid with spray.'

'And she'd be regarded as one of my main competitors, would she, Caryl Fargo?'

'She was jealous as hell of Saskia,' said Tara. 'It really irritated her that *StreetSmart* and Saskia got so much positive press. Far more than she got, even though Incorporated is a public company and has twelve titles in the stable.'

'So they're bigger than us?'

'A lot,' said Tara, 'but not as hot as they were. They've got strong brands – *Ladies' Home Cookery*, *Girls on Top* and so on – but they're sort of coasting right now. That's what the agencies think. They haven't launched anything for ages. You can see why Caryl hated Saskia. If Caryl is trying to stitch us up with Bercuse, it is because she thinks she can capitalise on Saskia's death. That would be typical Caryl.'

'Incidentally,' Max said, 'something you've just said reminds me. Just before Bob Troup left, he mentioned that *StreetSmart* isn't considered quite as good as it was. That it's becoming boring. Is that just Bob's opinion, or is it the prevailing view?'

Kevin and Tara looked momentarily nonplussed.

'Total rubbish,' said Kevin. 'The magazine's on a roll.'

'Bob was right,' said Tara. 'Editorially, we need a big kick up the pants.'

They left it that Max would ring Étienne Bercuse later that morning, and report back to Kevin on how he'd got along.

'Best of luck,' said Kevin. 'This is important. If Bercuse is a wipeout, the implications are serious. I don't want to exaggerate, but – commercially – *StreetSmart* could move towards meltdown. With Saskia dead, the advertisers might bolt for the exits.'

Before ringing Paris, Max wandered down the corridor in search of the fashion department. It occurred to him that Kitty might have some scoop on Étienne Bercuse, to bolster Kevin Sky's rather cursory character sketch.

The *StreetSmart* fashion room turned out to be a narrow black-and-steel chamber with two windows overlooking the rear of the building. One whole wall was covered with black cork, on which were pinned model cards and pages torn from magazines. Much of the floor space was taken up with rails of clothes on castors, from which hung dozens of outfits, some in bags, others thrust across the rail itself, or in crumpled piles on the floor where they'd slipped from their hangers. Two fashion assistants in black leggings were unpacking metal trunks. In the corner stood a glass kiosk, inside which Max could see Racinda Blick paging through an Italian magazine.

Kitty was blowing on a cappuccino in a Styrofoam cup. 'Hi, Max,' she said. 'I was just thinking about you.'

'You were?' Why did this please him quite so much? he wondered.

'Racinda and I were saying that we don't know what you think of our pages at the moment. The fashion stories, I mean. Are we going in the right direction?'

'Christ. I couldn't say, to tell you the truth. I'll have to give that some thought.'

'Then can I ask Jean to put a meeting in your diary? We'll need to know what you think before Milan. The collections begin next week. If you hate what we're doing, we should know before we go, since we plan the next six months' sittings during the shows.'

'Fix a time, whenever you like. The reason I dropped by is to ask what you know about Étienne Bercuse. I've got to ring him later on. Have you come across him?'

'Only once, in New York. Last week in fact. When I was with Saskia at the ball at the Waldorf, just before she died.'

'So Saskia knew Bercuse?' That could make things easier.

'She might have met him before,' said Kitty, 'but I don't think they really knew each other. When Saskia went to say hello that evening, she was more introducing herself. She went over to complain to him about his advertising in *StreetSmart*.'

'That's interesting. So Saskia already knew he'd cancelled everything in the magazine. She knew a week ago.'

'The conversation wasn't about pulling space, definitely not. Saskia gave him a lecture about how he wasn't advertising *enough*. I know I'm right about that, because Bercuse said something like, "We do support your magazine." And Saskia replied, "Yes, but not enough." She was going to call him the next morning, to discuss it.'

'The next morning? You mean the morning she died?'

'She promised she'd ring him.'

'Which presumably she never did.'

'I suppose not. She was going to call him at seven o'clock at his office. I remember thinking, how impressive – actually how depressing – that they're both up and working at seven in the morning.'

'Maybe Bercuse is annoyed Saskia never called him,' Max said, half to himself. 'Maybe that's why he's pulled the business.'

'He'd know she's dead though,' said Kitty. 'It was reported everywhere. And anyway, loads of people who work at Bercuse sent flowers. He'd certainly know.'

'Well, something happened in the past few days to upset him. That's for sure.'

'Do you want me to check it out?' said Kitty. 'I've got some friends at Sensi, working in the design studio.'

'People close to Étienne Bercuse?'

'Probably not that close. The ones I know work in the Via San Spirito. That's the Sensi headquarters in Milan. I don't think they see much of Étienne, though. His own office is in Paris, some modern building.'

'You might as well ask. Try and find out what's happened.'

'I'll call them right away. Oh, and by the way, how's your arm? Are you seeing anyone about it?'

'I keep meaning to, but what I really need now is exercise. I've got to start rebuilding the muscle.'

'There's a gym behind Oxford Street, if you want somewhere to work out. Quite a few people from here use it. I usually go after work.'

'Sounds great. How about this evening?'

'OK,' said Kitty. 'Collect me on your way out and I'll take you along.'

For some reason Max felt a whole lot better about cold-calling Étienne Bercuse, knowing he had a date with Kitty.

'Now, where've you been?' asked Jean as he arrived back in the outer office. 'I was about to send out search parties.'

'In the fashion room. I was hoping to get some lowdown on Étienne Bercuse.'

'From Racinda? I doubt she'd know anything.'

'From Kitty. She's making some calls to Milan for me.'

'Oh, I *see*,' said Jean meaningfully.

'It turns out she has friends who work for his company.'

'Yes indeed,' said Jean. 'I'm sure she has.' Then she said, 'In future, would it be a good idea if you let me know roughly where you'll be, when you wander off? Saskia always did, and it was quite helpful. In case I need to locate you. Some people rang, by the way, while you were along the corridor.'

She handed him a typewritten list of names and phone numbers. 'When you want me to get them on the line, let me know. Probably the character at the top needs his call returned sooner rather than later.'

Max studied the list. 'Marcus Brooke? Should I know him?'

'He works for Freddie Saidi. His official job title, I believe, is Head of Corporate Relations.'

'Which means what exactly?'

'Sort of a front man. Talks to the press on behalf of Mr Saidi.'

'And did he say what he wanted, when he rang?'

'I tried to get him to leave a message, but he said he could only talk to you.'

'So he didn't say anything about wanting to buy *StreetSmart*? That's the big rumour.'

'He didn't give a clue, but what a hideous prospect. Shall I try him for you?'

Max went into his office and shut the door. A couple of minutes later the telephone rang and it was Jean. 'Marcus Brooke. He's in a car.'

He could hear traffic down the line and then a treacle-voice said, 'Max Thompson? Marcus Brooke. We haven't yet had the pleasure, but permit me straight away to convey my condolences for your sister, my sincere condolences, and also those of Mr Saidi, who was devastated when he heard about it. *Such* a talented girl, *such* a waste.'

'Thank you. Much appreciated. Did Mr Saidi know Saskia, as a matter of fact?'

'Oh yes, they were great friends,' said Marcus. 'Mr Saidi makes a point of knowing all the most talented people in the arts, the media, all the movers and shakers. He entertained Saskia on more than one occasion, and regularly sponsored special events she was doing with the magazine.'

'I see,' Max said noncommittally, waiting for Marcus to come to the point.

'I'd like to drop round later today and discuss a little idea we've had. Mr Saidi's had, I should say.'

'OK. But you do realise the magazine's not for sale.'

'Max, if I've learned only one thing in my life,' said Marcus, 'and *particularly* since working for Mr Saidi, it's that nothing in this world isn't for sale. Not really. There's always a price, and I don't doubt for one moment there's one for *StreetSmart* too. I do take your point, though. Your sister put a lot of effort into that publication, and you won't want to say yes to the first offer that comes along, not without careful reflection. Which is why I want to come and see you. Is four o'clock convenient?'

'Fine. You know where we are?'

'Along the street from Fournels et Fils, the jewellers. Another fine old institution that's looked to Mr Saidi to keep them in business.'

After he'd gone, Max glanced at the list of who else had rung.

'Please call Cody at your parents'.'

He dialled the number and heard the phone ringing in Farnborough.

'Cody?'

'Hi, Max. I rang you all by myself.'

'Shouldn't you be at school?'

'School's boring. Anyway, I've got a belly ache. That's why I'm not going today.'

'So what are you doing?'

'Eating candy.'

'With belly ache?'

'Oh, that's got better now. Anyway, you know that high cupboard where Granny hides things she doesn't want me to have? The one in the kitchen, where the chocolate cookies and sugar lumps live?'

'Er, yes.'

'Well, I can climb up there. I can fetch a chair and balance it on the pedal bin, and I can reach. That's how I got the candy.'

'Where's Granny, then?'

'Out. Now those men have gone away, she can go shopping.'

'And Grandpa?'

'Asleep. At least I think so. He's watching racing on television.'

'And now you've rung to tell me how wicked you're being.'

Cody chuckled. 'No,' he said. 'I'm just wondering when Saskia's going to take me on a treat, but Grandpa says she's still in America. And, anyway, it's boring with Granny and Grandpa, they're *old*. And they *never* take me on treats.'

'If I took you instead, where do you want to go? Legoland?'

'Yuk, that place sucks. It's for kids. I want Planet of Adventure, and to go on the whitewater log flume.'

'Look,' Max said, 'I'll have to ask Granny, but maybe at the weekend. Until then, behave.'

'Huh. I bet we *don't* go. That's always what Saskia says: "Maybe at the weekend." And then we never do go, because she never even takes me. It's not fair.'

'Cody, we're *going*, OK? That's a promise, and I don't break promises. So long as Granny hasn't planned something else, we'll be there.'

'Huh,' said Cody. 'I bet Planet of Adventure won't even be open when we go. It'll be closed, or the queues will be too long to get in. Or the log ride won't be working or something. It's *always* unfair, when I have treats.'

Max got the number for Bercuse from Jean and rang Paris. Jean had offered to line up the call, but he still didn't feel comfortable with that particular manifestation of executive privilege. If the call was so important, he'd rather dial it himself.

'Bercuse SA.'

He asked in French for Monsieur Bercuse's office and was asked in English for his name.

'Max Thompson ... I'm the editor and publisher of *StreetSmart* magazine.' The first time he'd used the titles. Now it was for real.

'One moment please,' said the switchboard, again in English.

He was put through to a brusque-sounding woman, presumably the PA who had torn a strip off Tara. She didn't ask who he was, so it must already have been relayed by the telephonist.

Instead, she said, *'Oui?'*

'May I speak to Monsieur Bercuse?'

'What is this concerning?'

'A business matter.'

'Naturally business.' She snorted. 'I mean the *actualité* of the business.'

'It's a commercial problem. Monsieur Bercuse's companies have apparently cancelled their advertising with my magazine, and I need to ask him why.'

She emitted a petulant sigh. 'It is not possible, truly, that Monsieur Bercuse can speak on matters such as this. I am sorry, but Monsieur Bercuse is not available to discuss this thing.'

'Are you saying I can *never* speak to him?'

'I must tell you this is not appropriate.'

'Well, I hope you'll at least pass on a message. Please tell him Max Thompson, Saskia Thompson's brother, called.' Then he made her take down the telephone number and read it back to him. From the fuss she made, he might have been dictating a four-thousand-word dispatch.

'You will definitely pass that on?'

'I have written the message. Of course,' she replied, 'but I can't say whether he will telephone you. He is travelling. First in New York, afterwards I don't know.'

'Just so long as he gets it,' Max said, and rang off, boiling with rage. He didn't think he'd spoken to anyone quite so obstructive since he applied for press accreditation from the Zaire embassy in London, a week before the fall of Kinshasa.

[15]

Jean Lovell appeared, trailed by a youth with a shaven scalp and a gold stud in his left ear. 'Barry's come to set up the conference,' said Jean. 'He's one of the few people here who can work the equipment. He's part of our information technology department.'

'Must be interesting,' Max said.

''S OK.'

Barry disappeared under a table and took the back off a PC. Wires trailed across the carpet. All that could be seen was a white T-shirt and the seat of his jeans, while he tapped at a keyboard and flipped switches.

'Everything all right down there?' called Jean. 'Mr Thompson's video conference starts in five minutes.'

''S OK.'

The PC was set up on the table, with a panel the size of a postcard set into the screen. On top of the white box sat a small spherical camera – it looked like a golf ball with a flat base – pointing in Max's direction. Barry adjusted the lens and he could suddenly see, with fish-eyed clarity, the purple wall of a room and a big, empty, violet-coloured cylindrical sofa.

'There you are,' said Jean. 'Canal Street, Tribeca. Take a good look at the sofa. It came from Milan and cost more than my flat.' She went on, 'I don't know where the others have got to. I clearly stated nine thirty East Coast time. I'll give them a ring and chivvy them up.'

Just then two bodies waded on to the screen, only their torsos visible at first as they walked across camera and flopped on to the sofa.

The man – Chip, Max guessed – had an orange fringe, baggy black suit and lime-green shirt. Max thought he reminded him of someone, then realised that he simply resembled half the male models in *StreetSmart*: cool, urban, ironic, unfazed.

Sitting alongside him was a dark-haired, hyper-looking female in beige, carrying a stack of files. This was presumably Anka Kaplan, the American publisher. She was noticeably anxious.

After a couple of false starts, while Barry adjusted the connection, they could hear each other quite clearly. Anka put out a spiel about how shocked and sorry everyone was about Saskia, and Chip nodded his agreement, and said that he had identified Saskia's body at the Office of the Chief Medical Examiner on First Avenue.

'Thanks for doing that,' said Max. 'Was it OK?'

'Kind of weird,' said Chip. 'Seeing your boss in the morgue. It made you think, like, this is unreal.'

'How long are they going to keep her there?'

Chip shrugged. 'Until they're sure they know how she died.'

'You mean they still don't know?'

'That's what they said. They wouldn't tell me much.'

'I hope it wasn't upsetting,' said Max. 'Seeing Saskia like that.'

'I think Saskia would have been upset being there,' said Chip. 'It wasn't the crowd she usually hung out with. The other stiffs were a bit of a D-list crowd.'

The video conference began and Chip went first. Max didn't pretend to understand everything he was told about the Internet project, but it sounded exciting. In addition to operating the *StreetSmart* website, which was updated daily with current events, beauty and fashion news online, StreetSmart Interactive operated sites for several independent clients: automotive and specialist travel companies, and a large sports-shoe brand, Akron-KickBack, that was giving Nike and Adidas a run for their money.

'On our own sites,' said Chip, 'the most popular sections by far are the regularly updated ones. We try to hook users in with a bit of a cliff-hanger, and then the page accesses go into orbit.'

'Which sections are drawing the biggest audiences?'

'As of yesterday? Well, we've issued a laptop to this young writer from New York City, and dropped him off in the forest, four hundred miles from Seattle. He's got to survive for a month in the wild. Hunt and forage, or die I guess. We've given him a GSM mobile. Each morning he e-mails a report. It's making quite an impact. Upwards of two hundred thousand hits daily.'

'How's he getting on in the forest?'

'He caught a chipmunk Thursday, but aside from that, he's living on berries. I guess he's running on empty now. He's yet to locate a source of fresh water, so there's a degree of dehydration.

'The other section that's attracting page traffic,' said Chip, 'is our Small Wars site. We've issued laptops to reporters on the ground in various conflicts too esoteric to interest the big networks. Rwanda, Sudan, Peru. There's a big involvement factor here too, a lot of return users. The correspondents file each morning before eight a.m. our time, and it's up online by nine.'

'Does enough happen each day for them to report? Wars are mostly hanging about, waiting.'

'On slow days,' said Chip, 'the correspondents kind of personalise their experiences: what they had for breakfast, things they miss about New York City. There's an element of soap, which keeps people coming back.'

'Great,' said Max, he hoped not too insincerely. 'These are local correspondents presumably, working for us freelance?'

'No, all the guys in the field are our own people, special to StreetSmart Interactive. Saskia believed the branding was more impactful that way. She had this big interest in war reporting.'

'She did?' Aside from the Sarajevo print hanging on her bathroom wall in Holland Park, Max was unaware that she'd had any interest in it at all. 'You sure about that?'

'Sure I'm sure,' said Chip. 'She forecast war reporting on the Net would supersede print reporting within a couple of years. Pictures online within minutes of any atrocity, any place in the world. Saskia was very competitive with the news magazines. She thought their approach was complacent, but I guess you knew that.'

Max thought, Thanks a lot, Saskia. While I was slogging across Afghanistan to Kabul, you were busy undermining my entire livelihood. Thanks, sister.

'So what else should I be aware of?' he asked Chip.

'Well, the next important date for us is a competitive pitch for a website. Bigtime contract, potentially. In fact Saskia had planned on coming along herself, she knew the client. He's based in London.'

'And the client is?'

'Freddie Saidi. He owns the East River Hotel.'

Jesus! Saidi again.

'One of his people is coming over for a meeting with me this afternoon,' Max said.

'Then put in a good word for us. We need that business. As you can appreciate from the numbers, we're still some way from payback.'

'I know,' said Max, though actually he didn't. He made a mental note to check out the profit and loss of StreetSmart Interactive.

'It's taking longer than anticipated,' said Chip. 'I guess all the online projections were a little optimistic. But when the return kicks in, it'll come in torrents. Two years from now, it'll be raining dollars.'

'When is the Saidi pitch?'

'Monday.'

'I could be in New York myself then.'

'Then come along,' said Chip. 'It could help.'

Throughout this exchange, Max was conscious of Anka Kaplan looking increasingly uncomfortable. This was no doubt partly attributable to the awkwardness of sitting on a violet sofa and staring at a television camera, without contributing to the conversation, but he sensed that Anka was about to deliver bad news, rather than good.

'Hi, Anka,' he said. 'How are things going for us over there?'

'I wish I could say, "Great." ' She had some kind of Polish Brooklyn accent which reminded Max of Stefan, his editor at Bullet. 'But there's been some weird news. We're still trying to figure it out.'

Max guessed what was coming before she said it.

'Bercuse,' said Anka, 'I don't know how much you know about the Bercuse account . . .'

'Enough. Serène, Tranquilité, Gaia, Sensi, Lockerjock . . . In the UK we sold 107 pages of advertising to Bercuse last year, plus quite a few, er . . .' For a moment he couldn't remember the technical term for those disgusting sealed Rizlas of pong. '. . . Scent strips.'

He could see Anka down the tube looking impressed, and also surprised. He didn't blame her. So far as she knew, he was this backwoods hillbilly who just happened to be Saskia's brother, and who hadn't worked one week in magazines. He felt oddly pleased with himself for remembering the Bercuse statistics.

'Our volume over here was seventy pages,' she said. 'We received a fax this morning that first seemed like a hoax. The whole schedule's been canned.'

'Same in London,' Max said. 'I just rang Étienne Bercuse's office in Paris but couldn't get to him.'

'Jesus,' said Anka. 'It's a big problem for us. They've scheduled eleven pages in the next issue, and we close Thursday. We'll never sell them to anyone else now, and it's affecting the make-up of the book.'

'Sorry, you've lost me. What's that last bit mean?'

'Well, we set the issue size two weeks ago. A hundred and twenty editorial pages and 110 advertisements. The editorial department are working to that pagination. If we need to pull eleven ads for Bercuse, we'll either have to drop editorial pages or close them up: pages designed to work against advertising will have to be converted into spreads.'

'Ah.'

'So what do you want us to do?'

'What would you suggest?'

'Drop editorial would be cleanest, but you'll need to tell us which stories to hold over.'

'When do you need to know?'

'Tomorrow noon, our time. That's latest.'

'I'll get back to you. Anything else?'

'One other thing. This is also kind of unsettling. About fifteen minutes ago, one of the sales executives took a call from the agency for Chrysler. Somehow they already knew about Bercuse pulling out. They were asking us about it. We denied it, of course. The automotive companies only want a presence in books that are considered hot. The bulk of their advertising goes on TV. So when they get confirmation about Bercuse, they're liable to pull out too. Which is a further forty-eight pages. Two point eight million dollars.'

On the steel-and-mesh editorial floor opposite the lifts, thirty figures were crowded into the art department. Gina spotted Max, and beckoned him over.

'Take a look at these, Max. They've just come in. Madonna with Igor Sergov. Both together in the same picture.'

Half a dozen transparencies lay on a lightbox. Two had been marked on their mounts with yellow chinograph dots. They showed Madonna dressed in exercise clothes and wearing a baseball cap, arm linked with a heavily jowled man in a belted camel-hair coat.

'He looks Chechen all right. We're certain this is Igor Sergov?'

'Definitely,' said Gina.

Marie-Louise Clay had joined them at the lightbox and was nodding. 'A freelancer brought them in,' she said. 'He's been stalking Madonna since the Igor rumour surfaced six weeks ago. They've been going to enormous lengths not to be photographed together, giving the paparazzi the runaround, but Jonti – that's the photographer – got to them last night. Leaving a restaurant on South Beach, Miami.'

'They're good pictures too,' Max said, peering through a loop.

'There are only two, maybe three choices,' said Gina. 'In the others, Madonna is covering her face. And in the final frame Igor turns nasty, and lashes out at Jonti, which is strong in a different way.'

'Did he hit him?'

'Jonti was on a motorbike,' said Gina. 'He'd kept it turning over.'

'Sensible Jonti. These Chechens are serious boys. They don't appreciate being mucked about.'

'We've made a start on some layouts for the Sergov piece,' said Gina. 'Spiro, can you take Max through the roughs?'

'Sure,' said Spiro, smiling. 'I think you'll be surprised.'

Ranged along a work bench were twelve double-pages of photographs and dummy text. The opening picture, of Igor Sergov swinging a punch next to a grimacing Madonna, was evidently Jonti's exit shot. The rest of the photographs were all too familiar to Max: they were his.

'You got these from Bullet?' They were big, grainy black-and-white pictures of Chechnyan lowlife, used much better than on their first airing in *Newsweek*. There was a great one of three Mafia gangsters outside a club, and another of a boy of twelve selling cigarettes on a street corner with an AK-47 over his shoulder.

'I see you've gone for the one of the corpse in Grozny market,' Max said. 'The dead man's a Georgian, by the way, from Tbilisi. Probably trafficking in drugs. Anyway, he'd evidently done something to seriously displease the Chechens. I was right there when they dumped him out of a car, twenty yards away. It was broad daylight in a square full of people. Nobody saw a thing. The police, when they arrived, didn't even bother taking statements.'

'It's a strong picture,' said Spiro.

'But too gruesome for publication. If you look carefully, you can see he's naked from the waist down. You can see his testicles. They'll never use it. Bet you anything they don't.'

Gina and Marie-Louise both turned to him and laughed.

'Max,' said Gina. 'Wakey, wakey. You *are* "they". It's your call now.'

'Jesus, I was forgetting. I'm still not used to this.' Then he said, '*Can* we though? Use a picture like that in *StreetSmart*? I mean, is it allowed?'

'You're the editor.'

'What I mean is, is it ethical?'

'It's certainly journalistic.'

'OK, let me put it another way. Would Saskia have run it?'

'Now, that's a difficult one,' said Marie-Louise. 'Trying to second-guess Saskia.'

'We should use it,' said Spiro. 'It varies the pace.'

'And tells the story,' said Marie-Louise. 'What kind of society does Igor Sergov come from?'

'What the hell,' Max heard himself saying. 'Go for it. If people are saying we've become boring ... And the front cover?' he asked Spiro.

'We're working on this one of them both smiling. We need to decide now if you want to run with it. The cover was going to be Leonardo DiCaprio – Bob's choice – but this is more current. It needs to go to the printer today.'

'Do we use the same cover in America too?'

'Listen,' said Gina. 'When you have exclusive pictures of Madonna with a new man in her life, that plays *everywhere*.'

[16]

Although Max had long ago ceased putting much faith in first impressions, he nevertheless took an instant dislike to Marcus Brooke. Marcus wore a velvet-collared blue overcoat which hung almost to the floor, and as he was shown by Jean into Saskia's office, his eyes darted around the room, blinking rapidly, as though his irises had been implanted with spy cameras and he was intent on recording every aspect of the place.

'Ah yes,' he said, his gaze alighting on a photograph on the bookshelf, of Saskia with the late Mother Theresa of Calcutta. 'Mr Saidi has a similar picture of himself in audience with Mother. I was privileged to accompany him on that moving occasion. He presented her with a cheque for two million dollars, to enable her to establish a new orphanage. I can honestly say that the time spent in Mother's presence was one of the defining moments of my life. A tremendous *aura*, if that's the right word, of spirituality. I know Freddie felt it deeply as well.'

'Two million dollars. That's very generous.'

'Freddie Saidi is motivated by acts of generosity,' said Marcus. 'I can honestly say that he's the most generous individual I've ever had the privilege of serving. Although many of his charitable bequests have remained anonymous, which is how he prefers it, enough have found their way into the public domain to bear witness to an extraordinary *breadth* of giving. Children's charities in Albania, research into osteomyelitis, his timely bequest to save the Norwich Velasquez for the nation, his campaign to reduce drug abuse across the trailer parks of the American Midwest.'

'I've read about some of those.'

'That pains me, because it means I haven't done my job properly. I must tell you,' said Marcus, 'that even my own role is frequently misconstrued. I'm invariably described in publications such as yours as a public relations man, when my principal job is to keep Freddie Saidi *out* of the press. He shrinks from publicity. He is a family man first and foremost, fiercely private. I would almost say obsessively private if I didn't think that too might be misconstrued.' He laughed tepidly.

Marcus settled himself on a chair across the desk, and Max could see him eyeing the Madonna–Igor Sergov front cover upside down, a colour stat of which had just been delivered for final approval.

'People imagine Freddie relishes being in the public eye, when nothing is further from the truth. If I can be a little indiscreet,' he said, 'on the understanding that it'll go no further: he recently turned down an invitation to become the next General Secretary of the United Nations.'

'Really? Why'd he do that?'

'Obviously it was a great temptation, to be given an opportunity to serve,' said Marcus, looking quite pained at the memory of all the soul-searching that had gone on. 'But in the end, you have to ask yourself, "How is all this going to affect my family? And can I do more good by diverse means? Quietly, surreptitiously, in a spirit of humility?" Freddie came to the conclusion that the price of publicity was too steep.'

'Well, he gets masses of publicity as it is, doesn't he? I've spent a lot of time out of the country lately, but I still feel I've seen and read plenty about him. Carving a Thanksgiving turkey at his hotel in New York. They even published a photograph of that in Sarajevo.'

'That was most unfortunate,' said Marcus. 'We were mortified that anyone should have obtained those pictures. Incidentally,' he went on, 'I don't know how often your work takes you over to Manhattan, but next time you're there, I do hope you'll stay at the East River as Freddie's guest. He particularly asked me to extend an invitation. I think you'll find it comfortable. No hotel is ever quite like staying in one's own home, of course, but the East River is truly the next best thing. You live at the top end of Ladbroke Grove yourself, don't you?'

How the hell did he know that? 'Yes ... You're very well informed.'

'You'll become accustomed to people knowing your every move,' he said lightly. 'Now you're a public figure.'

'Hardly. I'm caretaking the magazine until we appoint a fulltime editor.'

'Or someone else does.'

'How do you mean?' said Max sharply. He was becoming slightly irritable with Marcus Brooke and all this disingenuous pap about Saidi.

Philip Landau had warned Max that Brooke would get under his skin. 'Don't let him,' Philip had said. 'Be totally noncommittal. Hear what he's got to say, and if he makes an offer, firmly and politely decline.'

Marcus began in a treacly voice. 'Now don't misinterpret what I'm about to say, Max, but there is a body of opinion that, sooner rather than later, you'll have to divest yourself of *StreetSmart*. And, if and when that moment does arrive, the perfect person to take on the responsibility and trust of ownership is Freddie Saidi.'

'As I've already made clear, *StreetSmart* isn't for sale. I don't know why you keep imagining it is.'

'Max,' said Marcus, soothingly. 'Let's not play games. You are a man of unusual and, dare I say, special talent. Some of your photographs of war and famine have made a profound impression. On more than one occasion, Freddie has been so moved by one of your images in the press that he's called me in and said, "Marcus, something must be done to help this hungry child. I want you to employ all the resources of my organisation and locate this child and fill her belly, give her as much as she can eat." All inspired by your work. The point I'm making is that I truly can't imagine you wanting to give all that up. Not for a magazine like *StreetSmart*.'

'If *StreetSmart* is so worthless, how come Mr Saidi is so keen to buy it?'

'It is more a feeling that it *ought* to be in his ownership,' said Marcus. 'For Freddie, there is always a strong element of sacred trust, as the guardian of fine institutions. You can see this in all his acquisitions: the East River Hotel, Fournels et Fils, Hadleigh & Hadleigh – Her Majesty's saddler by appointment. In every case, there are only three questions that really matter to Freddie: Is this business worth saving in terms of quality? Do they really understand the *concept* of quality? And what can I, Freddie Saidi, do to further enhance that concept?'

'Go on, then, what does he think he can do to improve *StreetSmart*?'

'Without presuming to put words into Freddie's mouth,' said Marcus, 'he can foresee enormous opportunities for promoting good causes. So many charities could benefit from the oxygen of publicity.'

'But I'm afraid the answer is still going to be no. *StreetSmart*'s definitely not for sale. My sister wanted it kept independent until Cody – her son – is old enough to take it on. That's if he wants to.'

'Ah yes, *Cody*,' said Marcus. 'Mysterious young Cody. Or, more accurately, the mysterious father of Cody. I did half wonder whether one of those fulsome obituaries in the papers might finally put us all out of our misery and tell us who he was.'

Max didn't reply. He had no intention of speculating on Cody's parentage with Marcus Brooke.

'But the rumours,' persisted Marcus, 'have certainly given us all plenty of enjoyment over the years.' He then went on, 'Well, think about what we've discussed, Max. Think about it carefully. And if you feel you do want to explore any aspect of how the deal might be structured, or you'd like to talk directly with Freddie, then give me a call and I'll do my best to facilitate it.'

'Thanks. I'll remember that.'

'But don't leave it too long, will you? Psychologically, there's an optimum moment for any transaction, and you can't expect Mr Saidi to be endlessly patient. A week, two weeks, fine, but no longer.'

'For the third and last time, we're not for sale.'

A new edge entered Marcus's voice. Beneath the solicitous charm was something darker and threatening. 'It's worth remembering one thing, Max. Mr Saidi would be unhappy were you to insult him by rejecting out of hand an offer that's been made in good faith. I should warn you that he doesn't respond well to being slighted.'

'Well, I'm sorry about that, but you can't expect me to sell out just because your boss wants to buy us.'

'There may come a time,' said Marcus, standing up and easing himself back into his velvet-collared overcoat, 'when you will reproach yourself for not reacting more intelligently to this open-handed overture.'

'There may indeed,' Max said. 'We shall just have to wait and see.

And, when you next see Mr Saidi, will you please thank him for his kind offer of a free stay in his hotel, but say that I'm perfectly happy to doss down at the company apartment in New York.'

Kitty met him by the lifts, already changed into exercise kit: sweat pants, T-shirt and a pale blue jersey knotted round her waist. Max thought she looked great in it too, fit and well toned. Her line about going to the gym most evenings was evidently no exaggeration.

'I've got a bag of assorted kit here for you, some of which I hope's going to fit,' she said. 'It's left over from a lifeguard story we've just shot in South Beach, Miami. The only thing I haven't got are trainers. I didn't know your size.'

'Twelves.'

'We can pick some up on the way. We've got to cross Oxford Street. It's one big shoe mart anyway.'

They bought trainers at some open-to-the-pavement boutique, then weaved between the traffic to a glass-and-brick building at the bottom end of Welbeck Street. Inside was a reception desk, piles of towels and an overpowering stench of armpits, deodorant and chlorine. Kitty flashed a membership card and checked him in as her guest.

A black instructor doing hamstring exercises against a wall called out, 'Looking good, Kitty. Who's your new squeeze?'

She laughed. 'Not a squeeze, Nat. My boss.'

Max carried his clobber to the locker room and arranged to meet Kitty up by the machines. 'You realise I'm going to have to feel my way today,' he said. 'Five days ago I was still in hospital with this arm. I'm not exactly going to be hanging from the wall bars.'

'I know,' said Kitty, 'but it's important you work out a bit. Your new job is quite stressful, you know.'

'Yeah?' he said. 'I'm not sure "stressful" is the word I'd choose. Selecting a few photographs, having some meetings.'

'You haven't been to the collections yet. You wait. Anyway, see you up there.'

The men's locker room was full of short, stocky jerks towelling their backs and elaborately blowdrying their hair. Some were wet-shaving around a mirror, defiantly naked, before slapping their cheeks with aftershave. For the first time in his life Max bothered to examine the bottles on the shelf: Gio by Giorgio Armani. Christian Dior's Fahrenheit Après-Rasage. Lockerjock Après Sport. Well, there was one that wasn't advertising in *StreetSmart* any longer.

He peeled off his shirt, prodded gingerly at the dressing on his arm, and flinched. It would be a few more weeks before it repaired itself. He opened Kitty's bag and shook out the kit on to the floor, and groaned. No wonder they'd used this on a fashion shoot – he couldn't imagine anyone normal choosing it: skintight black bicycling shorts in Lycra with a yellow padded crotch, red and white sleeveless singlets and ridiculously narrow Speedo swimming goggles.

Kitty was already on a running machine, towelling-covered earphones on her head, watching motor-racing on TV. She smiled when she saw Max come in, and decreased the speed. 'You look good in that stuff. It suits you.'

'Hardly. I've drawn the line at the goggles.'

'I'd forgotten about them. Yando – the photographer – insisted I get them for the shoot. He loves lifeguards in goggles and swimming caps.'

They were in a large eaved room at the top of the building, with a glass ceiling and mirrors the length of one whole wall, reflecting the Nautilus machines and Gravitrons. A man on a Cybex leg stretch waved at Max from the far end of the gym, and he recognised Spiro, the picture editor. Lisa – the macrobiotics and shark-oil expert – was working out on a Stairmaster. Kitty was right: the place was crawling with *StreetSmart* staff.

He stepped on to the adjacent running machine to Kitty's, entered his weight in kilos and set the timer at forty minutes. He selected an average-endurance programme with plenty of troughs as well as peaks. No point killing yourself, first time out.

Kitty was already ten minutes into her programme. He was impressed by how effortless she made it look. Her legs moved rhythmically beneath her as they pounded the rubber belt. She had set the speed on her machine at fourteen kilometres an hour. A cracking pace. He increased his own speed to match hers. They were running side by side. Her thick blonde hair was flailing about behind her, a light film of sweat discernible for the first time above her upper lip.

'OK?' she mouthed. She was still tuned into the earphones. Max gave a thumbs-up sign, and jogged on.

His arm was giving him less pain than he'd feared and his legs felt rock solid beneath him. The walk from Peshawar to Kabul and back must have built a lot of stamina.

Kitty pushed the earphones back from her head and draped them round her neck. 'Was that Marcus Brooke I saw coming down the corridor from your office?' If she was short of breath, it didn't show.

'Sure was.'

'And what did he want, if it's OK to ask?'

'Buy *StreetSmart*.' Max could reply without panting, he was relieved to discover. 'Not himself. He was representing Freddie Saidi.'

A look of anxiety crossed Kitty's face. 'You didn't . . . you wouldn't . . .'

'Accept? Why not? I'm sure he'd pay a lot of money. He's into these trophy businesses. He promised to maintain the quality – enhance it, in fact.'

'But I thought you said you'd be editing *StreetSmart* yourself?'

'That was before the offer came along.'

Kitty looked crestfallen.

'Cheer up, only joking,' Max said quickly. 'I sent him packing.'

'Genuinely?' Suddenly she was all smiles. 'You really turned him down?'

'Yep.'

'How did he take it?'

'Badly, not to put too fine a point on it. I got the impression it doesn't often happen, anyone saying no.'

'You should watch out. Saidi can be vindictive.'

'Marcus did imply that.'

'I mean it. He has a dodgy reputation.'

They were still running in step, beating up on the revolving rubber belt. Kitty had a great ass, Max noticed.

'In what way dodgy? I thought he owned all these venerable old companies. The Queen's saddler and so on.'

'You just hear awful rumours about him. I'm only warning you.'

Max leaned forward to the control panel, and increased the speed to sixteen kilometres per hour. He resolved to check out Freddie

Saidi as soon as possible. But if Kitty imagined he'd be intimidated into selling, then she didn't know him at all.

'I think I can look after myself,' he told her. 'I've come up against harder men than him before, you know.'

[17]

There was a message on the machine to ring his father urgently. 'We've heard from the New York police,' was all it said. 'Not good news, I'm afraid.'

Colonel Thompson picked up the receiver at first ring, sounding tired and impatient. 'I was hoping it was you, Max. I've been trying to get hold of you. Where've you been?'

'At *StreetSmart*. Attempting to sort out Saskia's magazine.'

'I tried you there earlier. They said you'd gone off to some health club.'

Max wondered why his father still had this unerring ability to wrongfoot him. It had been going on for ever, all his life.

'Anyway,' he said, 'you're here now. I've had the American police on to me. The detective who rang before. To be honest, it's difficult to know what to make of it all. Your mother and I are sitting down here, quite shaken.'

'What did he say, Dad?'

'That's just it. The first time we spoke, remember, they were saying it was a suicide, that's what was printed in all the newspapers, but now they're not so sure. There were bruises on Saskia's neck, and they think she could have been strangled. They say they can't release her body until they've done more tests.'

'Christ,' said Max. 'They're saying someone might have *murdered* Saskia? *Why?* I can't believe it.'

'It is unbelievable,' said the Colonel. 'Though I did say at the time that suicide made no sense. Saskia had too much to live for.'

'But you didn't suspect murder, did you?'

'It's always been there in the back of my mind. Saskia wouldn't commit suicide.'

'That's what everyone in her office says too. What do the police think happened? Had someone broken into her apartment?'

For a brief moment, he imagined his sister in a white bedroom somewhere in Manhattan, while an intruder watched her from the corridor, waiting his moment.

'They didn't say anything much,' replied his father. 'Not beyond what I've told you. But all this has devastated your mother. I'm ringing you from downstairs. Margaret's lying down on her bed, I don't want her to overhear this conversation. She's under a lot of strain. We both are. We wait around all day for news, can't leave the telephone in case anyone calls. Apart from shopping, we stay put.'

'And how about Cody? What have you told him?'

'Nothing so far. There didn't seem much point, not until we had definite news.'

'You still haven't told him his mother's dead?'

'We thought it better to wait.'

'But hasn't he said anything? He must have noticed Saskia hasn't rung. It's been over a week . . .'

Colonel Thompson sounded uncomfortable. Max could picture him standing in the narrow front hall where the telephone lived in a recess by the window. His parents were of the generation that still believed the telephone was intended for emergencies and making plans, and that calls should be made in the upright position, and kept short.

'The fact is,' the Colonel said, 'Saskia wasn't always very punctilious about keeping in touch with Cody. Don't get me wrong, Cody meant the world to her. She was a wonderful mother in many ways. But she had a lot of commitments. She couldn't always find the time to ring.'

'So Cody hasn't noticed. You're saying it hasn't made any difference to him, whether his mother's alive or not?' Max felt suddenly furious with his sister.

'That's putting it a bit strongly, but no, Cody hasn't said anything.'

'So when are you going to tell him? And what will you say? We'd better make sure we're all saying the same thing.'

'Probably no need to rush into anything,' said the Colonel. Max sensed that his father would delay breaking the news for as long as possible. As a soldier, he had been fearless, and an effective administrator, but at home, he prevaricated.

'Actually, there's every need,' said Max. 'There's been enough rubbish in the newspapers. If you don't tell him soon, someone'll say something to Cody at school.'

'Your mother and I were talking about it last night. We were wondering how to tell him. What *do* you say to a six-year-old in a situation like this?' There was a long pause before he said, 'You wouldn't consider breaking it to him, would you, Max? It might come better from you. You're closer to Cody in age . . .'

At that moment there was nothing in the world Max wanted to do less, but it was important that Cody be told soon, and he didn't altogether trust his parents not to fudge it.

'OK,' he said. 'I'll collect him from High Hatch tomorrow morning, and take him to Planet of Adventure and tell him there. You inform the school he's taking the day off, and I'll tell my office. It's not great timing, but it's got to be done.'

Afterwards, on some impulse, he rang Kitty Marr. Her address and telephone number were in the *StreetSmart* staff directory that Jean had given him to take home. She lived in a flat in South Kensington, in Rosary Gardens. Max hoped she'd gone straight home from the gym.

'Kitty? It's Max Thompson.'

'Oh, *Max*.' He could hear other people in the background, a man's voice, laughter. 'Just a moment, I'll transfer you to another room.' There was some rattling on the line, and she picked up an extension. 'Sorry about that. I can hear you properly now.'

'You may not be up for this,' Max said, 'but I've got to break it to Cody tomorrow about Saskia. He still doesn't know. I can't go into it all now, but something else has happened too, something terrible. I'll tell you when I see you. Anyway, I wondered whether you might be prepared to come along tomorrow? I may need moral support.'

'Sure,' said Kitty. 'If you think it would help. I'm meant to be spending tomorrow on appointments, but they can be rescheduled. You're the editor, so Racinda can hardly complain.'

'Thanks, Kitty. I really appreciate it. I'll pick you up at Rosary Gardens about nine thirty.'

That night, Max sat up late, thinking through everything that had happened, and struggling to make sense of it. The murder of his sister seemed, on the face of it, inexplicable and motiveless; one of those random New York homicides that hardly any longer qualifies as news. But was this really a random killing?

In her letter to him, Saskia had hinted at something going on in the background. What was it she'd said? 'For the first time since I started *StreetSmart* I'm nervous. There are a lot of predators out there.' For Saskia to write that – most of all in a letter to him – must mean it was serious. Max was the last person she would normally have confided in. He was conscious that his sister had always slightly resented the way that Max, the war photographer, was assumed to have greater physical courage. Saskia needed to be Number One in everything, even in areas in which she didn't compete.

Could someone have killed her to get the magazine? It was possible. *StreetSmart* was clearly worth a lot more than he'd realised, and there must be people who'd love to sink their paws into the advertising revenue. With Saskia dead, they'd have expected the magazine to be put up for sale. They wouldn't have known about her plan to keep it going for Cody.

In which case, who would try and buy it? So far, only Freddie Saidi's name had been mentioned. At the gym this evening, Kitty had warned him about Saidi. Would he commit murder to get the magazine? Max had no idea.

And, anyway, there could be any number of other suitors for *StreetSmart* still to declare themselves, or people who wanted Saskia dead for entirely unconnected reasons.

Unless Max discovered more about his sister's life, he would never begin to comprehend her death.

He could scarcely have left it later, but he would have to start getting to know her.

[18]

Max could tell that Kitty wasn't that impressed by the old white Citroën when it drew up outside her flat, but she put a brave face on it and slithered into the battered passenger seat.

'You know something,' she said, 'I'm quite touched you've asked me along. I hope I won't be in the way. With Cody and everything.'

'It'll be a big help. Cody's not that easy a kid. I've no idea how he'll react.'

'How are you planning on telling him?'

'Not sure. I'm trying to work out whether it's best to do it right away, in the car, or wait until we've had some fun first.'

Kitty furrowed her brow. For the second time, Max noticed how attractive she was when she looked serious.

'How about lunchtime?' she suggested. 'After he's got some food inside him. Then if he becomes hysterical he'll have eaten something first.'

They resolved to spend a couple of hours trying out the rides, and then they'd find somewhere quiet, if such a place existed, some restaurant, and break it to Cody about his mother.

Driving down the New King's Road, Max filled Kitty in on how the New York police were saying it could be murder, not suicide, and how nobody seemed to know what had happened.

'What's so frustrating,' he said, 'is that I've been abroad so much lately, I hardly feel I knew Saskia that well. Who'd want to murder her? Even in the last few days, you and Jean have told me more about my sister than I knew myself.'

'That's how everyone felt, I think: that they didn't really know her.'

'How do you mean?'

'She kept parts of her life secret, that's what people said, anyway.'

'You mean like the identity of Cody's father?'

'Exactly. Presumably you know, though?'

'No one does, as far as I'm aware, my parents included.'

'So you can't confirm it was Kiefer Sutherland? That was the office rumour.'

'Not a clue. Could have been Bill Clinton or Colonel Gaddafi for all I know. Which gives me an idea: if Saskia was murdered, could the father have anything to do with it? Maybe he wanted custody of Cody or something and had to get rid of Saskia?'

'It's possible, I suppose. It sounds a bit farfetched.'

They were driving up Putney High Street towards the motorway and Max asked Kitty to hunt about the car for a road map. She rummaged in the side pocket and produced a stack of them.

'Namibia. Chechnya. Chad. Honestly, Max. Don't you ever go anywhere normal?'

'Where's normal, then?'

'Well, places normal people go. For fun. On holiday. France, Italy, the United States. I don't know. Sardinia, Cyprus.'

'I've been to Cyprus. The northern-Turkish part. Not a spot I'd recommend for a holiday. The biggest transit point for hard drugs into Europe. Backdoor to Beirut.'

'One day,' said Kitty, 'you're going to have to take a proper holiday. Tobago or Mustique or somewhere. You'd love it, at least I hope.'

'I'll probably have to take Cody with me on holidays from now on,' said Max. 'I can't see my parents managing it.'

'Cody came into the office a few times with Saskia. He's very high spirited, isn't he?'

'Is that a polite way of saying delinquent?'

'People did wonder whether he's a bit hyperactive. He's not that great at staying in one place. He preferred chasing up and down the passages. Saskia used to get mad at him, so usually some department was told by Jean to look after him.'

'You've met Cody properly, then?'

'He likes playing in the fashion room, making little camps in the clothes. I remember once Chanel had sent round a messenger to collect some evening dresses and when the man tried to lift them off the rail, Cody had climbed inside the clothes bag and zipped himself in. The dresses weighed a ton. Then we saw these little legs kicking inside the bag.'

'Typical Cody.'

'The one place he'd really shut up was in the IT room, playing with the computers. Once we'd sussed that out, it made things a lot easier. Jean shunted him down there to play computer games.'

'Cody's always loved computers. He's like his grandfather, interested in technology.'

'I wonder whether he'll come into magazines too, one day?'

'That'll be up to Cody. Maybe he'll become a computer genius, the next Larry Ellison or Bill Gates. But, yes, in theory he's going to inherit *StreetSmart*. That's what Saskia wanted to happen anyway. She's left it to him in her will.'

'She'd really planned that far ahead, her succession and everything? That's organised.'

'You knew my sister. It always struck me that nothing in Saskia's life was left much to chance. She worked everything out, every move. You know that song by the Police, or was it Sting on his own, the one that goes "Every step you take, every move you make"?'

'*I'll be watching you.*'

'I told Saskia she could have written it about herself. It was almost as though she was watching herself in action, dispassionately manipulating her career. She was so alert to the consequences of every move, how it would be perceived and interpreted.'

'How did Saskia react when you explained that to her?' asked Kitty.

'How do you think? Badly. She never liked home truths. From a brother, it was even more annoying because you have the built-in advantage of family intuition.'

'You think there's such a thing as family intuition?'

'I hope so. I'm going to be depending on it in the next few weeks.'

'And then what?'

'For *StreetSmart* or for me? Right now, I'm taking it one day at a time. I feel quite out of my depth actually. I should probably start looking round for an experienced editor.'

'Don't do that,' said Kitty quickly. 'The magazine needs stability. There's been too much change already, what with Saskia and then Bob and everything. Promise you won't walk out on us.'

They were well on to the A30 now, passing the exit for Dorking and some grey ponds and a gabled Italian restaurant with peeling white paint. Kitty was looking at him with the same grave anxiety that he'd noticed yesterday at the gym, when he'd pretended to be selling out to Saidi.

'No promises,' he said. 'Not long term. But I do promise to stay for the next few weeks.'

His parents were listening out for the car when they arrived at High Hatch. Max saw his mother's face at the leaded pane of the sitting-room window. The Colonel came out to greet them in a brown herringbone overcoat, and Max introduced Kitty to his father as one of Saskia's staff. While Max went inside to collect Cody, Colonel Thompson gave her a guided tour of the garden. As they set off, Max heard him saying, 'So you worked for Saskia? I should think that kept you on your toes. Best way to learn, working for someone like that.'

He found Cody sitting on the side of his bed, absorbed in a Nintendo Gameboy. 'Hi, Max,' he said, not looking up. 'Don't jog me, I've nearly reached the next level.'

Max hadn't been into Cody's bedroom for years, though it had once been his own childhood room. In the gaps between the posters, traces of the original blue wallpaper were visible. His school desk stood in its old position in front of the window, its white lid now plastered with transfers and metallic decals.

Long after he'd left High Hatch for a succession of shared flats in London, the room had remained his to return to on visits between assignments. He remembered coming back after a particularly shattering tour of Somalia – a trip that achieved nothing journalistically and almost got him killed when a jeepney overturned – and climbing exhausted into his old narrow bed with its candlewick cover. He still felt sentimental about the room. At the time Cody had been born, he had resented having to shift his kit, when Saskia had arrived there straight from the maternity hospital with her newborn son, and handed him over like a parcel to her mother to look after.

Cody's bedroom was a little shrine to America: baseball bat and leather mitt, New York Giants cap, a real cowhide stetson hanging from the dressing-gown hook on the back of the door. Whenever Saskia went to the States, she'd returned with some authentic American gift, or laden with merchandise from the hot new American movie. Cody had *Toy Story* posters, and mugs and badges from *Batman Returns*, eighteen months before anyone else at his school, and the latest interactive computer games. Last time Max had seen his nephew, he was trialling the prototype of a Gulf War game in which you had to guide a smart bomb from a mobile rocket launcher in the Saudi Arabian desert, across Baghdad and down the air-conditioning vent of Saddam's bunker. Saskia had been given it by the president of Sony. Max had always assumed that a strong measure of guilt lay behind this largesse. Saskia reminded him of a divorced father, arriving every third weekend with a bag of love-me-do presents.

'OK, Cody, we've got to make a move. Got everything?'

Cody grabbed a Chicago Bulls bomber jacket and tugged on a pair of boots with thick, ridged soles like tractor tyres. When he smiled, he was unmistakably Saskia's son: the bright, observant eyes, long, narrow face. He found schoolwork easy; it was a problem for his teachers, keeping him quiet once he'd learned something, which he did at twice the speed of his classmates.

Before they set off, Max drew his father aside into the study. He left Kitty in the kitchen with his mother, where she was unwrapping tiny pieces of cheese from greaseproof paper, and arranging them on a plastic cheeseboard. The two women seemed to be rubbing along OK, though it was never easy to tell with his mother.

'Any more news from the police in New York?' Max asked his father.

'They've confirmed it was murder. The sleeping pills weren't the cause of death. Saskia was strangled. They can tell from the bruises on her neck, the blood vessels. They're treating it as a murder investigation.'

'But who did it? Are there any suspects? They must have some ideas.'

'If they have, then they haven't told me. The police officer is called Przemysi. Detective Przemysi. We've just spoken.' His voice shook a little bit. 'He sounded like he knew what he was doing.'

Colonel Thompson looked as though he hadn't slept for several days, and for the first time that Max could remember, he hadn't shaved carefully either; there was a patch of white bristle on his chin the size of a ten pence piece. On his desk Max noticed a long list of bulbs, meticulously handwritten in pencil, with their quantities and catalogue numbers, that his father was ordering for the steep bank behind the house.

Max told him about Saskia's will, and the letter she had left for him, and said that he was full of misgivings about it.

When he'd finished, the Colonel said, 'She's absolutely right, you know. *StreetSmart should* pass to Cody. He may be a handful at the moment, but I can tell you that young man could make a first-class editor one day. All that energy and intelligence, straight from his mother.'

'What do you think about me getting involved?'

'Oh, you must, if Saskia thought you were up to it. Keep the chair warm for Cody.'

Max couldn't help finding his father's endorsement rather half-hearted, but he let it pass. 'What I actually meant was, do I even want to do it? I've got no qualifications. Mightn't it be better to sell *StreetSmart*, and get shot of it? Put the money in the bank for Cody?'

'No, it would not,' replied Colonel Thompson, speaking more emphatically than Max had heard him for many years. 'If Saskia wanted her magazine to pass to her son, we must respect that. She put everything into it, and made it an immense success, and it should continue as she intended, not be sold within five minutes of her death. I feel very strongly about that.'

'You're really sure?' asked Max. 'That I should run *StreetSmart* until Cody is old enough? It could be years.'

'Beyond a shadow of doubt. I'd say it was a duty. A duty to Saskia and a duty to your nephew.'

Max and his father sat in silence, while Max evaluated his obligations to Cody, to his sister and to his family. It was true that, with Bullet in trouble, he didn't have any other commitments. And the prospect of letting Marcus Brooke and Freddie Saidi take over his sister's magazine struck him as dishonourable. He had more or less given his word to Kitty that it wouldn't happen. And, as editor of *StreetSmart*, he might be better placed to discover who had murdered Saskia.

'OK,' he said at last. 'I'll give it a go.'

Even as he said it, Ken Craig rushed into his thoughts, and he could feel his disapproval. 'Don't sell out, Max,' Ken had said. Well, too late now, Ken.

Colonel Thompson heaved himself up from his chair, and surprised his son by shaking him by the hand.

'I knew you'd make the right decision,' he said. 'Good luck. I'm certain we shall all be very proud of you, as we were of Saskia.'

Max retrieved Kitty from the kitchen, and Cody from the garden, and they all piled into the car and headed for Planet of Adventure.

'Hi, Cody,' Kitty said. She was leaning across the back seat to talk to him. 'Do you remember me? You came to my office: the one with all those rails of clothes hanging up.'

'Yeah,' said Cody. 'I built that hideout, except that man in the motorbike helmet came and ruined it. It's cool playing with clothes. Whenever I go to Saskia's flat I like to play in her cupboards. You can crawl right into the back, on your belly. Only Saskia gets mad when I do that, she says it muddles everything up.'

Remembering the chaos of overflowing rails, Max didn't see how Cody could have made much difference, but instead he said, 'Do you go to Saskia's flat often?'

'Not much. She keeps promising I can come for a sleepover, but then it never happens. Whenever it gets to the weekend, she says she meant a different weekend.'

'But you do go sometimes?'

'Sometimes. Before Christmas I went. Saskia took me for my treat to the Trocadero to do virtual reality, and then, after lunch, Jean – you know, Jean who works in her office – took me in the car to buy toys.'

'Didn't Saskia come too?'

'She had to go back to work, as usual, but she came later. We went to this big huge art gallery where you go through a little metal door to get in, and then inside it's gigantic and they have this whole sheep, a dead sheep with all its fleece still on, floating in special fluid in a glass tank. Jean said it was really disgusting and yucky, but Saskia liked it.'

'What about you, Cody? Did you like it?'

'It was really good, because it was dead but it looked like it was still alive. You could trick people. If you hid behind the tank and went "baa, baa", all the people got really scared.'

They left the car in a ten-acre parking lot and bought tickets at a turnstile got up as a pioneer stockade. Cody ran on ahead towards the log ride while Kitty and Max hurried along behind, past the toytown carousel and the Wild West main street with its souvenir shops and pizza houses.

'He's a smart kid,' said Kitty. 'I guess he's going to be pretty devastated about his mother.'

'He'll miss the toys more than he'll miss her, probably. No, that's cheap, I didn't mean that. But she wasn't exactly involved. You know what my mother once told me, she let this slip: Saskia never even bathed Cody. Well, maybe once or twice at the beginning, but not for years. She didn't know a thing about bathtime or bedtime or reading him stories.'

They queued for the log ride, snaking their way backwards and forwards between grey metal crush barriers, like sheep waiting to be dipped. Cody did somersaults on the bars, his boots kicking air as people in adjacent lines dodged to avoid his heels. A spur of rail track jutted out above them. Ahead lay a monster roller-coaster that cranked a log-shaped canoe up a steep slope and then forced it back down into a splash pool, all designed like some old gold-prospecting town.

'Are you going to scream and yell like a girl?' Cody asked Kitty.

'Not sure yet. It looks very scary. What about you, Cody? Are you going to scream?'

'No way. Only girls scream.' But then he said, 'Actually I *am* going to scream. If you scream it makes it scarier.'

Shortly before they reached the front of the queue, Max took Cody's small hand in his own, and squeezed it reassuringly, but Cody pulled away, and turned his back on his uncle.

They sat in single file in the scooped-out log like three divers in a midget submarine: Cody at the front, Kitty in the middle and Max at the back. As the log clattered and jerked its way up the steep incline, Kitty's weight pressed back on him; her ass pressing into his groin and the back of her neck against his face. Her hair smelt of lemons. Max slipped his good arm around her waist and felt the warm flesh of her stomach where her jersey had ridden up.

The log had reached a plateau at the summit and was juddering its way around a semicircular loop towards the descent. You could see the narrow track below, plunging almost vertically towards a tiny square of blue. The log ahead of them disappeared over the hump, its occupants screaming in terrified pleasure.

'You OK, Cody?'

'Fine.' His eyes were shining, he didn't look scared at all.

In profile, Cody looked so like Saskia it was unsettling: the same intense blue, almost flirtatious eyes, which could suddenly turn petulant, and the stubborn line of the mouth. But sometimes you picked up on some other, alien strain, the paternal genes. There was a wildness about Cody that was quite different from the cool calculation of Saskia. It wouldn't have surprised Max if Cody's father had turned out, as the press kept speculating, to be some Hollywood principal brat. Tim Roth, Matthew McConaughey, David Arquette, Kiefer Sutherland. Even Nicholas Cage. He'd seen all of them nominated at one time or another.

Now it was their turn to plunge over the edge. Kitty was muttering, 'No, no, for God's sake, no, somebody get me out of here, please, *somebody* . . .' and then they hurtled into the abyss, the wheels shooting sparks beneath them, the blue pool getting closer and larger each second. Max could feel Kitty's body being forced up against his own by the G-force, his arm squeezing her more and more tightly, his hand pressing against the soft skin of her belly, until they hit the water in a skeel of spray.

'That was brilliant,' said Cody. 'Can we go again?'

Kitty looked at Max meaningfully.

'Maybe later, Cody,' he said. 'First we need lunch. What do you want, hamburger or hamburger?'

'Great, yeah, lunch. Large fries, large Coke, milkshake, cheese-burger. And not just a quarter-pounder, OK?'

They found somewhere called the Old Cowpoke Hamburger Haven, or maybe it was the Tex Mex Hamburger Corral, with saloon doors, orange plastic tables and backlit slides depicting the various available combinations of hamburger, bun and garnish. Cody squirted his bun with ketchup, mayonnaise and brown sauce, then smeared it across the patty with the handle of a plastic knife.

'Cody,' Max said, 'while you're doing that, I've got something important to tell you.'

Cody didn't look up, but Max thought he had his attention.

'Something very sad has happened. You know Saskia went to America to do some work?'

'Yeah, she's bringing me back the new *Godzilla* interactive. She promised.'

'Well, while she was in America . . . ' Suddenly Max wasn't sure how he was going to put this. Everything he'd rehearsed in the car seemed trite or inadequate. He felt Kitty's hand move supportively on to his knee. 'While she was in America, a very sad thing happened, and she's died.'

Cody glanced up from his burger. He was looking intently at Max, as though working out whether or not he was serious.

'It's very, very sad,' Max went on, 'but don't worry, you'll still live with Granny and Grandpa who love you very much, and I'll take you on holidays, and there are lots of people who love you, and who'll look after you.'

'Was she wasted?'

Max felt a chill. *'What?'*

'You said she'd died in America. Was she gunned down on the sidewalk from a moving car?' He imitated a burst of machine-gun fire and people at the next table turned round. 'Or did a psycho park up outside her place and stalk her wherever she went, just follow her everywhere. And the cops didn't believe her, they thought she was making it all up. And then one night, when she was walking down this creepy alley in the dark, past the trashcans, suddenly she heard footsteps . . .'

'Cody, you must stop this. Nothing like that happened to your mother. That's just in films.'

Cody looked disappointed. 'It's not just in movies people get wasted. Saskia says if you take a walk in Central Park, even in the middle of the day, you might easily get murdered, probably stabbed one million times. That's why she always goes through the park in a stretch limousine as long as a house, that can fit twenty people and even has drinks and a TV inside.'

Then, as though he'd suddenly thought of some devastating new aspect, Cody stopped and asked, 'If Saskia's dead, who's going to get me my *Godzilla?*'

[19]

They dropped Cody back at High Hatch, declined Max's parents' offer of a large drink and hit the road. For the first part of the journey they drove in silence, drained by the whole episode of telling Cody, and disquieted by his reaction, or rather lack of reaction. When they'd left him with his grandparents, he'd been furious they wouldn't let him put on a video during tea. His temper tantrums were sudden and awesome; something else he'd inherited from Saskia.

After a while, Kitty said, 'You know, we probably shouldn't be surprised he's unfazed by his mother dying. He's not that old. He doesn't really understand what death is.'

'But no tears, nothing. My grandmother died when I was six or seven and I can remember crying about it. With Cody, it hardly seemed to make an impression.'

'Maybe he's bottling it up.'

'Maybe there's nothing *to* bottle up. Maybe he just doesn't feel anything.' Max was genuinely worried about his nephew and how he couldn't get through to him.

'Come on,' said Kitty. 'All children love their mothers. At that age, anyway. It's automatic.'

'Then why didn't he show any emotion? I'm serious. If your theory's right, he should be devastated.'

'I'm not a psychiatrist, but perhaps it'll express itself in other ways, later on. Like he'll start misbehaving at school.'

Max laughed. 'I doubt they'd tell the difference. From what I hear, Cody's disruptive enough already. Alternatively, perhaps he'll wait till he has *StreetSmart*, and then he'll come in one morning with a handgun and start firing at the staff at random. That's what emotionally repressed people do, isn't it?'

'Sounds like Saskia actually. Arriving at the office and firing staff at random.'

'Was she really like that?'

'Is Armani Italian? Saskia was a serial sacker. The turnover of people was so high, it wasn't worth learning their names till they'd survived six features meetings. One writer joined us from *Elle* on a Monday morning and she was out by eleven o'clock the same day. Two hours. That was the record.'

'Why? What had she done wrong?'

'Hadn't heard of Julian Schnabel.'

'Well, neither have I. Who the hell *is* Julian Schnabel anyway?'

'You're fired! Out, out, out! Now, this minute. Go, just leave. Are you completely out of touch with the zeitgeist? Haven't you got a fucking clue?' Kitty was prodding him in the arm, and laughing. 'I think that's a pretty accurate impression of Saskia in sting ray mode. The poor *Elle* girl was terrified, her mouth fell open. Bob Troup was told to march her off the premises.'

'Sounds like I'd better fire myself, then. So who is this Schnabel person?'

'American artist, originally hyped up by the Saatchis. Paints huge canvases, sometimes with bits of broken china stuck on. They sell for millions of dollars. Most of the important modern art galleries have at least one.'

'And what about *StreetSmart* readers? Do they know about him?'

'In theory, sure. Saskia was always publishing pieces about him. Schnabel in his studio. Schnabel at the Venice Biennale. Schnabel's wife modelling Isaac Mizrahi or something. I'm not sure how much the readers really registered it. Saskia liked using his paintings in fashion stories: a Julian Schnabel canvas on one half of a spread, a photograph of an Alexander McQueen evening dress on the other. A visual counterpoint.'

'You know, when you tell me that sort of thing, it makes me apprehensive. I can tell you all about a Steyr Aug but nothing about a Schnabel.'

'Steyr Aug? Who's that?'

'Advanced assault rifle. Austrian, developed for the Armée Universal Gewehr but used by most NATO soldiers, notably the SAS in Northern Ireland. Looks a bit space age, but bloody effective. Rate of fire, 650 rounds per minute.'

'It's going to be rather a novelty having someone like you around in magazines,' said Kitty. 'Most of the men in our world wouldn't have the first idea about a Steyr gun or whatever. They'd think it's a sculpture park, or a German fashion company. I'm not trying to creep up to you, just because you're my boss, but I tell you, you're going to go down bigtime with the fashion crowd. They love macho men, especially straight ones.'

They had reached Rosary Gardens when Max remembered something he hadn't done. 'Blast. What time is it? Six o'clock. I should have rung the New York office. I promised to call them before noon their time. Something to do with deciding which articles not to use if the Bercuse advertising has been cancelled and we have to print a thinner issue.'

'You can use my phone if you like. Come up to the flat.'

He dialled Canal Street and asked for Anka Kaplan.

'I'll see if she's available,' said a bored voice. 'Who is this speaking, please?'

'Max Thompson.'

It might have been his imagination, but he sensed the receptionist speeding up her act.

'Max? This is Anka. Thanks for calling. I've got the VP of production and creative services right here with me, and we need to take a decision on pagination.'

'Any development since yesterday with Bercuse?'

'Nothing. Except they've confirmed they're pulling the space. A hard copy of the fax arrived.'

'Are they entitled to pull out, this late?'

'Absolutely not. The cancellation date was sixty days ago. Whether we can get them to pay is something else.'

'There must be something in writing.'

'Sure, there's a contract, the terms and conditions are specific. I'm just saying that with a company like Bercuse, with all that volume, you don't want to antagonise them.'

'And there's still no explanation?'

'I've been calling Bercuse headquarters on Fifth Avenue all morning, but no one's returning calls. We don't know what's happening.'

'So what about dropping these editorial pages? Should we?'

'I guess,' said Anka. 'Saskia always insisted we stick to the ad–ed ratio. Otherwise it erodes the profit and loss. You know how much it costs to add every extra page of edit, with paper, print, repro, manufacturing, manuscripts and illustration.'

Max hadn't a clue, actually, not a clue. That was something else he needed to check out fast, along with the performance of Chip's Internet operation.

Somewhere in Kitty's flat he could hear the sound of running water. She must be taking a shower.

'If we're planning on holding over eleven editorial pages,' said Anka, 'that really gives us about five choices, and we'll have space to run only two of them. The regular columns we can't touch, of course, so liquor, sex, personal finance, motoring and Smartass are immovable.'

'Smartass?'

'You know, the mixed-media notebook Short takes from Hollywood and Eighth Avenue. Gucci Eyewear has it as a guaranteed adjacency, so it's a given.'

'I see. So, what *can* we drop?'

'Excuse me, I'll call up the flatplan.'

While Anka downloaded her electronic pagination, Max took a proper look around Kitty's flat. It was evident that whilst, in terms of square footage, it was probably no larger than his own place, in all other respects it was smarter and cooler and conspicuously superior. The sitting-room had a high ceiling with elaborate cornicing, sisal on the floor, tall bookcases and a marble fireplace incorporating two dancing marble caryatids. The walls were painted hot fuchsia pink. Opposite the fireplace was a deep four-seater sofa, also upholstered in pink. Dotted about were several pale wooden tables, on which stood glass and crystal lamps and photographs in black frames. However, the thing that made the greatest impression were the paintings: two huge canvases, hung at opposite ends of the room, one uncompromisingly modern – a charcoal drawing of lemon grass – the other a seventeenth-century classical Italian landscape, with columns, garlanded maidens and a ruined temple next to a sun-starved lake.

'Which do you prefer – the Old Master or the new?' Kitty entered the room in a dressing gown. 'It's a personality test.'

Max was still holding the telephone receiver to his ear. He could hear Anka saying, 'I have it now. It's right in front of me.'

Kitty's dressing gown was silk, printed with a yellow paisley design. Her hair hung down over her shoulders. The dressing gown was loosely tied, and as she leaned towards him, he caught a clear glimpse of one breast. It was impossible to tell from her expression whether or not this was intentional.

'Let me read you through the schedule,' Anka was saying. 'These are the five front-of-book stories. "Slaying Bob: Jakob Dylan comes out from his father's shadow." '

'Is this Bob Dylan's son? I've never heard of him before.'

Kitty, who was listening in on Max's end of the conversation, nodded emphatically and mouthed, 'He's really current. Don't kill that.'

'Then there's a story here about the fashion designer Michael Kors, and an address book of America's top hundred plastic surgeons: "Shopping for collagen, coast-to-coast." '

Kitty beckoned him over to the sofa. 'The cord stretches,' she said softly.

He repeated the ideas back to Anka for Kitty's benefit, and she wrinkled her nose. 'There's been too much about Kors already, he's been everywhere,' she hissed. 'And I *hate* surgery stories.'

'Alternatively,' said Anka, 'there's a piece about fashion designers and their pet architects. Donna Karan and Peter Marino. Calvin Klein and Claudio Silverstrin. Issey Miyake and . . . Toshiko Mori, I think that's how you say it. It's about which designers are using which architects for their flagship stores.'

Kitty nodded her approval for this one.

'Or, finally, there's a preview of the Yando retrospective of portrait photography at the Whitney. Yando does a lot of work for the magazine, I guess he's family.'

Kitty slipped her arm around his shoulder and whispered, 'Keep Jakob Dylan and the architects. I promise you.'

For some reason Max didn't just want to nod through Kitty's choices, so he asked, 'What about pictures? How are these articles being illustrated?'

'I'm afraid I don't have that information to hand,' said Anka. 'Do you want me to find out? The production department will have page proofs.'

He could hear the vice-president of production and creative services sigh as she went in search of pages. The issue was due on press. Doubtless she thought his question a further unnecessary delay. He could sense her thinking, What does he know about it anyway?

'I think it's worth finding out,' Max said to Anka, though equally explaining himself to Kitty.

'Sure,' said Anka. 'In our most recent Reading and Noting subscriber survey, seventy-three per cent of all *StreetSmart* respondents concurred with the statement "The visual appearance of a feature is a significant factor in my involvement." '

Max was conscious of Kitty's proximity: she was suddenly very close. She had tucked her long bare legs underneath her on the sofa cushions and now leaned forward to whisper something. Her breath was warm against his ear.

'You know something, Max,' she said. 'I'm impressed. You're really getting the hang of it. That's exactly what Saskia would have asked: "What are the visuals like?" '

She kissed him softly on the cheek and he felt a surge of sexual energy. He slipped his good arm around her back and steered her towards him, so her head pressed gently against his shoulder. Her skin felt soft. His arm was round her thighs now, and he felt Kitty shiver and arch her back like a cat, when he slid his hand higher to her ass.

She twisted on to her back, her head resting in his lap, and smiled. As smiles go, it was difficult to categorise, being simultaneously tentative and quite brazen. Her dressing gown had fallen open, and her small, pink breasts stood upright to the ceiling. As he cupped one of them with his good hand, he cursed that he didn't have the use of both.

'Max?' Anka was back on the line. Her Polish-Brooklyn vowels sliced through the room. 'I have the proofs you requested. As far as visuals go, we have a portrait photograph here of Dylan, looking somewhat like his father. Michael Kors is a stock picture from his publicist. Top Surgeons has this studio shot of a bruised apple being peeled by a surgical scalpel . . .'

Max was struggling to concentrate as Kitty rolled over on to her stomach, resting her chin in his lap. 'Could you explain that last concept to me in a little more detail, please, Anka?' he asked.

Kitty looked up at him with wide baby-blue eyes and smiled.

'The fruit is being held by a pair of steel forceps, at least I guess that's what's going on. The picture is kind of moody at the extremities, like the art director's gone to town here.'

Kitty was shaking her head, gently, from side to side. She was listening to Anka while rotating her lips against the seam of his chinos.

'The whole idea,' she whispered, 'sucks.'

'Go on,' said Max. 'I'm still not clear what's going on here.'

'The apple has been partially peeled, there's this spiral of skin, and the scalpel is kind of gouging out a chunk of rotten brown flesh around the core.'

Kitty's hand moved to his groin, loosening the metal fasteners of his fly. Her fingers were smooth and nimble. He felt his breath shorten.

'The concept's quite neat, I guess,' Anka was saying. 'It's kind of in-your-face, but that's OK.'

'Sure,' he gasped. He was struggling to control his voice, keep it steady. 'And the architects? What's the approach there?'

'Very graphic.'

He felt the coldness of a ring against warm flesh. He'd noticed in the car that Kitty wore a plain gold band on her little finger.

'What exactly do you mean,' he gulped, 'by graphic?'

'Columns of type, mostly. With head shots.'

Kitty must still have been half tuned in to Anka, because her head suddenly flipped up and she whispered, 'Ask her about the column measure. If it's a typographical solution, that's a factor.' Then, without waiting for a reply, she sank back to her lapside position.

'Er, how about the column measure there, Anka?'

He heard Anka relay the question to the VP of production and creative services, who sounded impressed. Maybe Max did know what he was talking about.

'Wide,' came the answer. 'Two column. It makes the presentation quite hard-nosed and masculine.'

Kitty gave a thumbs-up from down below, and Max replied, 'Great.' His voice sounded distinctly breathless, as though he'd stepped off the running machine at the gym.

'Alternatively there's the Yando preview. Not many words, mostly portraits from the show. I can see they've used one of Michelle Pfeiffer here. And Tommy Mottola from Sony. And Keith Haring. And Galliano.'

Max had heard of Michelle Pfeiffer, anyway.

Kitty was going gang-busters, her hair whipping about his groin. This girl was so attractive, incredible, he was squirming. Jesus Christ . . .

'So have you come to any decision?' said Anka. 'I know it's kind of hard.'

'Sure,' he spluttered. 'Please, I mean it, just give me one moment.'

'Take your time, Max. Your sister was the same. Always held off for as long as possible.'

'Je-*sus*!' He doubled up. He couldn't even hear properly any more. He was deaf and blind. Jesus, Kitty. He gasped, shuddered, Jesus.

'Max? You still there?'

He couldn't answer. Fireworks in the head.

'Max? Max?' He heard Anka say, 'We might have lost the connection here.' Then, more loudly, 'Max?'

'Uh, sure. Sorry, Anka, lost you there for a bit. Line went down. Still happens in England, you know, time to time.'

Kitty was smiling up at him, raising her eyebrows inquiringly as if to say 'OK?' But he didn't think she was in much doubt.

'Anyway,' he said, gradually recovering focus, 'decision time. Let's run with Jakob Dylan and Yando. The portraits. I think people like celebrity pictures. We'll go with them.'

'Good choice,' said Anka. '*Good* choice. That's the selection I hoped you'd make. It's exactly in line with our latest reader research: they asked for more rock music and more celebrities. That came through strongly.'

Afterwards, Kitty walked over to the bookcase, and slid open the central section to reveal a cupboard-sized kitchen. Max could see black granite surfaces, a fridge and ice-making machine.

'Here you go,' she said, handing him a whisky.

'Clever of you to know my drink.'

'You're a war reporter. Whisky's part of the profile, isn't it?'

He laughed. 'Am I that obvious a stereotype?'

She looked him up and down, smiled and said, 'Max, mind if I ask you something? Do you possess such a thing as a full-length mirror in your flat?'

'No. There's a mirror above the basin, not full-length.'

'If you did, and you took a good objective look at yourself, you'd see why people guess your background. You don't exactly make it difficult. The boots, combat jacket. You're either a war reporter or a model from the Milan menswear shows.'

'Why do I suddenly feel I'm being got at here?'

'You're not,' said Kitty. 'I prefer men who don't give a damn. Most of the time, anyway. If you're coming to Milan next week, which we all think you should . . .'

'Why Milan?'

'Womenswear collections. You ought to make an appearance, it's kind of expected.'

'Expected by *whom*?' He was astonished. If there was one thing he knew damn-all about, it was women's fashion.

'The industry,' said Kitty. 'The designers. Their PRs. They expect to see the editor-in-chief of *StreetSmart*. If you don't show, they'll think you're not interested.'

'But I'm *not* interested.'

'Irrelevant. They spend a fortune with us in advertising. You've seen the budgets from Milan.'

He hadn't actually. That's another thing I need to wrap my head round, Max thought.

'You don't need to come to them all,' said Kitty. 'Just the big ones. Armani, Versace, Gucci, Prada. And you ought to make a face check at Sensi this season, as it's their first collection since being bought by Bercuse.'

'Does that mean Étienne Bercuse will be there?'

'Possibly. He doesn't go to much, but he might for Sensi, since they're repositioning the brand.'

'Then I should go. I definitely need to meet Bercuse. I haven't had much luck through his office. Incidentally, do you know anyone in Milan I can stay with?'

'How do you mean?'

'I'll need somewhere to sleep. A spare room, or a sofa I can doss down on.'

Kitty stared at him as if he were crazy. 'Come off it, you've got a suite at the Principe di Savoia. Saskia had it booked for months: the Presidential Suite. Last season, she gave a Gucci dinner there for Tom Ford and Domenico de Sole.'

Kitty put her arm around his shoulder, and kissed him tenderly. 'Don't change,' she said. 'Promise you won't. Even when you're a magazine superstar, I want you to stay exactly as you are now.' She looked up at him, very solemn, as if his commitment on this issue really mattered.

'You've gone very serious all of a sudden,' Max said. 'What's the problem? You think I'm going to transform into Saskia by next Friday?'

'Modest men are quite rare in this business,' she replied. 'They don't survive. They get trampled on. So they turn into monsters.'

'Well, I'll try,' he said. 'I've got a lot to be modest about, not knowing the first damn thing about it.'

'You don't need to go *that* far,' laughed Kitty. 'Not self-effacing. If you go round telling people you don't know what you're doing, they'll believe you.'

'Well, it's true.'

'Better to say nothing. Half the people you'll meet haven't a clue either, and they've been at it for years.'

'OK,' he said, 'it's a deal. I'll come to Milan, I won't open my mouth, not even to breathe, and I'll slope about looking thoughtful and inconspicuous.'

'*God, no,*' said Kitty. 'That would be fatal. You've got to ride around in a Mercedes, sit in the front row at the shows, make sure you've got the best table at Bice and give a cocktail party on the terrace of your suite. Otherwise they'll think you're a total non-event and cancel their advertising contracts. And that's all true, by the way.'

'Do you know what this sounds like?' Max said. 'The last days of Mobutu. That's exactly what it was like in Zaire. People driving pointlessly around in Mercedes, throwing lavish cocktail events and puffing their own sense of importance, and then a week later they were all deposed. Rounded up and shot, most of them.'

'You see, you *do* understand this business,' said Kitty, laughing. 'It'll be a breeze. You've got the whole thing sussed.'

Now it was Max's turn to kiss Kitty. He was genuinely touched that she believed he could hack it. Although he didn't for one moment imagine that *StreetSmart* would be a breeze, he did at least, for the first time, feel the challenge was important, and that he might conceivably be equal to it.

Somehow it just seemed natural, when the time came to leave, that he didn't leave at all.

Instead, Kitty and Max gravitated to her white bedroom at the side of the building. And it seemed inevitable, when she slipped out of her dressing gown and climbed naked into bed, that he should follow her.

For a while they lay side by side, just staring at each other. Kitty had the most beautiful smile, almost childlike. Her skin was smooth and white, which gave the blue of her eyes an extra intensity. She seemed very small and delicate next to him; Max was conscious how much bigger each part of him was. His feet, next to hers, looked enormous – big pink rafts of flesh and gristle. A few years back, during a spot of R & R with a bunch of fellow photojournalists, he'd been cajoled into joining a visit to a Thai brothel in Chiang Mai. Max saw them as characters from a shaggy-dog story: there was this Englishman, Frenchman, Italian and American, who one evening went to this cat house . . . Except that it wasn't that funny, even at the time. The girls were half their age. He remembered feeling like this gross, galumphing, whisky-on-the-breath Westerner, shut in a cubicle with this exquisite Asian flower. Now, with Kitty, there was a similar sense of being altogether too big and uncouth for her white bed.

Kitty was leaning up on her elbow, with her serious face on. 'When you rang me last night and asked me to come with you to Planet of Adventure,' she said, 'did you guess that this might happen?'

'You mean, did I plan it? No.'

'Promise?'

'Not consciously, anyway.' He leaned over and kissed her. 'But I'm glad it has.'

'Sure?' asked Kitty. 'It worries me slightly, you and me.'

'Why?'

'Why do you think? People in the office could get the wrong impression. You know how these things can be misinterpreted. Especially somewhere like *StreetSmart*.'

'I've never worked in an office, but I can imagine. Racinda Blick might not appreciate the idea of you spending too much time with me.'

'Exactly. And, by the way, that was the most romantic thing you've said all day, you know.'

'Really? What was that?'

'That we'd be spending time together. In the future. That was the implication, at least I hope so.'

'Well, I hope so too,' Max said. 'I'm relying on you to guide me through Milan. And to give me the lowdown on the magazine. Though, while we're on the subject, it might be better if next time I can talk to Anka Kaplan in New York without that particular form of lowdown. It was rather distracting.'

Kitty laughed. 'Sorry, boss. I won't ever do that again.'

'That's not what I said. I only said, not when I'm on the phone.'

Then they made love.

Max had never regarded himself as some great international Casanova figure, though he hadn't spent his twenties and thirties hanging about on the periphery of small wars without getting a fair amount of sex. Nurses, journalists (Bosnia was swarming with beddable Italians), United Nations observers, documentary makers, aid-workers. The combination of adrenalin and boredom and human misery promoted casual encounters. One day Max was going to come home for good, and settle down with a good woman. He was sure that they existed, just not in war zones.

But that night, with Kitty, he had better sex than he had ever known before. She made love with an intensity, focus, desperation and fervour which amazed him. As though she actually meant it.

Afterwards, as they lay together, watching the night sky through her undrawn curtains and the patterns made by car headlights on the rose cornice of her bedroom ceiling, it struck Max that one chapter of his life was closing, and another had begun. Already, when he thought of his long march from Peshawar to Kabul, it seemed that a quite different Max Thompson had undertaken it. It had assumed a hazy quality, as though it were really quite surprising that it had ever happened at all.

Now, his life had been hijacked by a new cast of scoundrels, even less reliable than the Mujahedin. Freddie Saidi, Étienne Bercuse, Caryl Fargo, Bob Troup . . . Who were all these people, and what might they know about Saskia's murder?

Just before he dropped off, he whispered, 'There's something else I meant to tell you. I made my decision about *StreetSmart*.'

He felt her spine tense against his stomach. 'What is it?'

'To become the editor. Properly, I mean. Not just a stopgap.'

She rolled over in the bed and he could see her face, lit up by moonlight. 'Genuinely? Promise?'

'I don't know whether I can handle it, but I'm giving it my best shot.'

'That's fantastic.' She kissed him on the mouth. 'You're just what we need.'

[20]

'Max, Max! You've got to wake up.'

For a moment he thought he was back in hospital in Peshawar and a nurse was shaking him awake, until he saw it was Kitty, already dressed in a pink suit, who was leaning over him. 'It's eight o'clock. I've got to leave in fifteen minutes, there's a breakfast launch for some new scent I have to go to. Are you coming?'

'I don't know anything about it.'

'You probably *should* come, you know. Anyway, don't you have a car service?'

'Blast! It'll be waiting outside my flat. I never guessed I was going to stay here.'

'No problem,' said Kitty. He heard her ring Belgravia Limousines and have the car diverted to Rosary Gardens. 'Then it'll be on to the Lanesborough Hotel, waiting outside for about an hour, and then drop off at *StreetSmart*. Yes, all on account.'

Max took a quick shower, pulled on his clothes and located Kitty in the kitchen fixing coffee.

'Black OK?' she said. 'There never seems to be any milk in this fridge. Oh, and I've found this.' She handed him a blue tie with a discreet pattern of white stars. 'To put on for the launch.'

'I really have to wear a tie?'

''Fraid so. These events aren't exactly formal, but they're not Planet of Adventure either.'

The entryphone buzzed and they went downstairs to the waiting Mercedes.

'Hi, Bartholomew,' said Kitty to the driver. She was evidently no stranger to Belgravia Limousines.

They drove along Knightsbridge and Kitty rummaged in her bag for the invitation. She produced a reflective silver card in the shape of a scent bottle with the words 'And God created Gentlemen ... and

Ladies.' On the back was printed, 'The Directors of Nocturnes de l'Homme request the pleasure of your company to celebrate the launch of Nocturnes de l'Homme Pour Elle.'

'Not Nocturnes de l'Homme!' Max said. 'Saskia gave me a bottle of that for Christmas a couple of years ago. A huge bottle. It wouldn't even fit on the shelf.'

'We all got one of those,' said Kitty. 'At the launch party in Paris. They retail at three hundred pounds in the shops.'

'And now they're starting another version?'

'For women. All the men's companies are launching women's fragrances this year. Last year it was the other way round, the women's brands diversified into men's. Before that was unisex.'

'And what exactly happens at a scent launch?'

'Nothing to it. There'll be coffee and croissants, a speech by the president, another one from the marketing people – two if we're unlucky – then maybe a video. They're usually quite slick and painless.'

A hundred yards from the hotel they hit a traffic jam of taxis and limousines. Some guests were abandoning their drivers and walking the short distance to the porticoed entrance, brandishing their silver invitations. Kitty pointed people out to him as they went by. The whole beauty and fashion industry seemed to have turned out for the breakfast: editors and their assistants from all the magazines, fragrance buyers from the department stores, the merchandise and sales team from Nocturnes de l'Homme.

'Christ, there's Racinda,' said Kitty. 'It's better if she doesn't see I'm arriving with you. And look, getting out of the grey Daimler, that's Bob Troup, isn't it? What's he doing here?'

'I suppose he was asked.'

'But *still*,' said Kitty. 'He's been fired. He doesn't work for us any more. He shouldn't turn up on a *StreetSmart* invitation.'

Just then a second figure stepped out of the Daimler, and Kitty gasped. 'I don't believe it. That's Caryl Fargo. Bob arrived with Caryl in her car.'

'The woman who runs Incorporated?'

'Exactly. What the hell's he doing with her?'

They watched Caryl walk with Bob Troup towards the hotel. Bob was wearing his trademark green suit and a white shirt and tie, and looked as though he'd shaved again too. He was taller than Caryl by eighteen inches, though her blonde helmet of hair did something to restore the balance. She looked purposeful in a purple power suit and glasses with ornate gold hinges.

Just before they disappeared inside, Caryl said something to Bob and he laughed and took her arm.

The room for the launch had been set up with a shallow stage at one end, on which stood two lecterns and a video wall. There was a long table with a white cloth, coffee cups and Danish pastries and a giant silver replica of a Nocturnes de l'Homme bottle. Several waiters were cutting through the throng with trays of buck's fizz, while pretty girls in silver 'Pour Elle' spacesuits spritzed guests with the new product. A vaporous mist of eau-de-parfum was already settling over the Danish pastries.

'I can see Racinda over there,' said Kitty. 'And Lisa from the beauty department. We're well represented this morning.'

'Good,' said Max, though, so far, he couldn't see that they'd achieved anything very much.

'Ladies and gentlemen. Or should I, on this very special *historique* occasion, be saying Gentlemen and Ladies.' A small Frenchman with silver-grey hair had mounted the stage and was standing at the lectern.

'Who's this?' Max mouthed to Kitty.

'Luc Grimaud. Runs Nocturnes over here. Been in London about two years. Before that did the same job in Johannesburg, I think. Maybe Tokyo.'

'*Alors,*' said Luc, 'let me first of all be thanking you for coming along so early in the morning. For we French, most especially, it is always a big problem to queet the bed so early. That is our reputation anyhow, ha.'

The crowd tittered politely at this allusion to fabled Gallic sexiness, while Luc Grimaud adjusted the microphone.

'Yes,' he said, 'today is for our company *une affaire de la plus haute importance*. As our friends in the beauty business know quite well, at Nocturnes we launch a new product only very rarely. And only when we believe we have created a brand that is *un nouveau classique*. Well, today, three years following the phenomenally successful launch of Nocturnes de l'Homme, which has remained the number-one fragrance for men in every market where it has been launched – a great sensation – today, we launch the natural successor, you might describe it. First men, then women. It makes good sense, *non*? First men, then ladies. What would life be without ladies, ha!'

Encouraged by further polite laughter, Luc forged on. He seemed to be trying to flirt with the whole room at the same time. The girls in the silver spacesuits, who presumably worked for the sad old roué, looked up in rapt attention. Elsewhere, Max noticed, some of the beauty editors were less indulgent and were starting to chatter amongst themselves.

As Max scanned the room, waiting for the speech to end, he again noticed Caryl Fargo with Bob Troup. Both looked like the cat who'd got the cream. It suddenly occurred to him: maybe she's given him a job. If so, she was welcome to him. Max needed team players on *StreetSmart* and Bob certainly wasn't one of those. Bob must have felt his stare because he turned, caught Max's eye and scowled. There was no doubt about it, he'd made an enemy.

'Maintenant,' Luc Grimaud was saying, 'I wish to introduce to you my Directrice of Marketing, who may be known to many of you already, at least I am hoping so, Cathy Spence, who is going to describe to you the positioning of the new brand.'

Cathy was a breathless, big-boned English girl with brown hair and a generous bosom. Unwisely, she had elected to extend the brand livery into her own outfit this morning, and was wearing a silver parka, like a turkey trussed up for the oven.

'Let me take you back through time,' she began, 'to the Garden of Eden. Let us embark together in a time machine, way back through history, past the cavemen, past the dinosaurs, past Jurassic Park, to the biblical Garden of Eden. Imagine it. Adam is all alone in this beautiful garden, surrounded by beautiful flowers and bubbling streams, dressed in nothing, of course, except his Nocturnes de l'Homme.' Cathy beamed round the room, to ensure everyone had clocked the product placement. 'But something is amiss,' she continued, raising her voice an octave. 'What can it be? Surely Adam isn't bored. But he is. He needs a helpmate. Someone to make his supper, fulfil his sexual needs and, dare I say it, gentlemen, drive the car?' There was further obligatory laughter.

'So, gentlemen and ladies, what does Adam do? He calls God. "God," he says, "I'm lonely. I need a woman to make my supper and drive me home from the pub at night." And God replied, "Adam, I have duly considered your request, and am going to send you a woman. Her name is Eve. She will be very beautiful, and will be cleverer than you, Adam, and more attractive in every way. And, one last thing, Adam, I am creating for Eve her very own fragrance, because I know you men, you never want to lend your own aftershave and moisturiser to your ladies, so I'm creating one especially for women. It's called Nocturnes de l'Homme Pour Elle." '

There was a smattering of applause, but Cathy had not finished.

'Seriously,' she said, 'we believe that in Nocturnes de l'Homme Pour Elle we have created a fragrance not only for this millennium but also for the next. The first of a new generation of fragrances that defies categorisation. A fragrance that is both a lifestyle concept and appeals directly to the emotions. A fragrance for the Eve in every woman – the first woman and Everywoman. Our research proves that the millennium woman doesn't any longer want to be categorised. She is literally a different woman at different times of the day and night: mother, lover, successful executive, child, romantic, home-maker, juggler, carer, eco warrior, artist, nurturer ... she holds her infant to her breast, runs barefoot along a deserted beach at midnight, climbs Mount Kilimanjaro, works out at the gym, flies Concorde to New York for that all-important business meeting, then winds down with a relaxing aromatherapy massage. It is for women like this – the millennium woman – that we have created Nocturnes de l'Homme Pour Elle. Now, before I leave you to enjoy your pastries and coffee, I would just like to show you a short video that will be part of our launch TV spend in the autumn. The girl this time is Tigra.'

The video monitors flickered into life, and they saw the naked supermodel running in soft focus along an empty white beach. Max was looking out for the baby at her breast, when Kitty hissed, 'Time to go, but you should say hi first to Luc Grimaud, otherwise he won't know you were here.'

Kitty introduced them, and Luc went through the motions of making his condolences about Saskia. 'I never knew her that well,' he said. 'I invited her to have lunch on a few occasions, but she never had time.'

Luc made it clear, without saying so, that Saskia wasn't his favourite person.

'Anyway,' he said, 'you will get a good price for the magazine, I am certain.'

Not another one, Max thought. 'Actually, *StreetSmart*'s not for sale.'

'It's *not*? But I heard . . .'

'I'm afraid you heard wrong. And if you hear it again, I'd be grateful if you'd help me put a stop to the rumours.'

'It's good to know that,' said Luc. 'I was about to cancel my advertising with you. If the magazine were changing owner . . .'

They were waiting for their car on the slipway outside the Lanesborough when Caryl Fargo and Bob came out behind them.

Caryl held out her hand. 'I'd like to introduce myself. Caryl Fargo from Incorporated.' She had white-tipped fingernails and a brutal handshake. 'We need to get together some time.'

'Er, fine,' said Max. 'I'm not sure what my plans are for the next few days.'

'Look, let's not get into this,' she said, with a touch of impatience. 'We could talk now.'

'Why not?'

They walked thirty yards towards Hyde Park Corner. Taxis and buses rushed past. Even in their tailwind, Caryl's hair seemed immovable, an igloo of lacquer. Max could see Kitty watching them through the open door of the Mercedes.

'*StreetSmart*,' she said. 'I need to know. Is it, or isn't it, up for sale?'

'Everyone's asking me that this morning. And the answer's no.'

'I thought Freddie Saidi was buying you. Are you saying I'm too late?'

'He's not buying us – definitely not.'

'So I'm in with a chance. Who's handling the offering?'

'Nobody.'

'You're handling it yourself?' She looked surprised. 'Could be a smart move, Max. No fees.'

'You still misunderstand me. The magazine isn't for sale. Seriously. I'm keeping it.'

Caryl smiled patronisingly. 'Yes, we all know that,' she said. 'It's a good position to start from, a smart bargaining position. You can't seriously operate it. Now you've lost Bob Troup, you haven't even got an editor.'

'Actually, I'm editing it myself.'

Caryl laughed. 'I heard that,' she said. 'It's very sweet. We're looking forward to the articles about bazookas and hand grenades.

And travel features from Bosnia. But let's be serious, one chief executive to another, I've got a proposition. We own a little magazine you may have heard of called *Town Talk*. It does OK, though not in the same league as our flagships like *Girls on Top*. You have *StreetSmart* in the same sector. What I'm proposing is that we take *StreetSmart* off your hands and fold it into *Talk*. On their own, neither property is worth much, but together, Max, it could be quite a meaningful business. Which is why I'm prepared to pay top dollar.'

'Look, I'm grateful for your interest, but it's not going to happen.'

'Get real,' said Caryl. 'This is a genuine offer. From Incorporated. We're a quoted company. A lot of publishers would give their eye teeth to have me stand here, offering to buy them out.'

'I appreciate that. It's just that I have an obligation to my sister not to sell.'

'An obligation to *Saskia Thompson*? You think she worried about obligations?'

'Well, I do.'

'Then you're a bloody fool. There's nothing more to say. And I hope you won't end up a poor bloody fool too.'

'How do you mean?'

'Because if you choose to play hardball, Max Thompson, then I can play too. I hope you understand that. I've appointed Bob Troup editor of *Town Talk* and told him to do whatever it takes. Whatever it takes. And that goes for our advertising department too. They're going to undercut you all along the line. I've told them to deal so far off ratecard, they won't even remember what a ratecard is. We can afford to do it. We're big enough.'

She turned on her heel, and strode to her car without looking back.

[21]

'Philip, I need to talk to you urgently. Something's come up – several things in fact.'

Max had called Philip Landau the minute he got into the office. Already he could see why Saskia had rated him: he was urbane and direct and gave the impression of being unshockable. Max reckoned that if you rang him from a payphone and said, 'Philip, I've just robbed an American Express office at gunpoint, and shot three people including a cop, and I've run over a child with the getaway car,' Philip would reply, 'Quite an eventful morning. Perhaps you'd better find your way over to Long Acre and let me give you lunch. Then we'll decide how best to sort this out.'

Max gave Philip a précis of everything that had happened in the past twenty-four hours. 'So now we have two people trying to buy us: Freddie Saidi and Caryl Fargo. And there's something else too. My father got a call from the New York police. They're saying it might not have been suicide. Saskia may have been murdered.'

'*Murdered?*' Landau sucked his teeth. 'The police are saying that? Well, my immediate reaction is one of shock but not absolute surprise. You'll remember when you came to see me at my office, I told you I'd never viewed Saskia as a potential suicide.'

'Gina David at *StreetSmart* agrees with you. My father too. I mean, who'd want to murder Saskia?'

'Tell you what,' Philip said. 'Would it help if we met up and talked it through properly? Tonight if you like. I'm having dinner with Karis – I don't believe you've met my wife yet – but I know she'd be delighted if you joined us.'

'You sure? It's not your wedding anniversary or something?'

Philip laughed. 'No, just dinner. Karis doesn't cook. Eating in this marriage equals a restaurant. Quaglino's at eight fifteen, meet at the table? We can talk about Saskia and devise a response to these overtures for the magazine. I suppose they were inevitable, now your sister's dead. You'll have to decide what to do about them.'

'But we've agreed I'm keeping *StreetSmart* for Cody. That's the whole point.'

'That was most definitely what Saskia *wanted* to happen,' said Philip. 'That was her intention, as her will makes plain. They're not very salubrious suitors, but you have an opportunity here to sell out, probably on very advantageous terms. With two of them, there's no telling how they might bid each other up. Neither party is short of funds.'

The conversation left Max feeling unsettled. Saskia's murder, if that was what it was, strengthened his sense of obligation to her magazine. He didn't see that he could change his mind now, even if he wanted to.

Marie-Louise, Gina, Kevin and Spiro appeared at the door of the office looking excited.

'First off the press. The new issue,' said Marie-Louise. 'They just couriered it from the printer.'

She handed it to him and it felt substantial. It must have been half an inch thick.

The cover shot of Madonna and Ivor Sergov was strong, even better than he'd imagined. Madonna looked sexy, while Sergov with his heavy jowls and camel coat was suitably sinister.

'This is clever,' Max told Spiro. 'The orange lettering up here, on the word *StreetSmart*, it's really eye-catching and bright.'

'We used a fifth colour,' said Spiro. 'I was hoping you wouldn't notice, actually.'

'Why's that? Is it expensive?'

'That's what the production people always claim.' He sounded evasive. 'You have to run the cover twice through the presses, for the extra intensity.'

'Did Saskia use it?'

'Only sometimes. But they're going to use a fifth colour every issue now at *Town Talk*. That was Bob's first decision as editor.'

'Anyway,' said Kevin, who was flicking proudly through the issue, 'it's not much money when you put it in the context of the advertising revenue. Look at all these colour ads. A hundred and seventy-six pages of paid space. Even without Bercuse – the bastards.'

'Still no news there?'

'Only that Étienne Bercuse personally made the decision to pull out. No one knows why.

'Just look at that,' Kevin went on. 'They're all in here. Guess Jeans, Dior, Jeep Cherokee, Nocturnes de l'Homme, and there's a lovely gatefold here from Salvatore Ferragamo.'

'Gatefold? You've lost me.'

'Four-page advertisement opening out of a front cover, like a concertina. Bags of impact, so commands a big premium. Anyway, *Town Talk* closed on 131, that's forty-five pages behind. Our yield's a lot firmer too.'

'Great,' Max said. 'That's a real achievement.'

'I'd love to be a fly on the wall over at Incorporated when they see our issue, I tell you they're going to wet themselves. A sixteen-page bound insert from DKNY. Those wasters at *Town Talk* couldn't get through the front door. Couldn't even get an *appointment to pitch.*'

Max laughed. There was something so joyful about Kevin in his triumph over the opposition. He was cock-a-hoop. A week ago, Max would have thought Kevin was stark staring mad, dancing around the desk over a few advertising contracts, but his enthusiasm was more understandable now. It was starting to get to Max too.

He located the Sergov article with his Bullet agency photographs, and felt unexpected pride. The pictures were three years old and had appeared before, but *StreetSmart*'s printing and art direction gave them new life. In *Newsweek*, you always got a little screen of dots across the photographs, as though they were printed through a teabag, but in *StreetSmart* you could see every detail. There must have been a hundred tones of black and grey in the mono repro alone.

On the final spread was his picture of the corpse in Grozny market. Even Max blanched a bit when he saw it so large. This was one occasion when some softer printing might have been in order. Max turned the page hurriedly, and found himself face-to-face with a colour advertisement for diamond earrings.

'One thing you've *got* to look at,' said Marie-Louise. 'I managed to get it changed at the last minute on press.'

She was leafing through the front section of the magazine.

'There you go,' she said. 'Masthead.'

He saw it at once. His own name, in giant type, at the top of the page. MAX THOMPSON, Editor, Chairman and Chief Executive. It was so big, you could have read it from across the room.

'Surely this is a bit premature. I mean, I haven't done anything yet.'

'Yes, you have,' said Gina. 'You chose the cover. And supplied a lot of the pictures inside. Anyway, that's not the point of a masthead, it's not an historical document. The names are meant to tell you who's there now, who to contact in the different departments. That was Saskia's policy. If you were fired, you were struck off the masthead the same day.'

'Well, it's certainly unmissable. There's no turning back now.'

Gina and Marie-Louise laughed. 'We weren't going to tell you this,' said Marie-Louise, 'but that's exactly why we did it, altered the masthead so quickly. So you couldn't change your mind. It makes it more official, with your name up in lights.'

'Actually,' Max replied, 'it scares me stiff. It makes me want to do a runner.'

After they'd gone, he asked Jean to bring in the various bits of information he'd make a mental note to look up: *StreetSmart*'s advertising revenues from the fashion business in Milan, the cost of adding and subtracting pages of editorial in the American edition, and the profit and loss of StreetSmart Interactive. For some reason, he sensed that the last of these was going to be bad news. How had Chip Miller put it exactly? 'I guess all the online projections were a little optimistic.'

Jean returned with a sheaf of computer printouts and statistics, and a slim orange book of accounts. 'I think you'll find everything here,' she said. 'These are the Italian advertising figures you asked for. I've given you year-to-date and also the whole of last year, which gives a fuller picture. The paper, printing, repro, manufacturing and delivery costs you'll find on this spreadsheet. Editorial contents costs are separated out over here into manuscripts and illustrations, travel, studio hire, operating expenses and kill fees.'

'*Kill* fees?'

Jean smiled primly. 'Not a contingency budget for murder, though I dare say we all feel we need one, sometimes. Kill fees are what we pay when we commission work that doesn't, for whatever reason, make it into the issue. Generally fifty per cent of the published rate.'

'I see.'

'If there's anything you don't understand, just ask,' she said, 'and I'll do my best to explain. The numbers are quite confusing. Nothing goes quite where you expect. Costs of the fashion department attending the collections in Paris go under travel and entertaining, but if you want to give a dinner party in Milan, that's operating.'

For two hours, he wrestled with the figures. Jean was right: until you'd puzzled out how they were structured, they were almost incomprehensible. Columns and columns of numbers indicating variances from budget, target, the previous year, market share – the permutations were baffling. There were statistics about issue size, paper tonnage, colour/mono split, whatever that might be, unsolds, postage costs on subscriptions, freighting, provisions for bad debts of ninety days or more. Had Saskia really understood this stuff? His respect for her was growing all the time, along with his own sense of inadequacy.

He began with the easy bits. Italian advertising. Kitty wasn't joking when she'd said it was important to *StreetSmart*. Last year, Milanese fashion companies had booked almost 200 pages into the British edition, and 129 in the American. Add those together and it was a ton of money. He began working it out, converting the dollars of the American revenues into sterling and then adding them to the British. It came to seven million pounds. Jesus, he whistled, no wonder Saskia could afford her place in Holland Park.

He could also see how important it was for him to go to Milan. If they put a lot of store by people turning up at their shows, he'd be crazy not to. For this amount of money, he'd move there for good.

Next he investigated the cost of editorial pages. This was more difficult, since there were so many elements. It wasn't simply the cost of the paper and ink, it was the editorial itself, and the nature of the editorial. Fashion pages, he could see, cost far more to generate than interviews or general articles, because the expenses were so high: hotel bills for eight or ten people, location van hire, air fares. Some of the models, Max saw to his amazement, flew first class. These girls were seventeen, weren't they? Even the articles worked out at six thousand dollars a page in the States. No wonder Anka had advised him to drop eleven pages from their New York edition. What would happen to those articles now, the ones he'd held over? Would they publish them next month, or would they be 'killed'? Max felt pleased with himself for remembering the expression. He was getting somewhere.

Finally he turned to the profit and loss accounts. These were divided into separate sections for the three divisions – StreetSmart Ltd, StreetSmart Inc and StreetSmart Interactive Inc (SII) – with a single sheet of consolidated P&L at the end. Altogether, the ringbound orange book must have contained thirty pages. He trawled through it line by line, using a ruler to keep his place. The computer-generated figures were hard to read and, after an hour, began to blur together. Gradually, he sussed out how the accounts were constructed, and how the various statistics fed together to arrive at the bottom line.

What Max discovered there, however, made him feel nauseous.

The London edition was plainly a big success, with annual profits of eight million pounds. Advertising revenue was running twenty-two per cent ahead of last year, with volume of space up by almost twelve per cent. The balance of this increased revenue came from soaring advertising yields. He could understand now why Kevin Sky had been so bullish: he was managing to squeeze his clients for eight or nine per cent more per page than they had paid the previous year. His first thought was: they must love *StreetSmart*, or Saskia, or both. His second was: would they still support the magazine now she was dead? It was becoming obvious that Saskia's personality and fame had been a big factor in *StreetSmart*'s commercial success. And Luc Grimaud's remark at the scent launch this morning hadn't been encouraging.

Circulation figures looked impressive too. So far this year, the British edition had averaged 407,000 copies a month, against 376,000 for the same issues a year ago. There was a separate line in the accounts showing returns – unsold copies – and these were diminishing. Now that he knew how much it cost to print each copy, he could see the double benefit of strong sell-through. A sold issue meant revenue, but an unsold was a negative, since you still had to print the thing. At the newsagent on the corner of Max's street, there were always piles of magazines left over at the end of the month; you saw the Gujaratis who owned the place tying them up with string. Max knew he would never be able to think of unsold issues in the same casual way again. Those bundles were pure money.

The Madonna–Igor Sergov issue lay face-up on his desk. He

looked at it again, more critically this time. Did *StreetSmart* readers really want to know more about Madonna and her latest squeeze? Madonna was everywhere, you couldn't get away from her. Was that an advantage or a disadvantage? He had no idea. Saskia would have known instinctively. He just hoped his first issue wouldn't end up as unsolds, half a million of them.

The American accounts were a different story. Circulation was booming – last month's issue with Tom Cruise and Nicole Kidman on the cover had sold 610,000 at newsstand plus 414,217 subscriptions – but the company was unprofitable. In fact, it had made a loss last year of almost eleven million dollars. It didn't make sense. True, they sold fewer advertisements than London, but the rates were much higher. Did they really get paid sixty thousand dollars for each and every page? That was what it said. Incredible. Sixty thousand dollars was about what he owed the mortgage company on his flat. And *StreetSmart* charged that to print one photograph of a swimsuit or a pair of shoes.

And yet, according to the accounts, the magazine wasn't even washing its face.

It didn't take long to locate the reason. *StreetSmart*'s subscriptions were sold so cheaply that they made a colossal loss: the price people paid for twelve issues mailed to their home didn't even cover the manufacturing cost. And the level of unsolds at newsstand was crippling too. To sell 600,000 Tom Cruise and Nicole Kidman, they'd distributed more than two million copies across America. It was hard to credit, so he buzzed Jean for a breakdown. Three minutes later, she handed him a distribution map of the whole United States. He read the statistics for the different wholesalers and then for the supermarket groups that were responsible for half *StreetSmart*'s sales. Kroger Stores, based in Cincinnati, Safeway in Oakland, PriceCostco in Kirkland, American Stores in Salt Lake City that traded as naff brand chains like Acme, Jewel and Lucky, Albertsons in Boise, Idaho, Publix in Lakeland, Florida; *StreetSmart* was available in thousands and thousands of drugstores and convenience stores, but at what cost?

He made a note to question Philip Landau about the American edition this evening at dinner. Was Saskia concerned about it? Had it worried her that they were losing so much money? And what about the American investors? They'd better be cool.

The third section was devoted to StreetSmart Interactive, and the numbers were so terrible Max hoped he'd misread them. In fact, they were catastrophic. Last year, the division had soaked up sixteen million dollars, and the results for this year were no better. Since the holding company owned fifty per cent of SII, *StreetSmart* was taking hits of almost eight million dollars a year. In relation to revenues, they were spending money at a frightening rate on technology and content. Max could hardly believe the cost of keeping Chip's online war correspondents in the field, their *per diems* were mind blowing. Where the hell were these guys staying, anyway? The Four Seasons?

On the final sheet of the orange book were the consolidated results. He guessed what was coming and had to steel himself to read them. The profits of the London edition were being blown away by losses in the States. In fact, last year, the company had posted an overall loss of five million dollars.

Along the corridor, on the editorial floor, Spiro was assessing photographers' portfolios while Marie-Louise and Tim, the features assistant, sifted through unsolicited ideas. Gina was processing contributors' expenses in her open-sided glass pod. Picture editors were marking transparencies with yellow chinographs. At a long bench in front of the window, news editors and reporters were occupied on the telephone or typing copy into PCs. Max noticed Bob Troup's acolytes – 'the talented ones' – huddled together in a glass meeting room. The bald youth with the goatee glared at him, and addressed some remark to the others, and they all laughed sourly.

'Someone else here offering an exclusive interview with Gerard Depardieu,' Marie-Louise was saying. 'Any takers?'

'There was a big story about him in American *Cosmo* last issue,' said Spiro from across the light box. 'Pictures by Yando.'

'I think we'll pass, then,' said Marie-Louise.

'How about this?' said Tim. 'Confessions of a Beverly Hills cocktail waitress. Claims to have kept a diary. English girl who worked the movie scene. Sex and canapés.'

'Depends how it's done. Could be us, could be *National Enquirer*. Bring it to the next ideas conference. Oh, hi, Max.'

Max dragged a metal chair across to the features desk and sat down. 'How's your article about data protection shaping up?' he asked Tim.

He looked pleased that Max had remembered. 'Not much to report yet, but I've put in some calls. I know people in the auction houses and they're going to dig a bit. One thing I've already discovered: it'll be pretty hard to get access. Only people at board level have the passcodes to the databases, for the interesting stuff, at least. Same with the Mandarin-Oriental hotel group. All the information's there, but it's hard to hack into.'

'Well, persevere. It's an interesting concept, and it would work in both editions, over here and in the States. People are obsessed by the whole idea of secret records, being spied on without their knowledge. Incidentally,' Max added, 'that reminds me of something. What does anyone know about Freddie Saidi?'

'Our would-be owner?' said Gina, emerging from her pod. 'Everything and nothing. We called in all the cuttings when the rumours began about him trying to buy us. There are plenty of articles, but nothing very illuminating. It's all PR generated. And most of the pieces are written by the same small group of journalists, which is always suspicious.'

'How do you mean?'

'Tame hacks. Malleable. I don't know this for certain, but I've heard Saidi pays retainers to five or six feature writers on national newspapers – cash or presents or both. In return, they line up favourable articles about him. It's all done through Marcus Brooke.'

Max was genuinely shocked. 'Would journalists really do that? Accept bribes?'

''Fraid so,' said Gina. 'And Marcus Brooke is brilliant at predicting who might be up for it.'

'So you mean those gushing articles about Saidi, they're all *bought*?' He felt particularly sore, since his own Christmas in Latvia feature had been syndicated by *Newsweek* to a British broadsheet, but was later bumped by a puff-piece about Saidi and his traditional British celebrations.

'Probably. And he's clever about preventing real journalists from getting too close. There hasn't been a single in-depth profile, despite all the rumours.'

'Kitty Marr said something about rumours too, but she didn't seem to know anything definite.'

'No one does. Arms dealing, drugs, money laundering. Everyone assumes that's where his cash comes from, but I've never seen it in print.'

'Haven't any of the newspapers investigated him? With all these companies he's been buying, I'd have thought he'd be a natural candidate.'

'They've all put people on to it, but it's difficult to stand anything up,' said Gina. 'Unless you're one of Marcus Brooke's patsies, you don't get access, and his employees won't say anything. They're totally paranoid. They won't even talk about him off the record. It's that bad.'

'So nothing gets written.'

'Or Brooke gets it pulled. He's very manipulative. Saidi's companies are big advertisers, don't forget; he can threaten to pull out. If that doesn't work, Brooke intervenes in some other way: bribery, blackmail or litigation.'

'I didn't realise it was so easy to suborn the press.'

'Legal action is effective, you know, because it's so expensive and time consuming. It ties everyone up for months, so there's a natural tendency to shy away from writing about litigious people. After a couple of libel suits, word gets around, even if they're settled out of court. Editors don't need it. Management hates it. And we can't be sanctimonious, because *StreetSmart* has never written about Saidi either.'

'Have we considered it?'

'He comes up all the time at ideas meetings. Contributors often suggest doing him.'

'But we haven't, for the reasons you've described.'

'Saskia was tempted, and I think we even commissioned someone to do some legwork. A couple of years ago, when he bought Fournels et Fils. But it never came to anything. To be honest, I think Saskia was always equivocal, because of the advertising. That was Saskia with her publisher's hat on. In the end, she didn't think it was worth it.'

'When Marcus Brooke came in to see me the other day, he said something about Saskia being a great friend of Saidi.'

Gina laughed. 'She couldn't *stand* him. He kept inviting her to things and she was always making excuses to get out of them. At one point, he was asking her to dinners and film premieres almost every week. He must have had a thing for her. These gross bunches of flowers kept arriving. And jewellery. And gifts for Cody. It went on for months.'

'When was this?'

'Oh, I don't know, six or seven years ago. The magazine was in Soho Square. We hadn't moved here.'

'Well, let me tell you,' Max said, 'whatever Freddie Saidi felt about Saskia, it hasn't transferred to me. Marcus Brooke became very aggressive when I turned down his offer to buy us. It was quite intimidating.'

'That's how those guys operate. They're over you like a rash, until you cross them.'

'All the more reason to get a better fix on them. Can you get me the Saidi cuttings? I'd like to take a look, even if they're bland. And let's try and remember who worked on the *StreetSmart* article about him, the one that never ran. Do we store that kind of information?'

Gina said, 'I should have that somewhere. If we paid anybody for research, it'll be on record.'

'Let me know, won't you? It's worth a shot. If the journalist went round doing interviews, there could be notes. And Tim,' he said, 'with your research into data protection, try and get some of these companies to run a search on Saidi. There could be useful stuff there too.'

[22]

It was lunchtime and Max was ravenous. He buzzed Jean. 'Tell me, where's the nearest place round here to get a hamburger?'

'A hamburger?' She sounded surprised. 'You mean an actual hamburger? With a bun and everything?'

'And french fries.'

'Well, I'm sorry, Max, but I'm afraid I haven't the faintest idea. A hamburger in Bond Street? I'm not even sure that's possible.'

Now it was Max's turn to be amazed. 'It's got to be. Don't people have lunch?'

'Of course,' said Jean. 'There's Chow Bene in the Givenchy boutique if you'd like me to see if I can get you a table.'

'God, no. I'm *hungry*. I need fuel.'

'Well,' Jean said doubtfully, 'I believe I might have seen a McWhatsits up towards Oxford Street, on the way to the Underground. Shall I send a messenger to buy you one?'

'No, thanks. I'll go myself. I could do with the air.'

He set off up Bond Street, past the sleek façades of the fashion boutiques and jewellers. In the window of Fournels et Fils was a large colour photograph of Freddie Saidi standing next to the Duchess of York at a polo tournament. He looked very small next to the Duchess, who towered above him, laughing as she handed over a trophy to some South American player. A banner showed that the tournament had been sponsored by Fournels et Fils.

As he passed the boutiques, he found that he recognised several of the names from his meetings with Kevin and Anka. Cerruti, Lockerjock, Sensi, Yves Saint Laurent. It was like learning a foreign language, certain vocabulary was beginning to come round again. Words that had meant nothing whatever a week ago, when he flew out of Peshawar, were becoming familiar.

At the top of Oxford Street, he caught sight of his reflection in a mirrored doorway. The hems of his chinos were concertina'd around his desert boots, which themselves looked scuffed and galumphing. The blue tie Kitty had lent him was smart, but seemed at odds with his worn shirt and combat jacket. And he urgently needed a haircut.

First, however, he had to have something to eat. A powerful stench of junk food, and the sight of Styrofoam boxes drifting about on the pavement, alerted him that he was approaching a hamburger bar. The place was crowded with tourists and office workers, though not the sort of office workers you found at *StreetSmart*. He reckoned he was the first person from the magazine ever to walk through the door.

As the queue shuffled its way forward, he looked out on to the street. Three figures were standing across the road, apparently waiting for someone. There was something strangely furtive about them. More than once they looked around, as though they wanted whoever it was to get a move on. A girl and two young men, one with a bald head and a goatee. Bob Troup's talent, Max realised with a start.

A bus pulled up, and for a moment they were hidden. What the hell were they doing there? Then the bus pulled away and he once again had an unimpeded view.

A taxi drew up at the kerb and a man with ginger hair got out. It was Bob Troup. He gave the girl a cursory kiss and shook hands with the men. He didn't pay off the cab, but kept it ticking over. Max strained to see what was happening.

He watched him hand each person an envelope – it looked like a letter – and then produce a larger brown envelope, which the bald youth tore open. The others gathered round excitedly. He pulled out something that looked like a brochure or a catalogue: no, it was a magazine. Not the new *StreetSmart*, surely? After all, it was Bob Troup who was showing it to his acolytes, not the other way round. Whatever it was, they all seemed well pleased.

Shortly afterwards, Bob stepped back into his taxi and the talent set off by foot, in the direction of Bruton Street.

Max ate his burger at a stool at the counter, and wondered what that had all been about. It didn't make sense, but it made him uneasy.

On the way back to the office, he stopped at a payphone with an acoustic hood and rang *StreetSmart*.

'Kitty Marr, please.'

A second later, she was on the line.

'Kitty? It's Max. I'm in a callbox. You doing anything right now?'

'Eating rice salad at my desk.'

'Look, you remember something you said yesterday about taking an objective look at my appearance? In a full-length mirror?'

'Er, yes. I'm feeling slightly embarrassed about that, actually.'

'Well, I just did. And you were right. I'm wearing the wrong uniform for the job. Kitty, I need to buy some clothes and get a haircut. Any tips?'

'Can you be outside the office in five minutes? Meet you in the lobby.'

Kitty was already waiting downstairs with a list of shops. 'Now, I bet you hate clothes shopping,' she said. 'All men do.'

'I wouldn't know. I never *go* clothes shopping. As you've already pointed out, I don't own any clothes.'

'Haircut first though,' she said, setting off up Conduit Street in the direction of Soho. They walked along narrow streets, lined with sushi bars and pizza places, before arriving at some kind of space-age barber's shop, with chrome basins and chairs formed out of treadless tractor tyres. Along one wall hung showcards featuring editorial work for magazines, including several for *StreetSmart*.

'We use this place a lot for hair,' Kitty explained. 'Hiro did Liv Tyler for the January cover.'

Hiro, who was Taiwanese, appeared less than eager to take Max on as a client. He was preoccupied in a back room dealing Tarot cards. Kitty made Max wait outside while she talked to him. He heard the words '*StreetSmart*' and 'Saskia', and eventually Hiro shrugged, and agreed to come outside.

He asked Max his star sign and then told him to hold a crystal close to his face. Then, with sudden resolve, he snatched up his scissors and a razor and began snipping and slashing at Max's thick, uneven hair, occasionally sighing, the blades of the scissors and the steel of the razor flying about his ears until his lap, and the floor around the chair, were strewn with clippings.

Afterwards, appraising the result in the mirror, Max found it difficult to recognise himself. The hair up his neck had entirely disappeared, and the top was cut short and spiky like a GI in an old movie. Kitty, however, pronounced it 'cute' and stated that, at sixty pounds, 'Hiro's given you a massive discount, the special magazine staff rate.'

They walked back in the direction of Bond Street, stepping out into the road to dodge the pedestrians in their winter coats who thronged the pavement. As they went along, Max told Kitty about spotting Bob Troup and the three *StreetSmart* staffers in Oxford Street.

'Those people are nightmares,' she said. 'The one with the shaven head is Phil. Phil Weber. He only recently came on staff. He does investigative stories, supposedly.'

'What do you think they were all doing there, with Troup?'

'God knows. Not showing Bob our new issue, I hope.'

'That was my first thought, but it was Bob who arrived clutching a magazine, not Phil.'

'Anyway,' said Kitty, 'Bob knows virtually everything that's in it already. He edited most of it. Not much altered after he left, did it?'

'Just the front cover.'

A hundred yards short of the office, Kitty stopped at a door between two shopfronts, and rang a brass-plated entryphone. A sign underneath read 'Creative Concepts, Public Relations'.

There was a crackle from the intercom, and she shouted, 'Hi, it's Kitty from *StreetSmart*. Can you buzz us in?'

Max trailed behind her up three flights of stairs to a bright attic space, flooded with natural light. Every inch of wallspace was filled by rails of clothes, three deep. There were carrier bags printed with the names of different fashion companies, with labels attached saying '*Vogue* – Urgent' and '*Marie Claire* – Must have by Fri pm'. There were trolleys of leather belts, Stussy caps, motorcycle boots and Y-fronts, and boxes of rayon and nylon jerseys.

'*Ciao*, Kitty.' A thin young man, pale like an albino, appeared from behind a rail, holding a mug of coffee.

'Hi, Marco. Mind if we try on some things? This is my boss, Max Thompson.'

'Be my guest,' said Marco. 'The Clements-Ribeiro stuff's nice. It's just come in.'

'Look, Kitty,' said Max, as soon as Marco was out of earshot. 'I'm not convinced we're in the right place at all. I can't wear any of this. I need a suit.'

'Relax,' said Kitty. 'They have everything. And you can get it here at wholesale less forty per cent.'

Fifteen minutes later, they were back in the street and Max was catching his sharp new silhouette in shop windows. The transformation was so total, it was hard to believe that this was him. Black suit, white button-down shirt, black loafers. With the haircut and everything, he resembled some smooth operator from a different planet. Kitty had reclaimed her blue tie, and made him dump the rest of his kit in a bin at the PR company.

'You won't be needing it,' she said. 'You promised to edit the magazine, remember.'

When they reached the *StreetSmart* lobby, the receptionist with black nail varnish failed to recognise him, and asked him to sign the visitors' book. When she realised her mistake, her jaw dropped.

The moment Max reached the third floor, he knew something was wrong.

'Thank God you're back, Max. We've been hunting everywhere for you.' Gina looked distraught. She was surrounded by an agitated group of staff, including Spiro, Tim, Racinda and Lisa. 'Marie-Louise has gone to Chow Bene, in case you were there,' said Gina. 'Jean didn't know where you'd gone for lunch.'

'I'm here now, anyway. What's the problem?'

'This!' said Gina. She was holding up a magazine. It took him several seconds to register that it wasn't *StreetSmart*. The front cover was identical: Madonna smouldering, with Igor Sergov scowling next to her in a camel-hair coat. But the logo across both their heads said *Town Talk*.

'That's extraordinary. It's virtually the same as ours.'

'It *is* our cover,' said Spiro. 'It's one of our pictures.'

'But how did they get it? I thought it was exclusive. The photographer – Jonti, the guy on the motorbike – took it for *us*, didn't he?'

'I've put in a call to him, but we already know what's happened. They've pinched one of our rejects.'

'You mean they've stolen it from here, from the office?'

'No question. Look, here's the envelope of transparencies.' Spiro held up a brown envelope, with 'Jonti/Madonna–Igor' scrawled across the front. 'Here are the two we've used – the cover and the inside shot – but there's a third one missing. Someone's cut it off the sheet.'

'Isn't that illegal?'

'Totally,' said Gina. 'We've got them by the short and curlies, legally, but that's not much help now. It's going to look ridiculous, two competitive magazines with exactly the same cover.'

'When do they go on sale?'

'Tomorrow. Same as us,' said Gina. 'Can you imagine? Two identical covers, side by side on the newsstands? Except they won't be displayed together, not at the kiosks, the newsagents will only display one. Readers will be confused. People who usually get both magazines will probably only buy one, because they'll think they've read it already. Oh God, *how* has this happened?'

And suddenly Max knew. *Of course*, Phil Weber and Bob Troup in Oxford Street. That's what they were doing: looking at the *Town Talk* cover. Phil and his friends – Bob's acolytes – had stolen the transparency from the art department. They must have taken it the evening after the cover meeting. Bob certainly hadn't wasted any time. He remembered Caryl Fargo at this morning's breakfast: *'I've told him to do whatever it takes.'* Well, she wasn't kidding.

Just then, Jean bustled on to the editorial floor. 'Max, if I can interrupt you for just one moment.' She drew him aside. 'Two things you need to be aware of,' she said. 'Neither of them good news. We received three resignations over lunchtime. Phil Weber, Stella Greenley and Matt Stein. They're all going to *Town Talk*.'

'Good riddance. I was about to fire them anyway.'

Jean smiled. 'You sounded exactly like Saskia when you said that. If anyone resigned, even to have a baby, she always said she'd been on the point of sacking them. She couldn't stand people leaving.'

'This is different. Those three should be prosecuted. Anyway, you mentioned there were two things.'

'We received a telephone message two minutes ago from our printer. It was rather garbled, I'm afraid. The customer services director of Gërstler-Begg rang from Doncaster – that's where the plant is. He'd been contacted by the police to say there's been a serious accident on the motorway, a lorry has overturned. There aren't many details yet, he was just alerting us.'

'And this lorry was delivering *StreetSmart*?'

'To the distributor. We print in Doncaster and the whole run is driven down to the main warehouse in Catford.'

'So what next? When will we find out what's happened?'

'They're going to ring the moment they know anything. Apparently the driver is badly injured. He was thrown through the cabin windscreen.'

'Poor sod,' said Max.

There was a message on Max's desk to ring Chip Miller in Hartford, Connecticut.

'Listen,' Chip said, coming straight to the point. 'There's been a development. Nothing definite yet, but it could be good news.'

'Really?' If any division needed good news, it was Interactive.

'You remember I mentioned we had this big presentation for the East River Hotel.'

'Sure.'

'Well, it's become a lot bigger than that now. We got sent a fresh brief last evening. They want to put everything up online, all Saidi's businesses. A three-thousand-page site.'

'The jewellers and everything?'

'Everything. The jeweller. The saddler. And they've asked us to come up with some interactive biographical pages about Mr Saidi, accessing relevant information about him and his charitable involvements.'

'There'll be a demand for that service,' Max said drily. 'Who will you be pitching to? Is a man named Marcus Brooke involved?'

'He sent us the revised brief, and he's coming to the meeting with Saidi.'

'Saidi's coming himself? They are taking this seriously.'

'That's why I'm calling you. You mentioned you might be over in New York. I think that could swing it. Saskia was going to be there, originally, and she was a great presenter. The proposal we're putting up to them is worth seven million dollars.'

Seven million was almost half the annual loss.

'Where's the presentation taking place? Up in Hartford?'

'New York. At the *StreetSmart* magazine offices, eleven o'clock, Monday morning.'

'OK. We have a deal. I'll be there.'

'Good man,' said Chip. 'I'll download some of the concepts we're working on, so you can see where we're coming from. You might like to present a segment yourself.'

The minute he put the phone down, Jean buzzed him on the other line. 'More bad news from Gërstler-Begg. They've just this moment rung.'

'OK, what happened?'

'It seems that the lorry with all our copies on board was involved in a major pile-up. The cause still isn't clear, except that it lost control on the M1 and smashed through the central barrier, then swerved into oncoming traffic. Six other vehicles were involved.'

'Christ.'

'The driver's dead. At least one other person died too.'

'What a disaster.'

'That's not all, I'm afraid, Max. The freight doors flew open when the lorry turned over, and magazines were propelled right across the motorway.'

'What, all of them?'

'A good number, from what they were saying. It's difficult to know, since the police won't let anyone near the scene, but according to the printers, about half the copies are ruined. The bundles spilled down the hard shoulder and split open, and a lot have been driven over.'

'So what happens now? Do we reprint?'

'That's the hitch,' said Jean. 'The printers promise they'll move heaven and earth, but there's not much flexibility in their schedule. They can't tell us anything until midday on Monday. Their machine-time's pretty much committed, twenty-four hours.'

'So what do they expect us to do? Skip a whole issue?'

'We're insured, of course. So are Gërstler-Begg. So we won't be out of pocket, and we'll be able to refund the advertisers. But a month off the bookstalls is a long time.'

'Has this ever happened before, Jean? Did this happen to Saskia?'

'Never like this. It's rotten luck, Max, your first issue. I'm so sorry.'

'Yeah, it is bad luck, isn't it? I can only agree.'

'Incidentally,' said Jean, 'I haven't had a chance to say anything about this new image of yours, the suit and everything. Very sharp. You look very much the part.'

'Ironic, isn't it? I'm walking around looking like a man in a movie playing myself, but half our issues are spread across the motorway and the other half have the same front cover as the competition. Hope I do this well every month. And on top of everything else, my arm's giving me hell. It's throbbing like a bloody steam engine.'

'I know what you need,' said Jean. 'A glass of Glenfiddich.'

'I thought you said we didn't keep strong drink on the premises.'

'That was the old regime. I went out and bought you a couple of bottles. Do you prefer it with soda or with water?'

'I like it just as it pours. Straight up. And make that a large one, please, Jean.'

'Gracious,' she said. 'I can see I should have ordered two cases, not two bottles.'

[23]

That evening, Max brooded in Saskia's office until he thought everyone else had gone home. One way and another, it had been a terrible day, and he needed a little time alone with a cigarette. There was certainly plenty to think about: Bob's duplicity over the front covers, and Caryl's bid for the company; the overturned truck and the tragic death of its driver; the American company's results, which had shocked him. Then there was Freddie Saidi, who sounded a dangerous enemy, and the continuing mystery over Cody's father, and the uncertainty over Bercuse, and Luc Grimaud's conviction that *StreetSmart* would soon change hands. And, above everything, who had murdered Saskia, and how did it all fit together? There must be a connection between all the bad things that were happening, but he couldn't work it out. When Philip Landau had sold him this job in his office – was it really only four days ago? – it had sounded to Max like a sinecure. Now it seemed anything but.

Jean tapped on the door. 'If you don't need me any more, I'll slip off home, if that's all right.'

He was on his third whisky now, and he saw Jean's sharp eyes settle, for the briefest of moments, on the fast-diminishing level of the bottle.

'Jean,' he said. 'This may sound a bit strange, but there's something I've been meaning to ask you.'

'By all means.'

'My nephew, Cody. It's just possible that his father might be connected in some way to Saskia's death . . .'

Jean looked at him noncommittally, while fractionally raising one eyebrow. 'Now I do hope, Max, that you're not about to invite me to speculate on his parentage?'

'I'm not asking you this for gossip reasons, it could be important. I wasn't in the country much around the time Cody was born, so I don't know who Saskia was seeing.'

Jean thought for a bit, carefully weighing her words. 'Let me put it this way, Max. I'm trying not to be indelicate. Your sister always had a number of admirers, at any one time: some quite well-known people, others not. I certainly wasn't aware of all of them. Saskia liked to keep her private life just that – private.'

'But you must have had your suspicions, when she became pregnant?'

'There were certain names mentioned around the office, but I can assure you I discouraged it. I've never approved of office gossip, particularly about my employer.'

She looked pointedly at Max, and he wondered whether she could be referring to him and Kitty.

'Sorry, Jean. I won't do that to you again.'

However, Max had the distinct impression that she knew more than she was saying.

'Oh, and Jean,' he said, 'I spoke to Chip Miller and I've agreed to join him at a meeting in New York on Monday morning. Do you think we can get a plane ticket this late?'

'Of course, I'll ring them right away. You'll stay at the apartment, I take it?'

Ten minutes later she came back, wearing her coat. 'All done,' she said. 'You're on the 1900 Concorde flight on Sunday evening. Here's the confirmation number, you can pick up your ticket at the service desk before the flight. And here is the spare key to Saskia's apartment. The police say they'll have finished by then. I've written down the address for you. I understand from Kitty Marr that you'll be going to Milan after that,' she went on. 'She was talking to me about show tickets and cars. I'll make those arrangements first thing on Monday.'

'It's not a problem, is it?'

'No, but it requires planning. If you're going to the important shows, it means Racinda will have to sit in the second row.'

'Why's that?'

'Because, as editor, you'll have front row of course. There's generally only one front-row seat per magazine. Incidentally, you might say something to Racinda, if you have a moment. It would be politic.'

'I haven't offended her?'

'Racinda's easily offended,' said Jean. 'I wouldn't worry about it. She was just a bit surprised to learn via her assistant, Kitty, that you're going to Milan, that's all. She'd probably prefer to have heard it direct.'

'God, sorry about that. I'm not used to office politics yet.'

'Racinda's a troublemaker, but she's good at her job, and the designers respect her. That was the only reason Saskia put up with her. You'll soon work out how to handle her, you'll have her eating out of your hand.'

Max was meeting Philip and Karis Landau at eight fifteen, and it wasn't worth going home first, so he sat at his desk, rereading the spreadsheets and book of accounts, and tried to get more accustomed to the way around them. Like most things, it required practice. Both the British and American accounts were structured in identical ways: statistics about print runs, followed by circulation revenue, advertising revenue in all its forms – display, advertorial, special sections and classified – then paper and manufacturing costs and contents. Finally, there was the cost of people: editorial and advertising salaries, production, media research, information technology, the cleaners who came in to empty the bins and the companies that serviced the computers and colour copiers. Each time he read through the numbers, he felt slightly less confused and more confident of his ability to navigate from one section to another.

It was seven thirty and he was in urgent need of a pee. He left the office and walked down the corridor towards the editorial department. The washrooms were situated between the lifts and the stairs.

It was dark in the corridor, the overhead lights had been turned low like night lights in the cabin of an aeroplane, and the offices on either side were deserted. Through the open doors he could see desks and computers, and wastepaper bins waiting to be emptied next morning by the cleaners. He passed a water dispenser with a turret of plastic cups, and a Coke machine. The water dispenser gurgled as he went by.

He turned the corner on to the editorial floor and everything was quiet. The forty desks stretched into the distance. The heels of his new shoes clacked on the steel floor.

Then, somewhere over to his right, near the lifts, he heard a noise. It sounded like someone moving about.

'Hello? Anyone there?'

There was no reply. The room was silent. He froze for ten, twenty seconds. Still nothing. Strange, he was sure he hadn't imagined it. Outside in Bond Street he could hear voices, and cars accelerating away from the lights.

He continued in the direction of the lavatory. There were swing doors leading to the men's and ladies', set in a small recess next to a Canon copier.

Twenty yards away, in the middle of the editorial floor, he noticed a square of light, a computer screen. Someone had left it on at their desk, and it glowed like a TV in the darkness of the large room.

He felt his way through the maze of desks to the PC. On the way, he stumbled against a metal bin, sending it clattering across the floor.

He reached the computer and hunted about for the mouse to close it down. The finger icon was still on the screen, the mouse lay at an angle on the pad. Whoever had been working here today must have gone home, and forgotten about it.

He was searching for the closedown button on the tool bar when a word on the screen caught his eye: Bercuse. The screen had been left on at a Bercuse file. There was a list of the various subsidiaries – Tranquilité, Sensi, Lockerjock – with notes about the products, plus the advertising spends of the individual brands.

At that moment, a shaft of light cut across the room. He spun round. The door out to the stairwell crashed shut, and he heard footsteps running down the stone stairs.

He bolted across the floor, dodging between desks and chairs. A fuzzy light from the stairwell filtered beneath the door, giving him something to aim for.

Max threw back the door and ran out into the corridor. Boxes of old magazines were stacked around the stairwell, and giant blow-ups of front covers. Evidently the back stairs were used as an unofficial storage area. Flights of tiled stairs, with black treads, led up to the higher floors and down to the ground. He leaned over the well and could just make out a figure two floors below, sprinting away.

Max pounded after him, taking the stairs four at a time, pitching himself from the banisters at each corner. The whisky had dulled the pain in his arm and heightened his bravado. He must have gained a bit on whoever it was, because now he could hear the slip and slide of his shoes on each tread.

The intruder reached ground level and accelerated across the hallway in the direction of the lobby. Blast, he'd lost him now. He was still three flights behind. Once he had left the building, he'd melt into the darkness, and Max wouldn't have a hope.

He had reached the double doors into the lobby and was pulling at them. As Max rounded the corner, he could see his backview, only a floor below, rattling and tugging at the handles.

Suddenly he realised what had happened: the doors from the stairs to the lobby were locked for the night.

The intruder turned, and looked around him for another way out. The angle of the stairwell prevented Max from getting a clear view of his face. He was wearing a dark-coloured baseball cap and some kind of tracksuit top with jeans.

Max knew he was almost on top of him now and hurled himself down the stairs, half a flight at a time. Another ten yards and he'd have him. However, the man had spotted some stairs at the back of the hall, leading down to the basement, and by the time Max reached ground level, he could only see his back, disappearing down them.

The basement steps were narrower than the main flight and led into a warren of passages. There were no lights, and the area was pitch black. Max felt about the wall for a switch, but couldn't find one. Somewhere ahead of him, in the darkness, he heard the roar and whoosh of a gas boiler.

He stood still, listening, waiting for his eyes to acclimatise to the darkness. Gradually, he was able to make out shapes in the passage ahead: a metal door with a no-entry sticker, doubtless containing the building's main electrics, and various storerooms. There was still no sign of the intruder, but Max knew he had to be close by.

He edged his way forward, holding out his arms in front of him to feel the way. His foot struck something hard and round, and he felt a smooth aluminium handle sticking up into the air: a floor polisher.

Then, from somewhere very close, he heard the sound of scraping on the floor, and a voice muttered, 'Shit' as something metal tipped over.

He could see the man now, his silhouette moving rapidly away from him, further down the passage, a shadow against the dark walls.

Now Max had the advantage. He had something to aim for, whereas the intruder was forging into the darkness. Another six strides and he'd be on top of him.

The man spun around, throwing a punch at Max's face. Max put up his arm to protect himself, and felt the force of the man's fist straight on to his shrapnel wound. He took a step back. The pain from his arm made him feel sick.

Suddenly the man bolted past him and flung himself against the horizontal bar of a fire exit.

A way out into the street.

It shuddered, and crashed open, sending him sprawling down a flight of steps into a service yard.

An alarm began ringing somewhere high above them on a wall. A moment later, the intruder had picked himself up and was sprinting round a garbage shed to the side of the building, in the direction of Bruton Street.

There were restaurants in Bruton Street and a popular pub, the Coach and Horses, always heaving with people. Now Max knew he hadn't a hope of catching him. He could have headed in any direction: down Bond Street, up towards Regent Street, or through Bruton Place to Berkeley Square.

Max lit a cigarette and found he had a bad case of the shakes.

It was infuriating that he hadn't got a proper look at the man's face. Who the hell had it been, spying on the *StreetSmart* offices? And what was he trying to find out?

He walked round to the front of the building, shivering without a coat, and re-entered through the lobby. His heart was racing and he could taste the adrenalin in his mouth. A night security guard in Corps of Commissionaires uniform was watching television on a portable under the desk. He glanced up as Max passed, and told him to sign himself in.

He picked up the biro and wrote 'Papa Doc Duvalier', before taking the lift upstairs.

'Remember to sign yourself out when you leave, won't you, sir?' called out the guard, returning to the quiz show.

Max sat on the sofa in Saskia's office and tried to calm down. He took deep breaths, in and out, filling his lungs with air. He poured himself another drink, and found his hand was still shaking. He kept thinking about the intruder. He had been medium build but fit. Why had he broken into the offices and what was he searching for?

Across the office, the fax machine was spewing out a mile of bumph. A long scroll had already spilled over the edge of the tray. The topsheet read, 'To: Max Thompson. From: Chip Miller. Here are hard copies of the visuals for Monday's presentation. We'll be presenting on a laptop. Do you want to open, giving a general overview of SII and what we can offer and I'll follow with the numbers and proposition for Saidi. Call me if you want to play it differently.'

Max gathered up the fax, reading random pages as he went. The presentation looked impressive, but he could barely understand a word. For a start, it was written in jargon, a form of code. *StreetSmart* was recommending an interactive chat room in order to guarantee a million eyeballs. The various Saidi websites would all be hotlinked, not only to each other, but also to the StreetSmart sites, which would help drive page traffic. The widespread application of java script, in conjunction with various proprietary applications of our own, would ensure their status as an appointment website.

Reading this stuff made Max see how little he knew about new media, and how crazy it was that he should play any part in the presentation. Even if he winged it, he'd be out of his depth if Saidi started asking questions. He considered ringing Chip and admitting he was in over his head. On the other hand, seven-million-dollar contracts weren't going to come along every day, and they needed to win this.

Max realised he needed someone who could coach him on the technical jargon and on accessing the World Wide Web via a laptop. His only thought was the guy who'd set up the video conference link with Chip and Anka – he'd seemed to know what he was doing. Max had forgotten his name, but remembered Jean saying that he worked for the in-house IT department. Four names were listed in the *StreetSmart* directory, including Barry Higgs. He was sure Barry was his name. A home address was given in Stoke Newington and he left a message on his answerphone. 'This is Max Thompson. Sorry to bug you at home, but please ring me over the weekend.' He gave his home number in Ladbroke Grove.

After that he stuffed Chip's fax and the orange book of accounts into his bag, and headed off for dinner at Quaglino's.

As he crossed the lobby, the security guard looked up and said, 'Have a pleasant weekend, sir. Sign yourself out, won't you?'

'Sure.' He wrote, 'Ex-President for Life, Mobutu Sese Seko Kuku Ngbendu wa za Banga of Zaire,' and forged out into the cold March night.

[24]

The Landaus were already at the table. Max got the impression they were regulars at Quaglino's, because the head waiter didn't need to look them up in his reservations book, but led him straight down a horseshoe staircase and across a room containing several hundred diners. On the horizon, occupying a prominent table beneath a display of seafood on crushed ice, were Philip and Karis.

Karis was one of the most striking women Max had ever seen. From a distance, she looked twenty-five, though closer up you saw she was a deeply tanned fifty. When she stood up to greet him, she towered two or three inches above him, which made her six foot three or four. She had thick blonde hair swept up into a glamorous knot at the back of her head, which accentuated her long neck. Her dress was a single, flowing garment that reached the floor in a mass of crinkly, horizontal, russet-coloured pleats and which she later mentioned was Japanese couture, designed by Issey Miyake. Her jewellery, which was conspicuously large and ethnic, was made of whalebone and pale twisted gold.

'The designer,' Karis said, 'is a very special person. He's an Eskimo. He has shown at the Guggenheim. All his materials are natural, he finds the bones washed up on the seashore.' Her accent was impossible to place. There was American in it, but also something singsong and Scandinavian.

Max asked her, 'Where are you from, originally?'

'Sweden. That is where I was living as a young girl, until maybe seventeen years. You know Stockholm? After that, Santa Monica, Paris, Tokyo, all over. It doesn't signify. Now there are no frontiers, only one world.'

'Yes indeed,' Max replied, remembering the trouble he'd had obtaining visas for just about everywhere. 'One world.'

'Max,' said Philip, who had been examining the upper reaches of the wine list, 'are you old world or new world when it comes to whites? They have some interesting Tasmanian Chardonnays, but you might be thinking more Loire valley. Alternatively, we could stick with champagne, since we're celebrating your first successful week at *StreetSmart*.'

Karis winced at the mention of *StreetSmart* and said, 'When Philip told me you were getting involved with the magazine, my heart went out to you. Truly, I have been praying for you, and chanting.'

'It's not so bad,' Max said. 'There are one or two problems, although the people on the magazine are helpful, by and large.'

'But it's so corrupting,' said Karis, patiently. 'All those consumer goods in the advertisements. Things people don't need. Today, it is better to live more simply, I think.'

'Well, that's up to the individual, I suppose. If you don't need a new dress or a new car, don't buy it.'

'I'm sorry, but I can't have your kind of magazines in the house any more,' said Karis. 'Philip used to bring them home for me, but I said, "Enough." At this stage of my growth, I don't need them. I look beyond.'

A waitress appeared to take their order, and Karis asked, 'This seared tuna. Tell me about it. In which ocean was it caught, and in what kind of nets? Is it from an ecosustainable shoal?'

'I'm afraid I'll have to ask Chef about that,' the girl replied doubtfully. 'All our fish comes fresh each morning from market.'

'Actually, don't bother,' said Karis. 'How are your aubergines tonight? My dietician has told me, "Karis, eat more aubergines. They fortify the *chakras*." '

Throughout this whole exchange, and his wife's homily on the immorality of glossy magazines, Philip Landau smiled benignly, betraying neither the slightest sign of impatience nor irritation, but not in any way endorsing, either by word or gesture, a single thing she said. He seemed to have perfected an ability – essential, Max imagined, for successful relations with Karis – of distancing himself completely from her views: his expression a mask of indulgent compliance, like a member of the Cambodian bourgeoisie under-going a programme of re-education at the hands of the Khmer Rouge. If anyone had reached the highest stage of enlightenment – the seventh wheel – it was Philip, not Karis, Landau.

'So, Max, how's it all going?' he asked, once they'd ordered. 'Apart from the ghastly news about Saskia and the distraction of all these predators.'

'Well, I'm still there. That's the most I can say. I've survived a week. Though something very strange happened just now in the office, while I was waiting to come here.' He told the Landaus about the intruder and the fight in the basement. 'He seemed to be hacking into our computer system. I haven't worked out why yet.'

'It's certainly disturbing,' said Landau. 'Especially after what you told me this morning about Saskia. I've been thinking it over, and the crucial thing, it seems to me, is that nothing should get into the newspapers. Apart from anything else, it might worry the American investors. We don't want the magazine destabilised.'

'How do we manage that?'

'By keeping our mouths shut,' said Landau. 'We won't be able to prevent it from leaking indefinitely, but we might buy some time.'

'Thanks,' Max said, 'that would be a big help, because it's getting quite hairy. The lorry delivering our new issue has flipped over on the motorway. And three more staff resigned today, so that's four gone including Bob Troup. Then one of our largest advertisers, Bercuse, pulled out without explanation. Now the new issue of *Town Talk* has exactly the same front cover as us. You'll need to issue a writ, by the way, since they've stolen our photograph.'

'Of course,' said Landau. '*Town Talk*'s Incorporated, isn't it?'

'Yes.'

'I thought they're one of the outfits that wants to buy you. Isn't that rather an odd way of going about it?'

'Caryl Fargo seems like a ball-breaker, but not stupid.'

'Probably she's trying to demonstrate how rough it could get if you don't sell to her. So you'll want out.'

'She threatened to play hardball – her expression – with the advertising too, undercut us on everything.'

'Well, Incorporated is big enough. They're well capitalised. If Caryl says she's going to take that route, she probably will. Incidentally, did you say Bercuse has pulled out?'

'From both editions, America as well.'

'You mean *all* their brands? Isn't that quite a hit?'

'And the worst thing is, we can't puzzle out why they've done it. Only Étienne Bercuse seems to know, and I can't reach him. He's travelling and not returning my calls.'

Landau looked thoughtful. 'Do you think Caryl could be behind this?'

'Behind Bercuse pulling out? Possible. Kevin Sky, our commercial director, suggested the same thing. He used an expression, "a one-time volume shut-out deal". He thought Incorporated could have booked a lot of business dirt cheap, on condition nothing comes to us.'

'It figures,' said Landau. 'Think of it from her position. She wants *StreetSmart*, *needs* it badly in fact. Incorporated's underperforming the market, and the analysts are getting restless about her performance. Revenues have plateaued, and there's been margin erosion. Caryl knows it's only going to get tougher. Paper prices are on the way up. *Girls on Top* is getting a run for its money from *Cosmo* and *Marie Claire*. And their other big one, *Ladies' Home Cookery*, has lost its way a bit too. All in all, Incorporated's looking jaded. Suddenly *StreetSmart* becomes available, or so Caryl hopes. If she could add it to her stable, it would be a coup. She could amalgamate it with *Town Talk* and solve two problems at once. *Town Talk* would become profitable – which it isn't now, whatever she may say – and Caryl's career would get a boost. It might even save it. *StreetSmart*'s a hot book. The media analysts all read it, or anyway their girlfriends do. It would be perceived as a sexy deal. Some of Saskia's lustre would rub off on Caryl.'

'Whoever was hacking into our computer system was accessing the files on Bercuse,' Max said. 'Does this sound farfetched, or could Caryl have arranged it? It would have been easy enough for Bob Troup to brief her on accessing the system. And they wouldn't have expected anyone to be working late on a Friday.'

'Do you happen to know whether your advertising rates are stored electronically?'

'I don't, but I'd guess so.'

'Then it's possible,' said Landau. 'It would certainly help Caryl to know what Bercuse were paying for their space. That kind of information just isn't in the public domain. If she's done a volume deal with them, she'll want to know what the damage is to *StreetSmart*. I could believe it of Caryl. She's devious enough,' he went on. 'She could be trying to force the eventual purchase price down too. If *StreetSmart* went to market, you'd arrive at a value by a multiple of revenues, so the lower the revenues, the cheaper it would be.'

'Isn't that quite an expensive way of doing it? For Caryl, I mean.'

'Not necessarily. If Bercuse's advertising investment with you is, say, six million dollars, and we're working to a multiple of one and a half times revenues – which seems not unrealistic – that's nine million dollars. It wouldn't shake down quite like that, but you get the general idea. *Town Talk* drops its knickers for a period on rates, but that's more than compensated by a fall in the acquisition price of *StreetSmart*.'

'Sneaky. And you think she'd have worked all that out, cynically, to get the magazine cheap.'

'Except she wouldn't think of herself as cynical. She'd call it best business practice.'

'Huh,' Max said. 'She can call it what she likes, but it's still unethical. Stealing candy from a six-year-old. *StreetSmart* belongs to Cody; Saskia's hardly been dead a week. No wonder Caryl was worried about Freddie Saidi getting in first.'

'As I said on the telephone this morning, you're in a strong position if you do decide to sell.'

'It's actually quite pissing off, the way these people take it for granted I'll sell out. Caryl was bloody patronising. She implied I'm only capable of publishing articles about bazookas and Bosnia. Marcus Brooke was patronising too. He invited me to stay at Saidi's hotel in New York.'

'Probably wanted to bug you,' said Landau.

'I'm sorry?'

'All the rooms are bugged at the East River. That's what people say, anyway. The suites have video surveillance. Cameras hidden in showerheads, two-way mirrors, that sort of thing.'

'Why?'

'God knows. Blackmail. Curiosity. Saidi would probably claim they're for security, if he ever admitted it happened at all. His personal security, that is. He's made plenty of enemies over the years.'

'Apparently he had a big thing about Saskia at one time. Showered her with jewellery.'

'Quite likely,' said Philip, looking pained. 'He's immensely wealthy. He lives up in Regent's Park, near the mosque. Big walled mansion.'

'Where did his money come from? That's something nobody seems to know.'

'People say arms dealing, but I don't know that for a fact. He only arrived in Britain about ten years ago. He was in Beirut right through the civil war. Allegedly supplied weapons to everyone: Christian Phalangistes, Hesbollah, Druze, Sunnis. The Syrians too, and Jordan. He was close to King Hussein. I know that because Karis saw them together, didn't you, darling?'

'At Petra,' said Karis. 'The rose-red city. I was attending a yoga and meditation retreat under the auspices of Deepak Chopra. Surrendering to Love. One morning, during the sun salutation, we were ordered to leave the temple area. Several truckloads of soldiers turned up, and cordoned off the whole site. Then the King arrived with Saidi in a jeep. Some members of the group felt quite violated.'

'I have to say, Max,' said Landau, 'that I admire you for not selling out to Saidi. It would have been a betrayal of Saskia's vision, if *StreetSmart* ended up in his soiled hands.'

'One way and another, I seem to have talked myself into rejecting everyone. Must be the idealistic war reporter in me, with his brain in his butt.'

Karis, having polished off the wild salmon with samphire that she had eventually settled on, now leaned confidingly towards him. 'Max,' she said, 'can I ask you a personal question?'

'Er, sure.' He wondered what it could possibly be. For an awful moment, he thought she was going to invite him to be her yoga partner, or attend a session of Gestalt scream therapy.

'Have you ever experienced death, Max?'

'In what way?'

'I mean as a reporter. Have you witnessed atrocities at first hand?'

'A few, since you ask. In some of the African countries. And in Sarajevo there were a fair number of fatalities, as they put it on CNN.'

'Did it affect you *very* much?' asked Karis. Her mouth was suddenly uncomfortably close to his face, her fawn lipstick outlined with brown pencil. 'Do you want to talk about it? Open up, Max, I'll understand. It's all right to cry, Max, we're all damaged. Don't fight it, listen for the still, small voice that's inside each one of us.'

'Excuse me please, waitress,' said Landau, gesticulating for his bill. 'Could you bring me my check, quick as you can? No, we won't bother with coffee or desserts, if that's OK with you, Max.'

As they were standing on the pavement outside the restaurant, Max said, 'Philip, there's something else I meant to ask you. Jean gave me the *StreetSmart* financial reports, and they look much worse than I'd expected. We seem to be losing a packet in the States.'

'The American edition is still in start-up mode, don't forget,' Landau replied. 'Magazine business plans generally work to a five-year breakeven.'

'But was Saskia concerned about it? To me, it looks terrible.'

'If she was, she certainly never mentioned it. She seemed fairly satisfied about everything. She always knew it would be a long haul in the States. She used the profits from the British edition to fund the start-up over there.'

'And these other American investors? The investment banks, et cetera. They're relaxed about it?'

'So I believe. Saskia never said much about them, but I'm pretty sure they're taking the long view.'

[25]

Max woke up with a hangover and a distinct feeling of unease. He had slept badly, unable to rid himself of the image of the man in the basement.

Normally, on a Saturday in London between assignments, he'd have holed up in bed until noon, then met up with Ken Craig and some of the boys at the bar of the Earl Percy in Ladbroke Grove, followed by a Greek or an Indian. Today, his head was cloudy with the aftermath of too much Glenfiddich and Tasmanian Chardonnay, and conspiracy theories about Caryl Fargo, Bob Troup and Freddie Saidi.

He stumbled into the kitchen, put on some coffee and cursed that, as usual, there was no bread in the place. In a cupboard underneath the sink he found a dusty packet of Ryvita, that must have been a year old, which he spread with peanut butter and carried with him into the bathroom. While the bath was running, he played the answer-phone messages that he'd been too tired to listen to before he went to bed.

There was one left on the machine at eleven p.m. the previous night. 'Max. This is Marie-Louise Clay. I've managed to find the information you wanted on Freddie Saidi. I've got some cuttings and have looked up the details on that piece we were thinking of doing on him. The journalist was Phil Weber, the one who's just quit to join *Town Talk*.' Max groaned. Phil Weber was the last person he could ask for help. Marie-Louise wasn't finished, however. 'He spent about a month doing some groundwork, but it doesn't sound like he got far. We paid him a research fee of £1,500. Saskia decided not to proceed with the piece.'

Marie-Louise had left a home telephone number, and he dialled it straight away. He'd like to read the Saidi cuttings over the weekend, in advance of Monday's presentation.

The telephone was answered by a child, who sounded about ten. 'Hello.'

'Is Marie-Louise there?'

'Who is this speaking, please?' asked the girl in a precise little voice. He imagined her in a pink gingham dress and pigtails.

'Max.'

He heard her call upstairs, 'Excuse me, Mummy. Telephone for you. It's *a man* called Max.'

Marie-Louise picked up an extension. 'Hi, Max, you got my message?' It could have been his imagination, but she sounded apprehensive.

'The Saidi cuttings,' he said. 'I'm keen to read them today. I don't know where you are now, but is there some way of getting them over to me?'

'I can drop them in myself. I've got to deliver Tamsin – my daughter – to her karate, so I'll be in your area. Also, I'd love fifteen minutes of your time, if that's possible – there's something I need to tell you, confidentially.'

They agreed to meet at Max's basement flat in half an hour. Max hoped she wasn't about to inform him that she too was joining *Town Talk*; the way things were going, he'd soon be the longest-serving member of staff.

He took a bath, examined his wound and ate another Ryvita.

He had barely dressed, when he heard the squeak of an iron gate and saw Marie-Louise's loafers through the sitting-room window, gingerly descending the steep area steps to the front door, followed by a pair of sandals and white socks.

'Hope you don't mind, I've had to bring Tamsin with me,' she said. 'Tamsin, say how-do-you-do to Mr Thompson.'

The little girl in a gingham dress and Alice band smiled up at him. She was a miniature version of her mother, neat and alert, with ash-blonde hair.

They shook hands, and Max suggested that she play in the overgrown back yard while her mother and Max talked.

'I love gardens,' replied Tamsin politely. 'We don't have one ourselves, so I'd enjoy playing outside in yours.'

Was she always like this, he wondered, or had she been told it was best behaviour? He left her examining a pair of old combat boots, that had limped home on his feet from Kinshasa, stunk out the place in ten minutes flat, and been flung outside into the yard.

Marie-Louise was waiting in the sitting-room, casting about for some pleasantry about Max's interior decoration. Max watched her examine the leather tribal footstool, a fragment of Russian shell and a wooden juju fetish he'd bought with the last of his local currency at N'Djamena airport. Eventually, realising that there was nothing she even half admired, Marie-Louise rummaged about in her bag for the newspaper cuttings.

'Are those the cuts?' Max asked, as she handed over a brown manila envelope. Half of them, he could see, came from an online retrieval agency, and were stored as raw data. The rest were facsimiles of actual newspaper articles, photocopied two or three to a sheet.

'I could have biked them over to you,' said Marie-Louise, 'but there's one article in here that requires explanation.'

'Which one's that?'

'Well, you see, this is embarrassing, but there's an article here written by me. Saying that Freddie Saidi is the greatest thing since sliced bread, and all the wonderful things he's done for this country. I'm so ashamed I wrote it.'

'Why did you, then? But wait, before you tell me, I'd better take a look.'

Marie-Louise passed him a photocopy of an article in the *Daily Express*. There was a picture by-line of herself at the top, looking slightly younger, and two large photographs of Saidi. There was one of him watching his polo team in action, sitting next to Her Majesty the Queen outside some kind of clubhouse, and another of Saidi dressed up as Father Christmas presenting a cheque to a child in a wheelchair. The headline and standfirst read, 'Santa Saidi brings Christmas cheer to wheelchair hero: Marie-Louise Clay meets a remarkable philanthropist with the Midas touch.'

Six paragraphs into the piece and already Max felt nauseous, it was like drowning in whipped cream. The article was so thickly larded with platitudes, he reckoned that Marie-Louise had simply looked up the words 'saint' and 'genius' in a thesaurus, and shoe-horned a fresh alternative into each and every paragraph. There was a paean of praise to his involvement with children's charities in Albania, including a tear-jerking tale about a nine-year-old orphan who had never slept in a proper bed until Saidi had lent him a stateroom for the night on his yacht, the *Princess Baalbek*. Marie-Louise had gone on to detail his charitable works in England and the United States, and the remarkable transformation he had wrought over the East River Hotel. The pay-off paragraph was so schmaltzy and corny, it made you want to throw up.

'Promise me one thing,' Marie-Louise had quoted Saidi as saying. 'When you write about me, please do not describe me as rich in possessions only. Of course I am very rich, my plane, my yacht, the houses, all those things. But for me, money does not matter. It is the satisfaction of giving, of helping others less fortunate, of enabling an old man to have a cataract operation, or a crippled child to walk, that for me is true riches. I want people to understand that.'

'Well,' Max said, when he'd finished reading, 'I expect he was happy with it.'

'No idea, I didn't hear a thing. I didn't want to hear anything. I was so angry and humiliated, I prayed nobody would notice it or read it. I didn't even buy the newspaper.'

'If you hated it, why write it?'

'Because I was stupid,' said Marie-Louise. 'It was a difficult time in my life, Tamsin's father and I had recently separated, it had been fairly acrimonious, and basically I was a bit screwed up.

'One evening,' she went on, 'I was invited to a private view at a gallery in Cork Street. I'd hardly left the house for a fortnight, and was right at the end of my tether, so I persuaded a neighbour to babysit and off I went. I needed a break, even a couple of hours, and some grown-up conversation. I can't even remember what the exhibition was, but at some point in the evening I was introduced to Marcus Brooke. He was very charming and solicitous, and asked me what I did for a living, and I found myself pouring out my life story: Jules walking out on me and how difficult it was to freelance with a young child, and how generally wiped out I felt. It was very un-me to bang on like that, but Marcus is a good listener, he gets people to open up and discovers their weaknesses. That's how he operates.'

'So what happened?'

'Not to put too fine a point on it, he offered me a freebie to the East River Hotel in New York. It had recently reopened, completely renovated – Saidi had poured millions into it – and Marcus said, "Come and visit it, we'll pay everything: flight, ten days in a nice room, all your incidentals." He even mentioned a courtesy car and driver.'

'I can see the temptation,' Max said. 'Is it normal for journalists to get these treats? They've never come my way.'

'A lot do accept them, especially travel journalists, but I told Marcus Brooke there was no way I could take it up, because of Tamsin. There was no one to leave her with.

'Anyway, I forgot all about it, and then a couple of days later I got a call from Marcus – which surprised me, that he even knew where I lived – and he said he'd been thinking about our conversation, and had discussed it with Freddie Saidi, and they were still very keen that I should experience the hotel, and why didn't I take Tamsin with me, they'd be delighted to pay for her too.

'I asked him what they expected in return, and he said, "Nothing. If you have a good time and want to write a travel article when you get back, we'd of course love that. But it's not a condition." He then became very smarmy and said that my opinion was worth a lot to them. His precise words were, "You get about, Marie-Louise. If you're able to tell your friends that Freddie has done a good job with the East River, bringing back a famous hostelry to its former glory, then that's enough for us. We want you to go along, put the hotel through its paces and not worry about a thing." '

'So you went.'

'So I went. And I wish to God I hadn't, because it turned into a nightmare, though that came later. Ten days later, to be precise.

'To begin with,' she said, 'it was incredible. A car collected us to take us to the airport – one of Saidi's own drivers – and when we checked in we discovered the seats were club class. At JFK, a stretch limo was waiting, with a video player inside, and someone had gone to the trouble of getting a Walt Disney tape for Tamsin, the *Jungle Book*, so as we crossed the Triboro' bridge we had King Louis singing, "I'm the king of the swingers, the jungle VIP", which is exactly how we felt, arriving in Manhattan in style.

'The room – suite, I should say – was out of this world. It was called the Mecca Suite. It took about five minutes to cross from one end to the other. One of the housekeepers told us the Crown Prince of Saudi Arabia had stayed in it the previous week. The decor wasn't totally my taste – too many gold swan-shaped taps and onyx ashtrays – but it was enormous. Tamsin had her own separate room, and there were two bathrooms plus a separate cloakroom, and a huge walk-in closet that was bigger than my bedroom at home, and then we discovered a terrace leading off the sitting room – with a *hot tub*. Tamsin and I stood there pinching ourselves. Then a bellboy – two bellboys – arrived with champagne and vases of flowers and bowls of fruit, pineapples, star fruit, kiwi, it was like a greengrocer's shop coming through the door, plus a letter from the manager of the hotel welcoming us, and a handwritten postcard from Marcus Brooke which said, "Freddie Saidi and I welcome you and Tamsin to the Big Apple. Enjoy the East River. As ever, Marcus." Then there was a PS: "In case you are stiff after your flight, I have booked you a massage at our health spa. Dial extension 92. I have informed Paolo the concierge that you are here as VIPs, and he will arrange all your expeditions. Tamsin will enjoy the Staten Island ferry."

'That night, we ordered hamburgers off the room service menu and ate outside on the terrace, with this incredible view of the river in one direction and skyscrapers in the other. We were so high up, you could see all the way across to Central Park, and I felt all my exhaustion falling away. It was just so lovely to be on holiday in New York with my daughter, I was so grateful to Saidi for making it possible.'

'Which is why you wrote that puff piece. A public thankyou letter.'

'No, it was more complicated than that. Matters were taken out of my hands.

'I should make it clear,' she went on, 'that we did nothing to exploit his hospitality. We had breakfast in our rooms, and supper in the coffee shop, but we were out every day sightseeing. We didn't order expensive wine or anything, or make many telephone calls. In fact it became embarrassing because the concierge and the manager kept ringing up, wanting to do more and more for us, arrange transport and tickets to shows. If I said no, it sounded rather ungrateful, as if we didn't want to see the city or try out the various restaurants in the hotel. Marcus Brooke had made it perfectly clear that everything was taken care of, and that we were guests of Saidi, so I allowed the concierge to arrange limousines to take us to the World Trade Center and the Bronx zoo, though we'd have been just as happy getting there in a yellow cab.

'And then finally – God, this was a mistake – on the last night, we agreed to have dinner in the main dining room and go to a Broadway show. The manager pretty well insisted. "Mr Brooke will be so upset if you don't accept, he keeps calling me up from London, asking have they taken in a show yet." So we had an early dinner in the dining room. We were virtually the only people there, just Tamsin and me and thirty waiters. It was all very stuffy, gold plates, Louis Quatorze chairs, you can imagine. The wine waiter arrived with a special bottle of claret, and kept pinching Tamsin's cheek, which she hated, and the food was far too rich, everything stuffed with foie gras. When I signed the bill and saw how much it had cost – $680 – I gasped. The wine alone had cost $200. I was just so relieved that we weren't paying ourselves. Anyway, another stretch limo was waiting and we watched a musical from the front stalls, and that was our last evening.

'The next morning,' she said, 'when I came to check out, was without question the worst morning of my life.

'I went to the cashier and told him who I was, and expected him to know all about the arrangement, and that would be that. He looked me up on the computer and smiled, and then this huge bill started printing out of a machine. It went on and on, this great roll of numbers, it wouldn't stop. I began to panic slightly at this point, but then I thought, No, they have to do this, it's a formality, I'll just have to sign it. Eventually the machine stopped printing, and the cashier tore it off, and folded it up and presented it to me.

'The total came to six and a half thousand dollars, and he was asking, "How would you like to settle the account, madam? By credit card or traveller's cheques?"

'I remember saying, "There must be a mistake, we are guests of Mr Saidi, your owner."

'The cashier went back to the screen to double check, and returned saying, "Yes, of course, madam, the suite is complimentary, I had already deducted it from the bill, the balance is simply your extras," and he showed me where he'd counter-credited $26,000 for the room. All I could see was item after item saying room service plus state tax, plus city tax, health spa plus tax, limousines plus tax, coffee shop, dining room – the $680 for that sickening meal – theatre tickets. I stood there staring at it, feeling I was going to die. The truth was, I didn't have six thousand dollars in the world. No way could I pay that bill.

'By this time a queue was beginning to form behind me. And the limo was waiting to take us to the airport, and our suitcases were in the lobby, ready to be loaded. I had to explain to the cashier that we hadn't expected to pay anything at all, and the cashier said, "Not even your extras? I'm sorry, but I have no instructions to waive your personal extras."

'Tamsin was tugging at my sleeve, and the queue was getting impatient. I asked to speak to the manager and had to wait for ages outside his office till he could be found. His secretary was so kind, which made it worse, asking Tamsin if she'd enjoyed New York and ordering a plate of cookies. I remember thinking, No, cancel those cookies. I'll probably be charged for them too.

'The manager was decent enough, if a bit disappointed. The only thing he could suggest was that we remain at the hotel until Marcus Brooke could be contacted. Since London is five hours ahead of New York, he was already out at lunch, which meant cancelling our flights. I had to hand over the air tickets, and our baggage was put in store, and we had to wait in the manager's outer office for three hours, while Tamsin did her colouring on hotel writing paper.

'Eventually they got hold of Marcus. He wasn't at all sympathetic, he made me feel like the biggest freeloader of all time. He kept saying, "I do find it surprising that you presumed even your breakfast egg would be on the house." They had faxed our bill through to London, and he kept picking on individual items. He went on and on about the theatre tickets and the two-hundred-dollar bottle of wine, which I hadn't ordered or even *wanted*. I'd left most of it.

'Then he said, "Well, Marie-Louise, this is an unhappy situation, but we'd better resolve it one way or the other. Shall we agree to split the bill for the extras fifty–fifty? You pay half, and we'll write the other half down to experience."

'I had to admit I couldn't manage even half. I was squirming. I felt like the most pathetic, insignificant, worthless person, a worm. And the worst thing was, I knew Marcus was enjoying it. It was giving him this massive kick, having power over me.

'He said to the manager, "Kurt, it doesn't sound like we've got any option here: put the whole bill on Mr Saidi's house account, and have Mrs Clay's limousine brought round to the front." Then he said, "Marie-Louise. You have now enjoyed in excess of thirty thousand dollars of hospitality courtesy of Mr Saidi. I think we'd better have a little talk, don't you, when you get back? So we can decide together what to do about this bill."

'A couple of days later he set up a meeting in Rutland Gate, at Saidi's head office. We met in Marcus's office, which was full of framed photographs of Saidi and various foreign statesmen. Arafat, Netanyahu, General Colin Powell, people like that. This time he was conciliatory. He asked how I'd liked the East River, and had Tamsin found the suite comfortable, and had we done the Staten Island ferry like he suggested? He told me how, on Independence Day, Freddie Saidi had ordered the hotel kitchens to prepare a thousand food parcels, which had been distributed to the city's homeless, supervised by Saidi himself, along with Mayor Giuliani and Whoopi Goldberg. When he asked what I thought should happen about the hotel bill, I'm afraid I burst into tears, because the whole situation was so hideous. I felt such a bloody idiot, crying in his office.

'Then Marcus proposed his deal, which I'm sure he'd planned from the start. He said that if I wrote a profile of Saidi for a national newspaper, the whole debt would be written off. He tried to make me feel better about it, claiming it would be an exclusive. The only condition was that Marcus would vet the article "and make sure no factual errors slip through". It was obvious what was being proposed.

'To my eternal shame, I gritted my teeth and did what he wanted. Marcus virtually wrote the piece himself. I had a ten-minute interview with Saidi, during which time he kept taking phone calls in Arabic. All the quotes were manufactured by Marcus. My main job was to find somewhere that was prepared to publish it. Eventually the *Express* agreed. Sorry the explanation's taken so long, but that's how that cream puff appears under my by-line. I expect most of the other journalists have similar excuses too.'

'Thanks for telling me,' Max said. 'I'm meant to have a meeting with Saidi and Brooke on Monday in New York. You really think they planned the whole thing?'

'It isn't the first time it's happened. They look out for writers without any clout, offer them a freebie, then pile on the extras. Those limousines cost a thousand dollars a day. I can see I was an ideal target, single mother at the end of her tether.'

'The more I hear about Saidi, the less I want to do business with him,' said Max, 'but we need it. The Interactive division is bleeding money.'

'Really?' said Marie-Louise. 'I don't know anything about the

American company. Saskia never shared the American results with anyone in London.'

'Why was that, do you suppose?'

'Your sister could be quite secretive. Everything was on a need-to-know basis. You only ever heard positive things about New York, like when they won a national magazine award, or gave a big party. You never got to hear about the problems.'

'There's a huge problem in New York right now,' Max said. 'The police are saying Saskia didn't commit suicide. She may have been murdered.'

'*Murdered?*' Marie-Louise looked horrified. 'But *why?*'

'God knows. I'm hoping to discover more when I'm over. It's a complete mystery. In fact, I was wondering whether you could think of anything – anyone who might want her out of the way?'

Marie-Louise screwed up her eyes. 'I can think of plenty of people who didn't like her much – staff she fired, et cetera – but no one who'd want to kill her.'

'Try looking at it a different way. Who stands to gain now she's off the scene?'

'Er, *you*, I guess.'

'Thanks, Marie-Louise. I don't mean me. I was thinking more of our potential purchasers.'

'But you keep saying we're not for sale.'

'They didn't realise that before Saskia died though, did they? They probably reckoned, with Saskia out of the way, *StreetSmart* would be in play.'

'Put like that, Freddie Saidi and Caryl Fargo both have motives.'

'And which is likelier to have had her bumped off?'

'No contest. Saidi.'

'That's what I think too. Which is why I have to find out more about him.'

'If there's anything I can do to help . . .'

'There is one thing, more of a personal than a work thing.'

'Try me.'

'Cody,' he said. 'I feel quite responsible for him, without Saskia around. My parents are trying their best, but they're getting on, it's not ideal, so I'm going to have to do more with him myself. What I was wondering is, would Tamsin ever be prepared to come over and play with him? She's a couple of years older, but maybe he might pick up some of her, er . . .'

'Manners, you mean?' Marie-Louise laughed. 'Saskia was always asking the same thing. She was always trying to enrol Cody in the Tamsin charm school. We love Cody, most of the time. You just have to keep him well away from Coca-Cola, chocolate, anything with sugar, or he goes berserk. But sit him in front of a computer and he's a honey. Send him over to us any time.'

Just then there was a tap at the door, and Tamsin popped her head round. 'Excuse me for disturbing your meeting, Mummy, but I think we should leave now for karate, or we'll be late.'

'Thanks for the reminder, darling. We've finished anyway. And, guess what, Tamsin? Max says Cody can come round again soon to play. Won't that be fun?'

Tamsin gulped. 'Oh yes,' she said bravely, in her polite, reedy little voice. 'It would be awfully nice to see Cody again.'

Ken and the boys were exactly where Max knew they'd be: at the table under the big mirror in the public bar of the Earl Percy. They had used the place as an unofficial club and information centre for six years. Twelve till three every Saturday, all year round, whoever was in London just turned up. If you wanted to know whether the ferry service had resumed between Brazzaville and Kinshasa, or when they'd next raise the *per diems* at *Der Spiegel*, the Earl Percy on a Saturday lunchtime was the place to be.

Other than Ken, Max hadn't seen any of the gang since his return from Afghanistan. A little cheer went up when he arrived, and cries of 'Let's see that arm, then, yer bleedin' skiver,' and 'Landmine, what bollocks. I bet some woman tipped yer out of the cot.' It was the custom in their group that, when any member caught flak or a stray bullet, he was bought a bevvy by everyone around the table. This was invariably accompanied by a good deal of joshing and healthy scepticism.

Max felt good to be back with the old crowd. There was a genuine *esprit de corps*, which so far had been in short supply in his new world. He found that, even after a week, he missed the gossip. Mick Paarl and Sam de Witt, both Afrikaaners and two of the best photojournalists in the business, told a great story about a journey they'd just made up to the Jaffna Peninsula in Sri Lanka, reporting the Tamil guerilla war. 'We had this driver, right,' said Mick. 'Sinhalese. Tiny little bloke, came up to my kneecaps. He was so scared shitless of Tamil Tigers, he hid in the bleedin' boot. I'm not kidding, he locked himself in for ten days. We tossed him the odd banana from time to time. Then, right at the end, when we were returning the car in Colombo, he suddenly re-emerged, combed his hair with this pink plastic comb, and took the wheel. Drove us into the garage.'

Mick Paarl had been Max's partner on two assignments. Nothing fazed him, and he was as strong as a wildebeest; Max had once seen him lift the whole back end of a 4×4 while they changed a burst tyre. Before becoming a journalist, Mick had seen active service with the South African Scouts in Angola, helping to bolster UNITA. He still spoke about that period as the happiest in his life.

'Here's a beer for the wounded hero.' Simon Scott put a pint of best down in front of Max, and twenty packets of crisps for the table. Max liked Simon. Physically and intellectually, he was the complete opposite of the Afrikaaners, and you could see the different approach in his work. Mick's technique was to stand four-square in the middle of the action, bullets winging around about him, while he shot off a roll of film. He was either very brave or stupid or blessed, probably all three. Simon was more circumspect, his trademark pictures were a little offside and oblique. He would give you two old men playing chess in Haifa, totally absorbed in their game, while students hurled stones at soldiers in the background. His most famous picture, which won all the prizes that year, was of a Cairo shoeshine boy buffing up some old gent's winklepickers, at the precise moment that a car bomb went off behind him. It was total luck, and Simon always had luck. The London *Independent* couldn't get enough of him.

'You look like you've been away somewhere yourself,' Max said to him. Simon was deeply tanned and had lost weight.

'Sudan. South, near the border.'

'Worthwhile?'

'Not really. I'd been promised a trek with the SPLA, crossing into Eritrea to see their training camp, but it didn't materialise. Instead there was a lot of hanging about, and not much to show for it.'

'All gong and no dinner.'

They both laughed at this old in-joke. Several years earlier, an Indian journalist had promised to guide them to a bauxite mine in Bihar, where children as young as six were allegedly being forced to work underground. Getting there had involved a long overland journey, not without danger. When they eventually arrived, and looked down on the place from a hillside, it was long abandoned. The children, if they had ever existed, had been shifted elsewhere.

'Very sorry, gentlemen,' their guide had said. 'A wasted journey. All gong and no dinner.'

'Another big drag,' said Simon, 'was the number of other journalists already out in the Sudan. I ran into three of them, all working for the Internet, would you believe? They spent all day tapping into laptops and filing copy to an outfit called SII in Hartford, Connecticut. God knows what about, they never went anywhere or saw anything.'

Max winced. His worst fears confirmed.

'Now, what about all these supermodels, then?' asked Simon. 'I should think there are some opportunities there, aren't there?'

'Ah, you've heard about my new job, have you?'

'Ken was telling us, before you arrived. You're running a fashion magazine. Mick said it could only be for the skirt.'

Mick and Sam, who'd been talking night-sights with Ken, pricked up their ears at the mention of women.

'Now, Max,' said Mick. 'No messin'. We want to know. Cindy Crawford. Are those tits on her the genuine business?'

Max laughed. 'I wish I knew, Mick. If I find out, I'll tell you.'

'What about those other two, then?' asked Sam. 'The snooty-looking ones. Marja and whatshername, the blonde.'

'Tigra?' he suggested.

'That's the one. Does she put out at all?'

'I haven't met her. I saw her in a commercial for scent yesterday. Big deal.'

'Fuck me, yer slipping, mate,' said Sam. 'We thought you'd have had them all on yer casting couch by now. Otherwise why bother? It can't be a barrel of laughs, choosing the latest hairdos.'

Max groaned. 'Don't start. I'm not rising to it. I'm not even going to discuss it. Anyway, I may not be there for long; everyone wants to take us over. It's getting quite dirty. You haven't come across a bloke called Freddie Saidi, anyone?'

'The Lebanese Freddie Saidi?' said Ken. 'Totally loaded and mad for sex.'

'That's him. Though I didn't know about the sex.'

'Famous for it,' said Ken. 'Can't get enough. I met him a few times in Beirut. This would be ten or fifteen years ago. I took his picture for *Time*. He was supplying weapons to everyone, it was an open secret.'

'Is that how he made his money?'

'Drugs were mentioned too. He isn't the kind of bloke you'd ask, not if you value your kneecaps. Nothing much stands in his way.'

'Well, the problem is, *I'm* standing in his way right now. He wants to buy *StreetSmart*, only it's not for sale.'

'That is a problem,' said Ken. 'One big problem.'

Mick Paarl returned from the bar with the next round. 'What's this we're talking about?' he asked. 'What's the big problem?'

'Freddie Saidi. Lebanese arms dealer.'

'I know him,' said Mick. 'I went along to one of his parties in Beirut. He had this big place near the American University. Great party. He'd arranged for a busload of Gulf Air stewardesses to come over, and these girls were wild, I'm telling you. Their drinks had been spiked with speed.'

'And why'd he ask you, Mick?'

'Probably felt he couldn't handle all those women on his own. He's an ugly bugger. About as attractive as a blind blacksmith's thumb.'

They finished their beers and the boys headed off for a curry, but Ken waited behind. 'Freddie Saidi,' he said. 'You want to watch out with someone like him. I'm not winding you up, but he's dangerous.'

'So everyone keeps saying. In fact, it's *all* they keep saying. I can't picture him, I haven't got a feel for him. I was intending to drive past his house, it's up in Regent's Park somewhere. Fancy coming for the ride?'

'Sure,' said Ken.

They headed down the Marylebone Road in the direction of the park. Opposite Madame Tussaud's, Max spotted a news kiosk with the new *StreetSmart* prominently displayed.

'Quick, Ken, over there. Our new issue. Madonna on the cover.'

He swerved into the slow lane, and pulled over. It was the greatest feeling, seeing his first issue on sale.

'I thought you said it's called *StreetSmart*, your one,' said Ken. 'That's *Town Talk*.'

'Then where the hell's *ours*? They were meant to go on sale today.' If the copies were still spread across the motorway, he might as well give up. With *Town Talk* out first on the bookstalls, it would look like their scoop. It was sickening.

They arrived at the park and drove round the inner circle in the direction of the mosque. The first daffodils of spring were already forcing their heads through the earth, and clumps of purple and yellow crocuses lay beneath the trees. A few solitary joggers pounded their way round the perimeter, or were engaged in elaborate stretching exercises against the railings. In a windblown playground, children dangled from a climbing frame, while their parents stamped their boots and slapped their arms to keep warm, and wondered how much longer they must stick it out before going home.

A couple of hundred yards beyond the Royal College of Obstetricians was an enclave of enormous detached mansions which had been put up by a property company in the early 'nineties with very specific occupants in mind. They had advanced infra-red security systems, steel gates, garaging for a dozen cars, indoor swimming-pools, a helipad and a minimum of twenty bedrooms. Surrounding each house was a nine-foot wall, ensuring absolute privacy while preventing the numerous bonded Filipino servants from escaping into the city.

Not one solitary English family lived in Regent Village, since none could afford to. Instead, it was Iranians, Russians, Malaysians, Qataris, Nigerians and Saudis who had gravitated to this secure, paranoid compound, where every visitor had to pass through a metal-detector at the gatehouse, and more than half the residents employed personal bodyguards. The largest mansion in Regent Village – an immense, bow-fronted, balconied palace, with three giant satellite dishes on the roof – was the London home of Freddie Saidi.

'When you said you wanted to get the feel of the man, is this what you had in mind, then?' asked Ken, as they tramped past the gatehouse for the fourth time.

'Just sniffing the wind,' Max replied.

They had embarked on their fifth circuit when two security guards emerged from the gatehouse. They looked fit and aggressive, kitted out in quasi-military dress with berets.

'You looking for anybody?' shouted one of the guards.

'No. Taking a walk in the public park,' replied Ken, in his thick Scots accent. 'Is that an offence down south?'

'These houses are private property,' said the guard. 'See those cameras?' He pointed to the security cameras mounted above the gate. 'You've been under surveillance.'

'For what purpose exactly, may I enquire?' asked Ken. He had become scrupulously polite, a dead giveaway he was getting angry.

The security guard didn't like being questioned. The muscles in his neck tensed, and he took a step closer to Ken. He had made the mistake of equating small stature with limited physical strength, and began imitating Ken's Scots accent, camping it up. 'And for what purpose exactly, may I enquire?' he minced. 'Now are you clearing out of here like I told you, yer fuckin' midget, or are you asking for a smack in the face?'

It was over so quickly that the guard never even saw it coming. Ken landed a left-hook on his chin, followed through with a rabbit punch to the solar plexus, and he was gasping for air on the asphalt path. His mate began muttering nervously into a walkie-talkie.

'Time to make a move,' Max said, propelling Ken in the direction of the car.

'Too right. I may not be all that tall, but I'm no fucking midget. I hope he comprehends that now.'

Ken was still brooding when they reached the car. 'Sorry if I over-reacted there, Max,' he said. 'I reckon I'm just sensitive about being a little Celtic dwarf.' And then he laughed, ruefully.

They were pulling out of the car park when they heard a loud beating noise from the direction of Regent Village, and a helicopter slowly ascended from behind the wall of one of the houses, tilted over the trees, and headed off above the rooftops. On the fuselage was painted 'Saidi Air'.

'Well, that solves that one,' said Ken. 'We know where the bugger lives. I wonder whether the man himself's inside,' he said, looking up at the helicopter, 'and where's he's going.'

'The airport, more than likely,' Max replied. 'He has a meeting with me in New York the day after tomorrow.'

[27]

Max arrived back at the flat to find the telephone ringing.

'Hi, it's Barry Higgs here, from the office. You left a message.'

'Thanks, Barry. Listen, I have to make a presentation in New York on Monday. It's going to be on a laptop, connected to the Internet. Chip Miller has faxed me over a hard copy, but I want to practise operating the laptop. I'm not sure how it works in conjunction with the Net.'

''S easy enough,' said Barry. 'I'll explain on the phone.'

'Ideally, I'd prefer a demonstration. I wouldn't be that confident if we did it over the telephone.'

'S'pose I could come over.' He didn't sound over-keen. 'You've got a modem at your place and an Internet connection?'

'Er, no.'

'We could do it at the office,' said Barry. 'Or at your sister's place. She's got a high-spec workstation and an ISDN line.'

'In Holland Park, you mean?'

'At her place, yeah. The department installed it all for her.'

Max still had Saskia's key, and Holland Park was a whole lot closer than Bruton Street. 'OK. How long will it take you to get over from Stoke Newington?'

'Forty minutes,' said Barry. 'In a cab.'

It wouldn't take Max more than ten minutes to Saskia's flat, so he filled in the time familiarising himself with Chip's presentation. He read it through twice, screen by screen, making notes in the margin of the fax. Chip had done a good job, but there were one or two assumptions Max didn't fully understand, and he didn't want to get tripped up by a rogue question from Saidi. He would need to get together with Chip before the pitch, for a final briefing.

The opening section was little more than a twenty-minute swank about the brilliance of *StreetSmart* in its magazine format – the 'tree pulp' version, as they called it – mentioning some of the awards and better-known contributors. Reading this stuff made Max feel suddenly apprehensive, in case the quality took a dive under him.

The presentation then moved on to the 'paperless' magazine, in which users logged on and grazed at will, like cattle on an endless electronic savannah, roaming from attraction to attraction, beauty, fashion, current events. Much was made of the quality of attention by Internet users, and how they were more completely absorbed by digital entertainment than by print. A jogger flicking through a running magazine might not register the colour advertisement for some new brand of sports shoe, but if the same message filled the whole of his screen, or pulsed from an electronic banner, then the recall was higher. That, anyway, was what they were telling Freddie Saidi.

At this point in the pitch, Max would outline their expertise as third-party website managers, showing some of their work for the car and sportswear companies and the digital travel agency. Then Chip would take over and demonstrate the things they could create for Saidi's companies. They had mocked-up a shopping plaza, in which all his businesses would have separate retail spaces, with software that enabled users to make purchases online. It was a smart concept, and well executed. Some sections of the site incorporated video, and you would be able to place your mouse on the entrance to the East River Hotel, pass through the revolving doors, and into the lobby. No doubt you'd even be able to visit the cashier's desk, assuming Marie-Louise Clay wasn't there first, sweating over her bill.

By the time Max had to set off to meet Barry, he felt he had pretty much mastered the content of the presentation. If only he could master the technology too, he was away.

He was pulling on his overcoat when the phone rang. It was Kitty, asking what he was up to, and would he like to come over?

'Sure,' he said. 'The only thing is, I'm on my way to Saskia's flat.' He told her about his masterclass in laptop orientation. 'It'll take about an hour, I reckon.'

'Why don't I meet you there?' she said. 'It's halfway between you and me.'

'You know Saskia's flat?'

'I've been before. I went to her party for Chinese dissident writers.'

Barry was already waiting on the steps when he arrived, smoking a cigarette. Max wasn't yet sure what to make of Barry. There was something feckless and cocky about him. The fact that he was about the only person at *StreetSmart* who could operate the computers and audio visual equipment gave him a kind of power.

They went up to the flat, deactivated the alarm, and Max followed Barry into Saskia's study. He had hardly noticed the PC on his last visit, buried on her desk under a mound of papers. Barry had brought along a laptop, and demonstrated how the two pieces of kit fitted together, and how the entire presentation could be controlled from wherever he chose in the room, freeing him from the PC itself. He showed Max how the various third-party websites – the automotive, sportswear and travel sites – could be bookmarked in advance, saving time during the pitch: he simply stored the designated sites under Bookmarks on the toolbar.

As a technician, Barry Higgs evidently knew his onions, but as a coach, he had a lot to learn. He had an annoying habit of talking exclusively in jargon, and if Max asked him to repeat anything, or explain it in layman's language, he did it with bad grace. When Max told him that he wanted to run through the whole procedure on his own, from start-up to shutdown, Barry stood behind the screen, rearranging his testicles through the pocket of his jeans.

Max felt that it was a merciful relief when the entryphone buzzed in the hallway, and Kitty rolled up in time to watch the final runthrough.

After Barry had gone, they poked about in the kitchen in search of a drink. There was an unopened bottle of Sancerre in the fridge, so they found a corkscrew and glasses and carried them into the drawing room, and flopped down on to one of the six white sofas. While Max opened the wine, Kitty adjusted the electric dimmers, until the huge space had been softened into a mosaic of diffused light. If it had been left to Max, the halogen bulbs would have blazed down on to their heads like an operating theatre, but Kitty conjured up something intimate and romantic.

Then, one by one, she closed the nine pairs of shutters on the windows overlooking the street. 'We don't want anyone looking in, do we?' she said, smiling at him meaningfully. 'You never know who might be watching, out there in Holland Park.'

Max felt the first stirrings of lust as Kitty recrossed the room. She had arrived by taxi, wearing a short suede dress that hardly covered the curve of her bottom. Her thighs were smooth and creamy white; her big blue eyes, as she came closer, the picture of innocence.

'Max,' she said. 'Can I ask you something?'

'Uh-huh.'

'This might sound rather odd, you mustn't laugh at me, but I want you to show me your war wounds.'

'*War wounds?* I've only had a piece of shrapnel in my arm.'

'I thought you'd have loads,' said Kitty, sounding disappointed.

'Look, I'm a photojournalist, not a mercenary. My job's to take pictures, not go round lending a hand.'

'So you haven't any scars at all?' She looked crestfallen. 'You're ruining my macho image of you.'

'Well, there is a small one above my hip, if that's any help. Six inches, when a jeep tipped over in Somalia. And then I've got this tiny scar where a bullet grazed my thigh.'

Kitty brightened. 'Why not strip off so I can see them properly? Then you can tell me how you came by each one.'

'Only if you will too.'

'But my only scar is an appendix scar.'

'So much the better.'

Max unbuttoned his shirt and let his old chinos and boxers fall to the floor. Kitty peeled her suede dress over her head, and stepped out of her knickers. Now they were both naked.

In the turmoil of their first night in Rosary Gardens, Max hadn't had a chance properly to appreciate Kitty's figure. She stood absolutely still for a moment, saying nothing, encouraging him to take it all in.

'OK,' she said, walking around the big silver metal coffee table in front of the sofa. 'Now tell me where you got everything.'

He gave her the full guided body-tour, ascribing each scar and blemish to a different war zone. 'That's a souvenir of Mogadishu in Somalia; that's from the Panjshir valley.'

'And what about this one?' asked Kitty.

'Tell you about it another time,' he said, 'because right now I've got this overwhelming urge to . . .'

'What about your arm, though?' asked Kitty. 'You shouldn't be putting any pressure on it.'

'Any ideas?'

'Yes, actually.' She swept a pile of art books off the coffee table on to the floor. *The paintings of Frank Auerbach*, and Gianni Versace's *Vanitas*. 'Lie down here, on your back.'

The metal felt cold against his ass and shoulders, but surprisingly sexy as he manoeuvred himself along the table. Then Kitty stepped up, planting the soles of her feet on either side of him.

'What do we call this?' he asked her. 'The mercenary position?'

For one moment, Max had this image of them both as figures in a temple relief at Konarak, enacting some ambitious tableau from Indian erotica. But then Kitty lowered herself into position, and whatever cultural allusion he was about to draw was overtaken by the more urgent matter in hand.

Twenty minutes later, when Kitty finally slithered back off him, and he staggered from the table, his outline was etched in sweat on the metal surface: shoulders, head, legs, the line of his spine. And, set slightly to each side, two perfect small footprints with every toe distinct.

They lingered in the drawing room, finishing the wine, and then drifted upstairs to Saskia's room, and lay together on the white bedcover watching the *Nine O'Clock News* on television.

This time tomorrow, Max thought, I'll be on Concorde to New York. Would he really be able to discover anything there about what had happened to Saskia?

'So, what have you been up to since Friday lunchtime?' asked Kitty. 'Your office door was shut most of yesterday afternoon.'

'Problems,' he said. 'I don't want to bore you with them. The lorry delivering the new issue to the distributors was involved in an accident. Half the copies are unusable.'

'I can't bear it,' said Kitty. 'My harem-pants story is in that issue. We shot it in Barbuda.'

'Apart from that,' he went on, 'I had dinner last night with the Landaus. Philip is the *StreetSmart* lawyer. Have you met him?'

'No,' said Kitty, 'but I know who he is. He's got a crazy wife.'

'Karis.'

'She keeps ringing up the fashion department, trying to get us to feature an Eskimo jewellery designer.'

'Maybe you should. He's very special, he finds all his whalebones on the seashore.'

'Max, we *can't*,' said Kitty. 'I've seen it. It's unbelievably tacky.' But then, realising from his face that he was teasing her, she said, 'You absolute bastard.' They both dissolved into laughter.

'For a moment,' said Kitty, 'I thought you were going to become one of those terrible owners who sits next to people at dinner, and comes in all fired up with ideas.'

'I am intending to *have* ideas, you know,' Max said defensively. 'As editor.'

'You know what I mean. Women like Karis Landau are the bane of our lives. They've got nothing to do, so they bug us with their little discoveries. She meets a Tibetan who makes earrings out of moonstones, or an Indian couturier who doesn't even have English distribution, and expects us to drop everything.'

'She told me she doesn't read magazines. She "looks beyond". She's into higher things.'

'Higher things like 747s,' said Kitty. 'She takes about ten holidays a year. And all this crap about not being a materialist. When she goes into the Jil Sander boutique, they bow. It's so pretentious, considering where she came from.'

'Which is where?'

'Oh God, she's an old rock chick. Can't you tell? She was a groupie for years, slept with every member of Deep Purple, or was it the Grateful Dead? That's how she met Philip, through the music business.'

'Have they been married long?'

'Years, I think. I'm not the person to ask. They were big buddies with Saskia.'

Kitty rolled over on to her side, facing away from Max, and said, 'Do me a favour, will you, and massage my shoulders? I think I must have pulled a muscle downstairs.'

He shifted up close to her, and began digging his thumbs deep into the muscle supporting her shoulder blades.

'That's magic,' she said. 'A little higher. Yes, just there.'

His face was buried in the nape of her neck, her hair still damp from their exertions earlier on. Her whole body smelt sweetly of sweat and sex. He felt himself harden slightly, as he brushed against the inside of her thigh.

'One question for you now, Kitty. That business earlier on about wanting to see my war wounds. Is that some kinky fantasy?'

''Fraid so,' she replied. 'I have this thing for real men with combat experience. You weren't ever in the SAS, were you?'

'No.'

'Pity.'

He suddenly realised that she was laughing.

'You *are* a sucker, Max. I couldn't give a stuff about war wounds. It was just a way of getting you to strip off.'

'I wouldn't have needed any encouragement.'

'Anyway,' she said, 'I enjoyed giving you the once-over. You know, check everything's where it should be, in full working order.'

'And did I pass?'

'You definitely passed.'

Max then told her about the intruder at the office, and his escape through the basement.

Kitty became increasingly alarmed as the story unfolded. 'Any idea who it could have been? Maybe it was just a burglar, doing over the office. There have been several break-ins, they steal the PCs.'

'Whoever it was was searching in the computer system. He was accessing the files on Bercuse.'

'Then who? Any thoughts?'

'I've been thinking about little else. Someone with something to gain by learning the details of our Bercuse business. Caryl Fargo has the strongest motive.'

'How about her, then?'

Max chuckled. 'It certainly wasn't Caryl under that baseball cap. Not with her hairdo. It could have been Bob Troup, though. He's the right build.'

'And he knows the layout of the office, and how to access the system.'

Max suddenly had another thought. '*Phil Weber.* It was his computer, I think. Or the one next to his.' Once the idea of Phil had come into his mind, it wouldn't go away. There was something about the intruder's posture that reminded Max of him. Maybe he just wanted it to be Phil, he didn't know.

'I'll keep my ears open while you're away,' said Kitty. 'If I hear anything, I'll ring you. Where are you staying?'

'Saskia's apartment, but you can reach me via the New York office. I'll be using it as a base. There is one thing you could do for me,' he went on. 'Can you get into the *StreetSmart* computer system yourself?'

'Sure. The whole staff has access to most of it. The only restricted files are the financial results. I can pull down all the editorial and advertising files.'

'What I'd like you to do is print off a full set of the Bercuse material. Whatever's on file. I want to see how commercially sensitive this stuff really is. Then fax it through to me at the New York office, marked Confidential.'

'I'll do it first thing on Monday, before the rest of the department gets in.'

'And I want to keep this quiet. There's no point the whole office knowing about the break-in. Other than Philip and Karis, I haven't mentioned it to anyone.'

'There's a fax in the fashion room. I'll send it from there. No one arrives before ten.'

They made love one more time. Afterwards, Max couldn't remember much about it, because it happened right on the edge of sleep; one minute they were gently screwing, the next they'd drifted off.

He felt very close to Kitty just then. And very lucky. With her help, he thought, it might just be possible to find a way through all this.

[28]

Max awoke at the first glimmer of dawn, which in London in March is no big deal, since it means about nine o'clock. He didn't wake Kitty because he liked the feeling of being awake while she slept on. Instead, he put on some coffee and padded through into the bathroom.

He had to concede that, compared with his own bathroom, Saskia's was a serious step up. The floors and walls, up to the height of the dado, were lined with grey marble like a Turkish bath and the sealed stone slabs on the floor were enormous, like in some ancient Roman amphitheatre.

He turned on the shower and was assailed from all sides by three hundred tiny jets of water, which powered into him with the velocity of a fireman's hose. His own shower in Ladbroke Grove consisted of a length of pink rubber tube, which attached to the hot and cold taps and dribbled.

After he'd showered, he crept downstairs and went out in search of breakfast. He'd noticed some grocery shops at the top of Holland Park Avenue where he'd be able to buy milk and bread, and maybe even the ingredients for a proper fry-up. Since returning from Peshawar, he hadn't had a single English fry-up, which was surprising, considering how much he'd been fantasising about them.

He bought the provisions, then stopped by at the newsagent's next door to pick up the Sunday papers.

The first thing he saw was a giant photograph of Saskia on the front of the *Sunday Mirror* under the headline 'SASKIA STRANGLED'.

He groaned. They were on to it. He paid for the newspapers, hurried outside on to the pavement and read the story.

Detective Karol Przemysi of the New York Police Department was quoted confirming that the death of Saskia Thompson was being treated as a murder investigation. Forensic reports showed that the magazine editor with the golden touch had been strangled in the early hours of the morning. There was a photograph of the exterior of Saskia's Manhattan apartment building, and a collage of pictures of her with various celebrities. The article itself was infuriatingly short on new information and detail. It stated only that the sleeping pills discovered by her bedside had been eliminated as the cause of death, which was no longer believed to have been suicide.

The article concluded, 'Sources close to the New York police reveal that they are focusing on Saskia's contacts in high society and the entertainment industry.'

Max hurried back to the flat and found Kitty in the kitchen, pouring herself a cup of coffee. She was wearing the fluffy white dressing gown that he'd noticed on the back of the bathroom door, with a grey 'S' for Saskia embroidered on the pocket, above the words Emporio Armani.

'Read this,' he told her. 'It's all we need.'

Kitty studied the paper while Max put sausages and bacon into a pan to fry. When she'd finished reading, he asked, 'What do you think?'

'It doesn't say much, considering it's the whole front page.'

'But enough to get everyone gossiping again, just when things are settling down.'

He turned the sausages, while Kitty blew on her coffee and stared blankly at the newspapers.

'Look,' she said suddenly. 'There's something else in the *Observer* about *StreetSmart*. They've done a story about us having the same cover as *Town Talk*.'

'I hope it exposes them for stealing our photograph. They're going to get into a lot of trouble over that.'

'Sshh, I'm trying to read. There are quotes here from Bob Troup and Caryl Fargo, it's quite long.'

Over her shoulder, Max could see the two Madonna covers reproduced side by side. The photo caption read, 'Copycat cover conspiracy ... *StreetSmart*'s espionage doesn't deliver.'

'Shit, I can't believe what I'm reading,' Kitty said. 'This is outrageous. They've gone and got the whole story the wrong way round.'

By now Max was halfway down the first leg of copy, and Kitty was right: it *was* outrageous.

'It makes out that we heard who was on the next *Town Talk* and changed our own cover at the last minute.' Kitty was beside herself. 'Bob Troup is even confirming it. Well, almost. He doesn't actually say *StreetSmart* copied *Town Talk*, but he implies it. And then they go on to say that Bob moving to *Town Talk* is a big coup for Caryl Fargo, and how you're not experienced.'

'That bit's true, at least.'

'*Stop* saying that. I've told you about it before.' Kitty was still reading the piece. 'This is *horrible*. It couldn't have come at a worse time either, just before collections. It more or less says we're on the skids. Listen to this: "Industry insiders are sceptical that Max Thompson is more than a caretaker editor, and predict that the award-winning title, founded ten years ago by his sister, Saskia, who was found dead last week in her $5 million Upper East Side apartment, would change hands before the summer. One media analyst told the *Observer*, 'The publication is already informally for sale. *StreetSmart* is a great property thats longterm interests will be best served within a major publishing conglomerate.' Possible purchasers being mentioned include Bertelsmann AG, Incorporated, H Bauer, Condé Nast, Hearst and Time Warner." '

'That,' said Max, 'is *not* going to inspire confidence. People like Luc Grimaud are going to read it and run a mile.'

'There's more,' said Kitty. 'The last paragraph. They know about the delivery lorry. It says almost our entire print-run is being withdrawn.'

'Let me see that.'

He read the paragraph, which suggested that *StreetSmart*s were going to be rarer than summer snow. It ended with a sick-making quote from Caryl Fargo, saying Max had all her sympathy, but that it was never easy for a novice to come into the business and get it right first time. 'I have met Max,' she had said. 'He's bright, but still very green. I'm convinced he can make a success in this business, if he can survive the first ten years.'

Well, thank you very much, Caryl Fargo. Max wasn't sure which he found more offensive: being threatened by her or patronised.

'The people I'm most worried about are the staff,' he said to Kitty. 'They'll read about the murder, and then all this rubbish. It won't do anything for morale.'

'It's bad timing that you're off to New York.'

'It's only for a few days. I need to meet everyone at the Canal Street office. And try and find out more about Saskia. The first thing I'm going to do when I arrive is ring that detective.' He suddenly said, 'Kitty, do you really not know who Cody's father is? I still think he might be significant.'

'Well, I told you there'd been this big office rumour about Kiefer Sutherland, but there were plenty of other names too. Nothing definite.'

'Were you actually working for *StreetSmart* when Saskia became pregnant?'

'Just. I'd only recently joined as a fashion assistant, the lowest of the low. I hadn't ever spoken to Saskia then, but I remember all the fuss. People talked about it nonstop.'

'So what happened?'

'Give me a second, I've got to remember when it was. I wasn't living in Rosary Gardens then, I shared a flat in the Munster Road with one of the features assistants, which is how I first heard. She asked had I noticed how fat Saskia was getting, and how it was all going on in one place. Then the whole office started gossiping. It became really obvious, but the weird thing was, Saskia never mentioned it.'

'She didn't?'

'Never. Which made everyone think she was planning on getting rid of it – an abortion. So every Friday we said, "She'll go in this weekend, I bet you," but she never did, and the bump got larger and larger.'

'Who did people suspect the father was, at the time?'

'Kiefer, Nick Cage, just about every movie star and rock star. Lucien Freud. Anyone she'd ever had lunch with, in fact.'

'And when did Saskia start acknowledging she was pregnant?'

'Like, never. She never, ever referred to it. At meetings she'd sit there with these cashmere jumpers straining over her bump, but she never said anything, so no one else did either.'

'Any idea why she was being coy?'

'That's what was weird. She was normally so upfront about everything. People wondered whether she was in denial.'

'How about Freddie Saidi?' asked Max. 'Was his name ever suggested as a possible candidate?'

'I do vaguely remember something about that.'

'Think hard.'

'Gina David or someone was speculating about it. Saidi used to send Saskia these amazing gifts.'

'So it's possible?' The idea of Saidi as Cody's father made Max feel sick, but it would explain Marcus Brooke's unhealthy interest in the subject, and Jean's discretion on Friday evening.

'Could be. A shame though, if Saidi did turn out to be the biological father. Not so glamorous as some of the other candidates.'

Max laughed. 'You people in magazines are hilarious. Everything is surface and appearances. Have you done anything unglamorous in your whole life, Kitty, or is it just parties, more parties and fashion shows?'

Kitty turned on him, suddenly angry. 'As a matter of fact, you don't know anything about me. If you did, you wouldn't have said that.'

'Sorry if I've misjudged you.'

'You have. When you've worked as hard as I have, it's bloody annoying when people suggest it's been one long party.'

'My fault for not asking. Do you want to tell me?'

'Not particularly, it's too boring, but I will tell you that I come from the Wirral – that's Cheshire in case you're wondering, you probably haven't been, there's no war going on. And my father owns a haulage company, with about thirty lorries that deliver gravel from gravel pits to various building contractors in the north. So there you are. Life before *StreetSmart*. Dad wanted me to come in to the business, maybe one day take it over, and when I said I wanted to come down south and work on a magazine, he never forgave me. So please don't lecture me about parties and fashion shows, because I do know about other things too.'

'What made you want to do it? Work for a magazine in London?'

'If you'd spent every Saturday and Sunday in a lorry park, you wouldn't ask. My mother walked out when I was ten, and I lived with Dad. He worked every weekend. I used to sit on a stool in the Portakabin office and read magazines and fell in love with them, and promised myself one day I'd become the editor of one.'

'Is that still your ambition?'

'It's everyone's ambition, isn't it? Everyone I know, anyway.' She laughed. 'Only of certain magazines, of course. Not *Woman's Own*. Anyway, I don't like talking about myself. I'm more interested in

Saskia: my role model. The speculation about Cody went on for months after he was born.'

'Did Saskia take maternity leave?'

'If you call three days maternity leave. She was back so quickly, you hardly noticed she'd gone. Even while she was having contractions, she was never off the phone, changing the coverlines for that issue.'

'She took Cody to our parents' house in Surrey after she left hospital. My mother looked after him from three days old.'

'There was an embarrassing incident when she turned up at *StreetSmart*,' said Kitty. 'Nobody was expecting her back so soon, and we were in her office looking at the flowers that'd been sent for Cody. People were opening the little envelopes to read the names on the cards, and the messages, to see if there were any clues to who the father was. You know, some incriminating message or an especially big bouquet.'

'And were there any?'

'I do remember a huge one from Freddie Saidi, but that might not mean anything: he's famous for sending over-the-top flowers.'

'And what happened then, when Saskia came back?'

'Well, people still speculated all the time about it. There was a lot of detective work, like finding out where Saskia had been nine months earlier, to work out where she'd conceived.'

'And where *had* she been?'

'Mostly here in London, but also in Paris and New York. So it didn't help.'

'In other words, it's wide open. Cody's father could be anyone.'

'There was even a rumour going round it was Bob Troup, but no one took it that seriously.'

Before he left for the airport, Max obtained the number for the 19th Police Precinct in New York, where he asked to be put through to Detective Karol Przemysi.

'Przemysi.'

Max introduced himself as Saskia's brother. 'I understand you're in charge of investigating my sister's murder. I'm coming over to New York and would like to meet up with you some time this evening.'

'Sure,' said Detective Przemysi. 'I'd like to offer my condolences about Saskia. Your sister, she made a big reputation for herself in this city. When I told my wife I was on this case, she was impressed. She reads the magazine, never misses an issue.'

'Good,' said Max. 'We need all the readers we can get. How about seven o'clock, if I come down to you?'

Przemysi consulted his schedule. 'In the afternoon I'm calling on Larry King. Isn't that something? He was big buddies with Saskia. But seven o'clock should be fine. Ask for me at the desk.'

Max sighed. Detective Przemysi sounded starstruck. Even after she was dead, the Saskia effect rolled on.

[29]

Étienne Bercuse sat behind his Arne Jacobsen iconic 1958 moulded desk, and paged his way through the magazine that had just been handed to him. It was Sunday afternoon and the office building was almost deserted; only Bercuse and a secretary were working. Through the window he could see the length of the avenue Montaigne, with its shuttered boutiques and couturiers, including his own Paris superstore with its *belle époque* façade.

As he turned the pages, he smiled. Not a single advertisement for any of his eleven companies appeared in the new issue of *StreetSmart*.

He buzzed his secretary on the squawk box. 'Chantal, will you please make an appointment for me to meet with Monsieur Thompson? He is the brother of Saskia Thompson.'

'Of course, monsieur. You prefer to meet with him here in Paris, or in London?'

'Either, but I would like everything to appear quite informal, just a quiet talk, no lawyers or attorneys at this stage.'

'You haven't forgotten he contacted you here at the office, while you were in the States? It was on the message sheet I faxed through.'

'Naturally, I remember,' said Bercuse. The message had pleased him: it had showed that his strategy was already working. 'Chantal, did you obtain the information I requested about Monsieur Thompson?'

'In the red folder, monsieur.'

He opened the folder and read the two closely typed sheets of biographical information. Max's life and career: the small wars, assignments and press accreditations.

When he had finished, Étienne nodded with satisfaction. He thought, This is quite fortunate. The brother proposes to run *StreetSmart* himself, with no experience. Previously, I had scheduled six to eight months before the magazine could become part of Bercuse SA. Now I am compressing the timeframe to one month.

He buzzed Chantal again. 'Don't worry to fix that meeting. It says here that Max Thompson has requested tickets for the Sensi show in Milan. Please ensure that he gets front row, and that he is seated directly next to me.'

PART TWO

[30]

The early evening Concorde flight to JFK was almost full, and Max found that he recognised several people in the Speedwing lounge. Rod Stewart was there with his children plus two nannies, and Jean Claude van Damme, and as they filed on board he realised he was standing next to Cindy Crawford, the supermodel. Remembering Mick Paarl's question about the authenticity of her tits, he gave them a hard, sidelong stare. They looked genuine enough.

He was in his seat, waiting for take-off, when he became conscious of a helmet of blonde lacquer approaching along the aisle, followed by an overweight man in a green cotton suit. Caryl was carrying a briefcase and a copy of the *Observer*, folded back at the section with the article about *StreetSmart*.

She didn't notice him until she'd almost walked past, then did a double take. She was evidently wondering whether Max had seen her, and whether or not to say anything. In the end she said, 'Hello, Max. This is a coincidence.' As she greeted him, Caryl became aware that she was holding the article, and tried to cover it with her briefcase.

'Thanks for the compliment in the *Observer*,' Max said. He was damned if he was letting her off the hook.

'Oh, you saw that? Those pieces can be quite silly. They never really get the story right.'

'They got that one badly wrong. Your front cover was stolen from us. I should warn you, we're taking legal action.'

Bob Troup, who was standing behind Caryl in the aisle, looked uncomfortable. It occurred to Max that maybe he hadn't told her where the transparency had come from.

'Well, have a good trip,' said Caryl, hurrying along.

When she'd found her window seat, Caryl turned to Bob and said,

'I hope that *Observer* quote isn't counter-productive. Max seemed annoyed. It was designed to impress the analysts, but I don't want Max selling *StreetSmart* to anyone else.'

'Relax,' said Bob. 'We'll get it, and soon. Incorporated's the perfect owner and I'm the obvious editor. Everyone knows that.'

'Let's hope you're right,' said Caryl. 'Anyway, our meetings tomorrow should be interesting.'

Just before they sealed the aircraft door, a tall man with a ginger ponytail, wraparound shades and parachute pants, was escorted down the aisle by a stewardess into the seat next to Max.

'There you are, Mr Yando,' said the stewardess. 'Just made it.'

He refused a glass of champagne before take-off, and when the food came round, waved it away. He stretched out in his seat and, in the private twilight world behind his shades, could have been either awake or asleep.

Shortly before landing, however, he became nervously alert, and said to Max, 'Hi, I'm Yando. I take pictures.'

'Me too.'

'Yeah? For anyone in particular?'

'Bullet. Photojournalism, mostly wars.'

'My agent wants me to get into this whole war scene,' said Yando. 'A big exhibition at MOMA. And a book: *Wars*.' Then he said, 'Can you recommend any wars that are, like, handy? It's tough for me to get away for more than a few days at a time. With my other commitments.'

The plane touched down and taxied along the apron to the terminal.

Jean had arranged for a limousine to take Max from the airport to Saskia's apartment, and he told the driver he wanted to go via the 19th Police Precinct at 153 East 67th. When Saskia's body had first been discovered by her maid on the morning after the benefit, it was the 19th Precinct that had first responded to her call.

If Max was going to discover what really happened that night, the Precinct was the place to start.

Detective Karol Przemysi was as tall as Max, but broader and heavier, with iron-grey hair cropped close to his skull. He led Max into a glass-fronted office and offered a cigarette. 'The people your sister knew,' he said, shaking his head. 'All the stars and celebrities. I was hearing about a party she gave for Jennifer Flavin and Sly Stallone.'

'Saskia enjoyed that kind of life,' said Max. 'Rather her than me.'

'Hey, I don't know,' replied Detective Przemysi. 'Reckon I could get used to it: the parties, the movie stars ...'

'How's the investigation going?' asked Max. 'I know you've spoken to my parents, but we don't know much.'

'I've spoken with Colonel Thompson a few times. He's a nice guy, I mean that. Comes over so proud of his daughter. Terrible thing to happen like that.'

'Well, what *did* happen? I've only read that she was discovered by the maid and she'd been strangled.'

Detective Przemysi raised the case notes on his personal computer. 'Carmelita Puentes arrived for work as usual around eleven o five next morning, found Saskia in the bedroom and dialed 911. Call was passed on to Central Dispatch and a patrol car arrived four minutes later. Officer Mitchell and Officer Sonnabend reported a DOA. I arrived at the apartment myself ten, fifteen minutes after that.'

'And my sister was where? Some of the English newspapers said she'd been found in the bathroom. They implied she'd been naked.'

'That would be incorrect. She was in the bedroom, fully clothed. She still had the gown on she'd worn to the benefit the previous evening.'

'Were there any peculiar circumstances surrounding her death? Sexual, I mean? I overheard some British journalists imply various things.'

'It's like I always say, Mr Thompson. The whores of the media. I reckon people's private lives are their own business, but there was nothing like that. Nothing perverted.'

'So when do they reckon she was killed?'

'Hard to be precise. Forensics estimate any time between midnight and four o'clock next morning. She'd been dead minimum seven hours when the maid found her, probably longer.'

'And she'd definitely been strangled? My father said they'd found sleeping pills next to the bed.'

'On the night-table and spread across the covers. There were tablets all over the bed, but they weren't what killed her, the autopsy confirmed that. She'd been strangled. The skin round her throat was bruised. And they identified petechial haemorrhaging – small spots around the face – consistent with constriction of the blood flow to the head.'

'And when you first arrived at the apartment, what did you find? I want to know everything, every detail.'

'What can I tell you?' said Detective Przemysi. 'She was on her back on the bed, red cocktail dress, no evidence of sexual assault. There was the bottle of tablets on the night table, which first made us believe she might have taken her own life.'

'And what were these pills?'

'Temazepam. Purchased five weeks earlier at a drugstore on Canal Street, two blocks from her office. Seems she had trouble sleeping after international flights. Temazepam helped her get off.'

'Are they dangerous?'

Przemysi shrugged. 'Take the recommended dose – two, three tablets – there's no problem. Plenty of folk use them.'

'What about the doorman?' asked Max. 'The guy downstairs. When Saskia got back from the Waldorf that night, was she alone?'

'Swears she was. And his recollection fits in with the driver: he confirmed there was no one else in the car, only Miss Thompson. He saw her pass through the lobby to the elevators.'

'Did Saskia have any visitors later on?'

'Not that he noticed. Visitors are supposed to be announced, they can't just walk up. He says he didn't announce anyone. It's possible he missed seeing them. The elevators aren't visible from the desk, and there are stairs at the end of the lobby.'

'So someone *could* have walked up.'

'You can't rule it out. These portered apartments make a big issue of security, but the guy could have bunked off for a while, to grab a coffee or take a leak.'

'Have you been able to establish whether Saskia's killer was known to her?'

'Nothing conclusive, one way or the other. It's standard procedure in a homicide investigation to interview the deceased's known associates. Family, friends, business associates. I must personally have interviewed forty people – that's when I can get to them, which I can tell you isn't easy. Agents!' Detective Przemysi shook his head. 'Everyone in this case has agents – speak to my agent, call my agent. This to a detective in a homicide! But the short answer to your question is, no, we haven't any definite leads. Could have been someone she knew, could as easy have been a fruit loop off the street.'

'And can you tell whether Saskia had invited this person, whoever he was, into the apartment? When I mean is, had the door been forced?'

'There was no indication of forced entry. Seems like she let the killer into the apartment herself.'

'Which suggests she knew him.'

'Could be. But what we can't say is how well she knew him.'

'I'm sorry?'

Detective Przemysi looked uneasy. 'All I'm saying here is that your sister, she was a single unattached lady. There were certain bars she used.'

'Are you suggesting Saskia might have picked someone up? A stranger?'

'I'm saying we're not ruling that out as a scenario. Your sister liked men. Seems she enjoyed sex. It isn't a crime. Sometimes she'd meet some guy and he puts the move on her and she entertains him back at the apartment. Sometimes it was the other way round – she puts the move on the guy. She didn't always get to know them first, that's all.'

'So my sister was into one-night stands?'

'Don't get me wrong, there's no moral dimension here, but it's possible she'd arranged to meet someone at the apartment. Not all of her men friends were nice people, you know what I'm saying? They expected to get paid for their services.'

Max looked at the detective. He knew he should have been outraged, but somehow nothing he was hearing surprised him very much. Saskia had always taken control of every aspect of her life. Why not her sex life too?

'Did the forensic people find anything – fingerprints or whatever?'

'Place was covered with prints. Forensic took thirty different sets. And that's only the bedroom.'

Max groaned: Saskia's toyboys.

'One more thing,' said Max. 'You mentioned the autopsy. Did anything else come out of it, apart from the evidence of strangulation? Anything significant?'

'Not pertaining to the homicide.'

Somehow, Max knew the detective was dissembling. He had

attended enough government press briefings in disintegrating sub-Saharan dictatorships to recognise it instinctively.

'Detective Przemysi, I've told you already, I need to know everything. Saskia was my sister. There's nothing you can tell me that's going to change my feelings for her.'

'OK, there was one other thing. When they performed the autopsy at First Avenue – that's down at the OCME – there were traces of seminal fluid in her vagina. She had sexual intercourse within twenty-four hours of her death. According to the report, it took place between midday and early evening on the afternoon of the benefit. Only thing, we don't know who put it there.'

[31]

By the time Max left the Precinct for Saskia's apartment at 67th and Park it was dark. He stood on the sidewalk looking up at the sand-coloured apartment block, thinking, So this is where she was murdered. Saskia had owned the place for more than six years, and it said something about their relationship that he'd never been there before.

Once she'd achieved celebrity status in the city, Max didn't ever feel comfortable about being in New York. It was her turf. It was as though they had an unspoken agreement: Saskia would take London and Manhattan, he'd have the rest of the world.

There was a doorman in the lobby behind a beechwood desk. His name badge said he was Jon Kalowski. Max explained who he was. 'I have a key. I'll be staying a few days.'

'Too bad about your sister,' he said. 'She was a successful lady. I used to read about her in page six.' When Max looked blank, he added, 'The gossip page in the *Post*. If they put you in page six, you've made it. That's what people say.' Then he said, 'Wait a moment, I won't keep you,' and dialled a number on the house telephone.

Max took a look around the lobby. It was very large, more like the lobby for a headquarters building than an apartment block, with leather-and-chrome sofas, mirrors everywhere, an arrangement of bullrushes in a vase, and a sculpture that resembled three large stone bagels. At the end of the lobby were two banks of elevators. A notice said that the penthouse floor contained a health spa for residents.

'Mr Thompson.' The doorman beckoned him over. 'I'm sorry to tell you this, but I can't let you go up. The forensics haven't vacated the apartment yet. I've just spoken to the Precinct.'

'But I'm meant to be staying here tonight. I was told they'd have cleared out by now.'

'I'm sorry, but that's what they're saying. If you want to take it up with anyone, I can give you the number for the guy in charge. While you're here,' said the doorman, 'we have a situation you can maybe help sort out. Carmelita Puentes, Miss Thompson's maid – the lady who found her that morning in the apartment – she doesn't know what's going to happen to her now, and she hasn't been paid for a month.'

'I see.'

'I was wondering if you could maybe talk with her. She's a nice lady, lives way up Broadway, neighbourhood of Fort Washington Park. Tell her whether you still require her to come in. Right now, she doesn't know what's expected.'

'Sure,' Max said, while the doorman searched about for her number. 'I'll call her later on.' Though where he was going to make the call from, he hadn't a clue.

'One other thing about Carmelita. You need to know this. It may be that she's not strictly legal, in the matter of her immigration. She didn't appreciate being questioned by the cops.'

The limo had long gone, so the doorman flagged down a yellow cab on the corner of 67th Street, and before he knew it Max's suitcase was in the trunk, and the driver was looking to him for a destination.

The names of half a dozen famous hotels came to mind, but for some reason he heard himself saying, 'The East River.' Probably it was just front-of-mind. He'd been hearing about the place for a week, and was intrigued.

Soon they were cutting back across town, along Sutton Place and past the River House apartments, and drew up outside a soaring landmark building with a canopy on to the sidewalk, and a fleet of hotel limousines parked up along the kerb.

A doorman took his suitcase and a minute later he was standing at reception, completing a registration form and having an impression taken of his credit card. It crossed Max's mind that, if Saidi had arranged to have Saskia bumped off, Max was certainly making it easy for him to go for the double.

He chose a standard room on the eighth floor, and as he trailed the bellboy towards the elevators, he took in the lie of the land. They passed the cashier's desk, scene of Marie-Louise's humiliation, a glass showcase filled with a display of Fournels et Fils jewellery, and the entrance to a grand restaurant with a peacock painted on the door. Inside, he could see tables laid for dinner, and chandeliers.

Max was waiting for the elevator when the doors slid open, and out stepped Marcus Brooke. He looked momentarily wrong-footed, then bounded forward and gripped Max by the hand. 'Max! I had no idea you were staying with us. Why didn't you let us know?'

'It's a spur-of-the-moment decision. I'd intended to stay at Saskia's apartment.'

'Well, you honour us. I only hope the girls behind the desk have given you a suite with a river view. They try their best, but they don't always pick up on the VIPs, unless they're briefed in advance.' Marcus turned to the bellboy and said, 'Let me see that key. What, room 838? Oh, no, no. I'm going to take that key straight back to where it came from, and upgrade you to one of the river suites, whatever's available. The Sidon suite, or the Gardens of Babylon.'

'Honestly, Marcus,' Max said, 'I'll be perfectly happy in the room I've been given. In fact, I'd prefer it.'

'Nonsense,' said Marcus. 'Freddie would insist. That terrible story in the *Sunday Mirror* about Saskia being murdered. So shocking and unbelievable. The least we can do is ensure you are comfortable.'

Max made several further attempts to avoid the upgrade, but Marcus wouldn't be deflected. In the end, it seemed easier to go along with it. He needed to ring Chip Miller and Carmelita Puentes, Saskia's housekeeper, and he didn't want to miss them.

'One last thing, Max,' said Marcus, 'then I'll bid you good night. Before your presentation tomorrow, which we're all eagerly looking forward to, Freddie will probably want a little word with you. He's keen to press forward with the matter we discussed in London.'

'I'm afraid he's going to be disappointed, in that case. Nothing's changed since last week.'

'That didn't seem to be the view of this morning's *Observer*.'

'The *Observer* was wrong.'

'Nevertheless, I am sure Freddie will raise it. I shouldn't be telling you this, or you'll ask him for more money, but he's quite fired up by the prospect of owning *StreetSmart*. He's talking about it all the time. Anyway,' said Marcus, as the bellboy returned with a new key, 'enjoy the Gardens of Babylon suite, and if there's anything you need, just ask. It's one of our modest boasts that we can provide our guests with absolutely anything, anything at all.'

As the lift doors were already closing, he called out, 'I'd ask them to send you up a pretty girl, but I hear you already have one of those in London.'

[32]

As soon as his luggage was delivered, and he knew he wouldn't be disturbed, Max began to search the suite for bugs.

He started with all the obvious places, unscrewing the voice piece of the telephone – all the telephones, there were four, including the wall-mounted extension in the bathroom – then lifted up the bases of the lamps, ran his hand down the back of the bedhead, tipped forward the bedside cabinets to see if anything was attached, limpetlike, to their wooden undersides. On the wall above the bed was a needlepoint tapestry of a Fragonard maiden on a swing, dressed up as some kind of milkmaid, and he felt his way across it, inch by inch.

Without ever having seen a bug, he wasn't sure what he was looking for. He was reminded of the story of the American businessman, on his first trip to Moscow, who became convinced that his room at the Hotel Nationale was being bugged. He spent every evening taking the place apart, knowing it was there somewhere and determined to find it. Eventually he rolled back the carpet and there, at last, was the bug: a large metal device bolted into the floor. The businessman was elated. Now he'd teach those Communists to eavesdrop on him. He went out and bought a pair of pliers, and gingerly unscrewed the bug. Just then there was an earsplitting crash of breaking glass. The central chandelier of the Hotel Nationale had plunged thirty feet on to the ballroom floor.

There was a large French cabinet opposite Max's bed, concealing the minibar and television, and he examined every drawer, every whorl of the wood, in case anything had been inserted. Then he lifted down the pictures from the walls, one by one, and looked behind them. There was a particular picture light, illuminating an old print of the Hanging Gardens of Babylon, that seemed unnecessarily bulky. Using a coin, he unscrewed the bronze plate covering the plug, but couldn't spot anything. He rolled back a rug in the sitting room, and the linen footmat next to the bed, then moved on to the bathroom.

What was it Philip Landau had said? 'The suites have video surveillance in the showerheads.' He balanced on the rim of the tub and dismantled the chrome fittings. It took more than half an hour, but there was nothing inside: no wires, no fisheye lenses. He stared hard at the bathroom mirror, in case it was two-way. He was removing the cover of the shaving point when the doorbell rang.

He jumped. He was expecting no one. Maybe Saidi's security men had been watching him on the cameras he'd failed to find. Now they knew he was on to them, and they were coming to do him over.

He opened the door with the chain on, and looked cautiously outside.

A waiter was bearing a basket of fruit wrapped in yellow cellophane and an arrangement of flowers in a brass pot. 'Mr Thompson? These are for you. Compliments of the management.'

Max took off the chain, and looked both ways along the corridor, before letting him come in.

A handwritten card from Marcus Brooke said, 'Freddie Saidi joins me in welcoming you to the Big Apple. I have informed the concierge, Paolo, of your VIP status. If there's anything he can organise for you, press extension 18. As ever, Marcus.'

After that, Max took a shower and sat on a yellow silk sofa munching on a fig from Marcus's basket, before he dragged across a telephone, and started making calls.

Chip Miller was still up in Hartford. He'd be catching the first flight out tomorrow morning. 'Hi, Max,' he said. 'It's really good you could make it over for this.'

'Let's wait till we win it first,' Max said. 'They're not the easiest people to do business with.' He didn't tell Chip that Saidi had *StreetSmart* in his sights as an acquisition target. It would only worry him. Instead, they ran through the technology, point by point, and tried to second guess the questions they might be asked.

Max put down the telephone and called Carmelita Puentes. He heard the number ring fifteen times before it was answered, and a shy, suspicious voice said, 'Who is it, please?' The accent was Central American. He was sure it was Carmelita, but she was evasive. She probably thought he was from immigration or a cop.

Eventually he said, 'Carmelita – if that's you there – I believe my sister owed you money. For the housekeeping. I need to give you that money.'

'OK,' she said. 'This is Carmelita speaking. She owe me one month, four weeks' working. Saskia said, "Carmelita, I give you your money tomorrow like normal," but when I walk in the apartment, what a shock, I can't believe it. Terrible. And now, I don't know, should I find other job, come in like before, what I do?'

'Carmelita, I'd like to meet with you tomorrow and talk about that. Not at the apartment, because the police are still there. Maybe at your place. In Fort Washington Park. Is that possible?'

She sounded unkeen.

'I can bring the dollars with me if you tell me how much.'

'OK, $290 a week, which come to $1160. Then $26 for cleaning materials, I have receipt. Coming to $1186.'

Max got her to dictate her address, letter by letter, and said he'd meet her around two o'clock.

Shortly before turning in, he had an overwhelming desire to talk to Kitty. The combination of his first ever business trip, and staying in a suite at the East River, made him long to tell her about it. Also, he really wanted to hear her voice. There was no doubt about it, he was falling for her heavily.

'Kitty?'

'Max! Hi, darling. How was the flight?'

'Apart from running into Caryl Fargo and Bob Troup, fine. And quick. I could get addicted to that plane.'

'Must be genetic. Saskia flew Concorde fifty times last year. Twenty-five round trips. Anyway, what were Bob and Caryl doing there?'

'No idea. I told Caryl we were suing her over the front cover, and Bob looked deranged.' He told Kitty about being turned away from the apartment, and his conversations with Detective Przemysi and Carmelita Puentes.

'Then where are you ringing from now, if not from Saskia's?'

'A hotel.'

'Which? The Royalton?'

'No.'

'The Mercer?'

'No.'

'Where, then?'

'The East River.'

'You're kidding. You crazy? Don't you realise all the suites are bugged?'

'If they are, they're well concealed. I've spent an hour searching.'

'Well, don't invite any call girls back to the room. Next thing you know, it'll be on video.'

'Would I?' Max laughed. 'Why would I need call girls when I've got you, Kitty?'

'Thanks for the compliment. You can be such a smooth-tongued charmer when you want to be. You really know how to romance a girl. Actually, I was just thinking about you when you rang.'

'Nice things, I hope.'

'Thinking how great it would be if you were here now, in Rosary Gardens. It's weird, but I'm feeling quite aimless without you. And quite sexy. I think I must be missing you.'

'Three days. Once this presentation's out of the way, and I've found out more about Saskia's murder, I'll be straight home.'

'I *think* I can wait that long. Can't promise anything, mind. But no longer.'

[33]

The New York offices of *StreetSmart* occupied the ninth floor of a converted dry-foods warehouse on the intersection of Canal Street and Greenwich Street. Max could see from the board in the lobby that the other suites were taken by fashion and public relations outfits, plus various graphic design companies on the upper floors.

It wasn't until he reached Saskia's own office that he understood why she'd chosen this building: the view was breathtaking, a wide open vista across rooftops and parking lots to the Hudson River. Even in March, the room was full of hard winter sunlight. Adjoining Saskia's office, through a sliding smoked-glass door, was the purple meeting room with the violet Milanese sofa. The walls were lined with framed *StreetSmart* covers, and there were two thirty-six-inch computer screens set into the wall. Chip had already arrived, and was busy downloading the latest build of the presentation. Max joined him and they ran through the final details.

Saidi and Brooke weren't due for forty minutes, and Anka wanted to take him on walkabout, and introduce him to the staff. 'I told them they had to be here, on pain of death, by eight o'clock latest, even the editorial people. And believe it or not, they're all here. *Incredible.*'

Max was already impressed by Anka Kaplan. A little tense maybe – you could almost smell the Prozac on her breath – but he'd marked her down as a good thing. A worrier and a worker. They could do with some of those on the team.

Anka led him around her own department first, introducing him to the sales team. He couldn't tell how effective they were at selling advertising, but they were great at selling themselves. At each desk, a different perfectly groomed blonde was locked into a telephone negotiation, toughing it out with one agency or another. 'No way is *StreetSmart* moving off ratecard,' each executive was saying. 'The only discount you get here is the structured volume incentive plan.'

For all Max knew, the phones weren't even plugged in, but it certainly made an impression.

As he passed one desk he heard an executive say, 'I can categorically assure you about that, Steve. *StreetSmart* is not, repeat not, on the block. We have a new editor in place, it's business as usual.'

'Who was that?' Max asked.

'Young & Rubicam. Agency for Revlon. They said we've been sold.'

'Well, they're mistaken. Keep denying it.'

Max addressed the group. 'I know a lot of people in the industry believe we're for sale. The truth is: a couple of publishers and individuals have approached me, but I've turned them down flat. We didn't even have a meeting. As for the other names being mentioned, there's been no contact whatever. I've said the same thing to your counterparts in London: *StreetSmart*'s remaining independent. Now if anybody has any questions . . .'

There was a protracted silence while he looked round the room. Nineteen blondes in beige suits smiled silently back, then a Chinese girl, who said she looked after the travel category, asked, 'Mr Thompson, will there be more editorial pages devoted to destination travel under your editorship? Considering your own background and everything.'

'I'm afraid I haven't given much thought to that yet. I've only been at it a week. But don't worry, the magazine won't be recommending vacations to the sort of places I used to travel to, if that's what you're concerned about.'

There was relieved laughter, followed by a second question.

'Mr Thompson. Mary-Ellen Gallagher Du Puis. I handle accessories and new business development in the fragrance category. I have a question.'

'Go ahead.'

'In the latest issue, there's a photograph of a corpse that some people may find offensive. I don't mean to interfere with editorial integrity or anything, but I think we could have a problem here with some of the advertisers.'

'I know the picture you mean. It's one of mine. All I can say is, let's hope we don't. Have you had any complaints so far?'

'At a breakfast meeting this morning, I showed a copy to the marketing manager for Tranquilité, and she was quite offended. She's not that easy a person in any case.'

'Thanks for the warning.'

Anka, probably feeling that the visit should end on a more upbeat note, said, 'Thank you, Max, for that reassuring message about the future of the magazine. I am sure that, inspired by this fresh commitment from you, we will all sell even harder, break new accounts, and achieve record revenues for the company.'

Turning to her team, she said, 'I think we should demonstrate our level of commitment with the *StreetSmart* chant. This, Max,' she explained, 'developed out of a motivational role-playing seminar at our most recent sales conference in Maui. *OK everybody*, go for it, on the count of three . . .'

The sales team formed up in a ragged line behind Anka, like college cheerleaders at a baseball game, then began beating out time with imaginary pom-poms.

StreetSmart, *StreetSmart*, A thru Zee
Strongest in its category.
StreetSmart, *StreetSmart*, inn-o-vate
Each new sale we cel-e-brate.
Sell! Sell! Sell!
Sell! Sell! Sell!
Meet those targets
Beat them well!

When they reached the line about Sell! Sell! Sell!, the team adopted especially aggressive poses, as though psyching themselves up for a street brawl. They reminded Max of the All Blacks doing their Maori intimidation routine – the Haka – before a rugby international.

Afterwards, he wasn't quite sure how to respond. At airports he had often seen those business books with titles like *Reignite Your Sales Force with Three Easy-to-remember Platitudes*, but had never even picked one up. So he just said, 'That was great, everybody. I promise you, if I ever need to buy a page of advertising, I'll come to you guys first.'

'Yeah! It's a blast!' called out Mary-Ellen Gallagher Du Puis. 'But don't even *ask* for a discount.'

Right across the lobby, on the opposite corner of the building, lay the editorial department.

Much to Max's relief, nobody showed the slightest sign of either singing or chanting at his arrival. Instead, the whole department looked hungover, and in danger of collectively throwing up.

Once again, he was steered from desk to desk, and given a brief resumé on what each person did.

Silas Cheung, the US art director, had a pigtail and a tiny tattoo of a dragon in the fold of skin between finger and thumb. 'Listen, there's something I need to raise,' he said. 'When you were deciding which stories to hold over from the issue, I understand you asked about page design.'

'That's right. We had to drop some pages. I wanted to know what they looked like.'

'Next time, it's better if you discuss that directly with me, OK, not Anka. After all, I'm the art director. I think I have a better feel for these things than someone from advertising.'

'Point taken. Another time, I'll consult you.' Blast, thought Max, I've succeeded in pissing him off before I've even started.

'It would help,' said Silas. 'The wrong choices got made for the balance of the book.'

The rest of the staff seemed curious rather than hostile, and were anxious to show him what they were working on. An editor called Ilsa Jane Pezzimenti handed him the draft of a profile of the author Thomas Pynchon, with some snatch-shots they'd obtained of him buying a tuna submarine at a coffee shop. 'It's a big, big scoop for us,' she said. 'He hasn't been photographed since 1953.'

A line editor called Jonny Tannenbaum said sorry to raise this, but Saskia had been on the point of reviewing his compensation when she was murdered, and could they discuss this some time?

Leah Sheinberg, a picture researcher, took him through the choices for a story on private yachts. Most seemed to belong to *Forbes* 400 CEOs, but one in particular caught Max's eye.

'Isn't that Freddie Saidi in that picture?'

'Yes, Saskia told me to call it in. His boat's one of the biggest. The *Princess Baalbek*.'

Leah gave him a lupe, and he studied the transparency over the lightbox. It was an immense white floating hotel with four decks, with a speedboat suspended from the quarterdeck and a helicopter pad on the roof. The staterooms all had full-sized windows, except close to the waterline where he counted twenty portholes for the crew.

Just then, Anka touched him on the arm and said, 'Max, message from Chip. Mr Saidi and his associate are on their way up.'

They waited by the elevator, watching the digital display, as it tracked the car's ascent to the ninth floor.

'Best of luck, Chip.'

Chip grinned, and punched the air. 'You betcha. We'll sell 'em.'

The car jerked to a halt, and the doors slid open. The first person to step out wasn't Saidi, but a three-hundred-pound bruiser in a dark suit. He looked swiftly around the lobby, sizing up the situation, then moved cautiously forward, all the time covering the elevator door.

Meanwhile a second bodyguard, black this time, edged out of the car. Max couldn't be sure, but from the bulge beneath his armpit, he'd have said he was armed.

'OK, let's *move* it,' shouted the first man, and the black bodyguard sprinted up the corridor on the balls of his feet, and took up a position next to the window.

Waiting inside the car for the all-clear, Max could see Marcus Brooke in his velvet-collared overcoat, and Saidi.

Marcus emerged with hand outstretched. 'Max, marvellous to see you. You slept well, I trust, in the Gardens of Babylon suite?'

'Yes, fine, thank you, very comfortable.'

'Now,' said Marcus. 'Let me introduce you to Mr Saidi. Freddie, may I present Max Thompson who you've heard so much about? He is Saskia's brother.'

Saidi regarded him noncommittally beneath hooded eyelids. He was slighter and shorter than Max had expected, but the thing Max noticed first about him were his eyes. They moved very slowly and very deliberately like the beam of a lighthouse, and struck him as wholly lacking in humanity.

'Saskia was my friend,' he said. His voice was soft, and heavily accented. 'Many times she come to my house. We make fucking good party together.'

'What did I tell you?' put in Marcus. 'Saskia and Mr Saidi got on together like a house on—'

'We need private talk,' said Saidi, cutting him short. 'Just you and me. You have some place?'

'Through there. My office.'

As they left, Max attempted to introduce him to Chip, but Saidi was already pushing ahead, sandwiched between bodyguards.

He waited just inside the door while the minders checked out the windows and lowered the blinds. Eventually, when they had finished, he sat down in a leather chair, and said, 'Too bad some bastard kills your sister.'

'Thank you. It's been a shock.'

'What the police say about it? They going to make an arrest soon?'

'I don't know.'

'Saskia should have married me, when I ask her.'

'You asked her to *marry* you?' Max was astonished. 'When was this?'

'If she'd say yes, she still be alive today, no question. It's not good for women to live alone in some fucking big place.' Then, abruptly changing the subject, he said, 'How much you want for the magazine?'

'I'm afraid it isn't for sale.'

'How much you want? Fifty million US dollar?'

'Like I said, I can't sell. I've agreed to keep it going for Saskia's son, Cody. Until he's old enough to run it himself.'

'He very good boy, Cody. Like my own son. Sixty million?'

Max had to admit it was tempting. Sixty million dollars for a magazine that wasn't turning a profit. But then he thought of his father, and Marie-Louise, and Anka and Gina and Kitty. He'd given his promise, and he liked to think that meant something.

'OK, no bullshit,' said Saidi. 'Seventy million. I pay big premium because it's worth it for me. We have deal?'

'I wish, but I can't. And, you know, we ought to go through and see the Internet presentation. It's all set up for you.'

'You shit-hot bargainer,' Saidi said. 'OK, we talk later.'

Chip and Marcus were already seated at the conference table. Marcus scrutinised their faces as Max and Saidi joined them, trying to work out whether or not they'd made a deal.

'OK, let's see this computer shit,' Saidi said. 'Who the fuck looks at the Internet, anyway? One of the pilots of my helicopter, he finds dirty pictures in there someplace. Gurt told me that.'

'If you'd like to sit down, Mr Saidi,' said Chip, 'we've prepared a twenty-minute presentation that covers everything. I think you'll be quite impressed by the high AB demographic.'

Saidi snorted and Max was on. One way and another, he didn't feel the audience was exactly rooting for him.

He embarked on the presentation as rehearsed, controlling it from his laptop and watching the images appear simultaneously on the two large monitors. Chip's graphics looked pretty irresistible in colour, and there were sections incorporating audio, too. When he brushed his mouse against a hot icon representing *StreetSmart*, there was a roll of drums and a fanfare of trumpets. When he reached the sequence about cutting-edge technology, the theme music from Zanneck's *2001: A Space Odyssey* blasted out.

Saidi, he was relieved to see, seemed increasingly absorbed. When the space music started up, he turned to Marcus and said, 'Fucking funny joke.'

Marcus, seeing which way the wind was blowing, replied, 'You were absolutely right to investigate this new media, Freddie. Five years from now, we'll be doing everything on screen. Shopping, brushing our—'

'Shut it,' said Saidi. 'And listen.'

Max forged on, proselytising the paperless magazine, advances in download times and the prospects for real-time video and push technology. The great thing about presenting via a laptop was that you didn't need to keep turning round to look at the big screens, which enabled you to maintain eye contact with your audience.

'Now,' Max said, 'I would like to show you some of the work SII has undertaken in partnership with third parties, including several blue-chip corporations with capitalisations of ten billion dollars upwards.' Chip had inserted that last line, hoping that it might appeal to Saidi's vanity.

'Let me start with the travel company ExpediCo ...' he read. 'Headquartered a couple of hundred miles north of here, in White Plains, ExpediCo had a medium-to-large-sized travel business based predominantly within New York State itself. The challenge for the CEO over there, Don Pepper, was how to grow the business right across the States, without the accompanying cost implication of several hundred retail sites.

'ExpediCo handed the problem to StreetSmart Interactive, with the brief, "Show us what you can do to meet this challenge electronically." After eight months of research and innovation, which included developing a bespoke software package to meet exactly our client's needs, we came up with ExpediCo Online, the fastest and most comprehensive travel database and booking system in the world. It is now being accessed by upwards of three million eyeballs a day, and more than four per cent of all adult Americans have switched to ExpediCo for their travel requirements, both business travel and personal.'

'Not me though,' said Saidi. 'These fucking geniuses don't make my travel bookings.'

'Hardly, Freddie,' chortled Marcus. 'You are in the enviable position of speaking directly to your own captains, both on the yacht and the—'

'I said, "Shut it",' said Saidi. 'So shut it.'

Max moved his mouse on to the toolbar, and brought down the bookmarked sites of clients. The column of hotlinks was all in place: ExpediCo, Akron-KickBack and the Mitsufushi motor corporation.

'We are now going live onto the Internet,' he said, 'exactly like any normal user.' He double clicked on ExpediCo, and gave the machine a couple of seconds to make the connection.

A moment later there was a sharp intake of breath from the audience, and he saw Marcus Brooke's eyes bulge in amazement.

'What you are looking at,' Max went on, 'is a geo-political map of the world. Click on any section, and your chosen zone enlarges to fill the screen . . .'

'Who the fuck is this?' Saidi was exclaiming. 'That's one big pussy she's got there.'

Max noticed Chip had gone deathly white, and was staring up at the screen with his mouth open. He spun round and the screen was filled by a naked woman, legs apart, sitting on a bamboo seat.

He couldn't believe it. Somehow they'd accessed a porn site.

He fumbled about for the mouse, but it seemed to have slipped his control. As he moved it up to the toolbar, it skeetered off in the opposite direction, towards the turn-page arrow.

What the hell was going on? Nothing like this had happened during Barry Higgs's demonstration. The laptop was bewitched.

In his panic, he scrabbled for the shutdown button, but the keyboard had developed a mind of its own.

The mouse had reached the turn-page arrow now, and was propelling them forwards to the next screen.

'Now, this girl I *like*,' said Saidi. His eyes were glued to the screen, where a rough-looking redhead was tied by her wrists to a bed. 'Big, big tits. Where she live, Marcus, that girl? Bet she like to party.'

'I'm sure we can find her for you, Freddie,' said Marcus quickly. 'I'll make some enquiries afterwards.'

Max was pressing all the keys now at random, and hitting the return carriage, praying that something would unlock the laptop. Then, as suddenly as he'd lost control, he found that he'd regained it. The mouse moved wherever he wanted it to. He moved it to the left, and it went left. He shifted it over to the right, on the keypad, and the finger on the screen followed.

He was sweating inside his shirt. Objectively, he'd have rated their chances of still winning the contract at less than zero, but, as the cliché goes, it ain't over till it's over, and the clients hadn't actually walked out. Maybe he could still salvage something if he moved fast.

'Well, I don't know what happened there,' he said. 'Some gremlin in the works. I don't need to tell you that that *wasn't* ExpediCo we were looking at there. Maybe it's best if we forget that site for now, and take a look at the work we've been doing for Akron-KickBack.'

He began his background briefing on the Atlanta-based sportswear company, and once again placed the mouse on the bookmarked hotlink. 'The client brief called for something hip, leading edge and genuinely interactive. This was our solution.'

This time he turned to watch the big monitor as the connection was made, so he saw the masked face of the dominatrix at the same moment as everyone else.

Jesus Christ, now they were into something *really* heavy. The site must have had audio facility, because groans and moans started to echo from inside the PC.

He shook the mouse and hit the return button, but for the second time the electrics had stalled or shut down, and the finger icon was accelerating across the screen under its own power.

He could scarcely bear to look up from the conference table at the others. When he did, he saw Marcus's face formed into an expression of prurient outrage, and Saidi slavering over the old boot in leather.

There was just one way to describe the presentation: a complete wipe-out. The only thing left to do was to thank everyone for coming along and apologise for wasting their time.

Marcus stood up and said, 'Not perhaps anyone's finest hour, but at least you had an opportunity to meet Freddie, and get to know him a little.'

Saidi said, 'OK, before we go, we finish that conversation.' He headed back into Max's office, and Max tagged along behind. 'Now,' he said. 'No more screwing about. We level with each other, OK?'

Max said nothing.

'I pay you one hundred million dollars for the company. Top fucking dollar. Everyone will say, "Freddie, you gone crazy or something? Why you give all that money for that magazine?"'

Max didn't even bother trying to interrupt, just sat there dumbly, staring back at him.

'What's the big problem?' Saidi said. 'Saskia was about to sell me the magazine when she got murdered. She said, "Freddie, OK, I'll sell to you, I give you my word."'

'She did?'

'We shake hands on it, we have a drink. You ask Marcus. You ask him, if you don't believe me.'

'And when was this "deal" made?' Max asked, his voice heavy with sarcasm. 'Was this before or after you asked my sister to marry you?'

Saidi's eyes narrowed, as he struggled to control his temper. 'We talk for one month, maybe six weeks. She come to my office, we have lunch, dinner. I fucking send my driver over to collect her from her place, you can ask him. We talk, we talk some more, we make deal.'

'At what price?'

'Ninety million dollars, no bullshit.'

'If this deal was really agreed, why aren't there any papers? There'd have been a contract, surely? And what's that expression, a "heads of agreement"?'

'I told you,' said Saidi, 'Saskia was a friend. We trusted each other. When she sells me her business, I don't say, "Sign this piece of paper in case you get yourself strangled."'

'OK,' Max said. 'Even assuming I believe you – which I don't, by the way – then why wasn't it made public? Why didn't anyone know about it?'

'Because Saskia wasn't ready. She needed more time. She say to me, "Freddie, don't push me, OK. We've shaken on it." That's what she said at our last meeting, in New York, on the day of that big dinner.'

'You mean at the Waldorf? You saw Saskia on her last day, here in the city?'

'At the East River. She came over at lunchtime for a meeting in my suite. I want to make a big announcement about our deal. She'd agreed to stay on as editor-in-chief for five years. For ever, if she like. I say to her, "You look fucking attractive in that red dress. Why you not marry me? What's the fucking problem? Cody like me, OK. If you want, I put a million dollars in his name in Switzerland."'

'And when she left, you felt you had a verbal deal to buy *StreetSmart*?'

'No question. So you will honour your sister's last wishes? We have agreed the price at one hundred million dollars?'

As he watched Freddie Saidi sitting across the office, so many different emotions went through Max's head, he hardly knew how to respond. Saidi's alleged friendship with Saskia, and these repeated references to marriage, contradicted everything he'd previously heard. Gina David had said Saskia couldn't stand him.

Could she really have considered selling him *StreetSmart*? As a business proposition, it wasn't such a crazy idea, considering how badly the company was doing, especially if he'd promised to keep her on as editor-in-chief. Maybe she'd simply been playing him along until the website deal had gone through, and then she'd have gracefully disengaged. Saskia was capable of duplicity in a good cause, he was convinced of that.

It was too convenient, the whole concept of the deal. If true, he was sure Saskia would have mentioned it to somebody – Marie-Louise or Gina or Chip. Or Philip Landau. Surely her first action, faced with a serious takeover offer, would have been to involve her lawyer. And yet Philip knew nothing about it. Whichever way you looked at it, the thing stank.

So, in the end, Max just replied, 'Listen, I've said no four times now. It isn't a bargaining position: it's final. I'm sorry, but I'm not about to change my mind.'

'What about Saskia's promise?' said Saidi. There was no longer any pretence at charm. 'You are breaking her fucking death wish.'

'The fact is, nobody knows about any deal except you, and Marcus Brooke who works for you.'

Now Saidi was on his feet, his face contorted with fury. 'OK,' he said. 'So you want to insult me. Well, go fuck yourself. Other people have tried that before, and have regretted it.'

With that, to Max's considerable relief, he left the office.

[34]

As soon as he was certain that Saidi was off the premises, Max rang Kitty.

'Hi, Max,' she said. 'I'm in the middle of faxing you that stuff about Bercuse. It should start coming through any time.'

'Can you talk?'

'Yes, everyone's out at meetings. I got into the system and printed it off. There are about twelve pages.'

'Well, you're not going to believe this. Freddie Saidi's just left. The presentation couldn't have gone worse, by the way. But afterwards he said the most extraordinary thing. He said Saskia had agreed to sell him *StreetSmart*, just before she was murdered. They'd made a deal.'

'That can't be true. I don't believe it.'

'Nor me, but Saidi was adamant. He insists they'd agreed a price – ninety million dollars – and Saskia was going to stay on as editor-in-chief.'

'I bet he's invented it, to make you feel you have to sell to him.'

'That's what I reckon, too. Otherwise he'd have mentioned it straight away, instead of making offers. When he arrived, he first offered fifty million, then kept raising the price. Whenever I said no, he added another ten million.'

'And suddenly he remembered the secret deal?'

'Only when he realised money wasn't going to do the trick.'

'Saskia despised him.'

'That was another strange thing. He told me he'd asked her to marry him on the day she died.'

'You mean Saidi was in New York too?'

'He claims they had lunch together at the East River, on the day of the gala. In his suite. We could probably check that out. Jean would know, wouldn't she?'

Then Kitty, suddenly excited, said, 'Max, I've just thought of something. If Saidi was actually in Manhattan that night, it makes it far more likely he had Saskia murdered. He was right there, and the motive's pretty obvious too.'

'That's the bit I don't get. If he'd struck a deal for *StreetSmart*, and wanted Saskia to edit it, he wouldn't want her dead, would he? Quite the opposite. What had he got to gain?'

'Don't you see?' said Kitty. 'He had her murdered precisely because she *wouldn't* sell. I bet you anything there never was a deal. I bet he'd made endless offers, just like he did to you, but she'd turned him down. Maybe she did have lunch with him that day, but it was to *reject* the offer. And he was so furious, he had her bumped off.'

'There's something else, too,' said Max. 'You remember you told me Saskia had spotted someone that night at the gala, someone across the room. Could it have been Saidi?'

'I didn't see him, but it could have been, there were about two thousand people. It's exactly the kind of thing he'd do, isn't it, turn up if he knew Saskia was at it?'

'To make a final offer.'

'Or spook her out. She seemed quite scared of whoever it was. She definitely wanted to avoid him.'

'Is there any way we can find out whether he *was* there?'

'If I ring the organisers, I bet I can get a complete guest list. I'll say we're writing about it for *StreetSmart*.'

'Try and get it today. If it turns out Saidi was at the Waldorf, that's important. He might have had her followed back to her apartment.'

The twelve-page fax from Kitty about Bercuse had disgorged from the machine, along with a second fax from London. This was from Tim, the *StreetSmart* features assistant who was researching data protection.

To: Max Thompson
From: Tim Anscombe, Features Dept.
Subject: Freddie Saidi

I've managed to obtain some information on Freddie Saidi. As I told you, none of the auction houses would co-operate, but I know someone who works in one of them and has access.

I promised we wouldn't drop her in it, or publish anything that could only have come from their database, otherwise she'll get the sack.

I am faxing through what she gave me. It is mostly biographical and quite informative.

There were six sheets, evidently downloaded direct from the auction house database, stamped Confidential: Limited Distribution Only.

The first section was devoted to Saidi's tax advisers and banking details. Auction houses routinely record the names of banks used to transmit funds to settle client purchases, and also the accounts into which proceeds are directed following any sale. Max could see that Saidi utilised a variety of overseas and offshore banks, including LGT in Liechtenstein; the London branch of the Beirut Riyad Bank SAL in Curzon Street; National Republic Bank in Geneva; the Paris branch of the Moscow Evro Bank on the Boulevard Haussman, and the Banco Rio de la Plata SA, which sounded Central or South American.

Immediately after the banking details came an inventory of all Freddie Saidi's purchases at auction over the past two years.

Reading the list, Max could see that Saidi's taste ran to heavily ornate antique furniture and nineteenth-century marble and bronze statues. In October 1996, he had bought in London for £139,000 a Regency library table after a design by Thomas Hope, with Eygptian winged ornaments on the end supports. The following month, at a sale in New York, he had successfully bid for an 1872 bronze by Emile Guillemin of an oriental maiden carrying a pitcher of water on her head. It had been inset with lapis lazuli, jade and other coloured hardstones and cost Saidi $260,000 plus buyer's premium.

There was a note from the credit-control department alerting directors that Saidi was a habitual late payer, with a history of cancelling cheques after issue. Payment should in all circumstances be cleared before purchases left the warehouse.

There were several anonymous file notes about his status as a boardroom lunch guest, and a directive that 'female representatives should not be permitted to visit him unchaperoned in Rutland Gate, Regent Village or on board his yacht, in view of the unfortunate episode involving the expert from Applied Arts'.

Finally, there were three sheets of biographical information, part factual, part anecdotal. It was evident that whenever auction house personnel had contact with Saidi, they logged all reports into the database, so the file had a rambling, repetitive quality.

Compared with the newspaper hagiographies Max had previously read, however, it was fascinating.

Saidi had been born in the Bekaa Valley in 1938, three years before the British and Free French invaded Lebanon and captured Beirut from Vichy forces. His father, Khalil Saidi, had been a successful trader with a large business based around the port, and the family had lived in conspicuous comfort. Khalil had formed an important collection of oriental carpets and rugs, which he had been forced to sell during the 1958 civil war, some of which Freddie Saidi had subsequently bought back at auction.

In the 'eighties, Freddie had repurchased several Heriz rugs and an exceptional Salor Engsi carpet from Turkestan, provenance Khalil Saidi.

Born and raised a Muslim, Freddie had by the 'seventies inexplicably converted to Christianity. This had not constrained him, after the PLO was driven out of Jordan and set up headquarters in Beirut, from selling them weapons for the 1975 civil war against the Christian Phalangistes.

Contemporaneously, Saidi was believed to have provided Maronite Christians with the hardware used to massacre Palestinian civilians at Karantina and Tel el-Za'atar.

By the time the Israeli army invaded Southern Lebanon in 1978, opening the way for the United Nations peacekeeping force, Freddie Saidi had become the biggest and most indiscriminate arms dealer in the region. An auction house representative who'd visited him at his villa at Baalbek had recorded the local gossip: Saidi had sold the Syrian army the ammunition with which to shell East Beirut and played middleman to the Israeli defence minister Ariel Sharon. He was implicated in the murder of Lebanese president-elect Bashir Gemayel, and had masterminded the plan to send Phalangiste militias into the Palestinian refugee camp at Sabra, with hundreds massacred. When Ken Craig and Mick Paarl had arrived in Beirut in 1983, Saidi was already the principal supplier of weapons to every faction in the city.

Then, in the mid-'eighties, Saidi abruptly quit Lebanon. The villa in Baalbek was closed up, and he had embarked on a new respectable existence in the West. He married a Lebanese Muslim named Halma, who had been educated partly in the United States, and they had a son, Mitch. The Saidis had begun to appear in the newspapers and join in the bidding at charity auctions. In 1993, they quietly separated. Around this time, Saidi hired Marcus Brooke to enhance his public image.

In the box marked 'Client Wealth Rating', the auction house had awarded Saidi a triple A. Max could understand why. In the period since leaving Beirut, he had acquired four prestige businesses at approximately two-year intervals, always for cash. The most recent being Fournels et Fils, bought two years earlier.

Having read the fax through twice, Max sat in Saskia's leather desk chair and gazed out of the window down on to the Hudson River, and the gantries and rooftops of Jersey City and Hoboken beyond. He watched a tugboat cutting a path in the direction of Battery Park, pursued by a flock of tofu-coloured seagulls.

He knew now that Freddie Saidi was perfectly capable of having Saskia murdered. Next to everything that had gone on in Beirut, he wouldn't think twice. He must have killed dozens, probably hundreds of people already, directly or indirectly. He certainly didn't have a moral problem with murder.

Kitty's version of events sounded plausible, too. Saidi wasn't accustomed to being turned down, and Max could believe that, sufficiently enraged about *StreetSmart*, he would simply have had Saskia taken out. What was it Ken had said about him? 'Nothing much stands in his way.' Saskia had stood in his way, and next thing she was dead.

Max had stood in his way too. He'd better watch out.

Chip sat on the violet sofa with his head in his hands.

'Max, I don't know what to say to you. I don't know what the hell happened back there.'

'Maybe the laptop had a loose wire. Or the Internet connection was faulty. Whatever it was, it couldn't have happened at a worse time.'

'I don't get it, that's all,' said Chip. 'I just tested the system and it's working perfectly. I ran through the presentation with no glitches – not one.'

'You saw what happened. The keyboard wouldn't respond. It seized up.'

'I've never known that happen before. I don't understand how it's even technically possible. The Web runs slow sometimes, sure, and it goes down occasionally, but it doesn't misdirect requests from one site to another.'

'I'd bookmarked ExpediCo and Akron-KickBack, and it worked perfectly at the run-through, so we know the URLs were correct. But in front of Saidi it went berserk. We kept hitting those damned porn sites.'

'You know what I think?' said Chip. 'This may sound paranoid, but I'll tell you anyway. I reckon someone sabotaged the presentation.'

'How could they do that?'

'Search me, but that's what I reckon. There's no other explanation.'

Max stared at the blank monitors across the room. 'Chip, we need to figure this out. Is it technically feasible to sabotage the Internet? And if so, who has access to this room? Do the whole staff use it or is it restricted, and was anyone seen tampering with the kit? And, finally, who stands to gain from screwing up the presentation?'

'I'll have to talk to our technical director in Hartford before giving definitive answers,' said Chip, 'but I can tell you who stands to gain by the presentation cratering. Any number of Web design houses, if the business goes elsewhere. The market is pretty crowded. Several companies would be in the running.'

'Any that stand out as the obvious second choice?'

'Not really. In any case, I'm not aware anyone even knew about the presentation. It wasn't an open pitch, it hasn't been mentioned in the trades.'

Max thought for a moment. 'Then it sounds like the motive was simply to screw us up.'

An idea crossed his mind: had Saidi somehow arranged it himself? And if so, why?

'OK,' said Max, 'who uses this room? Can anyone wander in and out?'

'Pretty much. When Saskia was in town, she used it as an extension to her office. The rest of the time it's used by everyone. The advertising department block it out for client presentations, and editorial for meetings. When I'm in New York, I dump my stuff in here and take it over.'

'So anyone could have come in and tampered with the modem?'

'If that's what happened. It wouldn't have to be the modem. It could have been the laptop.'

'But I've had that with me,' said Max. 'It hasn't left my sight, except when I was asleep of course.'

'That's why I need to ask the technicians. I don't know what's technically possible. The laptop could have been sabotaged several days ago.'

'The only person, apart from me, who's been near it is one of our IT department in London, Barry Higgs, but it wouldn't be him. If you saw him, you'd agree.'

Even as he said it, though, Max thought, Could Barry conceivably be involved? He knew what he was doing technically, and he'd have had access to the PCs for Bercuse information too. It was possible. And Barry had a similar physical build to the intruder that night. Had the intruder been Barry Higgs?

'Do this, will you, Chip? Investigate every option. We've got to discover what happened. It looks like someone's out to fuck us up.'

'I'll have something for you by this evening, latest. Will you be here, or shall I call you at the hotel?'

'Best try both. I've got to go, I'm running late. I've an appointment in fifty minutes in Fort Washington Park.'

'*Fort Washington Park?* That's way up beyond Harlem, near George Washington Bridge.'

'I know. Strange as it may sound, I'm visiting Saskia's maid. I owe her for mops and soap flakes.'

[35]

The yellow cab headed north through Midtown, past Grand Central Station and the Helmsley Building and up Madison Avenue. Through the window, Max found himself noticing fashion stores which, a fortnight earlier, would have meant nothing to him at all. Sonia Rykiel, Armani, Valentino, Prada, Sensi, TSE Cashmere, Homeboy, Barneys, The Limited, Moschino ... this stretch of the journey was the plateglass and bricks-and-mortar manifestation of the entire advertising content of *StreetSmart*.

At the top end of Central Park, the cab turned west on to Broadway, and the neighbourhood no longer contained a solitary shop or business liable to advertise in Max's magazine. Instead, there were wine and liquor stores with boarded-up shopfronts, nail salons and hairdressing parlours with wild afro wigs displayed on planks in their windows, hardware stores and Rodriguez mini-market delis. Increasingly, the shop signs were in Spanish rather than English.

By the time they crossed West 170th Street, Max doubted that anyone within a radius of three miles had heard of *StreetSmart*, still less bought a copy.

The cab drew up outside a brick apartment building in the projects backing on to Henry Hudson Parkway. Three black youths in Homeboy caps and Hilfiger vests were cooling their heels on the sidewalk, while two Hispanics booted a ball about. Max asked the driver to wait, but he preferred to take his $35 and get out.

Carmelita's apartment was on the sixth floor and Max stood in the hallway waiting for the coffin-sized metal elevator to jerk its way down. The stairwell smelt of urine and singed rubber, and leaking out from behind the front doors he could hear the dull rhythm of gangsta rap.

The car reached the sixth floor with a jolt. A dozen front doors led off a stone hallway, and Max searched for 6K.

When he found it, the door was open.

'Carmelita? Carmelita Puentes?' There was no reply. '*Carmelita?* This is Max Thompson.'

He pressed the doorbell and heard it ring inside the apartment. He looked both ways up the hallway. She'd probably called on a neighbour, and would be back before long.

After two or three minutes, he called out quite loudly, '*Carmelita?* You in there? It's Max Thompson.'

He went inside and saw a small kitchen behind the door, with something cooking over low gas. Steam was billowing from under the rim of a pan. Good, thought Max, she hadn't gone far.

At the end of a short passage a door stood open into the living room. The room was neat and tidy with a couch along one wall with lace-covered bolsters and cushions, and a wooden crucifix hanging from a nail. There was a small table with a television, and another table between the windows with a display of framed photographs. Max took a look: four Dominican women, small and middle-aged, on an outing to the zoo, and a picture of Saskia like a filmstar in a sequinned dress. Well, he was in the right place.

In front of the couch stood a low sewing-table, with a *TV Guide* and some pristine copies of *StreetSmart*. Max wondered whether Carmelita enjoyed the magazine more than the landlord of the Drovers pub, his parents' local in Surrey.

He stood by the window, looking down on to the cars on the expressway alongside the river. The Hudson glinted in winter sunlight, and the steel beams and cables of the George Washington Bridge gleamed against the sky.

He was wondering how long he should hang about waiting when he noticed blood on the carpet in the passage. There were three livid streaks of it, like skid marks left by a tyre, leading towards the bedroom.

Max pushed the door open with his foot. The top of a dresser was arranged with bottles of scent, a hairbrush and some small silver boxes. Then he saw Carmelita in a heap by the bed. Her neck was slumped sideways on the carpet in a puddle of blood. He knelt over the body, taking care not to touch anything, and saw that the blood was fresh.

He looked at her face. He could just about recognise her as one of the women in the photograph next door, though she was badly cut and bruised. Her cheeks and the skin around her eyes were swollen, and had gone a dark bluish purple, and the bridge of her nose looked broken. Someone had beaten her viciously before cutting her throat.

Max ran back into the living room, found the telephone and dialled 911. He reported a murder at an address in Fort Washington Park and then sat down to wait for the police. Already a sick-making odour was beginning to circulate in the apartment.

While he waited, Max wondered who the hell could have done this – and why. Carmelita's murder must surely be connected to Saskia's, but he couldn't figure it out. Why had someone needed to kill Carmelita Puentes? Was there something she hadn't told the police that she might now have been prepared to tell Max?

There was a crackle of radios and two cops from the 34th Precinct arrived at the apartment. Max told them how he'd come up to Fort Washington Park by cab, and how he'd found Carmelita dead in the bedroom.

One of the cops, Officer Hanandez, radioed the Metrotex facility at Central Dispatch in Brooklyn and requested paramedics and the crime scenes investigation unit. 'We have a DOA,' Max heard him say. 'Suspected homicide. Female Hispanic, fifty years of age . . .'

A second squad car arrived with a detective and the coroner's assistant, followed by a third. An ID officer set to work coating the surfaces in the bedroom with black dusting powder; a second officer began capturing everything on videotape. Already a crowd of neighbours had formed in the hallway outside the apartment, and a cop was sealing the area with yellow tape, warning: CRIME SCENE – DO NOT CROSS. Max heard someone say, 'These scene-of-crime buzzards. What is it with these people?'

'Whaddaya got?' asked Detective Luis Amaya as he came in.

The coroner's assistant leaned over the body to begin his examination while Amaya interviewed Max.

'You the guy who found her?'

'That's right. I owed Carmelita Puentes some money, or rather my sister did. I was delivering it. When I arrived, the door was open and she was dead.'

'And your sister is where right now?'

'I'm afraid she's dead as well. She was murdered in the city ten days ago.'

Detective Amaya looked at Max suspiciously. A second murder.

He was a dark-skinned Costa Rican with twelve years' service, six as a sector cop, six in the Homicide Bureau. One thing he had learned was an instinct for self-preservation, and what his instinct was telling him now was that this was the sort of case that could turn into a big headache. 'If you could come down to the Precinct house, Mr Thompson. We'll need to file a report, get the paperwork right.'

'Sure.'

'You live here in the city?' he asked, as they got into a squad car. An ambulance, its tailgate open, was backing up to the kerb, and lights were flashing from a half-dozen black and whites.

'I'm in the States on business, staying at a hotel on 52nd and First.'

'That the East River Hotel?' said Detective Amaya. 'That's a pretty fancy establishment.'

The Precinct house at 4295 Broadway reminded Max, from the outside, of a Pizza Hut: low-slung with a timber and concrete frame and a rampway leading to a wraparound car park. Inside, it reminded him of every TV cop show he'd ever watched: a dozen policemen in blue caps, pants, Kevlar vests; a steel barrier, metal benches, a safe like a maildrop with a chute for seized narcotics.

Detective Amaya checked him through the barrier and told him to wait on a bench. A sergeant with a leery Irish face looked him up and down, shrugged, and resumed his conversation with a female black cop. Max heard the cop say, 'I told him, "Wiseguy, you do that one more time and I'll issue you a sixty-one." '

On the wall hung a Stars and Stripes flag, patrol rotas and public notices: 'Police Department, City of New York: NYPD Narcotics Division – Operation Lefrak City'; 'NYPD: Reinforcing a commitment to community relations.' A bronze plaque read, 'In honor of those members of the 34th Precinct who made the ultimate sacrifice for the people of the City of New York.'

Max sat on the bench, unable to get the image of Carmelita's beaten face out of his mind. Whoever had done that to her had made damn sure she was dead.

Who, he kept thinking, could it have been? And what was it that was so important they had to prevent Carmelita from telling him? Had Carmelita Puentes known who'd murdered Saskia?

Who had even known that he was going to Fort Washington Park that afternoon? Chip Miller had known, but Max had only mentioned it as he was leaving Canal Street. Surely Chip couldn't have organised a hitman in that time? Anyway, the idea was preposterous. Chip was a friend of Saskia's. He had identified her body.

The doorman at Saskia's apartment – Jon Kalowski – had known about the visit too. He had given Max Carmelita's telephone number. Was it possible he was implicated in this thing?

Detective Luis Amaya led Max up a flight of stairs to an interview room. The passageway was painted the same muddy-orange colour as the floor. The interview room had no windows, just a table and two grey plastic chairs and an ashtray containing cigarette butts.

'So your sister owed money to Carmelita Puentes?' said Detective Amaya. He made it sound significant, as though the money might have some bearing on the murder.

'When Saskia was killed, she owed Carmelita a month's pay. I rang her last night and said I'd bring it up to her.'

'How well did you know Carmelita Puentes?'

'I'd never met her in my life. She was my sister's maid. She cleaned her apartment on 67th Street. The doorman there might know more, if you ask him.'

'So you've no idea who killed her?'

Max considered the question, and the fact was: he didn't have any idea who'd killed Carmelita Puentes, so he replied, 'None. As I told you, I took a cab from downtown, found the door open, went in, saw the blood on the carpet, then discovered her body in the bedroom.'

After that, Detective Amaya concentrated on compiling a witness statement. 'State your name for the record, please. And your full address.'

Max told him.

'Zip code?'

'The postcode in London is W10. Not sure about the rest.'

Detective Amaya logged it on to the form. 'Age?'

'Thirty-six.'

'Profession?'

'Photojournalist. No, make that magazine editor. Or magazine executive. I think that's how you'd describe me. Excuse me, it's a new job, I'm still getting used to it.'

Somehow, it contrived to take two hours to get his statement down. He described the cab ride across town, and the boys on the sidewalk outside the building on Henry Hudson Parkway, and how he had been surprised to find the door open. He described his progress around the small apartment, room by room, and everything he had touched. More than once, Detective Amaya said, 'So, you're saying you never met with this lady before, not on any previous visits to the city?'

Afterwards, Max was taken to another room with a white computer with a sheet of glass on top. They told him to press his hands flat on the glass, and there was a flash of white light like a photocopy machine as they took his prints.

'Technology,' said Detective Amaya. 'Beats inking your thumbs. That's what they say anyhow. OK, Mr Thompson, that's everything finished for now. We have your details. Don't leave the city for any reason, or switch hotels without informing us.'

Max found a minicab outside the Precinct house and was heading back downtown when it hit him. Of course that was how they'd known! A third person had known he had an appointment with Carmelita Puentes: *Freddie Saidi.*

He had rung Carmelita from the East River. The telephone could have been bugged, probably was in fact. True, he hadn't found anything in the handset, but these things could be done at the switchboard, couldn't they?

Then something else occurred to him. The fruit! The basket of fruit Marcus Brooke had had delivered, and the arrangement of flowers. The waiter had placed them on the table in the sitting room, right by the telephone. They could have been bugged. Why hadn't he thought of that? One way or another, Saidi must have listened in on his conversation with Carmelita, heard Max agree to meet her at two o'clock the next day, and arranged to have her killed.

[36]

Max arrived back at the hotel to find a red light flashing on the telephone panel by his bed: Message Waiting. There was a voice mail from Kitty, saying she'd got hold of the guest list from the Waldorf benefit and could he ring her as soon as possible. There was also a message from Chip Miller: 'I've spoken with the team in Hartford and we think we've figured out what happened this morning. It kind of confirms what we discussed. Can you call me at *StreetSmart*.'

Max felt weak and realised that it was almost six o'clock and he'd had nothing to eat all day. In the minibar concealed inside a cabinet like a sarcophagus, he found a bottle of Tuborg, a Toblerone and a jar of jelly beans. He lay down on the yellow silk sofa with his eyes closed, sipping the German beer from a toothglass and delving with his fist in the jar.

The image of Carmelita Puentes's smashed face wouldn't leave his mind. Since his visit to Detective Przemysi, he found it easier to picture Saskia's murdered body too; the abrasions on her neck and, still wearing the red cocktail dress, lying on her back on the bed. If Freddie Saidi had killed her, either he or one of his goons must have slipped past the doorman, or found some back way into the apartment through a service entrance. Or maybe it wasn't Saidi. Maybe Przemysi was right, and Saskia had been strangled by some crazy with a kink. But then why had Carmelita been killed too?

He reached for the telephone to ring Kitty but stopped himself. He didn't want this conversation being listened in on.

Instead, he took the elevator down to the lobby and found a bank of payphones behind reception. There were five phones, well spaced from each other, with acoustic hoods. In one direction he could see the cashier's desk and in the other a news kiosk selling newspapers, confectionery and magazines. The new *StreetSmart* with Madonna and Igor on the cover was prominently displayed.

'Kitty?'

'Hi, Max. I was hoping it was you.'

'So you've got the guest list. Well, was he there?'

'No question.' Kitty sounded excited. 'He took a table. Freddie Saidi and eleven guests, I've got their names.'

'Anyone interesting?'

'His wife. Marcus Brooke. Several people with Arab names I've never heard of. The general manager of Fournels et Fils in New York. And a couple of bodyguards, it sounds like.'

'So Saidi and Brooke were both at the Waldorf that night. That really is helpful, Kitty. No wonder Saskia was annoyed when she saw him, if they'd had a big bust-up.'

However, even as he said it, Max remembered the autopsy detail about the semen. Was it possible that Saskia had had sex with Freddie Saidi on the afternoon before the benefit? But why would she have done that, if she'd just rejected his offer to buy *StreetSmart*? Why go and fuck him?

'Shall I fax you the guest list?' asked Kitty. 'It's an incredible list, we should seriously consider publishing the whole thing as an historical document. It was so starry, I hadn't even realised all those people were there. I'm reading names at random now: Michael Eisner from Disney, Bruce Willis and Demi Moore, Goldie Hawn, Ron Perelman, Rupert Murdoch, Étienne Bercuse ... what do you reckon?'

'I'm standing here thinking how much I'd pay not to have been there myself. But sure, fax it through. I'd like to take a look, particularly at Saidi's table.'

He told Kitty about the disastrous visit to Carmelita Puentes in Fort Washington Park. 'Her body was still *warm*, Kitty. She must have been alive half an hour before. I'm telling you, Saidi knew I was going up there, and precisely what time – he must have listened in on my call.'

'Explain something to me, Max. Why would he need to have her killed?'

'I've been thinking about that. She must have known something about the killer. I don't know, maybe she was trying to blackmail

Saidi. Whatever it was, he had to get her out of the way before my visit.'

'Then for God's sake tell the police about him, if that's what you believe. Just tell them.'

'I *can't*. Seriously, what would I tell them? That Freddie Saidi was at the same fundraiser as Saskia, so he must have trailed her home and murdered her? Well, so were two thousand other people at the Waldorf that night.'

'I still think you're taking an unnecessary risk, staying at the East River. Saidi murdered Saskia. He probably murdered Carmelita. And you've only gone and checked yourself into a suite in his own hotel, surrounded by his employees, who are listening to everything you say and are probably having you followed around the city too. I mean it, Max, it's *unsafe*.'

'One more day, two at most, then I'll be home. I can't switch hotel now. I've told the police I'm here. They may need to get hold of me.'

'You're off your head.'

'I promise you, Kitty, I'll watch out. I won't use the phones in the room for anything important. I'll open the door on the chain. They're not going to bump me off in a five-star hotel: the publicity would be terrible.'

'Just be careful, OK? This isn't meant to sound sickly, Max, but I need you back in one piece.'

'We reckon we've cracked it,' said Chip. 'It's kind of hard to believe.'

Max was making his second telephone call from the lobby payphones. He had waited several minutes after his conversation with Kitty, because a businessman with a crocodile briefcase had shown up at the next booth, and seemed to be trying to listen in. The man had moved away now. Max could see him saying something to the cashier.

'Go on,' said Max.

'Have you ever heard of RAS – remote access software?'

'No.'

'Neither had I, but it's probably what they used. It's a specialist piece of kit that can be installed in a computer and also on the target computer. Days or weeks in advance, if need be. Anyway, it sits there undetected, nobody knows anything about it, until the time of the presentation. Then the saboteur, whoever it was, logs on to the target machine and takes control.'

'You mean they hijacked our presentation?'

'They'd have been able to see the target screen on their own computer, and everything that was happening.'

'And then violated it.'

'Apparently it's quite straightforward, once you've installed the RAS. It stalls the host laptop and the interloper takes over. It's like dual controls on an aeroplane, when either pilot can steer.'

'So when I clicked on ExpediCo and Akron-KickBack, the mystery hacker diverted us to completely different URLs.'

'He'd have entered the Internet addresses for porn sites. Simple as that. Probably set them up in advance and bookmarked them.'

'And remote access software gives you control of the mouse too?'

'Everything. Originally, it was developed for two people sharing one PC in an office. It enables one of them to use a laptop but still download data on to the parent PC. Nobody foresaw the potential for long-range manipulation.'

The businessman with the crocodile briefcase had returned to the booth next to Max. He was turned to face the opposite direction, but was neither dialling nor speaking into the phone, and Max felt sure he was being eavesdropped on. He cupped the mouthpiece in his palm and talked in a hushed voice.

'But Chip, how far away would the pirate laptop have to be geographically? I mean, would it have to have been in the next room, or across the street, or could it be anywhere?'

'Anywhere, theoretically. The other side of the country, it shouldn't matter. But chances are the hacker was somewhere in the city, within a radius of a few blocks.'

'And still no clues to who it was?'

'None. Someone who knew about the presentation and wanted it to crater.'

'Saidi himself?'

'Sure, but *why*? What's in it for him? If he'd wanted to pull the plug on the websites, he wouldn't need to go to those lengths.'

'Well, if it wasn't Freddie Saidi, then who?'

Max had replaced the handset and was walking to the elevators when he noticed the man with the briefcase leave the bank of phones, and walk back towards the cashier.

* * *

As Max unlocked the door to his suite, the telephone was ringing.

'*Are you watching?*' Anka Kaplan sounded hysterical.

'Watching what?'

'Channel Seven. You're not going to believe what you're seeing.'

Max reached for the remote.

The screen filled with the face of a young man in a blue serge suit, white shirt and striped tie. His blond hair was cut short and neat, and he was standing outside a shopping mall speaking to camera.

'What we are saying to Americans all across the country is that you don't have to allow this filth into your communities. You can say, "No, I am tired of cursing the darkness, I am tired of my children being exposed to pornography, I am ready to light a candle for decency and traditional family values." '

'And your message to members of your federation is what?' A female interviewer with big hair was pressing him for a wrap-up soundbite.

'To boycott the magazine, and boycott all neighbourhood convenience stores that keep it on their shelves.'

'Thank you, Bud Casey of the American Federation for Decency, commenting there on the latest issue of *StreetSmart* magazine, where pictures described as "gratuitously violent and pornographic" have angered federation members.'

A flash of the offending photograph – the dead body in Grozny market – came on to the screen, plus an inset of the front cover with Madonna and Igor Sergov.

Max stood frozen in front of the television as he watched the camera linger on the corpse. He felt the muscles contract in his stomach, like cramps, and his palms were damp with tension.

'That was Ellen Shenk there, reporting from Ruston, Louisiana … And now, joining us on ABC *World News Tonight* from Bay Springs, Mississippi, headquarters of the American Federation for Decency, we have the Reverend Jesse Egan, President of the Federation. Jesse, you were a minister of the United Baptist Church before devoting yourself fulltime to leading the campaign against violence and pornography in the media. What is it about these particular photographs that you find so shocking?'

A bellicose pastor with a shock of ivory hair like an Old Testament prophet sat four-square in the studio. 'Well,' he replied, 'as a father myself of eight children and with twenty-two fine young grand-children, it is a question of fundamental standards of decency. You have to ask yourself, "What kind of society do I want for my family?" A society in which our children and grandchildren are daily subjected to filth, profanity and indecency over the airwaves, on television, via computers and through the media? Or a society founded on the traditional Judaeo-Christian values of decency?'

'If I might just interrupt you there, Jesse,' said the anchorman, 'let's get into some specifics here. The photographs in *StreetSmart*. You find them personally offensive?'

'Let me answer that with a question, Peter. Would you like *your* grandchildren to be exposed to them? Naked, dead bodies, porno-graphic in their explicitness? This magazine is being sold, with no warning at all, by supermarkets and convenience stores across America. Any unwitting parent could pick it up. A child of five, six years old could open the magazine . . . Is this what we really want for the next generation of Americans?'

'And exactly how harmful do you believe photographs like those in *StreetSmart* can be?'

'Let me share some statistics, Peter. A recent study by FBI researchers into thirty-six serial killers showed that twenty-nine of them were attracted to pornography and incorporated it into their sexual activity. That's twenty-nine out of thirty-six. And here's another one that's going to shock you. There are more outlets for hard-core pornography in this country – an estimated fifteen to twenty thousand – than there are McDonald's restaurants. That is a fact. And this in a society in which a woman is raped once every seven minutes.'

'A sobering thought,' replied Peter Jennings. 'But you aren't categorising *StreetSmart* as a pornographic publication, are you, Jesse?'

'Any publication that chooses to bring pictures like those into the public domain is pornographic. Which is why we are saying to our 780,000 members, "Boycott the magazine, picket the retailers that display it. Take affirmative action." It is our belief at the AFD that the entertainment industry and the media have played a major role in the decline of those values on which our country was founded. Only by fighting back – by saying publicly, "Enough, already" – can we make those companies accountable.'

'Finally, Jesse, how confident are you of having the issue pulled from shelves?'

'With the help of the Lord, and his principles of truth, righteousness and love, we will surely succeed. Our association is already mobilised, coast to coast, to cast this magazine back into the outer darkness where it belongs.'

[37]

'Did you see it?' said Anka, who had rung back the moment the segment ended.

'I'm sitting here in shock. Who the hell are those people anyway?'

'The AFD? They're a Bible-belt pressure group who go round censoring the media, or trying to. They're getting to be quite powerful.'

'Should we be worried?'

'Oh yes, the AFD is dangerous. If they're campaigning to get *StreetSmart* pulled, it's bad news for us.'

'But could they? The photographs in the issue aren't breaking any law, are they?'

'That's not the point. I'm telling you, these people are obsessed, and they've got this whole network of Baptist fundamentalists who carry out their orders. If they're told to picket convenience stores, then most probably they will.'

'How will the stores react?'

'Officially, they won't give in to them. If you speak with any of the VPs, they'll offer their full support. But unofficially, the managers of the individual outlets will take the issue off sale. They'll put it out the back. Wouldn't you, if you had an angry group of religious rednecks stood in your parking lot, holding placards and accusing your store of being sacrilegious? Not good for business.'

'Has this happened before?'

'Oh yes, it's getting to be quite a feature here. The AFD may still be a minority, but they're effective. Remember those Calvin Klein advertisements, the sexy ones? The federation played a big part in getting them withdrawn. Same thing with Madonna's world tour after that ad with the crucifix. Pepsi were going to be the main sponsors until the AFD piled on the pressure, and in the end they pulled out.'

'They really are that powerful?'

'They're tenacious. They're good at making a lot of noise. They've learned how to work television, and their members are big letter-writers and e-mailers. They bombard the chief executive of whatever organisation they're trying to influence: he might get twenty thousand pieces of mail and his voice-mail is flooded with abusive messages. In the end they usually get their way. People find it easier to give in.'

'But what about our magazines?' asked Max. 'We've just put out two million copies of this issue. If we get them all back, we're bust.'

'It's a serious problem,' said Anka. 'Not here in the city so much or on the West Coast, but everywhere in between. I've been figuring it out, and I reckon seventy to eighty per cent of the copies are at risk.'

'*Jesus*. As many as that?'

''Fraid so. Have you ever heard of the Southland Corporation?'

'No.'

'They're the owners, or rather the franchisers, of 7-Eleven, one of the biggest magazine retailers.'

'I know 7-Eleven.'

'They move a lot of *StreetSmart*s. Anyway, a couple of years back the AFD unleashed this big campaign against them to stop them selling pornography. Television, radio, the media was flooded with AFD spokesmen laying into them, telling decent Americans to boycott them until *Playboy* and *Hustler* were pulled. It wasn't even the heavy stuff. And eventually they won. Southland just didn't need the publicity.'

'So what you're telling me is we don't have a hope. The issue's a write-off?'

'Actually I think it could go either way. Not all their campaigns take off. A year or so ago they tried to influence television advertisers against sponsoring *The A-Team* because of the violence. They set themselves the target of driving away a million dollars in ad revenues per episode. They wrote to all the burger chains. But that one didn't play.'

'So what do we do?'

'Keep our heads down and hope for the best. We'll know in a day or two how seriously the AFD are treating this. The distributors will tell us soon enough if there's a problem.'

'How about our advertisers?' asked Max. 'What are they going to make of it?'

'Too close to call. If the issue gets pulled, and they become aware of it, they could ask for their money back. Which would be a big, big problem on an issue this size.'

Once again, Max felt his stomach contract. It was one disaster after another, his whole world was falling apart. So far as he knew, the British edition was still spread across the tarmac like mail on a giant doormat, and now the American edition was about to be pulled by the Mississippi chapter of the Taliban fundamentalists.

'Is there anything we can do to prepare them? I mean, a lot of people will have seen the evening news. I'm wondering whether I should put out some kind of statement about the photograph, pointing out that it's a legitimate piece of reportage. It really pisses me off to hear that nut say on TV it's pornography. It's not pornography. That picture was in *Newsweek*. If I were a porn photographer, I wouldn't go all the fucking way to Grozny, would I? And I'd get paid better too.'

Max was genuinely angry now. At the same time he felt guilty that it was his own photograph, and his decision to publish it, that lay behind the whole fiasco. Saskia would have known exactly how far she could push it. Max didn't like the idea that her judgement on a matter of taste was more acute than his own.

'One thing we could do, I guess,' said Anka, 'is put ourselves around a bit this evening. There's a cocktail party at Bercuse Plaza from six thru nine. Several of our key advertisers will be there if you want to come along.'

'You think it'll help?'

'It can't do any harm. If they have a problem with the picture, you can tell them what you just told me. It's probably better than issuing a press statement, which might escalate things.'

'I'll meet you there, then,' said Max.

'Twenty minutes, in the lobby. By the display of Étienne Bis briefcases as you come in.'

[38]

The cab that took Max from the East River Hotel to Bercuse Plaza on 57th and Park was driven by a maniac. The driver cursed as he accelerated from lane to lane, weaving between the tail-lights of the Midtown traffic, and he cursed as he jolted to a halt at each intersection. The surname on his ID looked Latvian. Max hung on to the handle of the door and prayed.

Outside, the sidewalks were teeming with people, making their way home from their offices or heading for the bars. The cab stopped at lights by a dingy singles place with happy hour in progress, and Max wondered whether it was one of Saskia's dives. He found the idea of his sister cruising for sex disturbing.

He yawned. Already the day felt like one of the longest of his life. This morning's Internet presentation to Freddie Saidi seemed weeks ago. Since then, he'd discovered the body of Carmelita Puentes, been interrogated by the police, learned that the online presentation had been sabotaged, become the target of a religious action group and found out that his sister was some kind of serial sex addict.

He reached inside his jacket pocket for his cigarettes and found a wad of fax paper. It was the guest list and table plan that Kitty had sent him for the Waldorf Astoria fundraiser on the night Saskia was murdered. Max had ripped it off the fax machine as he left the suite. He held it up close to the window and found that he was just able to read it as the cab swerved through the traffic.

Kitty had been right: it was an impressive list. Even Max could recognise most of the big-hitters. Some of the hundred tables had been reserved in the names of individuals, others in the name of corporations. All the big cosmetics and fashion companies had taken tables that evening. Ovarian cancer must be a fashionable charity, Max thought.

He searched for the *StreetSmart* table and found it close to the

278

dance floor, adjacent to the *Vogue* table and a couple of tables along from the Bercuse table. There was an asterisk next to Saskia's name, identifying her as the table host. The other names in her party didn't mean anything to him, apart from Chip Miller, Kitty Marr and Silas Cheung, the US art director.

He was scanning the long fax for Freddie Saidi's table when he noticed her name: Caryl Fargo. He hadn't realised Caryl had been there too, but there she was in black and white, a guest of L'Oréal.

Max found it creepy that both predators for his magazine had been in New York the night Saskia died. In fact the entire cast of his new existence seemed to have been there: Caryl, Saidi, Marcus Brooke, Étienne Bercuse. It wouldn't have surprised him by now to learn that the Reverend Jesse Egan had been there too, strutting his stuff to the steel band.

The cab drew up in front of Bercuse Plaza, where a stone-and-steel canopy projected on to the sidewalk. While Max stuffed a ten-dollar bill through the driver's window, the passenger door was opened for him by a Bercuse doorman dressed in a black leather trenchcoat like a Gestapo gauleiter. On his head was a tiny headset and microphone of the sort worn by bouncers at pop concerts.

Just inside the entrance three more bouncers wore leathers and headsets, and Max was relieved to spot Anka waiting for him with a spare invitation.

'What do you reckon?' said Anka, rolling her eyes around the triple-height atrium.

Max paused by a glass-and-stainless-steel display case containing men's jockey briefs, and tried to absorb the sheer scale of the place. The atrium was larger and sparer than in any department store he'd seen in his life. It was more like the concourse of a railway station, with soaring limestone walls and a triumphant sweep of stone stairs leading up to the mezzanine. Suspended on tensile-steel wires above their heads was a giant concrete B. The entire floor of the atrium was constructed of steel mesh surrounded by a rim of travertine marble.

What struck Max most about Bercuse Plaza was the almost total absence of things to buy. The place reminded him of a Soviet berioska shop. Half a dozen handbags were displayed singly on glass shelves along the back wall. A rosewood case displaying atomisers of Serène fragrance contained only three bottles. Inside a transparent acrylic column, artfully bathed in the warm glow of incandescent tubes, sat an orphan leather loafer.

'Tell me if I've missed something here,' Max said, 'but there's nothing for sale. This is a shop, isn't it?'

Anka smiled. 'The merchandise is mostly on the upper levels. That's the way Étienne Bercuse likes to play it, I guess, make a big statement in the lobby. You get to chill out a bit before you shop.'

Other guests were streaming across the steel-mesh floor and making for the elevators: women in black suits with red lipstick, and women in red suits with black lipstick. Max wondered how many were wearing Estée Lauder Deep Blackberry and how many had chosen Revlon Raisin Rage. From the look of them, some were wearing both.

'Now, quickly, Anka, brief me. What's this event all about, and who's going to be here?'

'It's to celebrate completion of the new womenswear style playground on the eighth floor. They're calling it Heat-on-Huit. All Étienne Bercuse's edgier designers have been grouped together to allow customers to edit the collections themselves.'

Max looked blank, so Anka continued, 'Like, you might want to create a personalised look combining a Sensi jacket with Homeboy sports pants. Now you can do that all on one level.'

'I thought that's what department stores did anyway. Isn't that what they're for, to provide a good choice all under one roof?'

'That certainly was the case when I was a kid in Indianapolis,' said Anka. 'The stores downtown sold everything from buttons to prom gowns. But for somewhere like Bercuse Plaza to mix the merchandise, that's kind of a seismic innovation. Hence the cocktails.'

Max laughed. He liked Anka's dry wit and the way she was right in amongst it – the whole fashion world – and showed serious commitment to her job, and yet she could still find humour in it too.

He said, 'I didn't know you'd grown up in Indiana. I thought you were a New Yorker through and through.'

'That's what you're supposed to think,' said Anka. 'My first six months in this city I told everyone I was from Indianapolis. I didn't know any different and my career went zilch. One day someone took me aside and told me, "Anka, you want to make it in this business, shut the fuck up about that place." And you know what? They were right.'

The cylindrical glass elevators gave a bird's-eye view of the atrium as the car rose soundlessly upwards like mercury in a thermometer. Max was staring down at the fast-receding lobby, and feeling suddenly queasy, when he spotted a familiar helmet of blonde hair.

'Anka, down there. Isn't that Caryl Fargo coming in?'

'Very likely,' said Anka. 'They asked a lot of the press along tonight. If Caryl's in town, she's sure to show up.'

'She's definitely in New York,' said Max. 'We were on the same flight.'

It occurred to him that it was quite some coincidence that Caryl was in town. Her last trip had coincided with Saskia's murder. This time, she shows up on the eve of Carmelita Puentes's murder. Maybe it was coincidence, maybe it wasn't. Max wasn't sure what he thought about anything any longer.

The elevator doors opened with a soft electronic ping on the eighth floor into another vast expanse of empty space, this time circular like a bullring. Around the circumference were half a dozen pavilions, each architecturally different, housing the various lines in the Bercuse empire. Anka told him that each pavilion had been designed by a celebrity architect to reflect the individual personalities of the designers.

They were greeted by one of the store's public relations affiliates. 'The pavilions are part of our programme of premium brand delineation in the luxury market,' he explained. He wore black jeans and a black T-shirt and had the blank zombie-like expression that Max associated with apocalyptic religious cults.

'Ah,' replied Max, noncommittally.

'Monsieur Bercuse appointed a team of style therapists,' he went on, his eyes virtually popping out of their sockets. 'Their brief was to pinpoint the various strands of the brand DNA, and this information was channelled to the interior designers.'

'Ah,' replied Max. 'Anyway, good luck with it,' he added, backing off as rapidly as possible into the throng.

There couldn't have been fewer than two hundred people in the bullring, and looking round, Max was sure he didn't know a single one. He felt equally sure that they all knew one another intimately. From the way they were kissing and hissing in each other's faces, he guessed they'd been lunching together and working together and copulating and stabbing each other between the shoulder blades for a couple of decades at least. The crowd made him uncomfortable. Where was Anka when he needed her?

A Moroccan-looking youth in a white wool jacket laid his hand on Max's elbow and said, 'I *know you*, don't I?'

'I don't think so.' Max was sure he'd never seen the boy, with his smooth coffee-coloured complexion, in his life before.

'Your face, it looks so *familiar*. Maybe you remind me of somebody, that could be it.'

Max shrugged.

'*I've got it*. I knew it would come to me. *Saskia Thompson!* You look like poor Saskia.'

'Actually, Saskia was my sister.'

'*No!* This is unreal, I've got to pinch myself. You're Saskia's brother, this has made my evening. I *adored* Saskia. I couldn't believe it when I read she'd been strangled.'

'So you knew Saskia?' For a ghastly moment Max wondered whether this could be one of his sister's toyboys.

'Not to *meet*. That could have spoiled it, like meeting Jacqueline Onassis or Björk. But you always felt you knew her anyway, didn't you, through *StreetSmart*?'

'Max,' said Anka, reappearing at his shoulder. 'We need to talk.'

Max followed her gratefully to the perimeter of the party. 'You disappeared. I'd been cornered by Saskia's fanclub.'

'We have a serious problem,' said Anka. 'I did a quick circuit to see who's here, and they all are. They've all heard about the AFD situation and are jumping up and down.'

'Saying what?'

'That we've made a big mistake. They think the photograph is in terrible taste.'

'But they must recognise the news value. Have they actually seen the picture?'

'Probably not, but that never stopped anyone from having an opinion. I'm telling you, the consensus round this event is that we've screwed up bigtime. Everyone's talking about it.'

'What about damage limitation?'

'That's why I've come to find you. We need to work this room fast. There are people here from rival magazines and they're milking it for all it's worth.'

'What bastards.'

'They *are* bastards. I've just overheard someone telling a group that *StreetSmart*'s been totally withdrawn from sale.'

'But that's outrageous. Not a single copy's come off sale. Not yet, anyway.'

'That's why we have to work the room,' said Anka.

They did it systematically, starting at the far end and schmoozing their way back towards the elevators. In the space of an hour, Max explained himself to twenty different marketing directors. Most were polite, though, as Anka had predicted, he could sense the hostility beneath the surface. Had they not been meeting him for the first time, and were it not for the circumstances surrounding Saskia's death, he knew they would have been a good deal more direct.

The people who were rudest were the ones who hadn't seen the issue, only heard about it secondhand or caught the newscast.

A fat man with a shaven head told Max, 'You don't think it would have been appropriate to inform your commercial partners in advance if you're changing the environment of the publication? It's seriously detrimental to my brand to market it in the context of naked stiffs.'

The marketing manager for Tranquilité – the woman who'd breakfasted that morning with Mary-Ellen Gallagher Du Puis – said she'd been 'sickened' by the image of the mutilated corpse and did not expect to pay one cent for her space.

'As a matter of fact,' said Max, 'there weren't any Bercuse advertisements in the issue.'

'I shall still be seeking compensation,' she replied. 'You editorialised our fragrance.'

In the end, Max couldn't tell whether he'd succeeded in defusing anything, but Anka reckoned he'd created some goodwill.

They were making for the exit when Max came face to face with Caryl Fargo. They were jammed together in a tailback for the coat check, with no chance of escape.

Caryl smirked at him, revealing a fleck of bright red lipstick on her tooth. 'Max, you *do* get around,' she said. 'Everywhere I go, people are talking about you.'

Max refused to be drawn

'I mean it, Max. I'm impressed. You even got *StreetSmart* on to national television I hear.' She raised one eyebrow meaningfully. 'You know what they say. All publicity ...'

'Actually, I'd be grateful if you didn't patronise me, Caryl, if you don't mind.'

'Stress beginning to get to you, is it, Max? It can be quite stressful in this business, if you let it get on top of you.'

'Listen,' he replied, his voice rising as adrenalin pumped through his veins, 'I am *not fucking stressed*. Have you got that? *Okay?*'

Caryl handed over the ticket for her coat, smiling thinly as though her analysis had been more than adequately vindicated. She wrapped herself in a knee-length mink, patted her hair and turned to address Anka. 'Let me know when you want to join us at Incorporated, won't you?' she said. 'We haven't got a publication in the States at the moment, but we soon will have. Sometimes it's best to make the switch while you're already in a job. Looks less desperate.' She stepped inside the elevator and the doors closed silently behind her.

'Bitch,' said Anka. 'I wouldn't work for her if she were the only gig in town.'

'I wonder what she meant about owning something soon over here,' said Max.

'Not *StreetSmart*, I hope,' said Anka.

'I hope not too. I've told her before, I'm not selling. She'd better believe me.'

[39]

Max and Anka were recrossing the atrium when they saw Chip coming in from the sidewalk, bundled up in an overcoat and snow hat with ear flaps.

'Hi, Max. I was hoping I hadn't missed you.' He looked absurdly cool that night, full of youthful energy. 'Anka said you'd be here. I wondered if you'd like a drink.'

'And how,' said Max. 'Anka and I have been through the mill upstairs. If one more person tells me I've screwed up over that photograph . . .'

'You haven't screwed up,' said Chip. 'It's a great image. Powerful. Only dickbrains can't see it.'

'Well, there are a lot of them about.'

'There's one outside now on the sidewalk. Giving an interview to camera. She's saying the magazine's lost it since Saskia died.'

'Who is?' asked Max. 'Describe this person.' But he'd guessed already.

'Creepy-looking dame in a fur coat. Big hair like a socialite.'

'I knew it. I just fucking knew it. And you say there's a *camera crew* out there?'

'NBC, I think. They're doing a segment for the local news about *StreetSmart* and the AFD. They're interviewing people as they leave, getting reactions from the fashion crowd.'

'Jesus, this is only getting worse.'

'How long do you reckon they'll stay?' asked Anka.

They edged closer to the door and could see the crew outside on the street. A woman interviewer in a belted trenchcoat was doing a piece to camera, while her producer covered the exit for further victims.

'So, what do we do?' asked Anka.

'Looks to me like we've got two choices,' said Max. 'Hang about here until they clear off, which could be hours, or step outside and face the music.'

'You won't speak with them, will you?' asked Anka anxiously. 'There's a chance they won't run the story if it's only vox pop, but if you go on record as editor-in-chief, they'll show it every fifteen minutes.'

'I'm thinking,' said Max. 'A part of me's just saying fuck it, let's go for it. Chip, what do you reckon?'

'Play it safe. Anka's right. These people are jackals, they manipulate everything.'

Max screwed his eyes tight shut. It was something he did only when he needed to concentrate very hard; the darkness inside his head enabled him to focus without distraction. Ken Craig had always ribbed him mercilessly about it. 'Blooming Ada,' Ken would say whenever they were in a tight spot together. 'Max is going into Stevie Wonder mode again. Blind leading the effing blind.'

'Let's go,' said Max. He still hadn't decided what to do. Sometimes the best plan is to have no plan.

The bouncers in headsets held open the door of Bercuse Plaza. There was a blast of cold air, and Max strode out on to the sidewalk, followed by Chip and Anka.

'Excuse me, sir,' called the producer. 'We're putting together an item for CBS news . . .'

The bright light of a mobile telecast was beamed on to Max's face and a microphone on a stick appeared beneath his chin. The interviewer in the trenchcoat blocked his way to the kerb. She had a thick mane of brown hair and the eyes of a mountain cat. 'Have you seen these controversial photographs in *StreetSmart*?' she asked. 'Do you concur with the American Federation for Decency that they ought to be withdrawn?'

'I have seen them,' Max heard himself saying. 'I happen to think they're important. I am the editor of *StreetSmart* and I'm also the person who took the photographs, and I'm proud that we've published them.'

Max watched the producer straighten up, scenting a scoop, and the interviewer take a step forward.

'That's an interesting point of view,' she said. 'We've been asking for reactions from influential opinion-formers across the industry, and I must tell you that yours is a minority viewpoint.'

'I can't help that,' said Max. 'We're not trying to please the whole nation. *StreetSmart* is edited for the most intelligent, best-informed group of readers in America, for readers who are concerned with what actually goes on in the world. At *StreetSmart* we don't dodge issues. We face them head on.'

'But wouldn't you agree that the photograph of the mutilated corpse is just gross?'

Anka and Chip had edged around the back of the camera crew and Max could see them clearly over the producer's shoulder. Anka looked sick, her face screwed up with tension.

'It isn't the photograph that's gross, as you put it,' Max replied. 'It's a society that allows acts of violence and terrorism like that to go unpunished that is gross. We're saying to our readers, "This happens on *your* planet. Take note. If you don't like it, change it. But don't pretend it doesn't happen." When I took that picture, the Chechnyan Mafia had just dumped that body out of a moving car. I watched them do it. It happened right in front of me. And do you know what? Nobody else saw a damn thing. It was broad daylight but nobody saw a thing. It's lawless over there, frontier country. Like America a hundred years ago when the pioneers were opening up the Wild West.'

The interviewer was losing control of the agenda. Max saw her glance over at her producer, who muttered something into her earpiece. 'But how would you feel, Mr Thompson, if pictures like the ones in your issue were seen by small children?'

'*StreetSmart* isn't a children's magazine. It's for grown-ups who have the motivation and breadth of education to read serious journalism on serious issues. If you only want to read about the latest powder puff, fine, don't read *StreetSmart*. But if you actually give a damn about global issues, and you actually care that human beings are tortured and mutilated in the former USSR, and the world community lifts not one finger to stop them, then maybe, just maybe, you'll find my magazine relevant.'

From the corner of his eye, Max saw Anka, eyes lit up, beaming at him. Chip had a big smile across his face, and was giving Max the thumbs-up.

'Finally, Mr Thompson, how do you respond to the criticism that *StreetSmart* has lost its way since your sister Saskia died? She would never have published these pornographic pictures, would she?'

'Saskia,' he replied, 'would have loved this issue, and she'd have admired the Chechnyan photographs most of all. They're everything she stood for: important, world-class, untrivial, timely, newsbased journalism. The photographs are almost a litmus test of contemporary American morality. The way people react to them says as much about them as citizens as the pictures do themselves.'

The camera stopped whirring, the lights shut out, and Max stood on the suddenly dark sidewalk, the adrenalin coursing around his system. He felt dazed and uncertain what he'd said. It was as though some inner voice had taken over. Suddenly, above the traffic, he head the sound of applause. Anka and Chip were clapping and hollering and even the crew smiled at him and nodded their approval.

'*Fabulous,*' said Anka. 'Just fabulous. You know something, I'm going to get a tape of that and incorporate some of it into the new media kit. It's kind of like the mission statement for *StreetSmart.*'

'You were great,' said Chip. 'A natural.'

The producer came over and pumped Max's hand. 'Nice,' she said. 'One minute forty. Four contained soundbites. You must have done this before.'

'Think you'll use any of it?' asked Max. 'I probably went on a bit. I got carried away.'

'It'll go out later tonight and all through tomorrow's breakfast show. It may go out national too. All the networks will be interested.'

'Grief. You serious?'

'Relax, you came over well. Good as your sister actually. We had Saskia on our Oscars special with Richard Gere.'

'How about that drink?' said Max. 'You joining us, Anka?'

'I'm bushed. If you'll excuse me, I'm going to turn in. Will you be stopping by the office tomorrow any time?'

'Probably. I haven't planned tomorrow. I'm having enough trouble keeping up with today.'

'I know, I'm sorry,' said Anka. 'We should speak anyway. We need to touch base about Bercuse.'

'Of course, Bercuse. I'd forgotten Bercuse. Tell me something, is it always like this in magazines? So remorseless? I'm beginning to feel like one of those targets in a rifle range at a fairground. A tin duck. Each time I pop up, someone knocks me down again with bad news.'

Anka laughed. 'You ever heard this saying: "Everyone dies. Not everyone lives"? It reminds me of magazines every time. If we weren't so exhausted, we'd notice what a swell time we're all having.'

'I used to think Saskia's life was one long party.'

'It was,' said Anka. 'And so is yours. Think about it. A suite at the East River, cocktails at Heat-on-Huit, more cocktails with Chip here – the badboy of the Bowery . . .' She flagged a yellow cab and kissed Max lightly on the cheek. 'You boys behave yourselves now. And, Max, thanks for coming along tonight. It helped more than you know.'

Chip took Max to a place called Speculum in the Village, which he said was famous for having the second-longest bar in Manhattan. Afterwards, all Max could remember about it was a chill cabinet containing 160 different kinds of vodka and the intense discomfort of the sharkskin stools. Chip knew a lot of people there and introduced Max as the editor-in-chief of *StreetSmart*, which seemed to confer celebrity status on them both. At first this embarrassed Max, but after three Black Labels he stopped minding.

'I've been thinking,' said Chip. 'Actually it's why I wanted a drink with you.'

'Yeah?'

'Something's bugging me about this business over the new issue. Something doesn't stack up.'

'Go on.'

'Tell me, would you say that members of the American Federation for Decency are the kind of people who regularly read *StreetSmart*? What I mean is, do you reckon they're hanging about their local Safeway in Hicksville, Mississippi, clutching their three dollars and waiting for the new issue to come in?'

'I'd say that's unlikely.'

'Then explain how they got on to the issue so quickly? The official US publication date was only yesterday. A few copies might have begun surfacing on newsstands the day before, no earlier. The photograph of the corpse isn't on the front cover, you've got to open up the issue and page right through to find it.'

'I'm beginning to see. The timing . . .'

'It's out of sync. It doesn't work. Even assuming one of the Reverend Jesse Egan's Sisters of Chastity bought a copy of *StreetSmart* on day one, it still doesn't give enough time for the message to filter up through the AFD hierarchy and for them to contact the networks and get it on to the six o'clock news.'

'So what do you reckon?'

'Someone tipped them off.'

'Like who?'

'Someone with access to advance copies of the issue. Someone in the *StreetSmart* office.'

'Someone on our staff? Why would they do that?'

'Beats me, but I can't see another explanation.'

Max tried to picture the people he'd met in Canal Street that morning: Silas Cheung the art director with his pigtail and dragon tattoo, Ilsa Jane Pezzimenti, Leah Sheinberg the picture researcher and Jonny Tannenbaum who'd asked him for a raise. Was it possible that one of them had slipped an early copy to the AFD? Max hated the idea they could be harbouring a traitor in the office, but maybe that was it. Maybe the same person had installed the remote access software in the computer.

Suddenly he saw it. 'Chip, I'm being slow here. It doesn't have to be someone in Canal Street. The leak could just as easily have come from London.'

'From London?'

'The British edition finishes printing first. The print run's shorter, the process doesn't take so long. We're producing two million copies in the States, but only a quarter of that in England, so we get bound copies sooner. There were finished copies a couple of days before I left.'

'What happens to them when they reach the office? Are they locked away?'

'I don't know, I don't think so. I think the subscription copies get mailed right away. Kevin said something about sending early voucher copies to his advertisers. And, wait a minute, we send early copies to celebrities by motorbike. It was something Saskia started.'

'In other words,' said Chip, 'there are thousands of copies out there.'

''Fraid so. Anyone could have passed one to the AFD, but it still doesn't explain who'd have done it. What would be the point?'

'Screw us up, I guess. Same as all the other things that have happened.'

'Whoever's behind this, they must be tonto.'

'That narrows the field,' said Chip. 'But not enough.'

'You don't think it could be Caryl?' said Max. 'Each time I bump into her she seems madder. Maybe she's a screwball.'

'This morning you suggested Saidi.'

'Him too. They could be in it together. Saidi always wanted to fuck Saskia, and Caryl wanted to fuck her up. Now they're working in concert on me. Oh God, who knows? I don't know that I'm tough enough or smart enough for this job.'

'Believe me, you're tough enough,' said Chip.

Max wasn't sure whether the implication was that he wasn't smart enough, but he let it pass, and shrugged.

'You're as tough as Saskia was, anyway.'

'I doubt it,' said Max. 'Everything I've been hearing, she was a ball-breaker. I thought that was her whole thing, the driving ambition, the will to succeed. That's what it says in all the articles about her.'

'She was ambitious, sure. She was a very competitive lady and good at psyching people out. You saw that watching her when the new issues of the competition came into the office. She used to page through them at her desk with all the courtiers gathered round, and she'd slag off everything in the issue – features, fashion, horoscope, it didn't matter. She did it with everything: *Vogue, Bazaar, Talk, New Yorker*. "Old story", "Old story", "Non story", "Yawnsville". It was probably a pre-emptive strike, in case anyone dared suggest the competition was better than her that month.'

'At least she knew what she wanted.'

'You are kidding?' said Chip.

'No. She had this great instinct, didn't she, as an editor? I read somewhere that she'd look down a features list of fifty ideas and go straight for the best one.'

'Saskia's instincts were spot-on a lot of the time,' said Chip. 'She had a good nose. For instance, she always knew which movies would make it and which would bomb, even before they'd finished production, so *StreetSmart* had the best movie coverage. And she was great at sitting next to important people at dinners. When she met anyone useful, she was on them like a condom. That's how the magazine got the Kennedy scoop: she'd been placed next to his attorney. But, she did change her mind a lot. She wasn't what you'd call decisive.'

'I'm surprised.'

'The issue got changed and remade about ten times a month. She'd put in a story, take it out again, put it back, get it rewritten five times, then drop it for something less good. If a story hung around for longer than a week, she got bored. She'd go out to lunch and come back fired up about something else, something newer. In the end, writers wouldn't give her their pieces until the issue was on press. It had more chance of making it in that way.'

'If that's true,' said Max, 'it makes me like her more. She sounds almost human. Chip, I heard something yesterday from the detective, the one investigating the murder. He talked about Saskia's sex life. He said she used male escorts, prostitutes. Had you heard that?'

Chip shrugged. 'People talked about Saskia all the time. You never knew whether the stories about her were true or apocryphal.'

'So you had heard it?'

'Sure.' He looked uneasy.

'Come on, Chip, you worked with her. Did Saskia pay for sex? It's important. It could have been a prostitute that killed her.'

Chip stared into his vodka. 'I guess she did, Max. I'm sorry, you probably didn't want to know that.'

'But *why*? I thought she had all these admirers. Rock stars and artists.'

'I always reckoned they were more for publicity, to keep photographers happy. She used the escorts purely for sex. I think she enjoyed the element of danger, it gave her a buzz.'

'The danger?'

'You should understand that. Dicing with death. With Saskia, it was more dicing with her reputation. She talked about it once, she said she liked the contrast. Like, she'd go to some big dinner, full of celebrities, and later she'd have sex. There was no hassle. She said it made a change from the writer–editor relationships she had in the office, which were always complicated and emotional.'

'Did you ever get to meet any of these escorts?'

'No way. That side of her life she kept completely private. A few of us in the company were aware of it, but it wasn't something anyone mentioned.'

'So she didn't have a regular man, far as you know?'

'I doubt that. The one time we discussed it, she said she requested a different guy each time. She used several agencies. She got bored, remember. She said she preferred fresh dick.'

[40]

He got back to the East River, ran a shower and held his head under an ice-cold jet until he'd sobered up a bit. There was a midget television set into the wall above the towel rail and he punched it on with the remote.

The first thing he saw as the screen flickered into life was Caryl Fargo on the sidewalk outside Bercuse Plaza. 'I don't normally allow myself to be drawn on the content of rival publications,' she was saying piously, 'but *StreetSmart* has overstepped the mark. I'm not a believer in censorship of any kind, but there is such a thing as self-censorship. My advice to consumers is to vote with their feet. Don't buy the issue. Simple as that.'

Max picked up a basket of cotton buds and hurled them at the screen. Just then, he had an overwhelming desire to attack Caryl's helmet of hair with sheep shears.

Now he saw his own face appear on screen. It was the first time he'd watched himself since his image makeover and it took a bit of getting used to. He looked cooler on the outside than he'd realised, almost as though he belonged.

He was surprised too by how fluently he came across. They had used almost everything he'd said, eliminating the interviewer's questions and broadcasting his replies unedited. Max thought he was a little too intense, but at least he sounded sincere and he hadn't minced his words. The stuff about *StreetSmart*'s commitment to global issues and campaigning for a better world was a bit rich, he thought – he sounded like Karis Landau, and he was glad Ken Craig hadn't seen it – but, all things considered, Max felt he had come over quite well. He especially liked that final soundbite about *Street-Smart*'s 'important, world-class, untrivial, timely, newsbased journalism'.

In the bedroom of the suite, his sheets had been turned back for the night and a peppermint and a spray of jasmine arranged on his pillow. Idly he zapped the bed-end television and there was his face again, lecturing America about *StreetSmart* as the litmus test of contemporary morality.

After he'd finished his little homily, the item wound up on a comment from an officer of the AFD. She was black and matronly and a member of the First Charismatic Gospel Chapel of Washington DC. She was ranting about the magazine, which she likened to the sinkholes of Sodom and Gomorrah.

'We have fought for the Good Lord before and triumphed,' she said. 'Remember how with His help we stopped production of the Satanic Freddy Krueger dolls? In His precious name we can do that again.'

The telephone rang next to the bed and Max picked it up. He guessed it was Anka or Chip who had caught him on TV.

'Max?'

'Uh-huh.'

'Where the hell have you been all evening? I've been leaving messages everywhere. Didn't you get my voice-mails?' It was Philip Landau. His voice sounded muffled and Max could hear music in the background.

He glanced at the Message Waiting light which was flashing on the bedside unit. He'd been so engrossed in the news, he hadn't noticed it.

'Sorry, Philip. It's been quite an eventful day, one way and another.'

'It's been eventful this side of the pond too,' said Philip.

'You're in *London*?' said Max. 'Isn't it the middle of the night there?'

'Four a.m. I'm ringing you because something's come up. I don't think it's a problem, just something you need to deal with.'

Max felt himself tense. Not another problem. He was becoming nostalgic for his old easy life, when stress just meant evading sniper fire or catching the last plane out of Burundi.

'I received a call last night from a guy named Dick Mathias. He runs the investment arm of Vision Capital Partners.'

'I've heard of that outfit somewhere,' said Max. 'Don't they own stock in *StreetSmart*? I'm sure they were on that list you gave me.'

'They're actually the lead investor,' said Philip. 'They have thirty per cent.'

'Right.'

'I don't know Dick Mathias personally, but Saskia used to pay him a courtesy call from time to time and keep him on-message about how the magazine was performing. They are based in New York, somewhere off Wall Street.'

'I see.'

'Dick said he'd like to meet with you, soon as possible. He thought you guys should spend some time together, get to know each other a bit.'

'Fine. If you've got the number, I'll give him a call tomorrow. Maybe I can see him on this trip.'

'I'm afraid I already took the liberty of scheduling a meeting for you. Sorry, I tried to call you, but Dick and his people were running tight on their own schedules. They'd said they'd like you to meet with them at seven a.m. tomorrow morning.'

'Oh Christ.' Max reached for an East River message pad and Landau dictated the address of an office building in Nassau Street. Vision Capital Partners occupied the twenty-seventh floor of the Galveston Assurance and Realty Building.

'You mentioned "Dick and his people",' said Max. 'Will there be several of them? What kind of meeting is this anyway?'

'Just an informal chat, far as I know,' said Philip. 'Should be straightforward. With a new CEO coming in, they obviously want to get a feel for you. They liked Saskia, so you're starting from a strong position. Talking to Dick Mathias, I got the impression he was quite in awe of her: she was in the newspapers all the time.'

'Bankers aren't impressed by that, are they? I thought they were impervious to hype.'

Landau laughed. 'Don't you believe it. Investment bankers are as impressionable as everyone else. Why else do you think those financial public relations companies are thriving? Dick mentioned that Saskia invited him along to some of the *StreetSmart* parties and introduced him to Uma Thurman.'

'Typical Saskia!'

'Smart move too,' said Landau. 'Most of the businesses Vision Capital Partners take a position in aren't that interesting. Automotive parts and floor tiles are Dick's other investments, I believe. *StreetSmart*'s sexy. They enjoy the association.'

'So, tomorrow at seven o'clock,' said Max. He wished the meeting hadn't been fixed for quite so early. His arm was starting to play up again, which he attributed to lack of rest. 'Philip, give me some advice. What should I say tomorrow? I've never met any financiers before. Is there anything I should watch out for?'

Landau thought for a moment before answering. In the background, Max could still hear music and the sound of a broadcast. Philip had mentioned that he liked to work with the TV on, generally VH-1 or MTV. Even in the night.

'Advice?' mused Philip. 'I'd say lay on the bullshit. Schmooze them up and lay it on thick. Bear in mind that bankers are often quite hazy about the detail of the various companies they invest in. They're big-picture merchants, they leave the detail to the executives on the ground.'

'Got you,' said Max. 'Thanks for that. I'll let you know how I get along.'

[41]

Max couldn't sleep. He was jumpy with exhaustion and the events of the day churned around in his head. He couldn't get his brain to shut down. It kept returning to the sight of Carmelita Puentes lying in a heap by her bed, her face bludgeoned to pulp, or else it produced crazy composites of the different interlopers in his life. The Reverend Jesse Egan would surface as a bouncer outside Bercuse Plaza, while Detective Przemysi suddenly transformed into Caryl Fargo. Or he imagined Saskia dialling one of her escort agencies on the night of her murder. Each time he was drifting into sleep, a fresh hallucination would take hold of him and he'd be wide awake again in a cold sweat.

The red Message Waiting light, still flashing at the bedside, began to irritate him. Even when he closed his eyes, he remained conscious of it, and there was no way of switching it off without first reviewing the messages.

He turned on the reading light and touched the button on the telephone for voice-mail.

A robotic pre-recorded voice said, 'You have eight messages. Hear them?'

He jabbed the star key to proceed.

'Message received 16.29. Hear it?'

Max relistened to Kitty's earlier message telling him she'd obtained the guest list for the Waldorf benefit. It was good to hear her voice. It seemed longer than two days since he'd been with her.

'Message received 17.20. Hear it?'

He knew that one was Chip Miller and wiped it off the system. There were six new messages.

'Max? This is Philip Landau. I need to speak to you at some point, but I'm not around much myself. I'll try you again later on. Hope you're having a successful trip.'

The second new message, timed 18.40, was also Philip. 'Max? Evidently you're still not back at your hotel. I'll try later.'

There was a third message from Landau, followed by a fourth and then a fifth. He had been leaving voice-mails every half hour. By the fifth, he was sounding testy. Max didn't blame him, he must have been dying to go to bed.

The final message, which had been left while Max was drinking vodka with Chip at Speculum, was from Colonel Thompson. It gave Max quite a jolt to hear his father's voice barking down the receiver.

'Hello?' it began. 'Hello, Max, is that you?' Max heard his mother saying something in the background. 'How's that, Margaret? I see, it's a *tape recorder*, why didn't you say?' Then: 'This is a message for Max Thompson at the East River Hotel in New York. I don't know whether you'll hear this, but if you do, please telephone your father in England. We're at *home*. I need to speak to you urgently, so ring whenever you can. It's the middle of the night here but don't worry about that, I'm not sleeping much anyway. I don't know what time it is in America, but please telephone urgently.'

Max dialled the number for High Hatch and the receiver was picked up almost before he'd heard it ring.

'Max?'

'Hello, Dad. You were quick answering that.'

'I was watching the phone. I didn't want it to wake Cody.'

'How is Cody?'

'Playing up his grandmother like nobody's business. It's got worse since, you know, what happened.' Max thought that his father sounded tired.

'Dad, I got your message. What's up? It's five in the morning in England, isn't it?'

'They've contacted us from America about Saskia's body. We've got to decide what we want to do with it.'

'Right. Have you and Mum got any thoughts?'

'We think the best solution is to bring her back home and have her buried locally. There's that pretty churchyard at St Michael's, overlooking the common towards Frensham. It's an attractive bit of country and not too close to the A30. I think the vicar will give his permission, even though Saskia wasn't much of a churchgoer. In any case, she should be buried somewhere where Cody can visit the grave.'

Although a churchyard on Frensham Common was probably the last spot on earth that Saskia would have considered an appropriate resting place, Max knew it would please his parents. Anyway, they could hardly bury her on St Barts or beneath the catwalk of some fashion theatre.

'I spoke to Jean, Saskia's old secretary at the office,' said the Colonel, 'and she told me you're returning from New York tomorrow.'

Was it really tomorrow? Max felt he'd only just arrived.

'I've done everything I need to here. I visited the *StreetSmart* office and saw Detective Przemysi. He's still interviewing Saskia's friends.'

Max wanted to tell his father so much more, but how could he? The conversations with Przemysi and Chip Miller, about Saskia's sex life, would have appalled him.

'I spoke to Przemysi myself,' said the Colonel. 'He says Saskia knew all the top dogs over there, not that their names mean anything to me.'

'Saskia met a lot of different people in New York,' said Max.

'Have you got something to hand to write with?' his father went on. 'I'm about to give you the address of somewhere called the Office of the Chief Medical Examiner of New York City.' Max wrote it on the message pad beneath the address for Vision Capital Partners. 'Five twenty First Avenue. I can't tell you where that is, but you can probably get a taxi to take you.'

Colonel Thompson told Max who to contact when he arrived and they discussed how best to transport Saskia's body home. The Colonel had an idea that corpses were generally repatriated by ship, but agreed that Max should do whatever he considered appropriate.

'I'll sort it out tomorrow morning,' Max assured his father. 'I've got a seven o'clock business meeting down in Wall Street and I'll do it straight after that.'

'What, seven o'clock in the morning?' The Colonel chuckled. 'I don't suppose you've been up that early in a long time. Dawn patrol, is it?'

'Something like that, Dad.' Colonel Thompson had a fixation, going back to when Max was sixteen and liked to lie in in the mornings, that his son never stepped out of bed before lunchtime.

'Actually,' said Max, 'I've got to meet a bunch of American investors. They're involved in *StreetSmart* and they've asked to see me.'

'Well, I hope you're well prepared,' said the Colonel. 'Got all your facts and figures together?'

'Not entirely,' said Max. 'I don't think it's that sort of meeting.'

'Max, I cannot believe I'm hearing this. Really, what is *wrong* with my children?'

'They just want to put a face to me,' said Max defensively. 'It's no big deal. There won't be a test or anything.'

He could hear his father sighing on the end of the line. 'I don't know how many times I lectured you on this as children. Dozens, I should imagine, but it evidently hasn't got through, and now you're nearly forty and I suppose it's too late. Saskia was the same. She'd float into those business meetings, flashing her eyes and hoping it would all be all right on the night. It distresses me to think of it. When there were high-level conferences at the MoD, you got your facts lined up. It was fundamental. You were *briefed*, prepared.'

'Honestly, Dad. Tomorrow's just an informal chat.'

'Not the point at issue,' said the Colonel. 'Nine times out of ten they won't be pitching bouncers, but the tenth time . . . *howzat*. Caught in the slips with your pants down. Look, I know everyone regards me these days as a silly old fool who nods off in front of the goggle-box, but please take my advice just this once: mug up on the key facts. Put them down on a postcard and memorise them. I told Saskia that, but she never took much notice. I was never convinced she understood the money side of that magazine anyway.'

After his father had rung off, and Max was lying in the darkness wondering whether the old boy had a point, he heard a soft clicking sound coming from the telephone. Guessing he must have replaced the receiver incorrectly, and the hotel operator was trying to tell him, he fumbled about on the table for the handset. He lifted the receiver to his ear and rattled the cradle to break the connection.

At first he thought that the Colonel must have rung him back. He could hear his father's unmistakable voice through the earpiece. He was saying, 'I know everyone regards me these days as a silly old fool who nods off in front of the goggle-box, but please take my advice . . .'

It was the weirdest sensation. Somehow Max was listening to a rerun of the earlier conversation. He sat bolt upright in bed, transfixed by the voice echoing down the line. 'I was never convinced she understood the money side of that magazine anyway.'

A moment later, Max heard his own voice cutting in. He was telling his father not to worry, and to give his love to his mother and to Cody. 'I'll try and take Cody out at the weekend,' Max heard himself say. 'Give you both a break.'

There was only one possible explanation: the line into his suite was tapped.

Philip Landau had been quite right: the rooms at the East River *were* bugged and now he had the proof. Something must have gone wrong with the electronics and the line intercept was giving blow-back. The tape must partially have rewound itself and switched into play mode.

Max's first reaction was sheer fury. How dare Freddie Saidi bug his private conversations? It was immoral and almost certainly broke the law. The Americans were even hotter on civil liberties than the Brits: there was probably something about it enshrined in the Declaration of Independence or the Bill of Rights. Did Saidi have all the rooms monitored or was it just certain suites? Probably the latter, which was why Marcus Brooke had been so keen to upgrade him. Doubtless they put all their VIPs into suites like the Gardens of Babylon.

A moment later, Max thought of something else. If Saidi had been eavesdropping on all Max's conversations, then he'd certainly have known about Carmelita Puentes.

He would have known about the visit to Fort Washington Park, the exact time Max would arrive, everything. Then, at the actual moment that Max was demonstrating the Internet site to Saidi and Brooke, they must have arranged to have Carmelita bumped off.

Carmelita's murder was all his fault. He'd been warned that the phones were bugged, but had still rung her. When he'd made that call, he'd as good as signed Carmelita's death warrant.

His first reaction was to ring the police, and he reached for the telephone to dial Detective Amaya at the 34th Precinct.

But – think – if his line was being monitored, that would blow it. The moment Saidi heard him report the existence of the tape, he'd remove the evidence. By the time the police showed up, there'd be no means of connecting Saidi to Carmelita's murder.

The more Max thought about it, the more he saw that there was only one solution. He had to get hold of the tape.

The telephone monitoring room had to be somewhere in the hotel. He looked at his watch. It was ten past midnight, and the hotel would be starting to wind down for the night.

Max slipped out of bed and pulled on jeans and a dark jersey. He opened the door on to the corridor and heard voices approaching from the direction of the elevators. An elderly couple passed by on their way back from dinner. Too early, thought Max, leave it another hour.

There was a galley kitchen in the suite with a kettle; a dozen different teabags and herbal infusions were displayed in a wicker basket, along with a jar of the East River's Specially Selected Bogotá Blend. Max made himself a cup of strong coffee and sat down on the sofa to wait.

His arm throbbed, and the coffee, as it flooded through his system, made him feel jangly. He wasn't sure he was thinking straight. He was bone tired. He breathed slowly in and out from his diaphragm, until he felt the tension begin to ebb away. Outside, the streets were almost empty of traffic. Only the occasional wail of a police siren as it cut across town reminded Max that he was in the centre of New York City.

He tried to work out where the telephone monitoring room would be situated. He reckoned that only a small number of East River staff would be aware of it, but that at least four people would be required to service it. There would be hours of tape to monitor and analyse, and transcripts and digests to be prepared. It would make most sense, and attract least attention, if the surveillance unit was sited close to the main hotel switchboard. It would need to be self-contained, of course, because the regular hotel operators would be unlikely to be in on the secret, but the surveillance team would need easy access to the telephone terminals.

Max guessed that the room would be situated somewhere on the ground floor of the hotel, in the labyrinth of offices behind the cashiers.

At one thirty he ventured out of the suite. This time, the corridors were deserted. He walked softly along the pastel-patterned carpet towards the bank of elevators. Dangling from doorknobs were East River shoebags, waiting to be collected by the shoeshine during the night. He passed a steel room-service wagon, strewn with the debris of dinner, parked at an angle in the corridor.

When he reached the elevators, he decided to use the service stairs instead. The elevator doors opened within sight of the reception desk and he didn't want to be seen.

He walked down ten flights without passing a living soul. On some of the half-landings stood industrial floor polishers with chrome heads like auto-hubs. On the fourth level, a trolley was piled up with towels and miniature bars of hotel soap.

He reached the ground floor and all was silent. The sofas and coffee shop were deserted. Behind reception, his back to the lobby, stood an assistant night manager.

Max ducked across the lobby in the direction of the cashiers. The desk was closed for the night. A metal grille had been hauled down and plastic hoods been placed over the computers.

Max slipped into the corridor behind the cashiers' desk. Several administrative offices opened on either side, all in darkness.

The corridor branched off left and right. In both directions were more offices with plastic signs on their doors: Payroll, Human Resources, Marketing. Ahead of him lay a flight of stairs leading to the basement.

He reached the bottom, and the hotel switchboard was directly ahead. Through a porthole in the door he could see a lone operator on night duty. She was black and she was painting her nails with some glittery green varnish. As Max watched her, she yawned. The telephones in the rooms were direct dial, and there weren't many incoming calls in the small hours.

Ten metres further down the corridor, adjacent to the switchboard, was a second room. A notice on the door said, AUTHORISED PERSONNEL ONLY. The moment Max saw it, he knew he'd found what he was looking for. This time, there was no window in the doorframe.

He turned the handle, but it was locked.

For almost a minute he stood motionless, wondering what to do next. He had to get inside the room and he had to get in tonight.

He listened at the door until he was satisfied no one was inside. The bugging equipment must be set up to operate automatically at night. The taps into the suites would be voice-activated.

He squared up to the doorframe with his shoulder. It felt flimsy, and he knew he could break it down. On the fourth attempt, the wood splintered around the lock and the jamb gave way.

The telephone monitoring room was hardly more than a cubicle. Telephone directories were piled up in a heap on a bookcase. Three work stations were positioned against the wall, each with a swivel chair upholstered in grey and a personal computer with a large external modem. The room was untidy and stank of cigarette smoke. Two of the work stations had items of electronic equipment spread about: batteries, microphones and dictating machines.

Lined up along a narrow shelf, Max spotted what he was looking for.

A dozen cassette recorders were each separately wired into a mini-switchboard. On each machine, the record button was depressed and a red standby light glowing in the unit. The cassettes themselves were stationary. Max guessed they would only be activated by someone in the suites lifting an extension. Each recorder had a number attached to it and Max hunted about the office for a key. He found it taped to the wall.

The key began: Tripoli Suite – 1014. Sidon Suite – 1016. Gardens of Babylon – 1018.

He located the machine numbered 1018 and pressed the eject button. The mini-cassette flipped up off the motordrive and he slipped it into his jeans pocket. Moving further along the shelf, he ejected a cassette from a neighbouring machine and substituted it for his own.

It wouldn't fool them for long, Max knew that, but it would buy him some time.

He got back upstairs to his suite at two o'clock, thrust the cassette into the bottom of his washbag, set his alarm for four hours later and collapsed on to the bed.

In less than a minute he was asleep.

[42]

At a few minutes before six thirty a.m., Max went uneasily down-stairs to settle his bill. Outside, the city was still dark and the traffic starting to edge its way through Manhattan had its headlights on.

The cashier spent an inordinate amount of time printing out the account, and cross-questioning him on whether he had drunk anything last night from the mini-bar. At every moment, Max expected to be detained by a member of the hotel surveillance unit. As he hung about in the lobby, he became increasingly conscious of the mini-cassette hidden in his washbag. He found himself glancing guiltily at his suitcase.

A bellboy insisted on stowing the luggage into the trunk of the cab, and Max was following it on to the sidewalk when he heard someone calling his name.

'Max, I'm most impressed that you are another early bird.' It was Marcus Brooke, incongruously kitted out in jogging pants and vest with a sweatband around his forehead.

'Er, yes,' he replied. 'I've got a breakfast meeting downtown.'

'You should have had your meeting here,' said Marcus, jogging on the spot on the hotel steps. 'The Cedar Room is the first choice among New York's power élite for business breakfasts. I always tell Freddie, "Half the deals that are done in this city are struck in the Cedar Room." '

'Maybe next time.'

'Of course,' said Marcus. 'I hope you will regard the East River as your club in New York from now on.'

The bellboy was standing by the open trunk waiting for his tip, and all Max could think about was the cassette. He had to get out of there.

Marcus placed a short leg up against the side of the cab, ostensibly to stretch his hamstring. Max was blocked.

'It's so important to have a place in the city where you are known,' he went on. 'Somewhere where they greet you by name, barman knows your favourite cocktail without asking, message desk can take a decent message. New York isn't always that hospitable a place to strangers. It can be dangerous, but of course you know that.'

He looked meaningfully at Max. 'Here in Midtown, it's not a problem. Nowhere much safer than a suite at the East River! But I wouldn't recommend anyone to venture much further north than 96th Street, even by day. That would be inadvisable. You read horrifying things in the newspapers. Half the murders don't even get reported.'

'I'm sure,' said Max. The threat was so circumspect and coated in honeyed charm, it was impossible to pin down, but there was no mistaking Marcus's intention. Max glared at him.

'Thanks for the warning,' he said. 'If I ever need to go north of 96th Street, I'll ask Freddie Saidi to lend me some weapons. He must have plenty left over from Beirut.'

'Max, we appreciate your being able to come on over and spend time with us,' said Dick Mathias of Vision Capital Partners. 'I'd like to introduce you to my associates, Yves Challon and Lee Kloepfer. Yves and Lee were both members of the team that made our strategic investment in StreetSmart Inc.'

Max circled the conference table, shaking hands. Dick Mathias looked forty, with a quiff of black hair, gunslit eyes, a white shirt and matching capped white teeth. His cheeks were mottled red as though he had a bad case of razor burn. There was something pugnacious and tight-arsed about him that made Max wary.

Yves was tall, sandy haired and French. Clinging to the corner of his mouth were little brown flecks of croissant, remnants of his breakfast. He struck Max as the only one among the three investment bankers in the room liable to have any kind of interior or emotional life.

When Max reached Lee Kloepfer and stuck out his hand, Lee shook it cursorily. 'Good to see you, Max,' he said, but his eyes were hostile.

Max poured himself a black coffee from a vacuum Thermos and surveyed the conference room. It reminded him of the waiting room in an airport, with grey and maroon upholstered seats and beech-wood cabinets.

'I don't know how conversant you are with our corporate investment policy,' said Dick Mathias. 'But, typically, we seek to identify and acquire positions in well-managed companies with good growth potential and opportunities to create significant value. Businesses that are rich in cash-generative abilities or businesses with a compelling story that isn't fully exploited.'

'I see,' said Max.

'It was in this context,' Dick continued, 'that we took our thirty per cent position in *StreetSmart*. Viewed from a five-year investment perspective, the potential for growth looked above average. For a number of reasons, publishing is a rewarding sector to be in. The cost base is low. There is limited overhead in terms of plant and manufacture. And in a buoyant economy the capacity for exponential revenue growth is considerable.'

Max took a long swig of coffee and tried to keep his concentration. He had barely slept in twenty-four hours and wasn't sure that he was equal to an economics lecture just then.

'A decisive factor in our decision to invest in American *StreetSmart* was the favourable impression we formed of the prevailing management. Saskia was an impressive executive. We found her to be highly focused, and capable of creating around her product a degree of excitement in the marketplace.'

Max nodded. He wondered whether this was an oblique reference to Dick's encounter with Uma Thurman at the *StreetSmart* party.

'As you can appreciate,' Dick continued, 'our primary concern now, as managers of risk capital, is to determine the degree to which our investment may have been materially affected by Saskia's death. We're having to ask ourselves, was Saskia so intrinsically identified with the brand that *StreetSmart* must inevitably lose some of its status and market impetus without her?'

'I wouldn't say that was the case at all,' replied Max. 'Saskia was very high profile, as you know, and was a genius at getting the magazine talked about, but it's the team that puts *StreetSmart* together each month. Over the past week I've been immensely impressed by the calibre of people working for the company. Anka

Kaplan, the American publisher, is incredibly committed. So is Chip Miller who heads up StreetSmart Interactive. There's a strong team in London too.' Max tried to remember who was still left in the Bruton Street office. 'Marie-Louise Clay is very smart. So is the managing editor Gina David. Racinda Blick, the fashion director, has an international reputation. Then, of course, there's Kitty Marr who is the hottest young fashion editor around.'

Max saw Dick Mathias exchange glances with Lee Kloepfer. For some reason, he had a premonition of bad news.

'Let me level with you, Max,' said Dick. 'Over the past couple of days we've received a number of approaches from parties interested in acquiring our equity in StreetSmart.'

'Really? Like who?'

'We're subject to confidentiality agreements on that, but I can confirm that there has been both trade interest and approaches by certain individuals representing capital outside of the publishing business.'

'You're referring to Freddie Saidi, I suppose.' Max felt suddenly furious at the prospect of him owning a slice of the magazine. He had already rejected him twice, and now Saidi was trying to push in through the back door. He was damned if Saskia's murderer was going to end up as a major shareholder in StreetSmart.

'I cannot comment on any individual approach,' Dick said, 'but I have to tell you that information has reached us over the last couple of days that gives us cause for concern. The fact that it has been relayed to us by a third party, and not by you, only adds to our unease.'

'What is this information?' Max looked around the table. Dick and Lee were poker faced. Yves was fiddling with his cufflinks. Max couldn't imagine what they could be referring to.

'Number one,' said Dick, 'we understand that a considerable portion of the print-run of the British edition has been destroyed before entering the distribution chain. Something about a truck overturning on the freeway?'

'Yes,' said Max. 'That is correct. There was a pile-up, it's not clear yet what happened there.'

'And can you estimate the approximate dollar variance that this accident will have on your business plan for this fiscal? As you appreciate, we don't own equity directly in the British edition, but the structure of our investment in terms of collateral means that there will inevitably be some impact.'

Max didn't have a clue what Dick was on about, but he replied, 'The lost copies were fully insured. There won't be a problem there.'

Dick nodded. He seemed content to leave the question of insurance at that. 'Let me move on to something else that's disturbing us. StreetSmart Interactive, in which we own equity via its status as a fifty per cent subsidiary of StreetSmart Inc. We understand that at a recent presentation, at which a seven-million-dollar contract was in play, your technology screwed up.'

How on earth did they know about the presentation? Saidi must have told them himself. 'We did have a problem,' Max admitted, 'but it wasn't our technology. Someone deliberately set out to sabotage the pitch.'

Yves Challon looked at Max in surprise. 'You are serious? Deliberate sabotage, you say? But who would do this?'

'Freddie Saidi,' replied Max.

'Saidi? But for what purpose? We heard that he was the client at this presentation.'

'I'm afraid I don't have an explanation. Not yet.'

Dick Mathias regarded Max quizzically across the tabletop. Lee was shaking his head.

'Let's move on, shall we?' said Dick. 'There are some other matters we need to ask you about. We understand that you've recently lost the substantial Bercuse advertising account worth some six million dollars. Then there's this business with the AFD and an offensive photograph in the new issue of *StreetSmart*. Talk us through that, will you, please? Did Saskia approve this image for publication?'

'No. The decision was taken after Saskia was murdered. It was taken by me.'

'That's what we'd heard,' said Dick. 'Listen, it isn't our policy as investors to second-guess the operating management of the various businesses in our portfolio, but it sounds as though you've pushed the envelope here, Max. *StreetSmart* is positioned as a premium upscale publication, kind of analogous to a Gucci or a Chanel. It strikes us as inappropriate to publish material of this nature. It mitigates against the brand.'

'I don't think so,' said Max. '*StreetSmart* has always had a reputation for provocative journalism. Saskia saw it as an essential part of the mix.'

'Correct me if I'm wrong, but this is the only time there's been a serious threat to the magazine's distribution? The publicity, anyway that I've seen, has all been negative. On CNN this morning they interviewed a committed Christian from Washington DC. She was setting fire to a copy of the issue. Have you made an estimate of the revenues at risk over this misjudgement?'

'Not yet. I'm afraid not.'

'I'm surprised,' said Dick. 'Lee, would you take Max through those numbers we were reviewing earlier on?'

'These are kind of down and dirty,' said Lee, 'but we're making an assumption here that fifty to sixty per cent of the distribution is in jeopardy, which equates to 1.45 million copies. Manufacturing cost per copy at one dollar is a straight 1.45 million dollars. We must then make a provision for the reimbursement of the same proportion of advertising revenue. This issue is carrying eighty-nine pages of paid space which, at 60,000 dollars a page, yielded 5.3 million dollars, indicating that approximately three million – or a total of 4.5 million dollars including circulation revenues – is at risk. We haven't factored in anything for incremental revenue loss from advertisers withholding business from future issues.'

Max felt sick. From the moment he'd seen the egregious Reverend Jesse Egan on ABC, he knew they were in trouble, but the financial ramifications for *StreetSmart* were even more serious than he'd realised. The American edition didn't turn a profit, and the hit on this issue would drive it deep into loss. And it was all his fault.

'What this adds up to,' said Dick, 'is a fundamental loss of confidence in management. One thing that we've learned at VCP – and it doesn't matter which sector we're operating in: autoparts, children's apparel, real estate – unless we have total confidence in our line management, it becomes impossible to recommend our investment strategies to the institutions and funds we represent. I'm sure you appreciate that.'

Max had a sinking feeling in his stomach. He knew what was coming next.

'Regrettably,' Dick went on, 'we have arrived at the point at which we have formed serious reservations over your temperamental suitability for the demanding role of chief executive officer.'

'I can assure you that I am temperamentally suitable,' Max broke in. He could hear a note of panic in his voice. 'And for God's sake don't sell out to Saidi. If he became a shareholder, it would be the end. I couldn't work like that.'

For the second time, Dick and Lee exchanged glances.

'Max,' said Dick. 'We've been making the assumption that you are fully familiar with the details of the structure of your sister's equity, but from your last remark, it is possible that you are not.'

'I know she owns forty per cent of the American edition and is the largest shareholder,' said Max.

'It is actually somewhat more complicated than that,' said Dick. 'Didn't Saskia confide in you her financial arrangements?'

'My sister never confided in anyone. It wasn't her style.'

'Four years ago,' Dick Mathias explained, 'when *StreetSmart* placed some of its equity, the company was in a mess. In terms of cashflow, it was critically overextended. Saskia had been using the profits from the British edition to fund the start-up over here in the States. The American edition was making progress in circulation and acceptance by the advertising community, but remained a long way from profitability. Saskia was looking for an anchor investor in her placement. We liked what we saw, but we told her and her attorney that we could only justify the degree of risk involved if we took some cross-collateral on the British edition. In other words, if the investment went belly-up or materially depreciated in the States, we would be able to recover our loss by realising part of her equity in the British company.'

'You mean Saskia mortgaged American *StreetSmart* against British *StreetSmart*?'

'That would be a fair analogy, I guess.'

'And you're saying that if you lose money on your investment over here, you can claim part of the British magazine.'

'That is correct.'

Max was appalled. 'Did Saskia realise that?'

'It wasn't a contingency any of us expected to kick in,' said Dick. 'We explained to her that our capital is patient. No one expected her to die.'

'So exactly what happens if you sell your stock to someone else?'

'Depending on the price we're able to realise, we would then review the four-year investment performance of StreetSmart Inc.

Stock has been changing hands at a significant discount to the placement price, so we have a book loss of some ten million dollars. Under the deal, we would look for reimbursement from London.'

'Ten million dollars?' Max was stunned. 'The magazine hasn't got ten million dollars.'

'Then I guess you'll have to put it on the block,' said Dick. 'I'm sure there won't be a problem disposing of it.'

The office was tilting. He couldn't see straight, the faces of Dick, Yves and Lee were shifting in and out of focus. All he could see were Dick's capped teeth, equine and dazzling white, as the room swam. He was losing *StreetSmart*. It was all over.

He closed his eyes. He needed to be absolutely calm, like Ken Craig at the Hutu roadblock outside Butare. Just like Ken, he had to talk his way through.

'Dick,' he began. 'I hear where you guys are coming from, and I understand your reservations about me as CEO. But I assure you that I can ride these problems out. My sister Saskia was tough, but I'm tougher. Much tougher. Let me tell you how tough I am, and then you tell me whether I can handle *StreetSmart*. Over the past ten years, I saw three hundred people killed, and then I stopped counting. There hasn't been one war of any significance – not one – that I haven't reported. When my arm was blown apart by a mine in the Panjshir Valley, I walked for four days across the mountains to get it fixed.'

Max glowered around the conference table like the platoon commander in *Die Hard*. He was gambling the farm on macho posturing, 'I've been under fire in Chechnya, Liberia, Somalia and Sarajevo. And, you'd better believe it, these situations are nothing like the sanitised versions they show you on CNN when you're eating your breakfast Fruit-Loops. You've heard the cliché, "When the going gets tough, the tough get going"? Well, I've lived that cliché. There's nothing anyone's going to teach me about tough.'

Max was into his stride now. In fact he was beginning to enjoy himself. Sometimes on assignment with Ken, they'd played a game similiar to this, trumping each other's stories on who was the toughest. Each round they raised the stakes, exaggerating more shamelessly.

Ken would say, 'Remember Srebrenica? The time we lived for ten days in a bombed-out basement on sewer rats?'

Max would reply, 'And then the rats ran out. So we had to eat that old Croat grandmother . . .'

Now Max was adapting the game for the benefit of Vision Capital Partners.

'As you're aware,' he forged on, 'I've only been in the publishing business for a week, but already I've formed an impression. Most of the people in publishing are wimps. They wouldn't last three days in a combat zone. They can't make tough decisions, they think slowly, they're flabby. They travel everywhere by limousine, eat in fancy restaurants . . . Gentlemen, I've seen more dead wood in one week in publishing than in the burnt-out ruins of Sarajevo.' He practically snarled at Dick Mathias.

Dick was listening intently, leaning forward in his seat.

'I want to strike a deal with you guys,' said Max. 'I want you to give me time. Just one week to kick ass, shake this business by its throat and unlock the value. A week's all I need. You know, people react in one of two ways to change. Either they embrace it or they resist it. Well, let me make something clear: I've never had much sympathy for resistance.' He fixed the three bankers with steely eyes. 'Gentlemen, do I have your backing?'

The conference room was silent for a full ten seconds before Dick Mathias responded.

'Max,' he said, 'we had pretty much resolved to liquidate our position in *StreetSmart*, and the likelihood is we will still take that route, but your observations there, some of your sentiments, they reflect the aggressive investment philosophy of VCP. We too have felt for some time that publishing as a sector is often managed with insufficient attention to the bottom line. I don't personally know what it is possible to achieve inside of a week, but if you can resolve the problems we spoke of earlier, we might be prepared to revisit our decision to drop the stock.

'That, however,' he said, 'will be contingent on your performance.'

[43]

The New York morgue stood on a particularly bleak stretch of First Avenue, across from the redbrick hospital called Bellevue. Three plate-glass windows overlooked the street, each covered with strips of plastic blind. The entrance crouched between expanses of brick and turquoise tiles, and the floors above ground level were concrete and had no windows facing the street. A wall bore the inscription 'City of New York. Office of Chief Medical Examiner'.

It was to the OCME that Saskia's body had been brought from her apartment, on the morning following the charity benefit at the Waldorf.

Max identified himself at the front desk and was taken to a viewing room on the first floor. He was told that an ME would be along shortly, who would explain the procedure for repatriating a corpse to a foreign country.

His heart was still palpitating from his encounter with the investment bankers. He couldn't work out how they were so well informed about the problems at *StreetSmart*. News of the Internet presentation could only have come from Saidi or Marcus Brooke: they were the only people there apart from Chip and himself. The AFD boycott was in the public domain – Dick Mathias probably did spot the woman from the Charismatic Gospel Chapel on CNN – but how had they known about the overturned Gërstler-Begg lorry? It was troubling.

Then he remembered the *Observer* report. Hadn't that referred to the truck accident? He was fairly sure that it had, but he doubted Dick Mathias read the British Sunday newspapers.

And then he saw it: Caryl Fargo. Caryl had been holding a copy of the paper on Concorde. Caryl must have shown the article to Dick Mathias. That was why she and Bob Troup were in New York. They'd been calling on Vision Capital Partners, trying to buy their equity in *StreetSmart*. It made sense now: Caryl's awkwardness when she spotted him on the flight and her remark to Anka at Bercuse Plaza about shortly owning a magazine in the States.

He knew Caryl was trying to destabilise *StreetSmart*. She had stolen his front cover, stolen his staff, intercepted the Bercuse ad-spend and now she was trying to steal the company.

Was it credible that she'd murdered Saskia too? He knew Caryl was jealous of her, and she'd been at the Waldorf on the night of the gala. On recent performance, she was certainly a little mad, but would she commit murder? And what about Carmelita Puentes? Was Caryl also implicated in that death?

An assistant medical examiner named Dr Basia Stern entered the viewing room. She had a strong, competent manner but made no secret of the fact that her workload was heavy and she didn't have a lot of time to spare. She told Max that she had been duty ME on the day Saskia's body had been discovered and that she'd been called out to the apartment on 67th and Park. She confirmed that initially the death had looked like an accident, but the autopsy had revealed abrasions on Saskia's neck consistent with strangulation. 'The blood had extravasated into the tissues.'

'Could you tell from the bruises whether the murderer was likely to be male or female? I mean, is there some difference in the degree of force?'

Dr Stern considered the question. 'In this particular case, I couldn't make that distinction. The neck was quite badly bruised, there was a pattern of multiple contusions. But I don't believe you could draw any reliable conclusion about the sex of the assailant. A lot would depend on the circumstances of the approach. If the victim had been taken by surprise, then the element of force could be less.'

'Which suggests she was caught off guard? Either by someone who entered the apartment, which could be anyone – an intruder off the street – or else by someone she knew and trusted who took her by surprise.'

'Possibly,' said Dr Stern. 'I don't think I'm an appropriate person to speculate on that. Down here we produce autopsy and toxicology results. The rest is police work.'

'Can I ask what the autopsy produced?'

'Beyond the abrasions to the neck? Well, I can tell you what your sister had eaten for dinner that evening, if you want to know that. Her gastric contents indicated salmon and asparagus, roasted guinea fowl with roasted Mediterranean vegetables and bitter chocolate.'

'You've got a good memory.'

'Most of the meals we diagnose in this job are less interesting. A body's brought in and maybe they've eaten a cheese cracker or a chilli dog. Not often we get to see a whole meal from a place like the Waldorf.'

Max sensed that Basia Stern resented the kind of high-society galas that Saskia frequented.

'Detective Przemysi mentioned you'd found traces of semen too?'

'That is also correct,' said Dr Stern. 'I told him there was evidence of sexual activity in the twenty-four hours preceding her death, most likely between lunchtime and early evening.'

'I wondered whether the motive for the murder could have been sexual?'

'The autopsy suggests not. The two incidents – the sexual intercourse and strangulation – were quite separate.'

'And the intercourse appeared to have been consensual?'

'There was no evidence of rupture to the genitalia.' Dr Stern looked at her watch. 'Excuse me, but I need to keep moving today. I need for you to identify your sister before we can release her body.' She lifted an extension and spoke to someone in another department.

Max felt suddenly apprehensive. He hadn't expected to be seeing Saskia's corpse. He wasn't sure how he would react.

A few minutes later a gurney bumped against the door, as it was wheeled into the viewing room by a black orderly. A pouch lay on the stainless steel surface of the trolley, secured top and bottom by Velcro straps. Max was surprised by how small and insubstantial the pouch was. It made him think of a child inside a sleeping bag.

Dr Stern ripped open the Velcro straps on the pouch, releasing a smell of formaldehyde.

And there, her head motionless against the black flap of the pouch, was Saskia.

The corpse was definitely that of his sister, and yet Max found it difficult to relate the grey-skinned cadaver with the exuberant Saskia he had known. Her red bob was lank and her eyes stared dully into the room. He realised with a start that he had never seen his sister's face in repose before. She had always been laughing, flirting, commanding attention. He thought of her tremendous energy and the way that her moods showed so clearly on her face: a rush of excitement about a great idea, followed by a sulky fury when it couldn't happen instantly. In death, she looked reduced and vulnerable.

He found he could recover her only in fleeting vignettes: the CNN newscast of her sweeping into the Oscars in her sequinned Armani dress; the memory of her tramping ahead across the flattened bracken of the common behind High Hatch; the little girl at the military camp in Kiplingweg.

Since her death, he felt that he had begun to understand her better. There was an element of tragedy about her that he had been oblivious to at those Christmases at High Hatch. Behind her remorseless pursuit of celebrity and success, Saskia had found personal relationships so complicated that she paid for sex.

He stooped over the body bag and kissed her goodbye. Her skin felt cold and damp against his lips. It was like kissing marble. He felt tears welling up inside him and he was overtaken by a sense of futility. Saskia had striven harder for success than anyone he knew, but what was she leaving behind? Ten years of old magazines – one hundred and twenty issues – and a son she'd never made time to see.

And already, within two weeks of her murder, Max had as good as lost the magazine she'd created. Saskia had never given Cody much love. Now she probably couldn't even give him *StreetSmart*.

Who *had* killed Saskia? The question went round and round in his head, but he couldn't make the pieces of the puzzle fit together. Saidi remained the obvious candidate: the cassette should contain conclusive proof that he'd known about Max's visit to Carmelita Puentes. He had motive, opportunity and a track record.

What, then, was Caryl Fargo's involvement? Could she really have formed some Faustian pact with Freddie Saidi? Bob Troup had seemed enthusiastic about Saidi as a potential proprietor that first afternoon when Max had dropped into the *StreetSmart* offices, and now Bob was working for Caryl.

Max was damned if he'd allow himself to be outmanoeuvred. There *had* to be an explanation for everything that was happening. He couldn't be approaching it in the right way, that was all. Think, Max, think.

He owed it to Cody and to his father and most of all to Saskia to save the magazine. And the only way he was going to do that was by solving the mystery of her death.

Well, he had a week.

Just then, it didn't feel as though he had a prayer.

[44]

Étienne Bercuse heard the bleep and whirr of the in-suite fax machine as it activated in the sitting room next door.

The digital Bercuse travelling alarm clock on his bedside table displayed the time in three cities: It was 02.14 local time, 19.14 in Paris and 13.14 in New York. For Bercuse, one of the particular pleasures of business trips to the Far East was the feeling of being perpetually a day ahead of North America. It made him feel ahead of the game.

He slipped out of the vast bed with its carved wooden bedhead in the shape of an Asiatic lion, and walked to the fax.

Outside, through darkened plate-glass windows, he could see the red and purple neon lights of downtown Taipei. The area surrounding the Formosa Regent Hotel was a virtual shanty town of wooden ryokans, hostess bars and sauna clubs. Bercuse had read somewhere that there were twenty thousand hostess girls operating in the city of Taipei alone. The number disturbed him slightly. He visited Taiwan six times a year and wondered whether twenty thousand would be enough.

He picked up the fax and made a face. 'I'm not believing this,' he muttered angrily. 'Bankers! What is the fuck wrong with these people?'

He snatched up a spiky pink lychee from the fruit bowl and lobbed it across the room. It was incredible. The offer he had made for their shareholding was more than generous. So why were they prevaricating?

Bercuse hated to be kept waiting. Whenever he conceived of a new acquisition, he agitated for it to be completed at record speed. Lawyers, attorneys, accountants and bankers routinely worked through the night while Bercuse abused them for lack of urgency. Today Li Fah Hsiang, President of Bercuse Asia-Pacific, had taken him on a hard-hat inspection of the new House of Bercuse concession at Taipei Metro shopping plaza. House of Bercuse was created as the prototype for a chain of pan-Asian malls-within-malls showcasing Bercuse merchandise with an emphasis on Chinese taste. There would be gold-plated pens with titanium nibs, gold and ruby cigarette lighters adjusted to shoot exceptionally high flames, jade Buddhas, five-litre crystal flasks of Serène fragrance and swimsuits emblazoned with oversized Bercuse logos. Bercuse was convinced that the product mix was perfect. It was all perfect. Except that the project was running twelve days behind schedule.

Walking through the lower floors of Taipei Metro up to the unfinished Bercuse level had made Étienne Bercuse feel impotent and enraged. The concessions of his competitors were open for business. They had passed a Gentleman Givenchy boutique, Chopard, S T Dupont, Montblanc, Pal Zileri, Fratelli Rossetti, Cerruti 1881, Jil Sander ... they were all there, but the House of Bercuse was twelve days late.

He had been returning to his hotel in the back seat of an air-conditioned white limousine, and wondering when to order the executive search company to identify Li Fah Hsiang's successor, when the idea had come to him.

He would launch separate editions of *StreetSmart* for the Asia-Pacific markets.

The idea – like all his best ideas – was so obvious that it only took someone half awake to see it. And once again that person was himself.

Ever since the economic crisis of November 1997, the luxury groups had all been wondering how to reactivate their Asian businesses. Bercuse would never forget the disastrous fortnight when the retail price of an Étienne Bis briefcase had to be adjusted more than a dozen times to reflect the nosedive of the baht, rupiah and ringgit.

Now, within his grasp, was the solution to reviving the businesses in Asia too. *StreetSmart* in Thai, Malay, Indonesian, Mandarin, Cantonese ... it would not be so hard to do, a little translation, maybe add a few local shopping pages. And, of course, reserve the advertising positions exclusively for his own brands.

All that stood in his way now was an American investment

company. Who had even heard of Vision Capital Partners? No, they would sell. He was convinced of it.

And if they didn't, *tant pis*, he would make a deal with Max Thompson in Milan instead. One way or another, he would be the proprietor of *StreetSmart* by next week.

As Étienne Bercuse walked back into the bedroom, he frowned. What the fuck did that tart think she was doing still in his bed? Her usefulness was over, he had never invited her to stay the night.

He touched the button marked Housekeeping on the bedside telephone. ''Allo. This is Suite 2010. Please send someone up immediately. There's a young lady here who needs to be cleared away.'

[45]

The traffic on the M4 into London had been brought to a virtual standstill by the rain. The Belgravia Limousines Mercedes that had collected Max at the airport was now immobile on the raised section by the Data General building. Max sat bleary-eyed in the back, having flown in overnight. He hadn't risked Concorde in case Caryl and Bob were on board.

For the duration of the eight-hour flight, he had wrestled with the enigma of Saskia's death. The facts kept blurring and refracting before his eyes like one of those Magic Eye holograms. There was a moment, shortly after the third Bloody Mary kicked in, when Max felt he could see it, but his clarity ebbed away along with the effects of the Stolichniya.

Dick Mathias had given him a week, but Max had no idea what to do with it. He was in any case only going to be in England until the afternoon. Racinda and Kitty had already flown out to the Milan fashion collections and he would meet up with them at the Sensi show that evening.

At some point over the Atlantic, he had returned to the mystery of Cody's paternity. There had been something about the way Freddie Saidi had spoken about him that made Max uneasy. What was it he'd said? 'He very good boy, Cody. Like my own son.' And later, 'If you want, I put a million dollars in his name in Switzerland.'

Max tried to fix Cody's features in his mind. Cody's complexion was very slightly olive coloured like Saidi's, and he wasn't particularly tall. And he was volatile and impetuous and could be a bully. Characterwise, it wasn't impossible.

The only topic on which Colonel Thompson resolutely refused to be drawn was that of Cody's father. On the level of social convention, he knew that his father disapproved of Saskia as a single mother. That the identity of the biological father had been widely speculated upon in the newspapers only added to the Colonel's unease. Max had noticed that the only articles about Saskia not to have been pasted into his parents' cloth-bound scrapbook related to Cody's parentage.

Once, when he was alone with his father in a car, Max had raised the question. They'd been driving together to the Esso garage to buy disposable nappies and Max had asked him right out, 'Has Saskia ever told you who Cody's father is?'

The Colonel had replied delphicly, 'Saskia may have learned only one thing from her military upbringing, and that's the old War Office dictum about sensitive information being on a strictly need-to-know basis.' His answer had left Max uncertain whether his parents had, or had not, been let in on the secret.

Today, Max meant to find out. The time for prevarication was over, this was too important. If his father knew anything, he must tell him.

Max got the driver to drop him at his flat off Ladbroke Grove. In the four days he'd been away, he noticed a new Korean place – the Kimchi Kafé – had opened up on the corner, and a shop selling Japanese topiary in glazed pots.

He descended the area steps and let himself into the flat. The front door at first refused to budge; then he saw that the doormat was piled high with envelopes and Jiffy bags with *StreetSmart* labels on the front. He ripped open the top one.

'Max. Welcome back from New York! Hope you had a successful trip. All these pages need to be signed off before midday today. What do you make of Lisa's piece on macrobiotic diuretics? It may need more work. *Also* how do you feel about classifying Hillary Clinton as HOT and Cherie Blair as NOT in the barometer of cool? Should these be switched round for the American edition? Marie-Louise.'

At the bottom of the note she had written, 'PS: We all watched you on CNN defending the magazine. You were GREAT. *Loved* your quote about not reading *StreetSmart* if you're only interested in the latest powder puff. Everyone in editorial cheered when you said that. Kevin Sky went puce!'

Elsewhere in the pile was a note from Kitty: 'Can't wait to see you in Milan and hear about the trip. I've been so worried about you.'

Max spent the remainder of the morning attempting to concentrate on the proofs, while all the time his mind kept reverting to the mystery surrounding Saskia's death. Who had strangled her? Who was it she'd had sex with on the afternoon before the Waldorf gala? Was it really Freddie Saidi, or some dick-for-hire she'd picked up at a bar?

Lisa's health-notebook item on shark-liver oil as a panacea for cancer struck him as specious, and he was busy toning it down when he thought, Chances are, I won't have anything to do with the magazine by the time this is published. He only had a week left, so what the hell was he doing, injecting a little objectivity into the research of some Japanese professor at Osaka University?

On the infrequent occasions that he travelled up to London, Henry Thompson liked to give his son lunch at the old General & Military Club in Albemarle Street. It had become something of a tradition that, before Max headed off on any overseas assignment, his father would treat him to a rollmop herring or chicken liver paté, followed by the club's legendary oxtail served with mashed potato and creamed carrots.

'There you go, you see,' the Colonel would say as the plate of disintegrating meat in brown gravy was placed in front of Max. 'Imagine it'll be a long time before you see anything that good again.' Colonel Thompson would then address a remark to one of the elderly Czech waitresses who served in the dining-room. 'This is my son, Yergena. He's off to Rwanda to take photographs of dead Africans. I was saying to him, I'm sure he won't find oxtail this good out there.'

The club waitress, Yergena, would then shake her head in disbelief at the whole enterprise, and ask them whether they'd like treacle pudding for sweet or would they prefer to see the cheese board?

With a slight feeling of foreboding, Max passed the pair of iron torchères on the club steps and went inside. A porter seated in a glass cubicle next to a tickertape machine regarded him with a watery eye.

'I'm joining Colonel Thompson. Has he arrived yet?'

'You'll find the Colonel and his other guest in the ladies' annexe,' said the porter. 'Straight down past the coat-stand, past the cloakroom, past the billiards room, door at the end on the left.'

Max's first thought was that his mother must be in London, which would be truly miraculous. He couldn't remember when Margaret Thompson had last made the fifty-minute train journey into town. From the day that her husband had retired from the regiment, she had never shown the slightest inclination ever to leave the neighbourhood of Farnborough again. It was as though she was compensating for moving house nineteen times in twenty-seven years.

However, when Max arrived at the ladies' annexe, it wasn't his mother who was the other guest but Cody.

'*Cody!* Hey, this is a surprise.' Max lifted his nephew off the ground and tossed him into the air. Cody always loved it when his giant of an uncle did that. 'And what's that round your neck, Cody? Am I imagining this? A *tie*?'

Cody made a face. 'Grandpa said I had to wear it or I couldn't come. Now I can't even breathe. It feels like I'm being strangled.'

'You look good, Cody. Grown up.'

'Anyway, where's my present from America?'

'Your present?'

'My *Godzilla*. You said you'd get me one, remember?'

Max groaned. He *had* promised, and he'd forgotten. He felt awful. With everything that had happened in New York, it had gone out of his head.

'Cody, I'm just so sorry, I forgot all about *Godzilla*. I'll have to get you something else.'

Cody shrugged. 'It's no big deal. I didn't want a *Godzilla* so much anyway. What I really want is a Freddy Krueger.'

It didn't surprise Max that theirs was the only table reserved for lunch that day in the ladies' annexe of the General & Military. The annexe – the one area of the club in which women and children under the age of sixteen were permitted to be entertained by members – was a desolate, cheerless room into which all the most rackety pieces of club furniture had gravitated, along with the least remarkable paintings and items of memorabilia. The Thompsons were shown to a table in the middle of a sea of white tablecloths, each laid with giant pieces of club cutlery – the soup spoons were as big as ladles – and baskets containing Melba toast.

In the interest of keeping things simple, Colonel Thompson announced that he would order lunch for everybody and that you couldn't beat the club specialities of a rollmop herring followed by oxtail stew.

Cody retched. 'Yuck. I'm not eating that, no way. I'd rather eat cat sick.'

'Cody. *Behave*,' said the Colonel sharply.

'I'm having hamburger, cheeseburger or chilli burger. Those are the only things. Otherwise I'm not eating.'

'You *will* eat, young man,' began the Colonel, but then he seemed to lose his will for the fight and turned wearily to Max. 'What are we supposed to do?' he asked. 'We don't know any more.'

'Listen, Cody,' Max said. 'It says here on the menu they do fishcakes. I'm going to order you fishcakes, chips and peas and I want to see a clean plate, OK? If I do, we'll see if we can find a Freddy Krueger after lunch in Hamleys. Is that a deal?'

Cody nodded his head sullenly.

'Geronimo, a deal,' said Max. Sometimes bribery was the only way.

'Now,' he said, 'it's going to take the kitchen a while to cook the lunch and I know how fidgety you get. If Grandpa doesn't mind, and seeing that we're the only people in the dining room, I think you can go over and look at those big paintings of battles above the sideboard. See if you can count exactly how many Zulus the British have killed. See the bodies all over the ground?'

'What's the prize if I get it right?'

Jesus. Cody, don't push your luck. 'Pudding. Peach Melba. That's ice cream with a peach on top, I think.'

'OK,' said Cody, sloping off as though he was doing Max an immense favour.

'Sorry about that, Dad,' said Max when he'd gone. 'I know you don't approve, but it seemed easier.'

'Everything's a struggle at the moment. Your mother's at her wits' end, it took over an hour yesterday just to get Cody to put his shoes on. And he's so *rude*. I'm sure you and Saskia were never like that. It makes your mother frantic. I had to bring him with me today just to give her a break.'

'It must partly be a reaction to Saskia. It's still early days. How's he taking it?'

'Never mentions her. *We* do, of course. We bring her into the conversation as much as possible: we don't want him to grow up thinking she can't be mentioned.'

Max gave his father an edited account of his meetings with

Detective Przemysi and Vision Capital Partners. It was difficult to know how to play it. He had no wish to worry his father, or denigrate Saskia. He went on, 'Dad, there's something I need to know, something important. I've asked you this before but you always evaded the question.'

'You're going to ask me about Cody's father, aren't you? I wish you wouldn't.'

'Why? What's the big secret? Why all the mystery?'

'Because I don't see that it's relevant, that's all,' replied Colonel Thompson. 'It upset your mother and me very much at the time. Saskia knew we didn't approve, but what can you do? It happened, and Cody was born and what else could we have done except offer our help? What would have happened to Cody otherwise?'

'I suppose Saskia would have had to take responsibility. If you and Mum hadn't been there . . .'

The Colonel looked suddenly wretched. 'If you must know, Max, Saskia made it clear that she wouldn't under any circumstances take Cody. If we hadn't agreed to, she was going to have him adopted.'

'*Adopted?*'

'That's what she said. Adopted, fostered. I forget the euphemism she used. She said she wouldn't have time to look after him as well as the magazine and commuting to and from New York. Margaret and I were obviously appalled. I questioned her about Cody's father then. I remember saying, "Won't the father have a view on this? Couldn't Cody go and live with him if you can't manage him yourself?" '

'And what did she say?'

'That the father wasn't in a position to.'

'Meaning?'

'You tell me. I assumed he was a married man.'

'But didn't she say *anything* about him?'

The Colonel thought. 'It was like getting blood out of a stone. You remember how Saskia was when she didn't want to discuss something. I told her, "Your mother and I are going to get landed with Cody for the next eighteen years . . ." ' His voice was rising and Max made a face for him to turn down the volume: Cody might hear.

He began again, more confidentially. 'I told her, "If your mother and I are going to bring Cody up, I hope the father, whoever he is, is going to chip in financially." It costs a small fortune in batteries just to keep Cody's computers going.'

'Does he contribute – the father, I mean?'

'Saskia implied that he wouldn't or couldn't. Try as I might, I couldn't get her to name him. Saskia used to send us whopping great cheques, but from the father: nothing.'

'I wonder why.'

'I can think of a couple of explanations. No, three. Saskia might have been too proud to ask. Wanted to show she could manage on her own. Or else the father doesn't have any spare funds. He could have had a dozen other offspring spread around the world for all we know.'

'And the third?'

'An out-and-out S-H-one-T. Which is the most probable of all.'

'So she never gave you the slightest clue? Not even a hint as to who he might be?'

'There was one thing she said. More of an implication than anything definite. I asked her where she'd met this prize shit and she replied, "Through work." '

'Through *StreetSmart*?'

'That's what she said, but of course that could mean anything, couldn't it? Journalist, photographer, film actor, Saskia knew so many people. At those parties of hers, I used to take a good look around, see if I could spot any resemblances. That's why I went.'

'I thought you went because you enjoyed them.'

His father looked sheepish. 'Well, I suppose I did enjoy them, up to a point. Saskia drew an interesting crowd. But I can assure you, I always had more than half an eye out for the father.'

Max couldn't help laughing. 'And what were you intending to do, Dad, if you spotted him? Hand him a bill?'

'And a bloody large one at that.' The Colonel shrugged. 'I often used to wonder, looking around those parties, if he were somewhere in the room. I glared at a few people.'

'The newspapers suggested various Hollywood film stars.'

'Feasible,' replied the Colonel, 'but I doubt it.'

'Why's that?'

'One very good reason: because if Cody's father *had* been a movie star, I don't think Saskia would have been so mysterious about it. I think we would have known. That isn't intended as a criticism of Saskia, but I knew my daughter quite well.'

Cody reappeared at the table in a crackle of rifle-fire. His eyes were sparkling. 'Two hundred and sixty-one,' he whooped. 'And I know I'm right because I counted them two times.'

'I'm coming to check myself,' said Max. 'Two hundred and sixty-one, you say?'

'I bet you can't even spot them all,' said Cody. 'It's really hard. Some of the dead Zulus are half-covered by their shields, you can only see their legs poking out. And some have been blown to bits by cannons.'

'I'll take your word for it in that case, Cody. Well done, you've won the prize.'

'If I don't have the peach with my Peach Melba,' he said, 'can I have extra ice cream to make up for it?'

PART THREE

[46]

Linate airport seemed to have been hijacked by Milanese fashion houses. A hangar alongside the runway had the words EMPORIO ARMANI spelled out on the roof in giant steel letters. The terminal building was draped with banners for Sensi ready-to-wear and accessories. Even the side of the bus that transported passengers to the arrivals terminal was freshly painted with advertisements for the new Versace fragrance.

Max took a taxi straight from the airport to the Sensi palazzo in the Via San Spirito. If the traffic was light, he should arrive in time for the show with fifteen minutes to spare.

He closed his eyes and tried to psych himself up for the challenge ahead. Somewhere at the fashion show would be Étienne Bercuse, and this was Max's chance to get to him. Somehow he had to make contact with Bercuse and find out why he'd cancelled his advertising contracts with *StreetSmart*. And how could Max persuade him to change his mind, before Dick Mathias's deadline ran out in six days?

The taxi was entering the centre of Milan. They passed some kind of triumphal arch and a Renaissance baptistry with elaborate coats-of-arms above the door. Banners for Versus and Trussardi were strung across the Corso Europa and the dusty plane trees on both sides of the road were plastered with posters for Moschino.

Max was increasingly sure that Kevin Sky's original theory – that Caryl Fargo had struck a one-time volume deal on the Bercuse business – was correct. Caryl had probably conceived it specifically to undermine Max's credibility with Vision Capital Partners. Having secured the advertising for Incorporated at a suicidal margin, she then represented it to Dick Mathias as a body blow for *StreetSmart* and proof that Max wasn't up to the job.

It maddened Max to think of himself being outmanoeuvred like that. Caryl must also have commissioned whoever it was who hacked into the *StreetSmart* computer that night. No wonder Dick Mathias was so well briefed about the Bercuse revenues.

Inside the folder that he was using as a briefcase, Max located the Bercuse fax that Kitty had sent three days earlier to the office in New York, downloaded from the *StreetSmart* database. He read the twelve pages, memorising the numerous subsidiaries and brands within Étienne's empire. Alongside each brand was detailed data on positioning and the price paid for each advertisement over the past five years. Max noticed that some Bercuse companies, such as Serène and Tranquilité, insisted that their advertisements appear within the first third of the magazine, and were charged more as a result. D Troit Denim was prepared to go in the second half, which was cheaper. The St-Cyr-le-Châtel champagne marque specified that their campaigns should face the drinks or food column, and they were charged a separate premium for this privilege.

If Caryl Fargo had accessed the database, then she'd known every last secret of the Bercuse business with *StreetSmart*.

Long before they reached the Via San Spirito, they hit a tailback of traffic heading for the Palazzo Sensi. The Via Monte Napoleone was already jammed with black Mercedes edging towards the show, and the pavement thronged with fashion editors and store buyers carrying invitations and bags of shopping and takeaway cappuccinos.

Max leaned out of the cab window, scanning the crowd for any sign of Kitty. After four days away, he was excited and slightly apprehensive at the prospect of seeing her again. He had missed her. There was so much he wanted to tell her. He hoped that, after the Sensi show, they could find some quiet restaurant and have dinner together, preferably alone. Kitty had already warned him that Racinda would expect to join them. And afterwards, Max looked forward to checking out the Hotel Principe di Savoia with Kitty too. If this ridiculous-sounding presidential suite really had been booked for him, they may as well both make the most of it.

A black tented *porte-cochère* had been attached to the façade of the Palazzo Sensi, and two thousand people were waiting in lines to be let inside. The first Sensi show under Bercuse ownership was evidently a hot ticket event. Three Italian television outside-broadcast trucks were double-parked in the Via San Spirito, with satellite dishes on their roofs, and the road was a spaghetti-swirl of rubberised electric cables. A dozen security guards in black suits manned the narrow entrance between metal crush-barriers, through which they occasionally permitted a hand-picked celebrity to pass, while several hundred guests at the front were squeezed against each other by the press of others behind.

Every so often the crowd was illuminated by television lights and the flashbulbs of the paparazzi as a star was ushered through the throng. Max, paying off his taxi, thought he recognised Leonardo DiCaprio stepping out of a Mercedes, trailed by Claudia Cardinale, the footballer David Beckham and Posh Spice.

He pushed his way into the crowd, looking out for Kitty. After he'd advanced a few yards, he felt that he'd been subsumed into one of the more grotesque and turbulent allegorical paintings of Hieronymus Bosch. On every side were dysfunctional and morbid human beings of a kind he'd never seen before, even in the aftermath of civil war or natural disaster: raven browed, noir lipped, preternaturally anxious, gum chewing, despondent like an army in retreat as they shuffled their way towards the crush-barriers. From the names and companies on their invitations, which they clutched tight with both hands as though they expected at any moment to have them snatched away, Max could see that every last inhabitant of Planet Fashion was there to witness the rebirthing of Sensi.

There were department store buyers from Neiman Marcus, Bloomingdale's and Saks Fifth Avenue in the States; from the Galeries Lafayette in Paris; from Harrods, Harvey Nichols and Browns in London; from Isetan and Seibu in Tokyo; from the Galleria in Seoul and La Rinascente in Milan. There were newspaper and magazine fashion editors, style directors, art directors, bookings editors, executive editors, editors-in-chief, editors-at-large, fashion markets editors, freelance stylists, model agents, cocaine dealers, publishers, copyists and style pirates, stock market analysts, boutique owners, personal publicists, self-publicists and breakfast television presenters.

He was elbowing his way closer to the entrance, where the crowd was now being admitted one by one, when a familiar voice made him tense up.

'What the fuck are we doing here anyway, standing about like some fucking fat hooker in the Bois de Boulogne? I thought I'd told you to fix this, Marcus. You said we'd go straight in.'

'Regrettably, Freddie, there does appear to be some kind of hold-up, but we are moving in now. I know your seat inside is excellent.'

'It had better be,' said Saidi.

As soon as Max realised that Saidi and Brooke were in the line, he ducked down behind a group of American buyers from Barney's. Sometimes he regretted being so tall. What was Saidi doing in Milan anyway? By now, he must have learned about the switched tapes at the East River. Whatever happened, he mustn't find out that Max was in Milan too. He was under no illusions: Saidi was dangerous. He could well have killed twice already.

Edging sideways he found himself face-to-hem with a familiar buttery, soft, indecently short suede dress. Somewhere way above was long fair hair and a pair of big blue eyes.

'Kitty!' He stood up, turning his head away from Saidi, and hugged her. 'It's so great to see you.'

Her black leather jacket was soft and smelt like the interior of a luxurious new car. Just then, he felt like jacking the fashion show and taking Kitty directly back to the Principe.

'You look pretty good yourself,' said Kitty. She appraised him critically. 'Definitely hunky.' She took his hand and squeezed it. 'How was New York? I've been so worried about you. I haven't heard a thing since you rang from that hotel lobby.'

'So much has happened, you won't believe it. I'm not kidding, it's been one horror story after another. I can't think straight.'

'What about the magazine? Are you more confident now?'

Max laughed hollowly. 'Actually, Kitty, I doubt I'll even own it by this time next week. It's falling apart around my ears.'

'You're not serious?'

'Deadly serious.'

They had reached the front of the queue. Security men were scrutinising invitations while Sensi public relations people hovered hawkishly in the background. Some way ahead, Max spotted Karis Landau mounting the steps to the palazzo. And, close behind her, Saidi and Brooke, escorted by a Sensi usherette.

'Got your ticket OK?' asked Kitty.

'Sure.' Max handed over the cream and black card.

'Christ!' said Kitty. 'You've got AA14.'

'Should I be impressed?'

'That's front row centre. Right at the foot of the runway. Probably the best seat in the place. You don't understand; normally the double A seats are reserved for the owner of the house, or someone like the mistress of the President of Italy.'

'Well,' said Max, shrugging, 'I guess that means I'll get a good view of the supermodels.'

Kitty laughed and kissed him on the cheek. 'Let's get one thing straight, Max, before the shows start. You have eyes for only one woman in this town, and that's *me*. No Helena, no Kate, no Naomi, just me. Got it?'

'I'll do my best.'

'Do that,' said Kitty. 'You're here to look at the clothes, remember.'

They entered the palazzo through a loggia with a mosaic floor depicting a chained dog and a Roman slave, and along a barrel-vaulted corridor lined with Renaissance sculpture. Eventually they arrived at the entrance to an immense black tent, with a catwalk down the centre and banks of raised seating on either side. The tent must easily hold two thousand people, Max reckoned.

'How do we know where we're sitting?'

'They'll direct you, but it always works in the same way,' Kitty explained. 'One side of the runway is reserved for press, the other side is for buyers – stores, boutiques, licensees etc. The press side is smarter, incidentally, we slightly look down on the trade side. Then you've got the photographers over there in their pen.' She pointed to a steep enclosure with what looked like three hundred lenses protruding from the darkness. 'And then – if you look down there – there are about five rows of seats at the foot of the runway. That's where you are. Sometimes the American press gets put there, because they're considered the most powerful since they're the biggest market. Otherwise, it's for the owner, film stars, rock stars, ministers of culture, whoever they can get, actually. Most of the celebrities are paid to turn up.'

'*Paid?* Why?'

'Well, bribed. The designers pick up their air fares and hotel bills and give them clothes to take home. It works for the stars too, because they get photographed everywhere. All they have to do in return is applaud. Great PR for all concerned.'

'It sounds very calculated.'

'You can assess anyone's clout at any particular moment by where they're seated at the shows. Editors in the front, then deputies and fashion directors, then assistants and so on back. I'm in D109. The more important the publication, the better your seat.'

'So where does *StreetSmart* rank?'

'Front row for the editor. Saskia insisted. She boycotted shows unless she got front row. At the beginning, the magazine didn't merit it of course. It used to drive Saskia demented, having to look over the shoulders of *Vogue* editors. But as *StreetSmart*'s prestige improved, so did the seats.'

An usherette in a taupe-coloured Sensi cocktail suit took Max to his place, which, as Kitty had predicted, was plumb centre of the front row. It occurred to him that, from this angle, he would virtually be looking up the girls' skirts.

On the back of his seat, a square of cardboard had been inscribed by a calligrapher: 'AA14. Max Thompson. *StreetSmart*, UK.' The seats on either side of him were not yet filled and he leaned forward to check out their cards. The place to his left read: 'AA15. Étienne Bercuse. Bercuse SA.'

Max closed his eyes and smiled. What an incredible piece of luck. There is a God! When he'd seen how big the tent was, he'd worried that he'd never get within a hundred feet of Étienne. And now he was placed right next to him. He mustn't blow it.

He turned to the seat on his right and groaned. No, it wasn't possible, it just wasn't possible: 'AA13. Ms Caryl Fargo. Incorporated Publications, UK.'

For one thing, Max wasn't sure how accountable he could be for his actions on seeing Caryl. Since discovering her duplicity with Vision Capital Partners, he didn't trust himself not to do something he might later regret.

'Max? Oi, up over here, yer big pooftah.'

Someone was bellowing at him from the photographers' pen, a voice he'd recognise anywhere: Mick Paarl.

Max went over to the pen and there, six rows into the scrum, was Mick giving him the finger.

'Mick, what on earth are you doing here? I thought you were in Croatia.'

'Postponed, mate. And then *The Sunday Times* asked me to do this for them. Some daft stunt for the magazine. They're sending war photographers to cover the fashion shows and the fashion department have all been sent to Baghdad.'

'You'll enjoy it, Mick. Maybe you'll solve the mystery of Cindy Crawford's tits.'

'She's not even here, mate. I'm serious, all the models are dogs. Flat-chested with it.'

'You're meant to be looking at the clothes, remember.'

Mick pulled a face. 'You'll never believe who I've just seen. I'm busting to tell Ken this.'

'Let me guess. Freddie Saidi?'

'The man himself. Large as life and twice as ugly. What the fuck's he doing here?'

'Same as you, I expect. Looking at the clothes. Maybe he's giving another party, Mick. For all the models. He's sure to ask you back.'

'Wouldn't touch them with a barge-pole, mate, not even for ready money. Bring back the Gulf Air stewardesses, that's what I say.'

'Well, don't tell Saidi I'm in Milan. I mean it. When you said he was dangerous, for once you weren't exaggerating.'

The tent was filling up fast. The aisles heaved with people and the Sensi PRs were imploring editors and buyers to take their seats. Every so often a fresh celebrity would be escorted to the front and the flashbulbs of the paparazzi would go mad. Max watched while several thousand frames were tossed off on Matt Dillon while he sat dumbly on his chair.

Étienne Bercuse had still not arrived, but as Max sat down he saw Caryl heading for her seat, closely followed by Bob Troup. Caryl was decked out for the shows in a fitted black suit and shades with a gold Sensi 'S' on the bridge.

Caryl and Bob, ignoring Max, struck up a conversation with someone in the row behind. Max heard Bob say, 'I'm *told* this issue of *StreetSmart* eventually made it on to the stands in some areas, but I haven't actually seen it myself.'

A tall, supercilious man in a conspicuously well-cut grey suit was escorted along the front of the catwalk by five Sensi usherettes. As he took his place, Max was momentarily overpowered by a warm front of citrus and sandalwood. 'Good evening. I am Étienne Bercuse.' He spoke stiffly and his French accent carried a slight American inflection.

'Max Thompson. Editor of *StreetSmart*.'

'Of course, I was introduced to your sister. I would like to say I am very sorry about what happened. It is bad news for you, *non*?'

'Yes. It's tragic, but we're trying to put it behind us now, we have to. The magazine is doing well.'

'I like *StreetSmart* very much,' said Étienne. 'It has – something. Quite chic, I think.'

'Thanks. I'm glad you think that. For some reason, though, the Bercuse companies aren't advertising with us at the moment.'

'Really? I am surprised.'

Max held Étienne's stare but the Frenchman didn't blink.

'You used to support us, but just after Saskia died, everything was cancelled.'

'It is possible.' Étienne pursed his lips. 'Sometimes, you know, an executive in a particular market will try some new policy . . .'

Max took a deep breath. 'I heard that you personally ordered the cancellation.'

Étienne regarded him sharply.

'In fact, that is quite correct.'

'Well, why, then?'

'Why? Because I was concerned that, without your sister, *StreetSmart* will lose its edge. I think it is better to wait and see what develops.'

'My first issue is out now, the first with my name in the front as editor. Now you've seen it, are you coming back in?'

Étienne looked at him for a long time before replying. 'Am I coming back in, as you put it? My answer is, yes, I would like to advertise again in *StreetSmart*. I could be prepared to do that.'

Max's heart soared. If the Bercuse business returned by next issue, he might be able to stave off Dick Mathias. If he could only get a firm commitment on the six million dollars.

Étienne hadn't finished, however. 'You know,' he said, 'I asked my office to place you next to me today: I need to talk with you.'

Max regarded him uneasily. So the seating at the show was no accident.

'As you may be aware, my company has a big commitment to the prestige market. At present, I believe we rank number five in net sales, but number two in terms of earnings per share.'

Max wasn't sure whether he was expected to say 'Well done', and decided to nod studiously.

'Our declared aim is accelerated compound growth at an annual rate of not less than one hundred per cent for each of the next three fiscals, by which point our revenues will exactly double those of our nearest competitor.'

'Impressive,' said Max, whilst thinking, If you're that big, what's the problem with our advertising?

'No doubt you are wondering, "How is Étienne Bercuse proposing to achieve this ambitious programme within such a limited time-frame?"'

'Yes.'

'One word: acquisition. Strategic acquisition, globally exploited by brand development and expansion.'

Even in the half-light of the tent, Max could see that Étienne's eyes were blazing intensely, and he wondered whether he might be a little crazy.

'Acquisitions need not be restricted to brand names in fashion, accessories and fine wine. At Bercuse, we will shortly own hotel and leisure marques with potential for franchise across all markets. Why should there not be a Hôtel Crillon in every large city? Or a Chantilly or Ascot racecourse in the States and Japan?'

Max still couldn't figure out where any of this was leading.

'To complete the circle, we are committed to building a position in publishing. For some time I have been exploring a number of options in this sector.'

'You have?'

'This is the reason I want to talk with you this evening. I have decided the next strategic acquisition for Bercuse will be *Street-Smart*.'

'*StreetSmart*?' It was unbelievable. Was there one person in the whole damn tent who didn't want to buy his magazine? 'You want to buy *StreetSmart*?'

'For us at this time, I think it would make good business, *non*?'

'I'm sorry, but the magazine isn't for sale.' How many times had he used this line in the last week? He'd soon be saying it in his sleep. 'I really am sorry, but it's a family obligation.'

Étienne smiled. 'I understand. There is the family honour to consider. I have bought businesses several times before from their founding families. Always it is painful to let go.' He shrugged. 'That is why, in such situations, we are prepared to pay above the market valuation. Believe me, we can be quite generous. One time, you know, when I was buying St-Cyr-le-Châtel, some of the family members were quite unhappy about it. Now they live in Monte Carlo and are quite happy, I think.'

'I'm serious, I can't sell *StreetSmart*. There have been other offers and I've told everyone the same thing. I have to consider my family and the long-serving staff . . .'

At that moment, Max became conscious of a disturbance further along the row. A female voice was shouting hysterically, and he heard his own name. Heading towards him was a demented-looking woman in leggings and mocha-coloured lipstick. Her face was contorted with fury, and she was shaking a ring-encrusted fist in his direction. Trailing behind her were several Sensi PRs and security men.

'Racinda!' Max leaped to his feet as his fashion director approached.

'I would like you to see this,' she screamed. 'Go on, look at it, please.' A cream and black invitation card was thrust beneath Max's face. 'Take a look at where *StreetSmart*'s fashion director is seated these days. I'd like you to appreciate the level to which this magazine has *sunk* since Saskia died.'

Max studied the card, which was numbered Q143. 'It does seem quite far back,' said Max.

'Far back? *Far back!* It's *seventeenth row*. I didn't realise the rows *went* that far back. The person in the next seat is a *Swiss newspaper journalist*. I'm humiliated, completely humiliated. And it's all your fault. Ever since you arrived, *StreetSmart*'s lost it.'

'There's clearly been a mistake,' Max said, 'but it's easily solved. You sit here in my place, and I'll take yours. We'll swap.'

'Oh no we won't,' said Racinda. 'The damage is done already. The whole industry is gossiping about it. Q143! They're all turning round and staring.'

Max was increasingly conscious of the attention that Racinda and he were attracting. He noticed Marcus Brooke do a double-take from the front row of the buyers' seats, and point him out to Freddie Saidi. Caryl and Bob were transfixed. He had never seen Bob look so happy.

'I'm resigning,' Racinda announced. 'In front of all these witnesses. You heard me. I quit. And I'll tell you something else, Max, I'm taking all my contacts with me – all the photographers, hairdressers, everyone. It's me they're loyal to. Not one of them will ever work for *StreetSmart* again.' She turned to Bob, two places along the row. 'If that offer is still open, Bob, I'll move to *Town Talk*.'

'Welcome aboard, Racinda. Sensible of you to abandon the sinking ship. At least with us your next sitting won't end up on the motorway.'

Caryl and Bob were still sniggering as the lights dimmed for the start of the Sensi show.

Étienne Bercuse leaned over towards Max in the darkness and said, 'I take it that woman was one of the long-serving staff you mentioned earlier. It is nice they are all so loyal, *non*?'

For the first full minute of the show, the runway remained in total darkness. The heavily amplified roar of a jet engine began somewhere in the roof of the tent and intensified until the banks of seats started to vibrate. The sound was deafening and Max's eardrums felt like they might explode. All around him, the audience were grimacing and covering their ears with their hands. Even during the siege of Sarajevo, when shells were landing in the marketplace at the rate of six a minute, Max had never experienced anything like it. The only thing that came close was standing without earplugs under the descent path of a Chinook helicopter.

Then, as suddenly as it had begun, the sound cut out and the tent was completely silent, and the runway was bathed in bright white light so fierce you had to shield your eyes against the glare.

A model – gaunt and entirely without expression – began to jerk her way along the five-hundred-foot catwalk. She was wearing a short grey skirt like a schoolgirl's, and a scrap of transparent grey chiffon as a top. It was impossible to guess her age. From a distance she looked twelve or thirteen, but by the time she reached the foot of the runway, Max thought she might be sixteen. Her breasts, which were on full view through the chiffon blouse, looked like two pink M&Ms balanced on poached gull's eggs.

The model paused for an instant while the three hundred photographers in the pen took her picture. The sound of so many camera shutters was like a plague of locusts swarming overhead.

As she began the return journey up the catwalk, two new models emerged from behind the trapezium. These seemed to Max to be wearing identical outfits to the first girl, but this time spontaneous applause broke out from all sides.

Caryl leaned across Max to Étienne and said, 'Bravo, Monsieur Bercuse. You've re-energised the whole brand.' With Caryl, it was always hard to gauge her precise level of insincerity.

Three new models, younger this time, embarked on the long journey towards the photographers. From the blankness in their eyes, Max wondered whether they might be on something. The third girl, blonde with the protruding ribs of a chronic anorexic, was topless and modelling a microscopic grey sarong. Freddie Saidi, whom Max could just see through the refracting light, appeared to be jotting down numbers.

Now the runway was full of girls. They were being sent out in waves, twenty at a time, like conscripts from the trenches. They slopped towards him four abreast, some barefoot, others in flatfooted sandals, their arms dangling limply by their sides.

This was the first fashion show Max had ever seen, and it absorbed him. It was the march of the living dead, and yet there was something perversely energising about this procession of sad, beautiful, gamine creatures. He kept thinking, I could make you happy, or else, For God's sake, lighten up, there are people on this planet with real problems, such as is there anything to eat today? But mostly Max thought how pretty they were, or could be. From time to time, he even remembered to look at the clothes.

It was swelteringly hot. Across the runway, Max could see the audience starting to glisten. Fashion editors, who were sketching the new silhouettes as the models passed by, mopped their brows with their sleeves. A fat American in the trade section began fanning himself with his programme. Sandwiched between Étienne and Caryl, Max thought he might be asphyxiated by the mingling odours of cologne and sweat.

As the show progressed, the soundtrack became more urgent and obscure. It seemed to incorporate fifteen seconds of everything: rock, soul, jungle, rap, folk, 'sixties, 'seventies, African tribal drums, all melding arbitrarily into each other. The rhythmic hammering of a blacksmith on a forge was followed by the muezzin call, followed by the whooping of Red Indians around a campfire. The girls processed to the heartbeat of a newborn baby, to random gunfire, to the ecstatic

344

shrieks and moans of orgasm, to the saw and crash of felled timber in a Brazilian rainforest. Sometimes a half-coherent voice was dubbed across the tape breathing, '*I am not afraid of the Big City, I am not afraid of the Big City, I am not afraid of the Big City.*' There was a snatch of the Velvet Underground and Nico that Max recognised from long ago, the keening of a blue whale, a French *chanteuse*, the humming of a kazoo. The eerie, digital larynx of a robot proclaimed, 'I-love-you-babe-with-my-heart-and-my-cunt.'

While Max watched, he analysed the implications of his conversation with Étienne Bercuse. It hadn't occurred to him that Étienne might also be in the market for *StreetSmart*. Whichever way he looked at it, it had to be bad news. For one thing, Bercuse had seriously deep pockets. Max guessed that they had access to unlimited corporate capital and could pretty well buy whatever they wanted. Next to Bercuse SA, Incorporated Publications and Freddie Saidi were nowhere.

It also occurred to him that Bercuse was precisely the kind of outfit that would impress Dick Mathias. Once he knew that Étienne viewed the magazine as a bid target, there was no way Dick would resist trading his thirty per cent.

Max resolved that, as soon as the show finished, he would ring Philip Landau from the hotel and talk it through with him. He wanted to chew it over with Kitty too, over a bowl of decent pasta and a large drink. Maybe they could still find a way through all this.

Some instinct told him that he was being watched and he turned his head slowly.

Freddie Saidi was glaring angrily at him. Max turned away. A minute later, he glanced again in Saidi's direction, and saw that he was still being watched.

[47]

'Kitty! Into this taxi, quick. Let's get the hell out of here.'

The moment the show ended, Max had legged it to the exit and out into the Via Monte Napoleone. He flagged a cab and had it wait on the corner while he found Kitty. He needed to get clear of the palazzo before Saidi or Brooke got a fix on him.

Kitty slid in next to him on the back seat. Her legs, in the pale suede skirt, looked wonderfully long and smooth. As the taxi headed for the hotel, Max felt the first stirrings of lust.

'Am I glad to see *you*!' he said. 'There's so much to tell you, it's unbelievable. I need to make a call from the hotel, then dinner. Did you manage to book anywhere?'

'Bice. For three, unfortunately. Racinda's insisting on coming along.'

'Not any more. She just resigned to join *Town Talk*.'

'You're not serious. *Why*, for God's sake?'

'Didn't like her seat at the show.'

'Well, if Racinda's resigned as fashion director, can I apply for her job?'

Max laughed. 'You don't hang about in this business, do you?'

'I know you'll get loads of applications, but I've been in the department for seven years. I could do it standing on my head.'

Max looked at her. Her big blue eyes were steady.

'Standing on your head, you say?'

'Or flat on my back, if you prefer,' she replied lightly, touching his knee with her palm. 'Oh look, we're here already. The Principe di Savoia. Maybe we should talk about this upstairs.'

Max checked in and was shown to the suite by a flunky in a bresaola-coloured jacket and matching toupée, who demonstrated how to unlock the mini-bar and the windows out on to the terrace. The suite was immense, full of tapestry chairs and dark Italian furniture. On the floor next to the bed was an ironed linen mat for standing on while you removed your slippers, and a fifteenth-century panel of the Annunciation, with the Virgin kneeling next to a vase containing a lily, hung on the bedroom wall.

Kitty was already half out of her clothes, and was peeling her suede dress over her head. As usual, Max was struck by how terrific her figure was, firm and slender.

He knew he should ring Philip Landau, but his priorities had suddenly been reset. Just then, he needed Kitty more than he could possibly express. He tipped her on to the linen bedcover and pressed his face against her breasts. Her body felt warm and slightly sweaty beneath him, and her skin and hair smelt of soap and Nocturnes de l'Homme Pour Elle.

'Four days,' pouted Kitty, as she directed him inside her. 'That's how long it's been. You left for America last Sunday.'

'It feels longer,' said Max.

'It feels exactly like I remember it. Very, very long,' said Kitty contentedly. 'I don't ever want to be away from you like that again.'

It was an hour before they finished making love, by which time Max felt all the tension of the trip to New York had been fucked out of his system. Kitty was curled up in a ball on the bedcover, breathing softly, her head pressed into his shoulder. Through the undrawn curtains, Max saw that it had become dark outside.

He moved softly out of bed and into the bathroom to take a pee. While he was standing there, he remembered he must ring Philip Landau. For one thing, Landau might have some advice on whether he should inform Dick Mathias about Bercuse's offer. Maybe he was statutorily obligated to tell Vision Capital Partners.

He wandered naked into the sitting room and slid open the doors on to the terrace. It was chilly outside but the air would help clear his head. He always felt more objective in the aftermath of making love. For some inexplicable reason, ejaculation defuzzed his brain.

The large terrace was dotted with terracotta pots and metal furniture, enclosed by a brick parapet – the terrace on which Saskia had given parties twice a year during the collections. Max pictured a long bar, covered by a white tablecloth, set up at one end, with waiters in those bresaola-coloured jackets dispensing Bellinis. Saskia would have stood at the entrance greeting guests. He wondered whether Freddie Saidi had ever attended any of the parties on the roof.

The view from the terrace was spectacular. Even in the darkness, he could see the skyscape of half of Milan. He walked round the perimeter of the terrace, spotting the spires of a dozen churches and the great dome of the Duomo, the Pirelli tower and the roof of the Fascist Stazione Centrale, a neon advertisement for Sensi on top, illuminating the night sky.

Sensi was everywhere. He could say this for Étienne Bercuse: he knew how to organise a marketing campaign. He'd left nothing to chance.

He went back into the suite and dialled Philip Landau. The answerphone was on so he left a message. 'Philip? It's Max. I'm in Milan but something's come up. You won't believe this, but there's a third – yes, seriously, a *third* – person trying to buy *StreetSmart*. This time it's Étienne Bercuse. It gets worse and worse. I do wish these people would just fuck off and leave us alone, don't you? Anyway, please give me a ring. I'm staying at the Hotel Principe di Savoia. It's ten past eight here, Italian time. I'm about to go and have dinner with one of our fashion editors, Kitty Marr.'

They threw on some clothes and headed back across the city in a taxi. Kitty was subdued during the journey, hardly saying anything, just staring out of the window.

Max put his arm around her. 'You all right, Kitty?'

'Fine.'

'You're so quiet. You sure nothing's the matter?'

She shrugged. 'I was only thinking. It's no big deal.'

'Thinking what?'

'I wasn't actually going to say this, but since you're asking, I was thinking about Racinda's job and how there's no way you'll ever give it to me.'

'Why do you think that?'

'Because you won't. You'll say there's a conflict of interest or something, because of us.'

Max liked that expression – 'because of us' – with its implication of an enduring relationship. 'Kitty, I'm not making any decisions about Racinda's replacement right now. I'm not even going to think about it until after Milan. But I give you my word: you're no less likely to get the job because of us. Quite the reverse.'

Kitty leaned over and kissed him. 'Thanks, Max. I told you before how ambitious I am, it goes back to my lorry park days. I just couldn't bear it if my career was screwed up, even for something like . . .'

'Screwing me?'

They arrived at the restaurant in the Via Borgospesso, which was pleasantly old-fashioned, with Italian dishes displayed on a narrow table down the middle of the room. As the waiter showed them to their places, Max noticed plates of mozzarella and basil and tureens of white bean soup and ravioli and fried zucchini. Until he saw the food, he hadn't realised how hungry he was.

It felt good to be sitting across a restaurant table with Kitty. They ordered steaming bowls of spaghetti with clams and then Max devoured a hunk of meat that looked like a boxing glove on a bed of spinach. They drank two bottles of Chianti and, for the first time in days, Max felt himself completely relax. Kitty demonstrated for him her favourite Italian snack, which was a slice of ciabatta soaked in olive oil until it was soggy like a damp flannel, sprinkled with salt and then eaten with her fingers.

'I'm amazed you even touch bread,' Max said. 'You're so thin.'

'That's because I *do* eat bread,' Kitty said. 'Bread and chips and pasta for dinner, salad or pulses for lunch. The *StreetSmart* Diet. Now,' she went on, 'I have to know. Tell me what's happening.'

He told her everything. It was a relief to be able to unburden himself to someone who knew the background. In New York, even when he was with Chip and Anka, he'd had to be selective about what he could tell them, but with Kitty he could talk frankly. He told her about the cocktail party at Bercuse Plaza, and his heated exchange with Caryl Fargo, and the meeting the next morning at Vision Capital Partners. He told her about the AFD campaign against *StreetSmart* and the sinister echo on the line in his suite, which had confirmed the room was bugged, and how he'd gone down to the hotel basement to recover the tape.

When he got to the bit about breaking into the surveillance room, Kitty looked terrified. 'You're crazy,' she said. 'What is it with you and danger? First you have to chase that burglar in the office. Then you book yourself into the East River, which is just unbelievable. Then you go and find Saskia's maid in Harlem or the Bronx or wherever . . .'

'Fort Washington Park.'

'Some no-go area anyway, full of crack dealers. And now – this is unreal – you're telling me you smashed your way into Saidi's bugging centre and stole the tape?'

'That's about it. You make it sound more dangerous than it was, though: there was nobody around in the basement. Only the night telephonist, and she wasn't paying attention.'

'So what's going to happen?' asked Kitty.

'With *StreetSmart*? Your guess is as good as mine. To keep it, I've somehow got to convince Dick Mathias I can turn the business round, and that he'll make more money holding on to his investment than selling out.'

'And how are you meant to do that?'

'Oh, lots of ways. By demonstrating my aggressive, dynamic leadership. By winning back the Bercuse advertising account. By holding the staff together and making sure nobody important quits. All of which, judging by today's events, I am singularly failing to do.'

'Racinda, you mean?'

'Precisely. You know something – I've been thinking about that whole episode, and there's something about it that doesn't add up.'

'In what way?'

'Let me try this out on you. Maybe I'm wrong and I'm just being paranoid, you know more about how this world works than I do. But Racinda's seat at the Sensi show. She gets given this invitation for row Z or wherever. Outer Siberia. And she's so offended, she quits her job. That's what happened, isn't it?'

Kitty nodded.

'Now the question is,' Max went on, '*why* was she put in Outer Siberia? I mean, that isn't normal, is it? Last season, which row would Racinda have been in?'

'B probably. In fact, definitely. Saskia got A and Racinda was sitting directly behind her.'

'And what about the other shows? Armani, for instance? And Prada?'

'B. Sometimes A. It depends how long the front row is, and how many people they can cram in.'

'So what you're telling me is: at ninety-five per cent of all fashion shows, Racinda Blick is allocated a first- or second-row seat?'

'Yes.'

'Then explain this: why would the Sensi public relations people, who I assume do the seating plan, suddenly decide to put Racinda at the back?'

Kitty thought. 'Because *StreetSmart* has upset them? Or Racinda has?'

'Feasible, but I've thought of another possibility. What if someone *wanted* Racinda to resign from the magazine? What if they were trying to undermine us – and undermine *me*? It would be a clever way of going about it. Everyone knows Racinda's crazy and status conscious. Even Jean Lovell told me that. So if you wanted to upset her, probably the quickest, most effective way would be to make sure she got a dud seat at the show. Public humiliation. The most insignificant player in the fashion industry. Isn't that how she's interpreted it? You know her better than I do.'

'You're right. I didn't realise you're a psychiatrist too.'

Max smiled, and signalled to the waiter to bring a third bottle of wine. 'Now,' he went on, 'let's take this one step further. We've established someone wanted to humiliate Racinda. Well, *who*?'

Kitty screwed up her face. 'Give me a second, I'm getting there. Caryl and Bob! They're the ones who've gained by Racinda leaving *StreetSmart*. She may be mad and insecure, but photographers love her. She's got a great reputation. I bet it was all a set-up by those two.'

'By fixing her a terrible seat, they've tipped her into joining them. But the question is: could they? I mean, is it possible to manipulate the seating arrangements?'

'I suppose someone could have altered the cards on the back of the chairs, if they arrived early enough,' Kitty said doubtfully, 'but then they wouldn't match the numbers on the invitations, which are sent direct to people's hotels. It wouldn't really be possible.'

They brooded in silence while the waiter uncorked the bottle.

Suddenly Max said, 'Hang on a minute. Surely it's obvious. Bob could have rung the Sensi press office, saying he was from *StreetSmart* and there had been some last-minute changes in the fashion department. He could have said Racinda was a freelance or something, and didn't need a good seat. I bet that's what happened.'

Kitty nodded dumbly.

'It couldn't have come at a worse time either,' Max went on. 'I even mentioned Racinda to Dick Mathias. I said she was a world-class fashion director, one of our key assets. I wish to God I hadn't. This isn't going to help, if he ever gets to hear about it. Which he will, of course, since it's all part of Caryl's strategy.' Max took a long gulp of wine. 'Fuck. That's all there is to say really. Fuck, fuck and fuck.'

'Don't blame yourself, Racinda and Bob are old friends. They're always having dinner together.'

'I know. They had dinner the night I fired Bob. Bartholomew the driver told me that.' He laughed ruefully. 'They must be celebrating right now. And Caryl's probably already rung Dick Mathias in New York. "Hi, Dick. Remember I told you about *StreetSmart*'s disaster with the overturned lorry? Well, I feel I should tell you this: now they've lost their fashion director as well." *Christ*, you disgust me, Caryl.'

It was almost eleven o'clock and Bice was heaving. All the tables were full, and more people were still spilling in. By the door, a small crowd was waiting to sit down. As he looked around him, Max thought that these were probably the best-dressed and best-looking group that he'd ever seen in one room. The Italian men, in their perfectly cut tweed jackets, laughed and flirted with pretty girls with tanned skin and gold jewellery. The standard of women in the restaurant was exceptional, but even here, Kitty stood out as the most beautiful.

'We got distracted into talking about Racinda,' said Kitty. 'You never finished the end of the story about Freddie Saidi and the cassette.'

'Yes I did. I said I removed it from the machine and substituted another one, from another suite.'

'But after that? What have you done with the tape? I mean, we know it's going to prove Saidi murdered Saskia's maid, or at least show that he knew you were going to see her. Have you handed it over to the police?'

'Not yet. I'm certainly intending to, but I need to get it transcribed first. Someone's got to go through the whole tape and type out the different conversations. It's going to be quite a job.'

'I thought you said you made most of your calls from the lobby.'

'I did, but that was only after I'd worked out what was happening.

There were still loads of calls, incoming ones too. Philip Landau rang me several times and I talked to my father, and to Chip.'

'So where's the tape now?' asked Kitty.

'Here.'

'It's in *Milan*?'

'It's in this restaurant, since you ask.' Max reached into his jacket pocket and placed the mini-cassette on the table between them.

'You're mad bringing it here,' Kitty said. 'What if you lose it?'

'What else could I have done with it? I didn't want to leave it at my flat, in case it got burgled again. I thought Saidi might arrange to have the place done over.'

'But Saidi's in Milan.'

'Don't panic, nothing's going to happen. I'm going to get the tape transcribed and then hand the whole thing over to the New York police. My friend Detective Przemysi, the starfucker. Or Detective Amaya, who's investigating Carmelita. You see, I'm so well connected with the NYPD, I have a choice. Incredible.' He laughed, and divided the remains of the bottle between their glasses. 'With the evidence on the tape, they have to investigate Saidi. And I bet you anything they'll discover he had Carmelita killed and Saskia strangled. So at least we'll know who murdered my sister, even if I fail to hang on to her magazine.'

Kitty went to the ladies' and Max signalled for the bill. While he was waiting for it to arrive, he surveyed the other diners in the restaurant. They all seemed to be laughing and having a good time. The fashion industry looked as though it might have been an entertaining and interesting, and certainly glamorous, way of making a living, but Max didn't rate his chances of being in it for much longer.

He glanced towards the door, where, even at half past eleven, people were still arriving, and got a shock. Freddie Saidi, Marcus Brooke, two bodyguards and several teenage girls who looked like models from the show were entering the restaurant. Max tried to cover his face but was too slow; Saidi had already spotted him.

A waiter began leading Saidi's party between the tables, in the direction of a round corner table beyond Max's own. In order to reach it, they would have to pass directly by him.

As Saidi approached, Max remembered the cassette. It was sitting in the middle of the tablecloth, beside a dish of amaretti biscuits. If he reached out for it now, he would only draw attention to it. He had to hope Saidi wouldn't see it.

Saidi stopped at the table and gave Max a steely stare. 'Have you changed your mind yet, about selling me that magazine? Or do you want to go down the fucking tubes instead?'

The teenage models stood about looking bored and out of it. Max wondered whether Saidi really suborned them with drugs. That was the rumour.

Marcus Brooke joined Saidi at the table, and shook Max tepidly by the hand. 'I trust you enjoyed the fashion show, Max. I was watching you watching the girls. You seemed to be having fun.'

'I couldn't take my eyes off the clothes, Marcus.'

Saidi roared. 'That's a good one. He couldn't take his eyes off the clothes. I like that, Marcus. He's a fucking funny guy.'

The cassette was burning a hole in the tablecloth. How could they miss it? Max was desperate. Any second now they'd spot it and it would all be over.

'Sorry I was so long, there was a queue.' Kitty returned from the cloakroom, and Max had never been more pleased to see her.

'Freddie, this is Kitty Marr, the fashion editor of *StreetSmart*. Kitty, I don't think you've met Freddie Saidi.'

Kitty nodded hello, and Saidi gave her an approving once-over. Max had a sinking feeling that he'd just provided him with an extra incentive for buying the magazine.

Saidi thrust his face close to Kitty's and leered. 'What you doing later on? You like to party back at the hotel?'

'Um, I'm sorry, I'm a bit tired tonight for that.'

Saidi slipped an arm around her waist, and squeezed. 'Come on, Kitty, my friend. Enjoy yourself! Hey, we can have fucking nice time together. Champagne, what you like, it's all there. Isn't that right, Marcus?'

'Perfectly right, Freddie.'

'All the same,' said Kitty, struggling to extricate herself from his bear hug, 'I think I'll pass tonight. Maybe another time.'

While Kitty was distracting Saidi, Max managed to palm the cassette off the tablecloth and into his pocket. For a moment he thought Marcus might have seen something. It was hard to tell. If he had, he didn't mention it.

They hurried out of the restaurant into the Via Borgospesso. Apart from several double-parked Mercedes, the street was deserted. They walked in the direction of the Via Monte Napoleone, past the shuttered windows of fashion boutiques, searching for a taxi.

Kitty was shivering. 'Sorry, it's just that Freddie Saidi gives me the creeps.'

'I know, I feel the same way. Whenever I look at him I keep thinking, You murdered my sister, you bastard. And he's not getting away with it either.'

A taxi cruised by and they flagged it down and climbed in. Max was telling the driver to take them to the Principe when Kitty said, 'Max, let's not go straight back. Seeing Saidi has wound me up, I know I won't sleep if we go straight to bed.'

'What shall we do, then? Nightcap in a bar?'

'I need air. Fresh air, a walk. I feel so cooped up, the shows always have this effect on me.'

'*Is* there anywhere to walk in Milan? I thought this was an industrial town.'

'There's one place I know, it's like a big park. Sometimes I go there to jog between shows. Up round the Castello.'

The taxi headed west across town while Kitty told Max more about the Castello. 'It's actually quite worth seeing,' she said. 'It's like a castle crossed with a Renaissance palace. Lots of loggias and courtyards, you can imagine. And Michelangelo sculpture. It was built by the Visconti family, but it's a museum now.'

'Won't it be closed? It's gone midnight.'

'The Castello will, sure, but not the park bit behind. It's like the Central Park of Milan, lots of jogging paths and leafy dells. And there's a funfair.'

The taxi dropped them on the corner of the Via Tivoli, and they walked along the back of the Castello, past some stalls selling snacks and cold drinks, in the direction of the park. After crossing a wide expanse of grass, dotted with boulders and rocks, they joined an asphalt path which headed gently down to a wooded hollow. There were benches every so often for people to sit on, and Max could see some small, dark ponds and a wooden bridge, but at this hour the park was almost deserted, apart from a group of black Algerians, who Kitty said were probably dealing drugs.

It had been a good idea of Kitty's to get some air, Max thought.

The Italian park at night was predictably beautiful, with sculptures strategically placed at turns in the path, and in the distance an elaborate triumphal arch which reflected the moonlight. Sometimes, when he'd been away on assignment to countries entirely devoid of culture, Max had visualised places like this – grand old European cities. He liked to remind himself that everywhere didn't have to be like Mogadishu or Bujumbura. Civilisation needn't only be a model in a World Bank report. It actually existed in cities like Milan.

He said out loud, 'You know something. If I do lose *StreetSmart*, I'm not sure I'll be able to return to my old job. All this high life is spoiling me.'

Kitty took his arm. 'You're not going to lose *StreetSmart*. You've turned down Saidi, you've turned down Caryl, you've turned down Bercuse. And that American bank will stick by you, I'm sure of it. So you won't need to go back to any wars. Anyway, I won't let you.'

'It's strange,' said Max. 'I've never thought of this before. Perhaps the reason I became a photojournalist in the first place was to put myself as far away from Saskia as possible. As her brother, I couldn't compete. She always had to win. So I took up something that didn't bear comparison. If parties and celebrities were her thing, I'd go to places where there weren't any parties or celebrities.'

'What about integrity, though?' asked Kitty. 'Weren't you taking those photographs because you wanted to show the world starving children, et cetera?'

'That too, I suppose. I guess we all have mixed motives, don't we? It all seems a long time ago now, I can hardly remember what I thought I was trying to achieve. Magazines seem more important now. More treacherous, too, I might add.'

They were seven or eight hundred yards into the park, walking along a path on the edge of a small wood. It was quieter and darker in this area of the park. You could just about hear the drone of night traffic from the main road, but it was easy to forget you were in the middle of the city. Somewhere above the treetops, Max could see the bright lights of a Ferris wheel from the funfair half a mile away. Kitty slipped her arm through his own as the tranquillity of the night hung around them.

Suddenly, close behind, they heard footsteps moving fast in their direction. Max turned round just in time to see a figure emerge out of the darkness. A moment later he felt the blade of a knife being pressed against his back. He froze. He was fairly sure it was one of the Algerians they'd passed earlier.

He glanced at Kitty. She looked terrified at what was happening. 'Whatever you do, don't move!' Max told her.

The man jabbed him in the back with the blade. He still hadn't spoken, but the message was unmistakable.

Very slowly, Max reached into his jacket pocket and removed his wallet. There were about two hundred American dollars inside and some Italian lire. He prayed it was enough. Very slowly and deliberately, he tossed the wallet on to the path close to his assailant. Max had been in situations like this before and knew the rules: no sudden movements, and don't look at their face. That way, you would probably get away unharmed.

He said to Kitty, 'If he asks you for anything, hand it over. Money, jewellery, give him whatever he wants.'

The man hadn't finished with Max, however, and continued prodding him with the blade. Max felt its sharp point pierce his skin. The man indicated with the knife that Max should empty the side vent pockets of his jacket.

Max tensed. There were only two things in the pockets: his hotel room key from the Principe and Saidi's cassette. Was it a coincidence, or was the assailant's real intention to get hold of the tape?

Max knew what he had to do. Whatever happened, he wasn't handing over the cassette.

As nonchalantly as possible, he slipped his hand into his pocket. He felt the metal keyring, like a fat bronze truncheon. Properly applied, it would make an effective knuckle-duster.

Slowly, slowly he eased his fist back out of the pocket. Then, swinging himself round, he lashed out at the man. The knife flashed, but too late: the knob of the keyring had connected with the bridge of the man's nose and he sprang back in pain.

Max could size him up now: he was of medium build and fit looking. Max sought his eyes, but they were impossible to see beneath a black balaclava.

For a moment the attacker looked ready to lunge. His shoulders were tensed. If he moved, Max would try and fend him off with his left arm while taking a second swing with the keyring.

The man hesitated, then turned and sprinted into the trees.

Max watched him go. He wasn't going to pursue him into a wood at night. Instead, he hastened over to Kitty and comforted her. She was shivering, and he could see she was on the point of tears.

'It's OK, Kitty, everything's OK. It's all over now.' He put his arm around her shoulder.

'I shouldn't have brought you here, it's all my fault.'

'It could have happened anywhere, any city in the world. Nobody's hurt. And he hasn't even got my wallet, look.' Max picked it up from where it still lay on the path, and slipped it back in his pocket. 'Let's get back to the hotel, away from this park.'

There was a taxi rank opposite the Castello and they headed back across the city to the Principe di Savoia. Max suddenly said, 'It had to be Saidi. One of his men. You do realise that?'

Kitty said nothing.

'Had to be. Marcus must have seen the cassette on the table in the restaurant. I thought he might have at the time, it was just a feeling I got. Then, when we left the restaurant, they must have followed us. It wouldn't be difficult. One of the bodyguards trailed the taxi in a car. I certainly wasn't watching, were you?'

'It never occurred to me. We know Saidi's dangerous, but I never imagined he'd go that far.'

'I don't think there's anything he wouldn't do, actually. Now he knows I've got the cassette, he'll do anything to get it back. It's the only piece of evidence that ties him to Carmelita's murder. And to Saskia's.'

'Would he try again?'

'I'm sure of it. I don't *think* he'll try, I *know* he'll try. He has to.'

'Doesn't that make you scared?'

'Honest answer, yes. It does scare me. But, even more than that, I'm afraid he'll get the cassette. I'm supposed to be here in Milan for another thirty-six hours. How many shows are there still to go?'

'Seven or eight. Including some important ones. They won't like it if you're not there, especially at Armani.'

'I must get the tape back to London. If I stay, the same thing is going to happen again. Except next time we might not be so lucky. Anyway,' he said, 'you can have my invitation. Row A something or other. Front row centre. It will annoy Racinda.'

[48]

By the time he reached the *StreetSmart* office in Bruton Street, Max was exhausted. He had sat up most of the night at the Principe di Savoia, convinced Saidi's men might attempt a break-in. The windows from the suite on to the terrace suddenly seemed vulnerable, and he had jammed a pair of hard-backed chairs under the handles.

Kitty had slept like a baby in the bedroom. She'd been shaken by the attack in the park, but the combination of melatonin and a miniature Glenfiddich from the mini-bar had worked its magic. In a strange way, Max felt the attack had brought them closer, because Kitty had for once allowed her vulnerable side to show.

For much of the night and the flight back to London, Max allowed the whole conundrum of *StreetSmart* and Saskia's murder to percolate in his mind. Each time he felt he was getting somewhere, some new factor entered his thoughts. What, for instance, was he to make of Étienne Bercuse's surprise bid for the magazine? Had Étienne only recently come up with the idea, or had he been planning it from *before* Saskia's death, and could he have played some part in the murder? Why not? He'd been in Manhattan at the crucial time: he'd been at the Waldorf and he had a meeting scheduled with Saskia for seven o'clock on the morning after her death.

Max felt his brain running ahead of itself. He was lurching from one conspiracy theory to another. Slowly, slowly: think it through step by step. What did he actually know about Bercuse? That he was a ruthless businessman who wanted to build the world's biggest luxury-goods empire. That he had never failed to take over a target business, once he'd set his sights on it. That he'd pulled the Bercuse advertising account from *StreetSmart* within a few days of Saskia's death. It all figured. If Étienne wanted *StreetSmart* as the latest arrow in his quiver, mightn't he have had Saskia murdered and then tried to lever the purchase price down by suspending his own investment?

At four o'clock in the morning, Max became convinced that Étienne Bercuse was Saskia's murderer.

However, long before the grey Milan dawn rose over the roof terrace, Max saw that his Bercuse theory was full of holes. Bercuse would hardly have needed to hack into the *StreetSmart* database to ascertain his own level of advertising in the magazine. Nor would he have any reason to alienate Racinda by giving her a bad seat at the show, nor to have him attacked in the Castello park. He didn't need the cassette. So far as Max could remember, he had made no reference to Bercuse from the East River Hotel, beyond arranging to go to cocktails at Bercuse Plaza.

No, the only person with a motive for repossessing the cassette was Freddie Saidi.

He reached the *StreetSmart* office around three o'clock and was touched by the welcome he received. Gina, Marie-Louise, Jean, Lisa, Tim, even people he hardly knew, all came up to ask, 'How was your trip?' or to say how good he'd been on television, defending the magazine against the AFD. The whole staff seemed to have watched him on CNN 'wiping the floor with Caryl Fargo'. As someone who'd never worked in an office before, Max appreciated the camaraderie.

He signed off on some layouts and headlines that Marie-Louise insisted were urgent, then drew Gina and Marie-Louise into his office and closed the door.

'I need your help,' he said. 'This is important and requires total discretion. Nobody must know about it, not even anyone else in the office.'

He placed the mini-cassette in the middle of Saskia's desk.

'Don't ask me how I obtained this, but it's from Freddie Saidi's hotel in New York. It's a tape of all the telephone calls from my room. It comes from his bugging centre in the basement.'

Gina's face lit up. 'Didn't I just *tell* you Saidi's corrupt? So he *does* bug the East River?'

Marie-Louise looked, if anything, even happier. 'Fantastic, Max. You should write a big story about it for *StreetSmart*. "How I was bugged at New York's top hotel." Serious scoop.'

'Maybe I will, but first we need a transcript of the tape. Every single word. I can't go into it all now, but I need to know exactly what Saidi heard.'

'Do we know how long the tape is?' asked Gina.

'No idea. There were several fairly long calls. Whatever happens, though, I need it finished today.'

'Gina and I can transcribe it ourselves,' said Marie-Louise. 'Ideally in here, if you can lend us your office, then we won't be interrupted. I've got some earphones on my desk.'

Gina and Marie-Louise began working on the cassette. It was a laborious business. They would let it run for a sentence at a time, tap into a PC, rewind, transcribe, rewind, transcribe. When Marie-Louise couldn't decipher some particular passage of conversation, Gina would have a go. Chip Miller's technical briefing about the future of the Internet required several attempts to decode.

Max sat at Saskia's old desk and wondered how much longer he could hang on to the magazine. He had three days left. He dreaded having to tell his father that he'd lost *StreetSmart*. There had to be a way to hang on to it, there *had* to be. If Saskia was still alive, he felt sure she'd have come up with something: some lifeline.

Jean Lovell came in with a tray of tea and a bottle of whisky. She was wearing her coat and Max, startled, realised it was already six o'clock. Marie-Louise estimated that they'd so far deciphered about one third of the tape. It was going to be a late night.

Max poured himself a drink and read through the first sixteen sheets of the transcript.

The conversation with Chip went on for pages. Reliving their exchanges, line by line, reminded Max how smart Chip was, and how determined. If *StreetSmart* changed hands, he doubted that any of the new owners would keep the Interactive division. It was a shame. Chip was a visionary, and he'd be out of a job.

Immediately following the conversation with Chip came Carmelita Puentes. He read:

CP: Who is it please?
MT: Is that Carmelita? My name is Max Thompson. I'm Saskia Thompson's brother. I think you worked for my sister at her apartment . . .

CP: [Long pause. Note: you can hear breathing, but no reply.]
MT: Carmelita? Is that Carmelita Puentes?
CP: [eventually] Sorry. Speaking little English.
MT: Carmelita – if that's you there – I believe my sister owed you money. For the housekeeping. I need to give you that money.

Max read on. He read the transcript about the money Saskia owed Carmelita, and his offer to deliver it to Fort Washington Park. And then – *yes, it was there, the proof* – Carmelita dictated her address, letter by letter, and they agreed to meet around two o'clock.

It couldn't have been clearer. If Saidi had listened to the tape, then he knew everything: the time, the place. The NYPD would have to sit up and take notice when he handed that over to them.

He read on.

'MT: Kitty?'

'KM: Max! Hi, darling. How was the flight?'

Max winced. *'Hi, darling.'* Were Marie-Louise and Gina aware of his relationship with Kitty? He supposed they must be, in an office like this one. Well, if they hadn't been before, then they were now.

He skimmed over the rest of his conversation with Kitty. It all seemed a long time ago now. Kitty was guessing which hotel he was staying at and telling him he was crazy when he said the East River. She'd been right about that. If he'd chosen somewhere else, Carmelita would still be alive. He had told Kitty about running into Caryl and Bob on the plane and the conversation with Carmelita.

'It's weird,' Kitty had said, 'but I'm feeling quite aimless without you. And quite sexy. I think I must be missing you.'

Max glanced over to where Gina and Marie-Louise were sitting with their earphones on. He felt embarrassed at the thought they'd typed out that bit. He'd forgotten it was on the tape.

The telephone rang on his desk.

'Max? That you? This is Anka.'

'Anka! Hi, I've just got back from Milan. How's the AFD?'

'That's just it, it's why I'm calling. There's been some incredible news. We just this minute heard.'

'What?' Max was wary. Was the news going to be good incredible or bad incredible? The way things had been going, he wasn't optimistic.

'First-week sales figures have just come through for the Madonna–Sergov issue,' said Anka. 'They're going through the roof: the best opening numbers we've seen in five years.'

'You're not serious? The issue's selling *well*? I thought half the supermarkets were refusing to touch us?'

'The publicity has worked in our favour. That interview you gave outside Bercuse Plaza. People are desperate to see the issue. Hudson News in Grand Central Station has reordered three times already. In Boston, they've sold out. Everyone loved what you said about the photographs being a litmus test of contemporary American society. The issue has become like an icon – people want one to keep.'

'Well, I'll be damned. It's almost unbelievable.'

Marie-Louise and Gina, who must have guessed from his face that something good was happening, took off their earphones and gathered round his desk. Max was shaking his head and beaming. The issue was a sell-out.

'Anka, you're quite sure?'

'I wouldn't have called you if I weren't. I'm telling you, every single monitor is positive. Coast to coast. Normally, by week one, we'd have sold around 240,000 copies. That's how many Tom Cruise and Nicole Kidman did. The best week-one ever was the Princess Diana memorial issue, which did 360,000. But Madonna–Sergov has gone supersonic. Six hundred and twenty thousand in one week! Several distributors are reporting sell-outs. We'll probably end up shifting more than one and a half million at newsstand, plus the subscriptions. We could hit two million.'

Max hung on to the receiver and just smiled and shook his head. '*Two million copies!*'

'Like *Glamour* and *Cosmo*. The team are ecstatic. We should think about raising the ratebase.'

'Maybe you should compose a new chant?' said Max. 'What was that last one again? *Sell, sell, sell . . .*'

'*. . . Meet those targets, Beat them well!* You're right. I'll get straight on to it.'

After Anka had rung off, Max said to Gina, 'You know something? For the first time since I stepped into this building, I actually think I might have done something right. One right thing. Not much, but it's a start.'

He went on, 'First things first, I'm faxing Dick Mathias.' He sat down at a PC and bashed out a few lines on the keyboard. 'How about this. "To Dick Mathias, Vision Capital Partners. Thought you'd like to know that the current issue of *StreetSmart* is up in single copy sales by three hundred per cent. You might like to have Lee Kloepfer factor this information into his business model. My American executives are recommending we raise the ratebase to reflect this dramatic unbudgeted growth. Best wishes, Max Thompson." What do you think, Marie-Louise? Reckon Dick'll appreciate it?'

'It's marvellous,' said Marie-Louise. 'Wonderful. There's just one thing about all this that's making me feel sad.'

'What's that?'

'That Saskia isn't around to see it. She'd have relished the twist – victory snatched from the jaws of disaster. She'd have got a big charge from it.'

Gina and Marie-Louise went back to the tape, and Max thought about Saskia. There was a part of him that desperately wished he could let her know what was happening, and hear what she thought of his performance so far. Her approval suddenly mattered to him very much. She had entrusted *StreetSmart* to him, and had believed in his ability to handle it. He would have enjoyed telling her how well the issue was selling.

His thoughts moved to Cody. Another thing he would have enjoyed reassuring Saskia about was that everything was in good shape for Cody, but that wouldn't be true. Even with the good news from New York, he still didn't rate Cody's prospects of inheriting *StreetSmart*.

It still bugged him that he hadn't solved the mystery of Cody's father, and the possibility that it could have some bearing on Saskia's murder. There were too many candidates: the Hollywood brat pack, Freddie Saidi, male escorts, Kitty had even mentioned Bob Troup. Saskia would never have chosen Bob as the father of her child, would she? She could never have been so desperate.

Colonel Thompson wasn't in on the secret, but Max still wondered about Jean Lovell. When he'd asked her about Cody, she'd seemed uncomfortable and he suspected she knew more than she was letting on.

On impulse, he looked up Jean's home number in the staff directory and dialled it. It was approaching eight o'clock and he guessed she'd be in. Jean didn't strike him as someone with an overwhelming social life.

She was in.

'Jean? It's Max Thompson. I hope I'm not interrupting anything?'

'Nothing at all,' she replied briskly. 'I'm looking at some half-witted comedy programme. It would be a positive pleasure to turn it off. How can I help you?'

'I need to talk to you, tonight if possible. Any chance I can come round to your flat?'

She sounded surprised. 'Fine. I think I might even have some whisky tucked away somewhere in a cupboard.' She gave Max her address, in a street off Warwick Way in Pimlico. 'It's the garden flat,' she said. 'Take care down the steps, they're rather steep.'

Max told Gina and Marie-Louise that he'd be back later, and took a taxi past Buckingham Palace and Victoria Station to Pimlico. Jean lived in the basement of a narrow brick house surrounded on both sides by small private hotels. There was an iron gate at street level, painted black, and then practically vertical steps down to the area. Hanging baskets swayed above his head.

Max pressed the bell and the door was opened at once. Jean must have been looking out for him.

She led him along a corridor to a sitting room at the back, overlooking a tiny, spotlit patio. There was a rockery and a well-kept flowerbed against the end wall without a weed in it. Max thought ruefully of his own back yard.

'You see,' said Jean, pointing to a table on which sat a half-full bottle of Famous Grouse, 'I found the whisky. I got it in for my brother when he came over at Christmas.' She poured a glass and placed it beside him on a mat.

Max looked round the small room, taking it in. The furniture reminded him of the furniture at High Hatch. Jean must be the same generation as his parents. A gas fire glowed red in the grate, and above the mantelpiece hung a watercolour of bluebells in a wood. A photograph of Saskia was propped up on a sideboard.

'Now,' said Jean, 'I know exactly why you're here, and I'm going to make it easy for you. I'm well past retirement age and I can draw my pension. So here you are –' she handed him an envelope – 'my letter of resignation. You've no need to sack me. I've never been dismissed from a position in fifty years and I don't intend to start now. Not at my age.'

Max looked at her, amazed, and said, 'Jean, I haven't come round to fire you. That's the last thing I'd want. Whatever made you think that?'

'Oh, I don't know,' she said. 'I thought you might prefer some luscious young thing as your secretary. What do they call those short skirts they all wear these days in the office? A pussy pelmet?'

Max laughed. 'After what I've just seen on the catwalk in Milan, I'm more than happy to ogle your tweed suit. No, that's not why I've come round. I have to ask you something, something important. I know you won't want to tell me – probably out of loyalty to my sister – but I really do need to know.'

Jean looked at him. 'This is about Cody, isn't it?'

Max nodded, and Jean made a face. 'I'll be honest with you,' she said, 'I do know who Cody's father is, but it's not important. Truly it isn't. You must trust me. It was something I chanced upon quite unintentionally, and should never have known about. I gave Saskia my word it would never, ever go any further. She particularly asked me not to tell anyone, her family included.'

'Jean, I'm sorry, I know you think you're doing the right thing, but I *have* to know. I *have* to.'

Jean shook her head slowly from side to side. Max could tell that he wasn't getting through to her.

'Listen, let me explain to you why it's important. There are things you probably don't know. *StreetSmart* is falling apart. The way things are going, I'm not even going to own it by next week. It's too complicated to explain right now, but Saskia had mortgaged it to the hilt, and the other investors want to sell. Unless I can do something, Freddie Saidi will probably take us over.'

Jean blanched. '*Not* Saidi.'

'It might not be him. It could be Caryl Fargo and Bob Troup.'

'Bob?' Jean shuddered. 'That would be the end. Saskia would turn in her grave.'

'Exactly,' said Max. 'Bob as editor. The man you said you wouldn't trust to walk your Airedale round the block. Incidentally, where is your famous Airedale?'

'I don't have one. It was a figure of speech.' She shrugged. 'But I still don't see what any of this has to do with Cody. I don't see the connection.'

'The connection,' Max said, 'is that if I can somehow solve the mystery of Saskia's death – which was murder, by the way, not suicide – and if I can do it in the next three days, then I might have a chance of keeping *StreetSmart*. Otherwise, next week you could be booking restaurants and fixing meetings for Bob.'

Jean emitted a long sigh. She closed her eyes and shook her head in anguish.

'All I need,' said Max, 'is to rule out every red herring. If Cody's father has nothing to do with it – and you say he hasn't – then it won't go any further. I won't tell anyone – not the police, not even my father, I promise – but I have to know. It could be the only way of saving *StreetSmart*.'

Jean sat in her armchair, saying nothing, just thinking. Eventually, she said, 'All right, I will tell you, but strictly on that understanding. You are Saskia's brother – and I must say that you have a lot of your sister in you, which is a very great compliment – so I'm going to trust you. Not without misgivings, mind you, but if it helps keep the magazine in the family . . .'

'Yes?'

'Let me explain what happened and how I came to know about it. I've told you already that Saskia always had her fair share of admirers. Men had a tendency to become slightly obsessed by her. The unusual thing was the range of men. Powerful men always found her attractive, probably because she was powerful herself. They were forever inviting her out to lunch, here and in New York. But your sister also had what you might call 'the common touch'. Photographers and pop stars, some quite rough, found her equally attractive, and – how can I put this? – sometimes I think Saskia was more receptive to them than she was to the tycoons.' Jean gave Max a meaningful look.

'Don't worry, I think I'd worked that one out already. When it came to sex, she wasn't fussy.'

Jean sighed. 'Anyway, one evening about seven years ago, we'd had a party in the old Soho Square offices to celebrate *StreetSmart* winning a prize. It wasn't one of our big parties, just a gathering of staff and some of the contributors, whoever we could get hold of. Yando was in town, shooting the couture, and he came along and some of the writers. There were probably about a hundred of us all told. At about nine o'clock the party started to break up, and people drifted off to dinner. I said good night to Saskia and headed off in the direction of the Underground station.

'I was halfway along Oxford Street when I realised I'd stupidly left my doorkeys behind on my desk, so I turned round and went back to the office. When I got there, the place was deserted, or so I thought. The desks were strewn with empty bottles and plastic cups. I found my keys and was on my way out when I heard noises coming from inside Saskia's office. The lights were off, so I thought I'd better check everything was all right. I still wish to goodness I hadn't. I pushed open the door and switched on the lights, and there was Saskia in the middle of the floor, with a member of her staff. I don't think I need elaborate on what was going on.'

Max was sitting on the edge of his chair. Who had Saskia been with that night? 'Jean, who was it? Which member of staff?'

'Barry Higgs.'

'*Barry?* You mean Barry who fixes the computers?'

Max was astonished. His sister had been screwing Barry? He had a sudden vision of him, fixing up the video conference on Max's first day at *StreetSmart*, surrounded by wires, the seat of his jeans protruding from beneath the table.

'I'm afraid so,' said Jean. 'You can imagine, I was quite taken aback myself. Barry isn't really my kind of young man, though I suppose there's a certain earthiness.'

'I find him rather cocky,' said Max.

'Quite,' said Jean.

Max's mind was rushing ahead. So Barry had been Saskia's lover. No wonder he'd known the way from Stoke Newington to her flat in Holland Park. He could have been over dozens of times.

He asked Jean, 'Were they actually having an affair, or was it a one-off?'

'Gracious,' said Jean, 'not an affair. Have you tried holding a conversation with Barry? I don't think Saskia ever spent more than fifteen minutes in the same room as him. I'm sure it was a fling, facilitated by too much champagne.'

Max gulped. 'And you think that this fling – at the end of the party – led to Cody's conception?'

Jean nodded. 'I know it did. Saskia told me. When I interrupted them that evening, I closed the door as quietly as possible, and went straight home. I wasn't ever going to refer to it again, it was none of my business, but Saskia did mention it, the next morning. She said that she'd decided to have a baby, and that she didn't want a husband, she had decided to get herself pregnant by someone who'd never even know he was the father. She had identified Barry Higgs as someone appropriately vigorous, but unlikely to want to play any part in Cody's upbringing. I'm afraid she put it rather more crudely than that.'

Max wanted to laugh. So many names had been put forward – film stars, rock stars, Saidi – but no one had suggested Barry. And it explained something: Cody's passion for computers. No wonder Cody was such a wizard with technology.

'And Barry really doesn't know he's Cody's father?'

'I don't believe so. Saskia intentionally didn't make anything out of being pregnant. She didn't mention it for the first seven months. By which time Barry had either forgotten the incident or couldn't make the connection.'

Max remained astonished. He thought of his father at Saskia's parties, scrutinising Hollywood film stars for physiological resemblances to his grandson. And he thought of Kitty's endless speculations. It was almost funny.

Max also felt frustrated, though. He couldn't see how Jean's revelation helped. He had hoped the identity of Cody's father would hold the key to Saskia's murder, but, beyond satisfying his curiosity, it didn't take him anywhere.

'And, apart from you, nobody else has ever known about Barry?'

'So far as I'm aware. Saskia seldom took anyone into her confidence, she could be quite a dark horse. I did wonder whether she'd ever told her lawyer, Philip Landau, but I don't think so, even when they were close.'

'You said "*when* they were close". They didn't fall out, did they?'

'Oh no, Philip remained a great confidant. Saskia was careful about that, she never fell out with old flames. All her old boyfriends stayed on the mailing list.'

'I didn't know Landau was a boyfriend. When did that happen?'

'A year or two ago. They kept it quiet because he's married. It went on for quite a long time – long for Saskia, I should say. Almost a year. They mostly saw each other when they were both over in New York.'

'And it ended when?'

'That I couldn't tell you,' said Jean. 'My impression was that Saskia ended it more than once, but it sprang back into life again, as these things have a tendency to do. Philip took it very badly. I was surprised how much he minded, but I suppose he must have taken it all much more seriously than Saskia ever had.'

Gina and Marie-Louise had almost finished the job, and a sheaf of fresh transcript lay on Max's desk. He picked it up and scanned the columns of dialogue.

Anka Kaplan had rung him at the hotel to tell him to switch on the television – *'Are you watching?'* Immediately afterwards, she'd rung back and they'd discussed the AFD. If it were Saidi who'd tipped off the Federation, he must have been delighted to know how much consternation he'd caused.

The second conversation with Anka ended, *'By the display of Étienne Bis briefcases as you come in . . .'* and a new one began. Philip Landau was calling him late at night.

PL: Max?

MT: Uh-huh.

PL: Where the hell have you been all evening? I've been leaving messages everywhere. Didn't you get my voice-mails? [NOTE: There's a lot of background noise and music, it's quite hard to hear.]

MT: Sorry, Philip. It's been quite an eventful day, one way and another.

PL: It's been eventful this side of the pond too.

MT: You're in London? Isn't it the middle of the night there?

PL: Four a.m. . . .

Max read on through the conversation. Philip had filled him in about Dick Mathias and Vision Capital Partners and the meeting the next morning in Nassau Street: *'Saskia used to pay him a courtesy call from time to time and keep him on-message about how the magazine was performing.*' Well, thought Max, Philip would certainly have known, if he was bonking Saskia in New York.

The next section of the transcript was Kitty's voice-mail, telling him she'd obtained the guest list for the Waldorf benefit.

Then five messages from Philip Landau, increasingly agitated, trying to get hold of him, and finally the conversation with his father about repatriating Saskia's body to Surrey. Marie-Louise handed him the final sheets as he read.

Gina and Marie-Louise started making coffee. They were tired. It had taken them a little over five hours to transcribe the tape. 'Some parts were actually quite easy,' Gina said. 'The conversations that took ages were Chip Miller, because of all the jargon, and Philip Landau. There was so much background noise.'

'It sounded like he was ringing from a railway station,' said Marie-Louise. 'It was echoey, like there were announcements going on over a tannoy.'

'I think he was watching television,' said Max. 'MTV or something. He watches it for his work.'

'There was definitely a TV on,' said Gina, 'but it wasn't MTV. I played that tape through so many times, I know it backwards. The music was the theme music for NBC *News at Eleven*. I watched that show all the time when I lived in the States.'

'It couldn't be though, could it?' said Marie-Louise. 'They don't show NBC over here.'

'I'm telling you it was,' said Gina. 'Monday nights at eleven, Channel Four. I never missed NBC *News at Eleven*. The jingle's unmistakable, those bells – *bong-bong-bong* – and then those trumpets.'

'If you're right,' said Max, 'then probably it was on video. All I know is that Philip was in London and it was four in the morning, British time, when we spoke. He'd been trying to get hold of me all evening.'

Max's brain felt as though it were being spun on its axis. 'Give me the tape, quickly,' he said. 'I want to hear it myself.'

He played and replayed it a dozen times, and each time he looked more thoughtful and more shaken. Eventually he removed the earphones, and placed them gravely on the desk.

He knew now what had happened.

He made two telephone calls – one short, one long – and then, giving nothing away, he left the office.

[49]

Ken and the boys were waiting in the public bar of the Frog and Three Chairmen on the corner of London Wall and Wood Street. It was almost eleven o'clock and the place was emptying for the night. Sam de Witt was grumbling to Simon Scott about the price of a pint in the City of London, while Mick Paarl regaled the group on the unfanciability of modern models. 'I'm not kidding,' he was saying. 'If one of those superslappers came up to me, and said, "Mick, I'm fucking desperate, I'm begging you to give me one," I couldn't go through with it. I'm serious, it was that bad.'

Ken had done well to assemble the team so quickly. Sam and Simon had been tracked down in the Earl Percy, and Mick had come straight from the airport. Ken had been demonstrating the strength of his elbows to some bird in Arundel Gardens, but put her on hold when Max's call had come through.

Max felt incredibly grateful, and quite moved, that the boys would turn out for him on trust so late at night.

He bought them a final round, and they went over the plan one more time, before slipping quietly out of the pub, singly so as not to attract attention, having agreed to meet up in ten minutes in the underground car park beneath the Barbican.

Ken and Max were the last to leave. They walked together through the empty streets of the City, past the darkened lobbies of insurance and commodities companies. Soon the brick and concrete balconies of the Barbican loomed over them, with its conference centre and restaurants, and expensive apartments above.

They strolled round to the back of the complex and down a ramp into the car park. There were four levels of parking and they had agreed to meet on level B.

Sam, Mick and Simon were there already, lurking behind a concrete pillar. Without speaking, they pressed the button for the lift which would take them up to the flats, thereby avoiding the porter in the front lobby.

The lift doors opened on to an upper storey and the five men followed the arrows until they were outside the flat.

Max looked at his watch. It was eleven twenty-five. He was fairly sure that Philip Landau would be inside. He guessed, too, that he wouldn't be alone.

The thought of it sickened him.

Sam de Witt was testing the resistance of the doorframe with his bovine shoulder. 'Nothing to it,' he said. 'One good smack and it'll split in two, no problem.'

Max paused, held up three fingers. Count of three. The doorframe cracked and splintered, but the door held. Sam kicked it hard, and this time it sagged open.

Simon and Mick were first over the threshold, and sprinted up the corridor while Sam and Ken covered the front door. Max stood in the hall, transfixed by a large charcoal drawing of a globe artichoke, framed in inch-thick steel. It was clearly the pair to the chilli pepper in Philip's office in Covent Garden, but it reminded Max of something else too: Kitty's drawing of lemon grass in Rosary Gardens. It had to be the same artist.

A girl's voice was audible at the far end of the flat, and Max heard Philip saying, 'What the hell are you people doing here?'

A moment later Kitty bolted down the corridor with only a hand-towel wrapped around her. When she saw Max, her jaw dropped and her eyes darted nervously about the flat.

'Back from Milan early, I see,' said Max. 'I thought you were staying on for Armani?'

Kitty stumbled, 'I needed to get back. A lot of work to catch up on.'

Before Max could say anything else, Philip appeared in a paisley dressing-gown, escorted by Simon and Mick. One of his eyes was blackened and puffy, but he managed a smile. 'Max! I didn't realise you were here: I thought your friends had come to do the place over.'

'They have,' said Max flatly.

Philip laughed. 'Anyway, it's good to see you, Max. I've been hearing about your successful time in Milan from your fashion lady here. She lost her flat keys and sensibly rang me for a bed for the night. Drink? Then you must tell me what brings you here at this hour.'

Max had to admit it was a virtuoso performance. Even with his black eye, Philip was so cool and relaxed, Max almost found him plausible.

'Strange, isn't it,' Max said, 'that Kitty should ring you when she loses her key? Considering she told me she doesn't know you.'

'There's modern women for you,' said Philip. 'Disingenuous. Pretty girls like this one, they will share it around, I'm afraid.'

From the corner of his eye, Max could see Mick and Sam eyeing up Kitty, who was trying to cover herself with the small white hand-towel.

'Honestly, fetch her a dressing-gown, won't you, Mick?' Max said. 'And let's move into the sitting-room. We can't stand around in the hall all night.'

They went into a large white sitting-room, full of chrome and white leather furniture. One entire wall consisted of a single sheet of glass, through which they could see the skyscape of the City, from the Lloyd's Building to the dome of St Paul's.

Philip went over to the drinks cabinet and said, 'Can I get you anything, Max? A whisky? Or some beers for your ... vigilantes?'

'Nothing,' said Max. 'And you'd better sit down. You can't smooth this over with a drink. I've worked it all out. Everything. Or almost everything.'

Philip looked at him. 'I don't know what you're talking about, Max. Though if it's about *StreetSmart* then I'm delighted. When we last talked about it in Quaglino's, you were full of the most intriguing conspiracy theories.'

Max said, 'You weren't in London when you rang me that night at the East River Hotel. I know that now, so don't bother denying it. You were ringing from New York.'

'From New York?' Philip tried to sound surprised.

'I can even guess where from. You must have been taking the overnight flight back to London, so you'd already have checked in. You were at JFK. Your flight had been called. That's why you were so anxious to get hold of me and couldn't leave a number to ring back. But your big mistake was ringing from a payphone near to a television.'

'For goodness' sake, what is all this?' said Philip, contriving to sound bored and exasperated at the same time.

'A television in a public area. We can place it because there are flight announcements in the background. If you listen carefully, you can hear them. In fact, I bet I know exactly where you made the call from. There's a bank of telephones in Terminal Seven next to somewhere called Chatfield's pub. They have a big television set on the bar. And the show that night was NBC *News at Eleven* – you can just make out the theme music – which proves you were in New York.'

Philip Landau still looked impassive, but Max saw that Kitty, perched on the edge of a white leather sofa, was tense.

'Even if I was in the States when I rang you, I don't see what you're getting at,' Philip said. 'Nor do I understand what you mean when you say, "If you listen carefully, you can hear them." Listen carefully to what?'

'You bloody well do know,' said Max, suddenly angry. 'Kitty told you about the tape. She must have rung you last night from Bice, at the end of dinner. You saw at once how potentially compromising it was, which is why you had to get it back, and why you got Kitty to suggest a midnight walk in the park, and why you attacked me with a knife.'

'Please,' Philip said. 'This is all rather pathetic. I actually find it more than a little annoying that someone – even a client – should feel that they can roll up here in the middle of the night, break into my apartment with a bunch of tattooed mercenaries, stinking of beer and cigarette smoke, and proceed to accuse me – without one scrap of evidence – of mugging them. Who actually gives a fuck whether I was in London, New York or anywhere else? We have offices in several cities. It's nobody's business but mine where I choose to work from.' He placed his whisky on a glass table with a crash. 'Now, if you don't mind, I'd like you all to leave. Saskia always told me you'd lost the plot, Max. She said the only reason you were drawn to wars was because you like to photograph people more inadequate than yourself.'

Philip stood up. 'Now – all of you – clear out of here. Go and join the French Foreign Legion, I don't care, go anywhere, but get out of my flat right now or I'll . . .'

'Or you'll what?' said Max. 'Call the police? Well, go right ahead.

Go on, ring them. I'd be very happy, because it'll save me the trouble. And I can turn you in for the murder of Saskia Thompson and Carmelita Puentes.'

Kitty, Max noticed, was looking terrified. Her whole body was rigid. Max turned to her. 'You knew about this all along, didn't you? You knew Philip killed Saskia.'

'I didn't, I didn't,' she burst out. 'I thought she killed herself, but then you kept saying it was Saidi.'

'Come off it,' said Max.

'All right,' Kitty said desperately, 'I did know Philip was trying to take over the magazine, and I was helping him. But not murder, I swear.'

'But why?' asked Max. 'Why did you do it? Because he's your lover? Is that it?'

'Don't answer,' said Philip. 'You don't have to. They're bluffing, he doesn't know anything.'

Kitty looked at Max, still saying nothing. Eventually she said, 'You don't understand, do you? You really don't. You're exactly like Saskia in that way.'

'I'm sorry, I don't know what you're talking about,' said Max.

'You wouldn't,' said Kitty. 'I was talking about me: my career, my life. I told you I was ambitious, but you didn't listen. I told you I want to be an editor, more than anything in the world, but you were never going to make me one, were you, any more than Saskia was going to?'

Max didn't say anything, just looked at her, wondering how it was possible to have loved this girl while knowing so little about her.

'You haven't answered my question,' said Kitty. 'I asked whether you'd ever have made me the editor of *StreetSmart*?'

'I've really no idea,' said Max.

'See, you *wouldn't*,' said Kitty viciously. 'I knew you wouldn't. When I told you which were the best two articles in the last issue – when you were talking to Anka on the phone from my flat – you ignored my advice. You don't appreciate how talented I am. All my life I've wanted to edit a magazine. I can see all these shapes on the page, layouts I want to do, photographers I want to use.'

'And Philip Landau would have made you editor-in-chief of *StreetSmart*, if he took it over?'

'He promised.'

'And you believed him?'

'We talked about it. I gave him all my ideas. He said they were brilliant. That's why I helped him.' Casting a nervous glance in the direction of Landau, as though trying to reassure herself, she said, 'You've always been wrong about the magazine world, Max, and I hope one day you'll recognise this.'

Max was frozen. That last sentence. He'd seen it before somewhere. And then he remembered. Saskia's letter, the letter she'd left for him with Philip Landau, asking him to take on the magazine: *You've always been wrong about the magazine world, and I hope one day you'll recognise this.*

He turned to Kitty, 'You wrote that letter. You wrote the letter from Saskia.'

Philip said, 'Careful, Kitty,' but she had already nodded.

'There never was a letter,' said Max. 'You and Philip invented the whole thing. Saskia never wanted me to edit *StreetSmart* or have anything to do with it.'

'Of course she didn't,' said Philip. 'Saskia was a smart cookie. She might have been a queen bitch, but she was smart. She wasn't likely to bequeath her magazine to some freelance mercenary in parachute pants. However, that doesn't prove I'm a murderer, you do realise that? You have no proof, not a shred. Sure I was over in Manhattan earlier this week, I go all the time. So what? It doesn't mean I murdered Saskia's maid. Nor did I have any reason to.'

Mick Paarl, who had been following the exchanges from a position behind the sofa, said, 'Do us all a favour, Max. Let me give this tosser a smack round the face. He's done nothing except take the mickey since we arrived.'

'That's OK, Mick,' said Max. 'We'll keep that offer open for now. First I want to explain to Philip exactly why he had every motive to murder Carmelita Puentes.'

'Go on,' said Philip. 'I'm fascinated. I never even met the woman.'

'You did. When you were going out with my sister last year. Jean Lovell told me that. You must have seen Carmelita dozens of times at the apartment.'

Kitty looked suddenly horrified and Max realised that she'd been unaware of Landau's relationship with Saskia.

'So what if I screwed Saskia? A lot of people did, you know.'

'But you didn't like it when she finished it, did you? You couldn't break it off. And when she began seeing other men, you were mad with jealousy. You had to be with her.'

Landau didn't reply, but his face gave him away.

'You were over in New York the week she was murdered, weren't you?' said Max. He glanced at Kitty, who looked stunned.

'I didn't know that,' said Kitty. 'Why didn't you tell me you were there?'

'Really, I can't remember,' replied Landau.

'It hardly matters what you remember or don't remember,' said Max. 'It will be easy enough to confirm with immigration and the airlines. But you were certainly there. You were furious that Saskia hadn't taken you on her table to the Waldorf gala. So furious and jealous that you had to turn up, to see who she'd asked instead. It was you that Saskia spotted that night across the ballroom. Kitty told me Saskia had seen someone, and had said, "I don't believe it, *he's* here." You were the "he", Philip. You'd been stalking my sister. Wherever she went, you followed, desperate to know who she was with. You were obsessed, you couldn't accept she didn't want to sleep with you any more.'

Kitty winced. It was obvious she genuinely didn't realise he'd been two-timing her with her editor.

'The next part of the story is supposition,' Max said, 'but don't worry, we'll make it stick, or the NYPD will. You were in New York. Wherever Saskia went, you stalked her. On the day of the gala, she had lunch with Freddie Saidi at the East River. You followed her, watched her go in. You were enraged, because you knew all about Saidi and how he'd always had a thing about Saskia.'

Philip's face screwed up at the memory of it. He seemed to be in some kind of pain. 'Saidi didn't have "a thing about Saskia", as you put it. He'd been her lover. I know he had. Don't you realise, he was the father of her son? He's Cody's father. She was going back to him. Saidi asked her to *marry* him. She told me that herself. He asked her at lunch that day.'

Max allowed the last remark to settle in the room, then said in a soft voice, 'Philip, I have to tell you this: Saidi isn't Cody's father. I know that for a fact. I know who the father is, and it isn't Saidi.'

It was hard to tell whether Landau had taken it in.

'Shall I go on?' said Max. 'Because, you see, you had driven yourself crazy about Saidi, hadn't you? The lunch went on and on, and still Saskia didn't come out. And the longer you waited, the more convinced you became they were in bed together. Probably they were. The autopsy found traces of semen, but we don't yet know whether it was Saidi's. Saskia could have had sex with someone else before the gala, for all I know.'

'She didn't,' said Philip. He had given up all pretence now. 'She went straight to her apartment from the hotel.'

'Thanks, Philip. You wanted to go up and remonstrate with her there and then, didn't you? But you couldn't, because you knew Carmelita would be in the apartment. So I guess you hung around outside, waiting for her to leave for the Waldorf. And after she'd come out, you went back to your own hotel, changed, then went over to the Waldorf after dinner to satisfy your curiosity.

'You stalked my sister all evening. You were watching her all the time. You saw her talking to Tom Cruise and Rupert Murdoch and Étienne Bercuse, and every minute you became more jealous. When she left the party, you followed her to 67th Street. You waited until the doorman left his post, and slipped upstairs to the apartment.'

Kitty was staring at the floor. She seemed to have gone into shock. Max realised that he could look at her quite dispassionately: she was beautiful, but he didn't feel anything for her any more.

'When you rang the bell, I suppose Saskia was stupid enough to let you inside.' Max spoke slowly and deliberately, trying to control his emotions. 'She probably told you that she'd seen you at the gala, and asked why the hell you were following her everywhere. You had a massive fight and you accused her of sleeping with Saidi. She might even have admitted it, to show that it really was over between the two of you. At some point the fight turned violent. You pushed her down on to the bed and strangled her. Then you noticed the bottle of Temazepam on the night table and thought you'd try and make it look like suicide. You stayed in the apartment until you were sure she was dead. The following morning you returned to London.'

Max stood up and walked over to the drinks tray. He would have that whisky after all. He tipped a couple of inches of Strathisla into a tumbler, and found that his hand was shaking. Ken and Mick took the cue, and cracked open Budweisers which they drained from the can.

'The one thing I don't yet know,' said Max to Philip, 'is exactly when you conceived your plan to take over *StreetSmart*. Your defence lawyer will no doubt try and sustain a plea of manslaughter, and argue that you thought of it after my sister was already dead. It hardly matters, considering you murdered Carmelita the following week.

'Whatever the chronology, you decided to target the magazine and run it yourself, but you knew it wouldn't be easy to pull off. You were aware of the losses in the States, and guessed some of the investors were getting windy. You also predicted – quite correctly – that several companies and individuals would be interested in acquiring the magazine.

'Somehow you concocted the idea of involving me as the fallguy. You specifically selected me because you thought I'd screw up. You needed to buy time. If *StreetSmart* went straight on to the market, then one of the big boys – Incorporated or Bertelsmann or someone – would definitely snap it up, so you forged Saskia's will, leaving the magazine to Cody, and concocted the letter manipulating me into taking it on. Naturally my father was all for it. He loved the idea of *StreetSmart* remaining in the family.

'Stupidly I fell for it. God knows why, since Saskia never made one unpatronising remark to me in the last ten years. I don't even suppose that photograph of mine in her bathroom, the one of Sarajevo, hung there in her lifetime. Did it, Kitty?'

Kitty muttered, 'I'm sorry, Max.'

'But I wanted to prove that I could hack it, and do the right thing by Cody and my father. Christ, am I gullible! I always knew Saskia was bad news, but I wanted to believe I'd been mistaken.

'So I took on the magazine and that's when things started to go wrong. I must say, Philip, you were very skilful, the way you systematically turned me against the other bidders, one by one, while pretending to be objective. After our dinner at Quaglino's, nothing would have induced me to sell to Saidi or Caryl. And you used Kitty to buoy me up, whenever I felt like quitting.

'Then, having installed me and secured my commitment, you began to undermine the operation, to drive the price down. First the lorry overturns on the motorway – which I guess you fixed – which means you will also be on a manslaughter charge, as the driver died. Then you sabotaged the Internet presentation, after Kitty spied on the runthrough in Saskia's flat. Then you tipped off the American Federation for Decency about those pictures in the issue, or Kitty did. It was certainly Kitty who arranged for Racinda's seat to be switched at the Sensi show – I rang Sensi earlier this evening and checked that out.

'It must have been invaluable having Kitty as a spy in the camp. I don't know how long you two have been together – at least a year, I assume. Long enough to have paid for the decoration of her flat, and given her that pretentious drawing of lemon grass. It's an indication of how devious you are that you encouraged Kitty to become my girlfriend, so you could know exactly what I was thinking and doing. It was Kitty who told you I was going to visit Carmelita Puentes. And you realised Carmelita might mention Saskia's relationship with you, which no one else knew about, so you had to kill her. It was lucky for you – and unlucky for Carmelita – that you were already in New York to screw up the Internet presentation. You knew exactly when I was going to Fort Washington Park, and got there just ahead of me.'

Max took another long gulp of whisky. He was trying to sound confident, but there were aspects of the story about which he remained ignorant, such as whether Philip Landau had ever genuinely loved Kitty Marr, considering his obsession with Saskia, and why he had needed to hack into the *StreetSmart* computer system on the night of the Quaglino's dinner.

'Philip, was it you in Bruton Street that night, hacking into the computer?'

Philip, sounding weary, replied, 'Truthfully not. Though I did know about it. Let's say I caused it to happen.'

'Then who?'

'Bob Troup.'

'Bob? *Bob?* I thought he was working for Caryl?'

'Only for now. If I'd got hold of *StreetSmart*, Bob would have been editor. He was my first choice.'

Kitty made a noise that came out like a whimper of fury.

'But why did you need to see the Bercuse numbers? Bob must have had a good idea of what they were already. I don't understand why you had to see them.'

'We didn't. It was meant to confuse you, and throw the suspicion on Caryl. We hadn't reckoned on the commissionaire locking the door through to the lobby.'

Then Max said, 'Last night at the Castello. That was you with the knife, wasn't it?'

'Regrettably so. And it nearly worked. I so nearly got the tape back. Without which . . .'

'Exactly,' said Max.

'How did you guess?'

'I didn't. Not at the time. Later I realised it couldn't be anyone else. I'd seen Karis going into the Sensi show and by some bizarre leap thought of you. I know that you and Karis are inseparable,' he added ironically.

He asked Philip, 'I'm curious. When did you start talking to Dick Mathias?'

Philip grunted. 'Dick and I go way back. I used to do dinner with him. He liked a restaurant called Da Silvano.'

'And after Dick had pushed me out, he would have given you *StreetSmart*? That was the plan? With Bob Troup as editor and Kitty out the door? And all the time I thought it was Caryl and Bob who were plotting with Dick.'

'That too,' said Philip. 'They were talking to him as well. I'd sold Dick on an endgame, good as. You've seen the numbers. The company can't make it as it is. We were going to break it up. I'd take the British edition, Incorporated would take the American. Totally separate operations. Two great franchises. Incorporated could have the headache of making America work. Caryl always wanted a way into America.'

'And what about Bercuse?'

'He was a factor no one had anticipated. That came right out of left field. We were betting on pushing the deal through before Étienne made a move.'

'And Saidi?'

'He wanted to take over *StreetSmart*, he tried to buy it from Saskia. I had to stop him, there was no other way. He screwed Saskia that lunchtime. I had to kill Saskia to save her from him.'

Philip sat on the sofa, head in hands.

He was still in the same position twenty minutes later when the police showed up.

[50]

The Sudan Airways flight from Gatwick to Khartoum landed with a series of bumps, and Max felt something close to elation. Ken was already standing up in the aisle, retrieving camera equipment and film from the overhead locker. They would stopover tonight at the Nile Hilton, then fly on to Nyala in Darfur the next morning, the staging post for Bahr el Ghazal.

Already the world of *StreetSmart* was receding into a distant blur. He hadn't ridden in a limousine for at least forty-eight hours, and looking around at his fellow passengers, Max doubted that a single one had ever heard of the magazine, or would recognise the smell of Serène, Tranquilité or Nocturnes de l'Homme Pour Elle, let alone have eaten at Chow Bene. Somewhere, he supposed, people were passionately debating the merits of the Arne Jacobsen stacking chair, and wondering whether to categorise Hilfiger or Hillwalking as Hot or Not, but it belonged to a world so remote from his present one that he couldn't really envisage it. He was pretty sure Khartoum was a Not rather than a Hot destination, and this delighted him.

He had appointed Marie-Louise Clay as editor of British *Street-Smart*, which was the edition the family had chosen to keep. One day, who could tell, Cody might actually take it on himself. That was what Colonel Thompson was predicting, though he probably wouldn't be around by then to see it happen.

Max had sold the New York edition to Étienne Bercuse, who had paid a hefty premium for the privilege as well as taking on the burden of debt. Étienne had bought out Vision Capital Partners and the other shareholders at the same time, and was now poised to activate his scheme to exclude competitive luxury advertising. Anka Kaplan, his publisher, was nervous as hell about the whole thing, but Étienne told her, 'I am buying so many new businesses, there will be no spaces for these other people to advertise. Already I look at

384

Sotheby's, at the Aman resorts, at the Hotel Bristol.' He flipped open his Apple PowerBook. 'It is here in the plan, *ça va?*'

Bercuse had acquired StreetSmart Interactive as part of the package, and instructed Chip to get a House of Bercuse Cybermall up online by Christmas, with electronic shopping for all his brands in every currency. The coding for the Indonesian rupiah and Dubai dirham were presenting complicated technical problems, Chip said.

For Chip, the jury was still out on Bercuse. If things didn't work out, he reckoned he might go and work for Freddie Saidi, who had already made overtures. According to Marcus Brooke, Saidi had been so impressed by the Internet presentation that he wanted to launch a major interactive porn site 'with the prettiest young ladies from all over the world. All in the best taste, of course.'

Marie-Louise, after a week of prevarication, had finally agreed to move into Saskia's office. Her fourth issue had just come out and already it was obvious she was going to make a fine editor. She worked all the hours God gave her, and her June gatefold cover with Liz Hurley, Jemima Khan, Naomi Campbell and Kate Moss, all photographed together in one Yando portrait, set new circulation records.

Caryl and Bob were still struggling on with *Town Talk*, though there was said to be tension already in their relationship. It was certainly a blow for them when Racinda defected back to *StreetSmart* after fewer than three issues. She had objected to being made to fly club class to Bali for a shoot, rather than sitting up front as she expected.

Having missed *StreetSmart*, Caryl's own position at Incorporated was looking precarious. Max had read somewhere, in one of the trades, that she was committed to launching eight new titles a year into the home interest and teenage markets. He'd believe it when he saw them. But then what did he know? As Caryl had said, he was very green.

Cody was still based down at High Hatch with his grandparents, though he spent every possible weekend with Max, staying at Saskia's old flat in Holland Park. Max had been persuaded to move in permanently, to provide continuity for Cody. It took some getting used to, and the Herat rugs and Somalian footstool looked rather lost in the white drawing room, but at least the boiler was reliable. Mick Paarl was flat-sitting while Max and Ken were away in the Sudan.

As far as anyone could tell, Cody had accepted the death of his mother with spooky ease. Max spent a lot of time with him, and had lost count of the visits they'd made to Legoland and Planet of Adventure, often taking along Marie-Louise and Tamsin. Tamsin and Cody had struck up a real friendship, which Max did everything to encourage.

After much debate, the Thompsons decided to tell Barry Higgs that he was Cody's father.

Max had taken Barry out for a drink at the Coach and Horses, next to the office, and broken it to him that he had a six-year-old son. Barry had at first refused to accept the biological possibility, but when Max explained that it wasn't going to cost him anything, and that he wasn't in any kind of trouble for bonking the boss's sister underneath her desk, he shrugged and said, 'Well, maybe I am. I'm not bothered.'

One Saturday afternoon, Barry had taken Cody to an information technology exhibition at Olympia, but didn't look set to get more deeply involved with his son.

Philip Landau's extradition to the United States went through that summer, and he was scheduled to stand trial in October for the murders of Saskia Thompson and Carmelita Puentes. If convicted, he faced a custodial sentence of not less than twenty years. Karis Landau, in anticipation of the trial, had already relocated to the States, where she divided her time between Guru Mayi Chidvilasa-nanda's ashram in the Catskills and the Jil Sander boutique on Madison Avenue.

As for Kitty, she was a subject that Max still couldn't think about too closely. It felt too raw. On the flight out to Khartoum, Ken had asked him, 'Whatever became of that great-looking bird you had the hots for, the one in the towel at your lawyer's place?' Max had rapidly changed the subject. The fact was, he didn't know what Kitty had ever really felt about him. If it was nothing, then she was a damn fine actress. He hadn't seen her since the night the police arrested her along with Philip at the Barbican. They hadn't pressed charges when she agreed to co-operate fully against Landau. The last he heard, she'd moved to New York and was socialising a lot around town with Étienne Bercuse.

The other person he gave as little thought as possible to was Saskia. Some subjects are just better left alone. It could take a lifetime to make sense of all the conflicting feelings he had about his sister, and he wasn't sure it was worth the journey.

What was that line Philip Landau had attributed to her? 'The only reason you were drawn to wars was because you like to photograph people more inadequate than yourself.'

He wanted to believe that Philip had invented it, but it sounded too much like authentic Saskia for that.

In forty-eight hours they would reach Bahr el Ghazal, the poorest province in the Sudan. Chances were, you couldn't buy a copy of *StreetSmart* for fifteen hundred miles in any direction.

Max reckoned he'd just about get by without one.